"*The Essence of Nathan Biddle* is a . . . beautiful work of fiction with characters that come alive on the pages. This is one of those books that keep you thinking of it long after the last page is read."

—*WriteKnit*

"The ladder is very high when it comes to novels that are good enough, deep enough, challenging and entertaining enough to be among the true classics. But this has definitely ascended that ladder and taken its place among the best."

—*Reader Views*

"*The Essence of Nathan Biddle* is a coming of age story that will resonate. . . . Author J. William Lewis has written a transfixing drama that will tug at your heart and mind from beginning to end."

—*Portland Book Review*

"Eloquent, provocative, and beautifully written, *The Essence of Nathan Biddle* is like discovering *The Catcher in the Rye* all over again."

—David Armstrong, author of *The Third Gift* and *The Rising Place*

jwilliamlewis.com

The

ESSENCE

of NATHAN

BIDDLE

The
ESSENCE
of NATHAN
BIDDLE

a novel

J. WILLIAM LEWIS

GREENLEAF
BOOK GROUP PRESS

Published by Greenleaf Book Group Press
Austin, Texas
www.gbgpress.com

Distributed by Greenleaf Book Group

For ordering information or special discounts for bulk purchases, please contact Greenleaf Book Group at PO Box 91869, Austin, TX 78709, 512.891.6100.

Design and composition by Greenleaf Book Group
Cover design by George Foster. Photograph of heron adapted by Phojoe Photo.

Publisher's Cataloging-in-Publication data is available.

Print ISBN: 978-1-62634-846-2

eBook ISBN: 978-1-62634-847-9

Part of the Tree Neutral® program, which offsets the number of trees consumed in the production and printing of this book by taking proactive steps, such as planting trees in direct proportion to the number of trees used: www.treeneutral.com

TreeNeutral®

Printed in the United States of America on acid-free paper

21 22 23 24 25 26 27   10 9 8 7 6 5 4 3 2

First Edition

To
Omar Khayyam

KIERKEGAARD'S LAMENT

It was early morning. Abraham rose in good time, embraced Sarah, the bride of his old age, and Sarah kissed her son Isaac, who had taken her disgrace from her, was her pride and the hope for all generations. So they rode on in silence and Abraham's eyes were fixed on the ground until the fourth day when he looked up and saw afar the mountain of Moriah. He turned his gaze once again to the ground. Silently he arranged the firewood, bound Isaac, and silently he drew the knife. . . .

Why doesn't some poet take up situations like these instead of the stuff and nonsense that fill comedies and novels? The comic and the tragic converge on each other here in absolute infinity.

Kierkegaard, *Fear and Trembling*

PART ONE

Climacteric

THE OPAQUE WALL

On the first anniversary of Nathan's death, we went to the sea. We may have been looking for the ungraspable image that Melville said is visible in all rivers and oceans, but I didn't see it. Maybe I wouldn't have recognized it if it were floating like flotsam on the surface of the water. In any case, I didn't see the image and I didn't find the key to it all. We spent two weeks in a little cottage my mother rented, walking on the beach in solemn silence and sitting on the deck in the evenings while the sun sank into the ocean. We talked some about Nathan but not really that much. Neither of us mentioned his death. We had exhausted ourselves in hours of anguished fretting over a death that in any sane world was inconceivable.

The ocean didn't provide any answers but it did envelop us in an almost mystical caressing balm. The beach house stood a couple hundred yards back from the water, built on pilings among the sea oats and bordered on the beach side by a large wooden deck. At twilight, when the sun left nothing but an orange tint on the waves, the ocean flooded the deck with a pungent fragrance and gentle gusting breezes. Even in the half-light, you could see the whitecaps cascading along the line of the beach. The hush of the evening was punctuated only by the incessant, rhythmic pounding of the surf like a gigantic heart.

The last night we were there, I was sitting on the deck looking absently toward the surf when I noticed a great blue heron standing alone about twenty yards from the deck. The bird stood on one leg at the edge of the area lit by the flood lamp on the beach side of the house. The wind off the ocean moved the lamppost gently to and fro, so that the ring of light on the ground moved back and forth and the solitary fowl was alternately bathed in light and sheathed in darkness. The bird never moved while I watched him. The light came and went but he just stood there looking wary and maybe perplexed.

I still think about that strange, gaunt bird standing on one leg in the pulsing light. It seems unbearably sad to be totally alone and uncomprehending: The heron had no way of knowing and no one to explain why the light came and went or why the ocean throbbed and the wind moaned along the shore. I don't worry all that much about Nathan's death anymore, but the bizarre monopode randomly sneaks back into my mind and roosts there like a spirit from another world. Maybe because he first showed up in the summer, the hint of warm weather always invites him to return. He seems always to be lurking in the shadows but in the summer he is a constant intruder, yawking wildly if I try to elude him or chase him away.

As far back as I can remember, I have expected summers to be wonderful. I don't know why I delude myself with that notion but I don't seem to have any control over it. It begins with a giddy sensation in the spring, and I can feel the anticipation rising inside me like a providential tide. But summer is never anything like the images I create in my mind. Last summer was particularly disappointing. My friend Eddie Lichtman's father hired us to deliver furniture again, and I was tired almost every weeknight. Also, Anna was gone the last month and a half of the summer, working as a counselor at a camp.

We had not been getting along very well when she left, and then right before school started everything collapsed. She wrote me a letter in early August saying that she just wanted to be friends. I was already getting more and more nervous and strung out worrying about the meaning of things, and I couldn't make the "friends" thing work in my mind. It was probably an illusion to begin with, but everything had seemed to be pretty much on track. I had been clacking along, more or less trying to stay with everybody's programs and schedules, and all of a sudden the trestle seemed to give way under me.

My last day of work at the furniture store was on Wednesday of the week before the start of the fall semester.

I was tired Wednesday night, so I decided to stay home and read instead of going out. But I really didn't do much of anything. I fell asleep on the couch. I don't even remember moving, but I was in my bed Thursday morning. The house was quiet and it was already nine-thirty when I woke up. My mother had left early because she had teachers' meetings, so I just lay there for a while. I thought about staying in bed all day but, after about thirty minutes, I started getting restless and my thoughts began to roam.

I probably would have loafed around and done nothing if I could have kept my mind blank, but I had been working on a poem during the summer, and it started nagging me again. The original version was nine wobbly quatrains about a preacher who had based his life on faith and then found that he could no longer account for anything. The poem climaxed in his attempt to administer last rites for a parishioner and his inability to utter the necessary soothing words to the family. The poem got to be too long and awkward, and I couldn't fix the glitches, so I pared it down and made a shorter poem out of it. It's a pretty depressing piece of work, but I had become obsessed with it and I couldn't let it go.

I got up, washed my face, then picked up the notebook containing my scribblings and went to the kitchen table. I was basically done with the short version except that I couldn't find the right word in several places and couldn't make the meter work precisely. Mr. Marcus says that you can't be a slave to meter and maybe he's right, but you can usually hear the words stumbling when the meter doesn't work. I poured some orange juice and sat down to try to fix the remaining wobbles. I was much happier with the short version, but a couple of lines still sounded like an old gasoline engine.

By the time I gave up, it was after noon and I was hungry again, so I fixed a sandwich and ate it, staring glumly at the product of my efforts. The back of my neck had begun to hurt. Ultimately, I made only a few changes, mostly diction, and then declared the poem finished. I wrote out two copies of it, one for me and one for Mr. Marcus. I left mine in my notebook and signed the other one and stuck it in an envelope. I wrote across the front of the envelope, "Mr. Marcus, please read." Then I folded the envelope and stuck it in the back pocket of my Levi's. I had decided to go running and swing back by Mr. Marcus' house, which is only a block over from school and a couple of blocks down on Bridgewater Parkway.

I was on the track team, which is the primary, maybe the only, reason I ran. When I started going to Bridgewater Academy, I felt sort of awkward. I stayed away from groups and team sports, but I liked running because I could do it alone. I also liked it because it seemed to help when something was bothering me. And I seemed always to have something bothering me. For the last couple of years, I'd been worrying about the meaning of things. I may have been fretting longer than that but I'm not sure, because when I first begin to worry about something it almost seems to be a feeling more than a thought. I get a vague impression of it before I find words to describe what I'm thinking. The fret I called the "willy-nilly problem" was probably in my mind a long time before I got it in focus, which didn't happen until about a year after Nathan's death.

I'm a fretter. I'll get something in my mind and it won't go away. It may begin as an indefinite hint of a concern, and then I find that some word or phrase comes into my mind at odd hours. I'll wake up in the middle of the night or I'll be running along the street and there it is, bouncing around in my head. The willy-nilly problem began to loom over me like a shadow and it has stayed with me. I had memorized the willy-nilly verses after I first read the *Rubáiyát* when I was about ten years old, but the verses didn't bother me back then. They did, however, stick with me because I would find myself from time to time repeating the words in my mind. The year I entered Bridgewater the verses became a serious burden, and I found myself increasingly haunted by the words:

> *Into this universe, and why not knowing,*
> *Nor whence, like water willy-nilly flowing,*
> *And out of it, as wind along the waste,*
> *I know not whither, willy-nilly blowing.*

The haunting of the willy-nilly lyrics persisted for a long time before I ever did anything other than brood about them. My first impulse was to talk to somebody, and I worked with that notion a little bit. I made a fumbling attempt to talk to my mother, but she gave me a bromide about life being an expression of God's love and deflected the subject as though she didn't want to discuss it.

I tried talking about it with Uncle Newt but that was, like all my recent conversations with him, more farce than drama. After I finally got out what was bothering me, he said, "Hang on a sec," and then he left. He just walked out the door. The next day my mother handed me an envelope and said, "Your Uncle Newt asked me to give you this." In the envelope was a single sheet with a handwritten note that said, "I couldn't decide which of these limericks provided the better answer, but it's got to be one or the other," and below were these goofy limericks:

> *Let's face it, you dumfounded dilly,*
> *Your bafflements aren't always silly.*
>   *But the source of your pain*
>   *Is most likely your brain:*
> *You just don't know willy from nilly.*

[OR ALTERNATIVELY:]

> *Forget your muddles and mismatches,*
> *Your foibles and gotchas and catches,*
>   *For despite your birth date*
>   *You got started too late:*
> *The subject is now closed by laches.*

I wasn't amused or mollified. The effect of these deflections was to push me into my own broodings. Brooding is probably what I do best. When I face it, here's what I find: The problem of meaning is strange and embarrassing. It is patently absurd not to know why or how you exist. You would think that the reason for existence would be one of those obvious things like why you breathe. It is bizarre that a person exists for years before ever even wondering why. Then it seems sort of late when you finally focus on the question, and it seems silly even to ask it. But I didn't like that answer because, in the end, don't you have to ask the question?

At the time, I didn't grasp that Newt was right in both limericks. Nonetheless, instead of dropping the subject, as almost everybody else seems to do, I decided that maybe I'd go to the library and do some reading. After I had some terminology to work with, I could talk about it with somebody who would take me seriously. Actually, I didn't rationalize it quite that well; the truth is I didn't do anything until I stumbled into it. I was trying to find Euripides in the encyclopedia, and I inadvertently turned to Existentialism.

The first few sentences got my attention because the subject seemed to be related to meaning. I read it and then went back through parts of it. I was so intent on finding an explanation of the meaning of existence that I couldn't understand the point of the discussion. I struggled with it for several hours before giving up. I don't know how long it took me to figure it out, but I finally realized that existentialism doesn't give answers; it just gives a person a theory for superimposing meaning on his existence. That wasn't what I was looking for.

The initial stumble into philosophy was not very encouraging. If the willy-nilly fret had gone away, I might have dropped it with a shrug. But the lyrics didn't go away and the questions began to weigh even more heavily on me. So I gradually resumed the chase, pursuing anything I could find on the meaning of existence (generally falling under the branch of metaphysics called ontology), first in the encyclopedia and then in philosophical histories and summaries. Sometimes I tried original sources, but not often, because philosophers are writers of riddles. It isn't philosophy unless it's written in the most vague, hazy, and abstruse language possible. After reading an explanation of the meaning of a philosophical oeuvre I had struggled with, my usual thought was, *If that's what the guy meant, why didn't he just say it?* Apparently it's not philosophy without the verbal haze.

I wasn't trying to become a philosopher. I was just trying to find answers to very basic questions. So, intermittently during my sophomore and junior years, I struggled to find glimpses into the nature of existence beyond the opaque wall (as my friend Lichtman called it), trying to penetrate the frequently bizarre ramblings of people who, according to somebody, are the greatest thinkers of all time. I cannot speak for them, but I can tell you that I wasn't all that happy with the fruits of my labors or theirs. The struggle produced an increasing level of frustration and stress but no answers to the questions of why or how we are here.

The one thing I got from my reading was a kind of confidence. By the middle of my junior year, Lichtman and I were talking reasonably comfortably, if not knowledgeably, about the various subjects. I'm not saying we had mastered anything or even that we understood everything we read, just that we had completely overcome the concern that everybody else had figured the stuff out and we were the only ones in the dark. The reason for the lack of common dialogue isn't that the answers are plain or certain. If people don't talk about meaning, it's because they don't know what to say. People don't talk about why they exist because, by the time the question comes into their minds, they know there's no answer. Or perhaps they just decide that the question is irrelevant. Either way, it's sort of depressing.

When I started running that afternoon, I didn't intend to go anywhere in particular; I was just running along thinking about things and I ended up going through the Loop and down Regency Street. And then, when I got to the front of the public library, I had run about five miles and I felt like stopping. I went into the basement of the library and bought a Coke and then went back and sat on the front steps. After I cooled off, I went inside and found a table in the corner. I sat alone for a few minutes and then got up and nosed around for something that looked good. I didn't know what I wanted to read, so I edged along the stacks like a prospector panning for gold. I didn't find any nuggets. Maybe my problem is that I'm always looking for the grand eureka moment, as Uncle Nat used to call them, the insights we get from special people, like Galileo or Newton or Einstein.

I ended up trying to make my way through *Thus Spake Zarathustra*, a little book that had lurked at the edge of my mind for a couple of years. Frankly, it seemed hazy and histrionic. After suffering through it for a couple of hours, I gave up and found a summary that said it was a poetic paean to the supposed denouement of evolution. I didn't like the verse very much (which may have been the translation but probably wasn't), and the creature lurching toward the Übermensch seemed to be angry about something (the darkness maybe?), which produced a peculiar response in the face of the imponderable: Nietzsche didn't know how to create life but he seemed to want to define what it should be and how it should behave. That notion bothered me. If you start with the premise that no human being has ever produced a living thing and no one has any inkling of how to do it, it seems absurd to extrapolate grandly from a blank slate.

FARDELS BEAR

It was after four o'clock when I left the library with nothing that remotely resembled a eureka moment, grand or otherwise. I didn't feel much like running so I walked along Regency and cut over toward Carapace at the Loop. All of my frustrations seemed to be piling up, and I was sagging again. And old Friedrich didn't help a whole lot. *Zarathustra* seemed awkward, almost silly, and for some reason that bothered me. Maybe what bothered me was the thought that Nietzsche was supposed to be a genius and his poem was supposed to be extraordinary; but I didn't appreciate either the content of the poem or the poetics. I wondered if there was something wrong with me.

I walked along looking at the sidewalk, trying not to step on the lines and getting more and more agitated when I heard "Fardels" almost as a whisper. I was so far off in my own thoughts that it took almost a minute to recognize my Uncle Newt. He was standing at the door of a bar called Emily's Tavern shouting at me, and I was on the sidewalk not more than ten yards away. He didn't say, "Hey, Kit" like any normal person would. He said, "Fardels!" When I didn't respond, he shouted louder, "Fardels Bear!" As soon as he had my attention, he completed the taunt:

> *There was once a lad who fell in despair*
> *When he found to his shock the world's not fair.*
> *So he's game as a tomb*
> *As he wallows in gloom,*
> *And lays the pain off on old fardels bear.*

"Fardels," he said in his most condescending tone, "you look, well, like you usually look. Come on in here and let me buy you some balm for the fret du jour, whatever it may be. There's hardly any fret a couple of beers won't soothe."

"Hey, Newt," I said nonchalantly, trying to convey a lack of enthusiasm. Newt is only eight years older than I am (and sometimes seems younger), so I've never called him Uncle Newt. He's always been just Newt. "I can't," I said. "I've got to do some stuff. And even if I didn't, I'm not twenty-one."

"As usual, Fardels, you're wrong. You've had at least twenty-one years' worth of fretting and moping. That counts for something. But your ace in the hole is that Emily doesn't really care how old you are. Half the patrons of this establishment at any given time are undergraduates at the U, not out of their teens. If you're old enough to sit on a barstool, you're safe in Emily's. I think what you need is a Pabst Blue Ribbon." As an aside, I might mention that Emily's was then at the end of a strip of stores called the Catawpa Center in a space that's now occupied by a children's clothing store. Emily's closed in 1960 after she lost her liquor license for selling alcohol to minors.

The real reason I wasn't all that eager to spend time with Newt is that he changed after Nathan's death. He had been witty and cool, but now he's really just cynical, irritating, and depressing. He looks like an older version of Nathan—and of me, I guess, because we all look so much alike—and he talks down to everybody, particularly me. Papa named him Isaac Newton Biddle, maybe in the hope that the name would inspire great things in him. Since he was the first known Escatawpa County resident to be admitted to Harvard College, the name must have looked like magic at that point in Newt's life. Things looked less promising after Nathan's death when Newt dropped out of everything except beer joints. For the first couple of years, he remained holed up in Uncle Nat's house reading tons of books but doing little else.

Since then he's "come out of his shell somewhat," as my mother put it, but he continues to be the world's only professional reader. He has almost dissipated the small trust left by Papa, so he complains constantly about an impending shortage of "actionable funds." He has developed a support plan of sorts: He has a knack for convincing women that he's an undiscovered genius who's on the periphery of great things. His current mullet is a sweet lady named Ruby, who has reputedly opined that the family has never understood Newt and that he will blossom once he finds himself. Newt is blessed with a mass of unruly blond hair, an engaging smile, and a con man's gift of schmooze.

He has found little difficulty convincing women that he is misunderstood; he has had some difficulty getting them to remain convinced for more than a year, sometimes even less than that. Since he's been with Ruby for almost a year, she is due for an epiphany unless she is particularly slow or needy. The pattern that has emerged, according to my mother, is that the new girl goes through four stages: Stage One, she enters the picture and avers that no one in the family appreciates Newt's genius; Stage Two, she undertakes a program to implement and deploy the perceived genius; Stage Three, she discovers that Newt has no intention to be implemented or deployed; and finally, Stage Four, she exits angrily, denouncing a totally unrepentant Newt as shiftless, deceptive, and self-centered, but usually not in those precise words.

When Nathan and I were little, Newt was often our babysitter. He was older, so by the time Nathan and I were three, he was a precocious eleven. I have no idea what Nathan thought (he never expressed views on anything), but I thought Newt knew everything. My mother made it clear I was supposed to listen to him. He spoke with authority and, for the most part, I did what he told me to do, at least up to the time of Nathan's death. In the last few years, I have seen him in a somewhat different light. I have also developed my own opinions and priorities. For most of my life, I thought that Newt was always right. If he said we should do something, it always seemed to be the right thing to do, both before we did it and after it was done. He always knew the answers to the questions, even the questions my mother and Uncle Nat didn't seem to be able to answer. Then, after Nathan's death, he no longer had the answers or even the will to do anything, much less tell me what to do.

I went into Emily's Tavern with Newt largely because of the past. I shouldn't have agreed but, ultimately, I did what I had always done. "Okay," I said. Then, maybe to demonstrate my new independence, I added, "You'd better be right about the ID. I'm not in the mood to be hassled."

"Faith," Newt said. "You must have faith, my dear Fardels, avuncular faith and, more importantly, faith in the sainted Emily." He pushed back the dirty crimson door and motioned me inside. I stepped into a small, noisy room with a jukebox blaring Harry Belafonte's "Banana Boat Song." We stood just inside the door for a minute or so, letting our eyes adjust. Newt swept his arm around like someone on the edge of the Grand Canyon and said, "This, Fardels, is life in its basic form: The post-pubescent students, the nearly senescent professors, and the random intruders from the neighborhood. Come in here and grasp the underpinnings of human malaise." I looked down the narrow rectangular room at Emily's patrons. Some were the older, tweed-coat crowd from the university and a few of the oldies were those Newt called the intruders, but most were, as Newt had suggested, undergraduate and graduate students. My immediate perception was that the young people were either having fun or pretending to, and that the older people, mostly older men, were just trying to regrip some prior time in their lives.

"Is this really life?" I said after studying the room. "Pretend life? Afterlife?"

"Good questions all," Newt said, "but the place has grit. The urgency and impetuosity of youth! The fresh glow of revelation! The irrepressible winking of coeds! The sag of life kicking against the goads. The grit in here is so rough you could almost sand a sidewalk with it."

"Really?" I said, looking around the room for the grit. "Is it grit or just detritus from the grind of life?"

"Hold judgment, Fardels, and observe. This place attracts some really interesting people. Not the college kids. They're really mundane. The interesting people are the detritus."

Emily had pickled boiled eggs in a jar on the bar, saltine crackers, and beef jerky. Newt asked if I was hungry, and I told him I'd take a Jax beer and two boiled eggs.

The jerky looked awful. When Emily saw Newt, she said, "Hey, Newtie, I've not seen you in a while. Where have you been?" She gave me a wry smile and said, "I've not seen you before, darlin'. Welcome to Emily's." She then put two frosted glasses and two beers on the counter. As Newt had predicted, she didn't ask me for a driver's license or how old I was. I guessed that Emily was on the other side of fifty but she dressed more like a coed, I assumed, because she wanted to blend. She seemed to ignore the older patrons except to serve them beer. The collegians pretended to welcome her presence but probably only because she let them drink beer. She had a paperback book on the counter, which she opened from time to time, but I never saw her turn a page. For the most part, she stood behind the counter looking slightly glassy-eyed, sipping on a mug of draft beer and randomly talking to the students at the bar or at tables near the bar.

Newt scooped out a couple of pickled eggs with a large wooden spoon that was lying on the counter between the egg jar and the jerky. I put the eggs on a paper plate and then took my beer and eggs to find a seat. The only available table was the one nearest the front door. Emily's Tavern was narrow, with the bar on the right and tables lined up down the left wall, broken about halfway down the aisle by the jukebox. When we sat down, Newt said, "Just look around you." I don't know what he wanted me to see. The collegians seemed to be posturing, some smoking pipes and speaking ponderously, some abandoning the scholarly guise and laughing or shouting. The older patrons, mostly middle-aged or older men, looked sort of out of place, trying desperately to mingle with the younger crowd. A few of the oldies sat alone at the bar looking straight ahead or ogling the coeds. I shrugged and turned to the beer and the eggs.

The pickled eggs weren't very tasty but I ate them anyway. I also nibbled saltine crackers and sipped my beer, which I really didn't like all that much. Newt and I sat in silence listening to the random chatter and the calypso music. The babble was so loud that I couldn't tell exactly what anybody was saying. "What about it, Fardels?" Newt said, smiling and leaning back in his chair.

"Grand," I said, "truly grand." I looked around the room, and I can tell you grand was nowhere in sight. Inane and mundane were everywhere. An emaciated man sitting on a stool at the end of the bar was talking to an obvious interloper, i.e., a man not a part of the college crowd. The interloper was probably forty-five years old but seemed to want to fit in. He was sitting on the first stool on the side of the bar facing the wall, diagonally across from the skinny guy. Actually, the skinny guy was trying to talk to the interloper, who seemed more interested in gawking at coeds on stools and tables nearby.

The skinny guy may have been trying to discuss religion because old skinny was holding a Bible and occasionally gesturing with it. The interloper seemed to be unimpressed with whatever it was skinny was saying and may have been making fun of him. Emily seemed to be more sympathetic because I saw her pat skinny's hand and smile at him. "Tell him to take it to church," I heard the interloper say to Emily. The skinny guy's eyes got watery and red and he held his Bible toward the interloper like a talisman. He had a desperate look on his face.

"Wait. May I please explain . . . ," he said, but the interloper turned away from him toward the coeds down the bar. The interloper must have ordered another drink, because Emily walked down the bar and put his glass under a spigot and filled it with beer. He continued to ignore the skinny guy, who sipped his beer and looked around the bar a few seconds. Then his attention seemed to be drawn toward the back of the room. He picked up a chipped and dented old cane and struggled to his feet. The arteries and sinews stood out in his spindly neck as he clung to the bar with his left hand and held on to the cane with his right. He was wearing a white dress shirt with stains around the sleeves and baggy gray trousers. He began edging his way around the bar, holding on to the empty stool next to the one he had been sitting on. When he rounded the bar, he stumbled slightly and tried to steady himself by grabbing the shoulder of the interloper, who muttered something and pulled away, causing the skinny cripple to lose his balance and begin tottering backward toward our table. Instinctively, I jumped up from my chair and caught him by wrapping my arms around his chest.

"Bless you, kind sir," he said, after I had steadied him. "You are very kind. May I have the privilege of buying you and your companion a drink? This is your brother, I presume." Before I could answer, he began maneuvering toward Newt, who was grinning broadly as though he were delighted to have skinny at our table.

Oh, no, I thought, but I couldn't figure out what to do, so I just held him up as he stumbled and lurched toward our table. I wasn't sure I wanted to be there, but I knew I didn't want to be there with some random derelict.

"Accepted," Newt said from behind me, "and we would be honored by your presence." Newt got up and helped the bony cripple into the chair next to mine.

"I am Jareb Bradford, but people generally call me Brother Jareb," the cripple said in very precise and unslurred speech. He didn't sound at all like he looked.

"We are pleased to meet you, Brother Jareb. I am Newton Biddle, and this is my forlorn nephew, Kit Biddle, often and more accurately known as Fardels Bear." I thought but didn't say, *Here we go again, Newt the clever intellectual accompanied for comic relief by his hapless nephew, the farcical Fardels.*

"Ah, yes," said Brother Jareb, "fardels bear. I believe from Hamlet's great soliloquy: 'Who would fardels bear, To grunt and sweat under a weary life . . . .' I am very pleased to meet you, gentlemen, and honored by your presence. And, young man, you should wear your sobriquet with pride. Hardships are the fingerprints of God."

"You know your Shakespeare, Brother Jareb," said Newt. "What did I tell you, Fardels?" Skinny had in one stroke elevated himself in Newt's estimation. If he had conspired to ratchet up his image, he couldn't have done better. "We are doubly honored to lift a glass with you, kind sir, the better to 'bear those ills we have/Than fly to others that we know not of.' With or without fingerprints."

Oh, Lord, I guess we're going to have a Shakespeare recital. I didn't say it. I just thought it. But I continued to sit there, knowing that things were likely to get worse. I thought about excusing myself and heading for the door, but I didn't. Instead of leaving, I just got irritated. And instead of directing my ire at Newt, who at least deserved a kick in the butt, I decided to attack Brother Jareb. Don't ask me why. Most of the time, I'm not all that rational. "I'm guessing you preach. You left your Bible on the bar. Are you a preacher?" I asked, not trying the least to hide the fact that I didn't think he was a real preacher.

"I taught theology and literature for a number of years at the university. Regrettably, I never achieved tenure because of personal lapses. I have preached for a number of years. I'm not currently affiliated with any denomination. The church, of course, is the body of Christ, not a building, as some seem to suppose, but the aggregate spiritual gifts of those who congregate. You probably find it hard to believe, but this very room can be a church."

"So, you don't really have a real church," I said, hammering away at him. Newt smiled and leaned back in his chair, probably thinking that I had become a real part of Emily's grit.

"Reality is in the spirit, Kit," said Brother Jareb. "There are many buildings with steeples and crucifixes that are not 'real' churches. The moment you enter them you can sense the vacuity of spirit: You may as well be in the lobby of the First National Bank."

"I would guess," said Newt, still smiling wickedly, "that you are retired, that you have hung up your vestments, so to speak." The reverend's hands had liver spots and wrinkles like a very old man, but his face had a peculiar youthful innocence.

"No, sir," said Brother Jareb. "I've simply made my venue comport with my circumstance. I have advanced the gospel in both formal and informal settings. In my most recent formal ministry, I was the pastor of a congregation calling itself the Christian Brotherhood Church. I did not retire. I must confess that I was relieved of my calling because of a 'fall from grace,' as the elders put it."

"May I be bold," Newt said with an almost gloating leer, "and ask whether the 'fall from grace' involved a comely female parishioner."

"No, sir," said Brother Jareb humbly but firmly. "The event described as my 'fall from grace' involved an actual fall. I regret to say that I became inebriated before a Wednesday evening prayer meeting and, as a consequence, fell spectacularly and ignominiously from the chancel into the nave. The limp you have doubtless perceived is a vestige of that fall, exacerbated by an apparently genetic susceptibility to osteoporosis." He paused and then said in a husky whisper, "I am very brittle, a glassy essence, as the bard would say, both physically and, I am ashamed to admit, spiritually as well."

"An actual fall from grace!" said Newt.

"Actually, no," said the reverend. "A fall from the chancel. The elders erroneously referred to it as a fall from grace. The doctrine of grace has nothing whatever to do with my inebriation or my embarrassing tumble into the nave. Grace has to do with the heart, my dear Newton, almost nothing to do with actions. It is generally true that one in a state of grace should behave more nearly in a socially acceptable way, but one's actions do not contribute to and can never attain to a state of grace."

"Yes," said Newt, "I'm familiar with the theology. We, Fardels and I, come from a long line of clerics, some of whom have not disgraced themselves. Let me ask you, Brother Jareb, what would you do if God ordered you to kill someone?"

"No!" I almost growled. "Newt, don't!"

Brother Jareb paused, perhaps because of the vehemence in my voice. He looked at me and then at Newt, who continued to look expectantly with eyebrows raised just slightly.

"I would question whether the order really came from God," the reverend said solemnly.

"What proof was sufficient for Abraham?" Newt persisted.

"Newt," I said, "let's not do this." I tried to put some edge and urgency in my voice to make sure Newt wouldn't just ignore me. Of course, Newt just ignored me.

"As you may have inferred," said Newt, turning toward Brother Jareb, "we have painfully close contact with a modern-day Abraham, my eldest brother, the Reverend Nathaniel Tyler Biddle, Jr., who killed his only son on direct orders from God, at least according to the reverend's account. We don't have the benefit of God's account."

"Oh," said Brother Jareb, settling back in his chair. "I read about that. How tragic. How terribly tragic. Your brother thought he heard the voice of God. Oh, my Lord, I'm sorry. I didn't make the connection."

"Yeah," said Newt, "so he's now in the nut house preaching to the goobers."

"I am very frail," said Brother Jareb. "If the Lord actually instructed me to kill someone, I would most likely fail the test of faith."

"Or is the question merely practical?" I asked. "To repeat Newt's question, how would you ever convince yourself that the voice wasn't a symptom of delusion or the voice of evil?"

"Yes, of course," said Brother Jareb, "you could never reach a question of faith until you overcame the evidentiary hurdle. According to scripture, God had spoken to Abraham before, so he had some basis for his determination that the order to sacrifice Isaac came from God."

"This heady theology is bracing," said Newt, "but let's regrip reality. For at least two months before the murder, the Reverend Nathaniel repeatedly referred to the hill beside his house as Mount Moriah and babbled incessantly about the obligations of faith even in contravention of societal mores. We can get carried away with deep theological truths, but the plain fact is the reverend was delusional."

"Yes," said Brother Jareb, "the Moriah thing does not sound good. Perhaps someone should have reached out to him. I don't know how one might have protected his son."

"You can't anticipate that level of delusion," Newt said. "Nobody picked it up. How could anyone ever anticipate that someone would kill his only son?"

"I would suppose," said Brother Jareb, "it could be argued that he would have been stopped, as Abraham was stopped, if the instruction had actually come from God."

"Well," said Newt, "that's a dandy way to confirm an instruction from God: If it's God, there's a ram in the thicket. If it's not God, oops, the boy dies."

"I don't follow any of this," I said irritably. "How different would it be if Uncle Nat had accidentally run over his son? If an omnipotent being could stop an evil, what is the moral difference between ordering the evil and permitting it? Just look at the primal mechanics of life—the heartless generation and degeneration, the brutal food-chain sustenance system, the insensible thrust of being—they all scream primordial evil or at least callous indifference."

"I don't know about any of that," said Brother Jareb, looking uncomfortable and uncertain, perhaps because of the intensity of my outburst. "I just know that I am not the author of this story. I am a mere player and thus constrained to follow the script even in the face of uncertainty or, God help us, total absurdity."

"And so," said Newt, "we come full circle. We're back to Brylcreem. A little dab'll do ya. I say we drink to the elegantly coiffed syllogism that leads inevitably to absurdity." He raised his beer glass and, not knowing what else to do, I raised mine too, but I really didn't know what I was drinking to. The reverend paused momentarily, then clinked glasses with us and took a large gulp of beer.

Just as we were putting down our glasses, the wall phone at the end of the bar rang, and Emily picked it up on the second ring. After a slight pause, she cupped her hand over the mouthpiece and said, "Newtie, it's a lady named Ruby. Are you here?" Without answering, Newt got up and walked over to the bar. Since I was facing the opposite direction, I didn't see Newt leave. I didn't hear anything—he obviously didn't say anything—but he was gone when I turned around to look.

"What?" I said to Emily. "Where did Newt go?"

"Newtie said to tell you he had to go," Emily said from behind the bar. "He paid for the beers."

Newt strikes again, I said to myself. "He left?" I said to Emily.

"Newtie said to tell you he had to go, he was late," Emily repeated mechanically. "That's all he said."

"Incredible! Incomprehensible! Beyond belief," I muttered out loud, despite the fact that it was a perfectly believable Newtonian maneuver. I wanted to raise my arms to heaven and say, "Why me, O Lord?" I didn't, because I was sure that no one would answer me. Besides, I knew why me: It was because I had once again fallen into the Newtonian snare, an all-too-common occurrence in my life, of assuming that my beloved Uncle Newt was a normal person and not a pathological trickster. I have too often been his shill, excuse, alibi, and decoy. Despite sincere efforts on my part to avoid his traps, I have often been the one who is left to explain his behavior: generally to my mother but sometimes to the baffled women in his life. With more than a degree of irony, I am thrown into the role of being Newt's apologist when I can't even account for myself.

PENUMBRA

When I realized that Newt had absconded, I stood up abruptly and leaned over to tell Brother Jareb that I also had to go. I was about to make up an excuse, but the sainted Emily came to my rescue. Smiling angelically, almost bathed in Shekinah glory, and clutching a bottle of Pabst Blue Ribbon, she held up Brother Jareb's Bible and said, "I got the preacher's book here." Then she began shoving a stool from behind the bar. I helped Brother Jareb onto the stool, and Emily helped me squeeze the stool between two accommodating patrons. She put the Pabst and a fresh frosted glass in front of Brother Jareb.

The reverend beamed and said, "Bless you, kind lady." I was very close to giving Emily a hug, but all I did was raise both thumbs in the air, and then I headed for the exit. "God bless you, Kit," Brother Jareb said. As the dirty crimson door was closing behind me, I heard him shout, "With joy and grace your fardels bear!" I didn't respond.

It was dark when I left Emily's Tavern. I wandered down to the end of the block and stood on the corner in front of Morrow's Drugstore waiting for the light to change. I was about to cross the street when it occurred to me that I might go in the drugstore and call Anna's house. I knew she wasn't supposed to be home yet, but I thought her mother could tell me something, maybe even give me reassurance. Anna had told me in her last letter that she was coming back on Friday but she didn't say exactly when. She had always ignored my questions, but the new "friends" relationship she talked about apparently meant I really wasn't even much of a friend. I wrote five long letters to her after I received her kiss-off note. In the last two, I told her that I would see her at seven-thirty Friday night but, of course, she neither confirmed nor denied.

The telephone booth in Morrow's is at the back of the drugstore over against the left wall beyond the magazine rack. The booth is one of those fancy walnut closets with little panes in the folding door so that you can see whether someone is using the phone. When I reached the magazine rack I could see that the door to the booth was closed, and I could see a faint outline of a person in the booth. I decided to browse around the magazine rack until the phoner finished. I tried *The Atlantic Monthly* first to see if it had any poems I liked. The only poems in the entire magazine were a series of haiku and a formless poem that seemed like loosely connected impressions of summer. I looked around for a magazine with pictures of girls, but I couldn't find anything really good. Mr. Morrow keeps the *Playboy* magazines behind the counter, so you can't look at one unless you buy it.

I looked at magazines for what seemed like an eon and the person in the booth was still talking. I could see through the panes well enough to tell that the person in the booth was a woman. Also, I heard her voice raised at one point but I couldn't tell whether she was laughing or shouting. I was tired of waiting and I was also hungry again. I didn't want anyone to squeeze in ahead of me when she finished, but I wanted to get a Milky Way up at the front of the store. Since nobody else was standing around waiting for the phone, I decided it would probably be safe to get a candy bar. As I walked toward the front of the drugstore, I passed the tobacco stand and had an urge to get a cigar.

I like to buy a cigar sometimes and smoke it and think about things. Everything seems more serious and consequential when you're smoking a cigar. I bought a Red Dot and a packet of folding matches and went out the front door of the drugstore. I looked around for a place to sit with reasonable comfort while I watched the door. Unfortunately, the only things out there were a fire hydrant and a mailbox. The decision was easy, particularly since the mailbox was next to the building, which provided a backrest to lean against.

I climbed up on the mailbox, draped my legs over the front, lit my cigar, and leaned back to wait out the seemingly permanent occupant of Morrow's phone booth. I wasn't looking at anything in particular because the only thing across from where I was sitting is a vacant lot. Beyond the vacant lot is the back of a house that has two windows facing the drugstore. The shades weren't drawn, so the light from the windows was bright even from the distance of a hundred yards, which is about how far I was from the house.

I was sitting on the mailbox with my head against the brick facade of the building, leisurely puffing on my cigar, when I noticed the shadow of a person's head against the light from the back right window of the house. At first, I thought the person was inside the house; but after I focused, I could see intermittent movement beyond the stationary shadow framed in the light of the window. I sat on the mailbox puffing for a while trying to decide what to do. When the shadow was still lurking outside the window after five more minutes, I decided to sneak across the street and surprise the guy.

I jumped off the mailbox, tossed the remaining butt of my cigar, and walked down to the intersection and across the street. I circled around into the vacant lot and sneaked behind the shadow, who appeared to be craning to see in the window. I could see someone inside the house, but I couldn't tell what the person was doing. I decided that I should try to find a weapon, a stick or something, to use in case the guy attacked me. I looked around for a few minutes in the dark but I couldn't find anything. I was so nervous I probably couldn't have found anything if it had been there. By this time, I was behind the house only twenty or twenty-five yards from the shadow, who was still standing at the window. The light from inside was shining on his face and, from my angle, I could see a portion of the right side of his head.

He was a thin white guy, youngish, dark hair, sort of, maybe a little like Mr. Marcus, but people can look alike in the dark. I moved laterally a few steps, watching the window, and in the dark I tripped over a tricycle. The thud from my fall plus the clanking of the tricycle scared the shadow, because when I looked back toward the house he had begun to slink off to the left. Emboldened by the shadow's flight, I jumped up and ran toward the windows, shouting, "Hey you, stop right there!" The shadow broke into a run, and I was right behind him until I got to the window. Two things caused me to stop: first, a woman in a white bathrobe was crouching just inside the window with her hands on the windowsill, and second, when I paused a few seconds at the window, the flashing lights of a police car blinded me.

"Stop right there!" someone shouted, echoing what I had said but talking to me rather than the peeping tom. Almost immediately, a floodlight beamed in my face and I covered my eyes.

"They had a peeping tom," I said to the flashlight. "He ran that way."

"Get on the ground spread-eagle," the flashlight said.

"I saw that guy looking in the window and I was chasing him." I shielded my eyes from the glare.

The flashlight closed in fast. I felt a hand on my neck and then I dropped to the ground, facedown in the grass. I heard the holder of the flashlight introduce himself as a police officer to the woman in the window. "You had peeping toms," he said, "and I've got one of them." The cop had placed a foot on my shoulder and pulled my left arm straight up, causing some serious pain. I was about to protest that I wasn't a peeping tom, but I didn't get the chance.

"Good evening, officer," I heard a male voice say. "I'm Watts. I called this in."

"We were watching from our back window over there," a female voice said. "This boy wasn't looking in the windows. He just showed up about the same time you did. He's not the one you're after."

"I was sitting on that mailbox over in front of Morrow's," I said, talking through the grass in my face but otherwise unable to move, "and I saw somebody over here looking in the window."

"Anybody get a description of the tom?" the cop said. He seemed to be accepting my innocence but he was still standing on my shoulder with my arm wrenched up in the air.

"All I saw was a shadow," the male voice said.

"How about you?" Only then did the cop take his foot off my shoulder. I didn't say anything at first. I just rolled over and sat up rubbing my shoulder. "Did you see the tom?" he shouted at me.

"He was a young white guy with dark hair," I said. "That's all I could tell." It occurred to me to make a comparison with Mr. Marcus, but I decided that that would be silly. "I might have caught him if you hadn't stopped me." This last statement probably overstated my real prospects, but I wanted to blame the cop for something.

"We don't need no vigilantes," he said, talking to me. "You just gon' get yourself hurt." He paused just a few seconds, then said to the woman who was sitting silently on the windowsill, still dressed in the bathrobe, "I don't suppose that description means anything to you?"

"I'm sure this young man was not peeping in my window," she said. "I know his mother. Kit, I'm Annie Brasher. I'm the assistant librarian at the college."

"That's all well and good, Mrs. Brasher," said the cop impatiently, "but it ain't helpful. I need to try to apprehend a miscreant."

"Well, I'm sure this young man is not a miscreant," Mrs. Brasher said.

"Okay," he said, "okay, I got it. Now if you'll excuse me, I may be able to catch this guy if he's still on foot." Then he hustled around the house and I heard his tires screech as he drove off. I could see his spotlight flashing between the houses as he drove down the street in the direction the shadow had run.

"Well, good night, folks," Mrs. Brasher said. "And

thanks for being vigilant. Kit, please say hello to your mother. I'm really sorry about the confusion." Right before she closed the window, a little girl appeared at her side and I heard Mrs. Brasher say, "It was nothing, honey. Some people going through the yard."

I was still nervous when I crept back across the vacant lot. I circled around the way I had come in order to avoid other traps in the darkness and crossed the street back to the drugstore. I went to the candy rack and bought a Snickers and some Milk Duds to settle my nerves. I was sure the phone booth would be vacant by then but when I got to the magazine rack I could see that the door was still closed. I sat down on a stack of *Saturday Evening Post* magazines to wait. When I finished my candy, I was still waiting and getting very irritated. I wadded up my last candy wrapper and threw it at the phone booth, then stalked over and banged on the glass door. Nothing happened at first. I could hear the drone of a woman's voice, then the door opened and a woman emerged enveloped in a cloud of smoke.

"You're a pushy young man, Kit Biddle," she said in her peculiar Louisiana accent. "You know that's rude maybe." I could have fallen over. The marathoner in the phone booth was Mrs. Ball, the mother of one of my best friends and the wife of Professor Ball, who was my mathematics teacher during the two years before I started Bridgewater.

"I'm sorry. I was just . . . ," and I made some confused

motions with my hands. I was so surprised that my mind jammed. I couldn't figure out why she would use the drugstore phone or why she would need to talk that long. Her vehemence also disconcerted me.

"Always good to see you, I'm sure," she snapped. She dropped her cigarette on the floor, stepped on it with the toe of her shoe and twisted her foot back and forth a few times. Then she put her purse strap over her shoulder and walked off toward the front of the drugstore. Her high-heeled shoes made a clacking noise on the tile as she wiggled her way out the door.

I reached in my pocket and came up with a dime and sat down on the seat in the booth. I didn't close the door because it was pretty stuffy even with the door open. No one answered at Anna's, so I decided to wait a few minutes and try again. I was fidgeting around in the phone booth when I remembered the envelope with my poem in it. I took it out of my back pocket and held it for a minute or so, trying to decide what to do. After I tried Anna's number again and got no answer, I decided to give up and take my poem on over to Mr. Marcus' house. I had already planned to leave it in his mailbox if he wasn't at home.

It's only a block from the drugstore over to Bridgewater Parkway, and Mr. Marcus lived a couple of blocks back toward my house, so it was more or less on my way home. It's hardly any farther to my house if I cut through Crestview Place rather than going around. On the way to his house, I tried to think of what I would say if he were at home, but I didn't need any rehearsal. When I got there, the house was totally dark except for the front porch light. I rang the doorbell a couple of times and then I stuck the envelope in the crack of the screen door to his porch. I walked back out to the street and turned right to go toward my house.

I had gotten to the front of the next house when I heard footsteps behind me. I turned and watched a man run up Mr. Marcus' driveway. I stood in the shadows looking back toward the house, so the man couldn't see me even if he looked my way. He first ran under the carport and stood in the dark for a minute or so and then he slinked around to the front door. My envelope must have fallen when he opened the screen door because I saw him bend down as if to pick something up. He looked back over his shoulder and then went through the front door into the house. I got nervous all over again. I didn't know what I was seeing, but I knew I wasn't going to go over and ring the doorbell.

I didn't want to draw attention to myself, so I just started walking toward what is known as the Ragg Swamp end of Bridgewater Parkway. Before they put in the drainage ditches, the area was swampland with a lot of gnarled old scrub oaks. You can get to my house by cutting through Crestview Place and then jumping over the drainage ditch behind Mr. Nacht's house. Unfortunately, you have to go through Mr. Nacht's yard, which he had already told me several times not to do. The alternative was to go all the way around Crestview Place back to Carapace, which added a couple of miles to the distance.

I was nervous and getting tired, so I didn't give much consideration to going around. Crestview Place has mostly large brick houses, much larger than our little frame house that looks like something built when Ragg Swamp was a refuge for muskrats. A wooded area encases the drainage ditch that separates Crestview Place from my street. I thought about going through someone else's yard and walking along in the woods until I got to my backyard, but I decided against that idea because trying to walk in the woods would be tricky in the dark. I concluded that the only thing that made any real sense was to go through Mr. Nacht's yard and run the risk of getting caught.

Mr. Nacht has a small white dog that usually barks at anybody who comes in the yard. My plan was to stay as far from the house as possible and hope the little dog wasn't outside. The plan actually worked perfectly insofar as getting through Mr. Nacht's yard without being yelled at. I slipped through the pine trees and then cut right and walked parallel to the ditch until I reached the narrow spot. I was about to leap across when I heard a whining noise back toward the house. I stopped and peered into the darkness.

At first, I couldn't see anything except the lights from the windows of the house, but after a few seconds I could see the little white dog. Instead of barking, the dog was standing with its tail down, whimpering piteously. I took a couple of steps toward the small dog, which cowered and ran not toward the house but along the ditch away from me. It was then I saw that the little dog was tethered to a wire like a clothesline, which Mr. Nacht had strung along the ditch at the very back of his yard. The tether was fastened to the wire so that the dog could slide the hook along the line and run back and forth across the yard. I don't care much about Mr. Nacht's dog, but the tether in the dark seemed cruel.

When I was in my room alone, I realized why the dog had bothered me. It was the way he was tethered to the wire. It was basically the same way Uncle Nat had tethered Nathan. I undressed and got in bed. I still felt very uneasy but I was tired. I closed my eyes and I could see Nathan with his long blond hair hanging down in his face, pulling the tether along the cable on the slope Uncle Nat had called Mount Moriah. Nathan was chanting and running, completely oblivious to the dangerous chaos around him. When I see Nathan in my mind now, the face I really see is my own, which is disturbing in a way. I've never told anybody that before. I lay there staring into the darkness for a long time thinking about the tether and Mr. Marcus, and worrying about everything. *Poccotola train broke down*, I kept repeating over and over in my mind.

FROST BITTEN

A few months before Nathan's death, we went to the city with Uncle Nat for a missions conference. The parsonage of the host church had extra rooms, so the four of us—Uncle Nat, Nathan, my mother, and me—moved in for the weekend. It didn't go well. Nathan had a bad seizure the first day we were there and then wandered off the next night. He was only gone for an hour or so but he caused a lot of stress. Our host alerted the neighbors, and we then fanned out in the neighborhood.

When I found him, he was standing at a neighbor's living room window muttering to himself. I shouted, "Nathan," but he ignored me, and then I saw the neighbors sitting in a swing on their front porch. I explained the situation to them, then we went around to the side of the house. Nathan was standing at the window, staring intently into a large window fan, his head making little circular movements. I don't know whether I can tell you what he was muttering but it sounded something like:

Esse by a sound,
Evolute abound,
Back into the ground:
Angle back around.

He repeated it over and over, probably five times in the few minutes we stood there watching him.

The peeping tom stuff was on my mind when I woke up Friday morning. The whole peeping tom thing made me uneasy. Not Nathan's incident, which wasn't really about peeping, but the guy looking in the window at Mrs. Brasher's house. I alternated between worrying about Mr. Marcus and fretting over Anna. She was not yet gone, and I didn't want to believe what she had said, but the truth is she was already getting hazy in my mind. I don't know how to explain it, but Anna had already begun to seem unreal, sort of a phantasm in my mind.

Since classes at Bridgewater were to begin on the following Tuesday, we could either preregister that Friday morning or we could register on Monday. I didn't have anything better to do so I talked Lichtman into going over with me on Friday. Since I started going to Bridgewater in the tenth grade, Lichtman has been my closest friend. Until last year when I got tangled up in things and got dropped from the honors program, Lichtman and I had been in the same classes but didn't become really close friends until we started practicing together on the track team.

That first year we started amusing ourselves with the

inverse proportionality axioms. The first one occurred while we were in class. The teacher was warbling on about stuff that was obvious, and Lichtman passed me a note that read: "The less you need to hear the more instruction you get." I grinned and passed him the following note:

> *It's an axiom of inverse proportionality called the Principle of Quantum Pedagogy. The axiom is stated thus: The quantum of pedagogy provided is always inversely proportional to the quantum of pedagogy needed. The symbol for all axioms of inverse proportionality is inversely laid triangles, thus:*

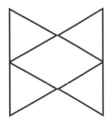

After that, we developed a lot of inverse proportionality axioms. If one occurred to us in class or somewhere we couldn't talk, we would just pass the symbol on a piece of paper. Sometimes that was enough, but often we had fun spelling it out later.

Lichtman is probably in most of the academic clubs at school. I think his mother causes it. You wouldn't believe the screwball stuff she wants poor old Lichtman to get in. His father doesn't get excited about anything except furniture. He's a pretty nice guy but furniture is his life. He talks about furniture like old people talk about grand-children and, so far as I can tell, that's all he talks about. He almost killed both Lichtman and me this past sum-mer, loading and unloading furniture. We told ourselves that we were going to build up our muscles and accu-mulate some money to buy a car, but at the end of the summer we had about as much money saved as we had new muscles, which was almost none.

We get along well most of the time, so the work wasn't all that bad. Actually, Lichtman and I are a lot alike. He broods about things, sometimes as much as I do. We resemble one another, except he's tall, lanky, and dark complexioned, and I'm tall, lanky, and light. We tend to think similarly but he's slightly more quantitative. He says that I think everything can be reduced to a word. He's wrong. After Nathan's death, I became so obsessive about prime and perfect numbers that my mother dropped my mathematics tutor for four months. I can obsess about almost anything.

Lichtman and I met at the administration building Friday morning at ten o'clock and went through our course selections. The purpose of preregistration was to simplify the process, but it turned out, as usual, to be total chaos. Instead of fifteen minutes, which would have been ample for normal people, the simplified pro-cess took about an hour and a half. I had hoped to run into Anna but she wasn't there. Instead of Anna, I ran into Coach Kern, the head coach who unfortunately coaches track. He walked up while Lichtman and I were standing in a disorganized line waiting to be shuffled around to more tables attended by teachers who seemed as confused by the process as we were.

The coach wasn't particularly friendly to either Lichtman or me, but he slapped Lichtman on the back and commented that he had done well with his summer running program. When he turned to me, he said, "You and I need to have us a little chat." He sort of spat the word "chat" and jutted his chin forward. "In my office, three this afternoon." His eyes squinted, his brow furrowed, his lips protruded and he raised one cheek in a twisted sneer. I have to say he disconcerted me. "Sure, Coach," I said, without even thinking about whether I could make it at three.

When we got through the preregistration obstacle course, Lichtman and I went over to the Frost Bite for lunch. The Frost Bite has floors and tables made of stained oak and exposed beams that crisscross the dining area. When we got there, it was full of students who had preregistered, maybe twenty of them girls, none of whom was Anna. Most of the girls were wearing shorts and most of them had on loafers and white socks.

I admit that the circumstances were not optimal for discussing much of anything non-carnal, but I had been trying to get Lichtman to focus on the concept of nothingness. I had tried, without success, to read *Being and*

Nothingness earlier in the summer, and I had come away with nothing (no pun intended), except one strange thing: When I tried to think of nothingness, I had a physical sensation in my head, like some peculiar electromagnetic impulse in my brain. I was thinking that the sensation must mean something, and I wanted Lichtman to try it and see what happened in his head.

During the past couple of years, Lichtman and I had talked a lot about meaning. It wasn't all that easy at first, because he pretended to know more than he actually did and he tried dropping some isms on me. After he found out that he couldn't bluff his way through, we confronted some real questions and grappled for elusive answers, but by the end of last year Lichtman was tired of talking about the stuff. He proclaimed himself an existentialist, which, according to him, relieved him from worrying about the opaque wall (which is what we started calling the boundary of our knowledge and understanding) and committed him to defining his own essence. I don't know what that means or how it is relevant, but okay.

I had a small book of poetry in my back pocket because I was trying to crib some ideas for a sonnet to Anna. The book was uncomfortable to sit on, so I took it out of my pocket and laid it on the table. It really had nothing to do with nothingness, the real subject I was about to mention, but as soon as I laid the book on the table, Lichtman looked at the ceiling with an expression of exasperation and said, "That's not the *Rubáiyát*, is it? Biddle, I think you're losing your mind. It's a pretty rhyme about the wall, a lot of very pretty words but ultimately nothing but lamentations without answers." For the record, I would offer that the *Rubáiyát* wasn't even in the poetry book I was carrying. "You ain't gonna find meaning in that rhyme," Lichtman said. "You want to know the meaning of life? There it is."

He was directing my attention toward a table across the room. Sarah Burchfield and a girl I didn't know were glancing at us as they carried on a fairly spirited conversation that we couldn't hear. Sarah's older brother Harry, whom Lichtman calls Odious Burch ("with homage and humble apologies to Charles Dickens"), was the first guy I met and my first friend when we moved from the country. It's hard to believe Sarah and Harry share ancestry.

Harry is a pluperfect ass and general emetic, but Sarah, according to my mother, has the highest measured IQ of any person—student or teacher—at Bridgewater. She's a year ahead of her age group and she still outscores everybody in the school. She is tall and thin and well proportioned, and happily she has become increasingly top heavy. When I looked up she smiled broadly and tilted her head a little without losing eye contact. She has a disconcertingly sultry mouth.

"Oh, man, Biddle," Lichtman muttered in a low voice, "Sarah Burchfield's looking at you like you were a Krispy Kreme doughnut and, as you may have noticed, she's got two of the largest meanings you ever saw. And she's very bright, which means, *a fortiori*, she defies the cranial calibration axiom." The "general theory of cranial calibration," as Lichtman and I formulated it, is that the size of a girl's brain is inversely proportional to the size of her boobs.

I had noticed Sarah's larval transformation, particularly the more prominent frontal facets. The change was pretty dramatic because Sarah hadn't been all that noticeable when I first met her. She had pretty auburn hair but she was skinny and formless, with large, almost spooky eyes and dark-rimmed glasses. The girl in the Frost Bite had bubbled out in the right places and nobody would describe her as spooky.

Several years ago, she sent me a note that I never answered. I started to talk to her a couple of times when I was at their house with Burch, but for some reason I never connected. I just wasn't very interested at the time, and she had actually seemed to avoid me. I waved to Sarah and smiled, but I still had no interest. I had been absorbed with Anna for almost a year and I could hardly fit Sarah Burchfield into my mind. The painful truth is that I had hardly been able to think of anything else since the first time I saw Anna.

"Yeah," I said. "I'm going with Anna, remember." I didn't mention that she had given me the old heave-ho or that in effect I may be going with her, but she was definitely not going with me. That is probably some kind of moron, maybe oxy or maybe just me.

"Oh, Lord, not the omnipresent, omniscient, all-powerful palindrome," Lichtman scoffed. "I read the other day that men have a tendency to see women as objects. The guy who did that study never considered your case. The palindrome is no object; she's all pluperfect subject. You've made her pure, singular and superlative subject. You've made yourself the object, totally unmodified and unqualified object. And saddest of all, I doubt there's a copulative verb anywhere to be found."

"You're being an ass," I said. "Do me a favor and try to focus a minute on something other than your libido. Here's the question for you: Have you ever tried to conceive of nothingness?"

"I'm trying. Lord knows I'm trying but you ain't helping a bit. As usual, you're not paying attention."

"You're not understanding the question . . . ."

"Wait, let me simplify this for you: The burden of your being is to take your hapless existence and create some essence. As you may have noticed, life has handed you a stone. For heaven's sake, Biddle, roll it and stop talking."

"I guess you know that makes no sense."

"You see, you're hung up on words again. You should love Sisyphus, the noble victim condemned to act out a mundane task over and over, no matter how inconsequential or irrelevant. Sisyphus is a Biddlesque character. Maligned. Put upon. Misunderstood. Noble. Mindlessly stuck."

"That's totally absurd, and I hate that metaphor. The mindlessness of rolling a stone up a hill over and over, that's what I hate. At least running around the track at school has purpose and consequence."

"Yeah, the purpose is to make the coach happy and the consequence is shin splints."

"Cynic," I said.

"Biddle, you're driving yourself nuts. I'm beginning to worry about you."

"How about worrying about the subject. And hold the ad hominem."

"I've held it as long as I can. It's getting harder and harder to hold. I'm tired of the questions. I don't know why you're continuing to flog this corpse."

"I don't either," I said after a pause.

"My father's answer is that if God had wanted you to know more, he'd have told you."

"Your father is a furniture man." The instant I said it I knew two things. First, I knew it would offend Lichtman. Second, I knew it was a boatload of irony. Every time he mentioned his father it really bothered me, but I don't know why.

"That's amusing coming from you. My father is a furniture man. You are *the* furniture man, remember? The palindrome has proclaimed it." As expected, irritation had bubbled up in Lichtman's voice.

"I just meant that he probably hasn't thought about this stuff."

"Yeah, maybe, but he knows what he believes, which is more than you can say for us." He looked across the room and reflexively I looked too. Sarah and the girl I didn't know were smiling in our direction. Lichtman gave them his most ingratiating grin. He has a small chip off the inside of his right front tooth. He isn't really all that chummy but his grin gives him a guileless, homey look. I could tell that he was trying to figure out a way to sit with the girls. We were sitting at a table for two, and they were almost directly across from us at a table, also for only two, against the opposite wall. The room was completely full and every table I could see was occupied. "People aren't supposed to be unhappy just because they don't understand everything clearly," Lichtman said. He wasn't even looking at me; he was staring at the girls across the room.

"Do you really think people are happy?" My voice was steeped in dramatic incredulity. "Lichtman, it's a vale of tears. The lot of man is tribulation. We lead lives of quiet desperation. Those are clichés because they're true. The only people really happy at any given time are those who are temporarily or permanently insane or people who revel in the sheer absurdity of their existence. We're subject to the laws of physics, which love no one. All matter is treated the same: It generates and disintegrates inexorably."

"Biddle," said Lichtman impatiently, "you may be right. Frankly, I think you like being a tragic figure.

Fine. Wallow in it. But I'm done. Go ahead and have a nervous breakdown. I may be back, but I hope not." He got up abruptly, walked across the room, and stood talking with Sarah and the other girl. I couldn't hear what Lichtman was saying, but Sarah looked over and smiled at me a couple of times. After a few minutes of unheard conversation, she got up and came over to my table, and Lichtman then took the seat across from the other girl. He smiled at me and made a sign with his thumb and index finger forming a circle. I didn't smile. I wanted to return a finger gesture of my own, but I didn't.

"Hi," Sarah said with far more diffidence than I expected. "Your friend Eddie asked me to trade places with him."

"Sure," I said, but I wondered what Anna would say if she walked in or heard about it and what I would say to explain it.

"He said I was a palindromic antidote. What does that mean?"

"He thinks he's a wit," I said testily. "He's only half right."

"I'm sorry. I think I've stepped into the middle of something." Then she shifted artfully away from the irritant. "I love this poem," she said, putting her hand on my book, which was only open because I was fumbling nervously with it. The book was opened at *When Lilacs Last in the Dooryard Bloom'd*, which was totally random and had nothing to do with anything. I didn't tell her the book was opened randomly or that at age ten I had almost gagged memorizing a bunch of Whitman ramblings. I was really uncomfortable and I didn't know what to say to Sarah. I was also annoyed with Lichtman for dumping important stuff and then leaving me in a situation that conceivably could be difficult. It also entered my mind that Anna probably didn't even care, but I didn't dwell on that dismal thought.

When the waitress brought the food that Lichtman and I had ordered, I asked her to take Lichtman's food to him at the table across the room. I looked at Sarah, who said sweetly, "I've already eaten, thank you." She smiled at me, maybe expecting me to say something. I wasn't in a great mood, so I didn't say anything. I just started eating one of my hotdogs. We had been waiting about thirty minutes for our food, and I had gotten hungry. Sarah sat across from me watching me eat and then said quietly, "Are you still going with Anna?" Bridgewater Academy isn't very large so it probably wasn't strange that she knew who my girlfriend was, but I was a little surprised at the question.

"Well," I said, trying to decide whether to tell her the truth, "I thought she might be here. She's been at camp half the summer. She's supposed to get back today."

"I'll leave if you think she won't like it," Sarah said in a sweet, sincere voice.

"Heavens, no," I said. I almost said, "She won't care," but I couldn't say it. Peculiarly I didn't want to appear to be in Anna's total bondage. I was also a little concerned that I might hurt Sarah's feelings. It was one of those situations where you don't know what to do. I didn't want to act unfriendly, but I didn't want to give the wrong signals either. She seemed content to watch me eat, so I decided not to make a big deal of it.

"Good," she said. It was nice to have an attractive and intelligent girl not only give me all of her attention but also act as though she approved of everything I did. Believe me, it was different from anything I had experienced with Anna. Sarah swept her hair back from the left side of her head and down her right shoulder so that it spread over her right breast like a radiant auburn shawl. She wore clear polish on her fingernails.

"Have you ever tried to imagine nothingness?" I asked.

"Nothingness, as in Jean-Paul Sartre?"

"Yeah," I said. "I've tried to imagine nothingness, no physical things, no spiritual presence, nothing existing. It seems to be an oxymoron. In some way, nothingness seems impossible. I think I know why, but I was just wondering whether you'd thought about it."

"Well, you haven't changed," she said after a slight pause. "We're sitting in the Frost Bite. The jukebox is playing Elvis and you're worried about nothingness." She reached over and took my right hand in hers. "You're priceless," she said, smiling broadly. "I haven't read Sartre, and I can't say I've ever worried about nothingness, but I'll think about it. Nothingness shows up as a zero in mathematics, but otherwise it's sort of slipped past me. I'll think about it, I promise." I extracted my hand and looked around the Frost Bite to see if anybody had seen her holding my hand. Nobody seemed to be looking. Lichtman was talking and gesturing, and the other girl was smiling like someone being royally entertained.

"Have you written poetry or anything recently?" Sarah asked, again shifting the conversation deftly to gentler territory. I didn't answer immediately because I was finishing the last of my hotdogs. It is flattering when people you hardly know ask about your stuff. Let me tell you, I puffed up like a frog, and I forgot about nothingness. It was as though she had asked whether I had won the Pulitzer Prize for poetry. She was getting better looking all the time. She certainly wasn't acting like her brother. Or Anna either, for that matter.

"I wrote a poem over the summer. Well, actually I wrote two poems. No, it's really one poem." I was in full swagger. You would have thought I was the poet laureate of the world. "I didn't like the form the first time I wrote it, so I changed it." I folded my hands behind my head and leaned back the way people do when they're pretty happy with themselves. When I slouched down in my seat, one of my knees came to rest against one of Sarah's knees. Her face reflected no notice of the contact, but momentarily her foot slipped behind the calf of my right leg. She was apparently sitting with her right leg crossed over the left one at the knee.

I was generally concerned about Anna but I became almost totally absorbed by Sarah's physical presence. Her smile was like a magnet. She also continued to press against my legs and casually touch my hands from time to time as she talked. A surge of testosterone flooded my brain, and the other people in the room disappeared. Sarah virtually never lost eye contact unless I looked away and, as anyone could have predicted, Moby began to expand territorially and throb uncomfortably in my jeans.

The effect of all this was to add to my confusion, which was already considerable. I was out of sorts anyway, and Sarah was unsettling some very basic assumptions. I had this vague sense that certain parts of my life were fixed. However confused, haphazard, and purposeless my existence, some things were definite and immutable. Among these were Anna, my mother, my running, and even my confused thoughts, all of which constituted a part of the permanent Biddlesphere that was real and there each morning when I woke up.

I was aware of the fact that nothing is forever, but I refused to think about the absence of any of these elemental structures of my life. Some things are supposed to be changeless, and the manifestations of them persist because they are true. Sarah evoked feelings that I associated in my mind with Anna, who, of course, remained the perfect, immutable form. I found myself struggling with the diversion of my feelings and the apparent contradictions.

"Biddle, you're going to be late for your date."

Lichtman's voice startled me. I sat up straight and disengaged my legs from Sarah's.

"What?" I said. I had become so charmed by Sarah's attentiveness that I didn't know what he was talking about.

"Coach Kern," Lichtman said. "You remember that sweetheart, don't you?" He and the girl I didn't know were smiling at us, and I had a feeling our tangled legs had become the subject of their conversation. I looked at my watch and immediately jumped up. It was a quarter till three.

"I've got a meeting to go to," I said to Sarah. I put enough money on the table for my food and a tip. "Nice to see you again."

"Nice to talk to you again," she said. "I really miss your coming by our house. My mother would love to see you again." She smiled voluptuously, then leaned back and put her hands behind her head as though straightening her hair. The effect was almost startling. I would like to say that I was thinking that she had a nice, attractive disposition, but you know that isn't remotely close to the truth. In fact, at that point in time (or, more precisely, at that stage of the interaction between two independent bundles of energy colliding in full complexity), Moby was doing most of the thinking.

"And don't forget about our game at Roby's," said Lichtman. "Four o'clock. And please don't forget to tell Kern how much I love him."

"Got it," I said and I went toward the door. I heard

"Bye, Kit" from Sarah but I didn't respond. "I'll be working on nothingness," she shouted. I just kept moving.

The coach's office is only about ten minutes' walking distance from the Frost Bite, so I really wasn't all that rushed. I think that I just wanted to get out because Sarah had disconcerted me. I was actually a little worried that she might come up to me when I was with Anna. As I walked back toward Bridgewater, I squeezed Sarah out of my mind. The testosterone in my system began to dissipate when I started focusing on what the coach wanted. I actually knew what he wanted in a general way. I had skipped more than a few track practices the year before and hadn't checked my summer running with him as he'd requested. Some things are obvious, if not easy.

SISYPHUS

The coach has an office in the rear of the administration building. It's underneath the main floor because the ground is higher in the front of the building than in the back. The walls of the room are concrete blocks painted white. Several small pipes, also painted white, run along the ceiling, and two fluorescent fixtures and a four-blade fan are suspended from the ceiling. I remember the screen door popping behind me when I went in and the spring on the door whirring for a while after the door shut.

Coach had his feet propped up on a beat-up old desk that was situated directly under the ceiling fan, and he was holding a fly swatter in his right hand and sort of tapping his right shoulder with the edge of the flap. Junk and athletic equipment were everywhere. The fan was moving the air around in the room and a stack of parental consent forms was rising and falling with the turn of the blades. The draft created by the fan felt good. I was damp with sweat, so I folded my arms over my head to let the air circulate around my body. I felt like a prisoner standing at attention.

He looked up at me without smiling. He started shaking his head slowly from side to side and pressed his lips. I assumed that he was struggling to find the right words. Finally, he stood up and said, "Straw," and then paused and wagged his head some more. He was referring to me. My hair is sort of long and coarse and it gets bleached out in the summer. Coach has a nickname for almost everybody. His put-down name for Lichtman is Light Man; my friend Q. Ball is Copperhead because of his reddish hair.

During the pause while he was standing there acting disgusted with me, I was looking at a stand-up frame on his desk containing a picture of a sandy-haired woman and a silky-haired little girl who appeared to be four or five years old. The little girl's hair looked very much like mine, parted in the middle of her head and pushed back on the sides, and I was wondering if he had a nickname for her.

He made an expression with his mouth and eyes that seemed to convey both exasperation and dismay. "Straw, sit down over here, son. We got to have ourselves a little chat." The coach was always telling us to sit down, maybe because he's not very tall. When he talked to us, we were always sitting on the ground or the gym floor. It didn't bother me a whole lot, but it seemed a little peculiar. He was wearing his gray Marine Corps pullover with the sleeves cut off at the shoulder. He wears pullovers most of the time, maybe because they show off his bulging biceps and partially hide the growing paunch that rims his khakis.

"Straw, do you want to participate in the varsity sports program?" I thought at first he wanted me to answer and I started to say something, but he kept on talking. "If you don't, you're going right back to gym classes. One thing for darn sure, Straw, we're not gonna have a repeat of last year. You miss one practice and you're off the team unless you're so sick you're dyin'." He sniffed for emphasis and pressed his lips.

One of the reasons I had dreaded talking to him was that I didn't know what I wanted to do about track. I enjoyed running when I was in the mood, but I wasn't usually in the mood at three-thirty in the afternoon when the coach scheduled the practices. In the afternoon I wanted to go to Anna's house, or, if I couldn't do that, I liked to get a Coke and just sit somewhere and read. I didn't want to be bothered in the afternoon except maybe by Anna. I preferred running late in the day when it's cooler and I could run along thinking about whatever was on my mind. I had been trying to decide whether I wanted to continue with the track team, and I had decided to see if I could just participate in the events but not practice every day.

"Why do I feel like I'm not gettin' through to you, Straw?" This time I knew he didn't expect a response.

He didn't pause long. "You got some ability," he said, his voice becoming almost a whine, "but, son, you're not gonna get anywhere in this world without discipline and hard work. Straw, it starts here!" His face was red, and he was leaning forward, pointing down at his desk with both index fingers. He was still holding the fly swatter, which seemed to confuse his gesture.

Then he settled back in his chair, carefully placed the fly swatter down on the desk as though it were breakable, and put his fingertips together. He sat for a while with his head bowed, staring at his fingers, maybe trying to regain his composure. I found myself staring at the top of his head. He wears his hair in a crew cut and his hairline is receding on the sides of his forehead so that the sprig in the middle forms a little fuzzy peninsula.

"Last year, Straw, your name kept comin' up in our teacher conferences, and we just finished this year's pre-registration conference. Straw," he said, shaking his head, his voice getting low, "you're pullin' the same stuff in your classes that you pull out here and it ain't workin'. You're not with anybody's program, here or in any class. You've been dropped from every honors class you were in." He tugged at the neck of his pullover. "Well, except maybe English, and even Mr. Marcus says you want to read books and do your poems mostly off on your own." He waved his hand in the air as though erasing an invisible chalkboard, lowered his eyebrows, and stuck out his lips. "That's fine." Then, with his voice rising, he repeated,

"That's fine, Straw. I like some poems. I like to read a pleasure book sometimes too."

I don't know why but that one got me. I wanted to say, *Whoa! Wait! You've gone too far! Way too far! Will somebody please help?* You won't believe this, but Dr. Ball once told me that a primary purpose of school is to teach patience and humility, because you usually have to deal with people who aren't as smart as you are. I don't know why he told me that, but I think I know why it came into my mind that afternoon in the coach's office.

I wanted to take the coach seriously but he was making it really hard. I'm supposed to believe that he likes some poems and he likes to read some "pleasure" books, and I'm supposed to pretend that I believe what he's saying and that I think it's meaningful. I looked at him and wanted to tell him the truth, maybe just go ahead and say it: In most of the interactions and conversations I have, I feel like a sewage treatment plant, not solely because of the dung shoveled on me at Bridgewater but particularly because of Bridgewater droppings. Actually, I didn't say anything.

"Straw, it ain't enough!" The strident voice jarred me back into the bowels of coach-world. "It ain't anywhere near enough," he said gravely. "You've got to work with the program." He got out of his chair and walked around the desk. He punched the palm of his left hand with his right fist and said, "You need discipline, son. You need to know what you're doin' every day. You need to stop wanderin'." He punched his palm again. "You don't know where you came from and you don't know where you're goin', Straw. Worse than that, you ain't tryin' to find out." He put his hands behind his back, apparently to demonstrate authority and composure, and walked slowly back around and sat down in his chair.

A fly buzzed in front of his face and landed on the desk in front of him. He stealthily picked up the swatter, but the fly zoomed away and made crossing sweeps while the coach swished the swatter through the air a few times and hit nothing. "You may be the fastest boy on the team, Straw," he said dismissively, "but you're still only half tryin'. If you could find out who you are, son, you might really do somethin'. I mean really do somethin'. There are college coaches all over the place who'd give you a scholarship in a minute if I assured 'em you'd cooperate, but I don't know what to tell 'em. I just don't know what to say." He jutted out his jaw and squinted. "Straw," he said, "are you with me? Do you understand the impact of what I'm sayin'?" I was staring absentmindedly at the stack of consent forms pulsating with the ebb and flow of the air current. I hadn't expected him to ask a question that he wanted me to answer.

"Yes, sir, I think so," I said after I focused on the question. I said that I knew what he meant but it just sounded very familiar: Get with the program and stay with the program. Maybe I should have gone to practice and maybe I ought to work on class assignments, but sometimes I think, "Aw, what the heck," and I just do something else that's more interesting. Everybody seems to know what I ought to do and it usually has something to do with a program. I used to enjoy running, but I was never all that interested in the program.

One of the things I was struggling with was why everything has to be part of a program. "I run a lot anyway," I said after a brief pause. "What difference does it make if I don't do it on schedule? I'm doing okay. I'm as fast as I've ever been. Maybe faster than last year. What if I didn't practice with the team? What if I practiced when it worked better with my schedule?" I was trying to work around to my idea of running in the meets and not being an official member of the team or at least not practicing with the team.

His face reddened again, and he came out of his chair, leaning over with his hands on the desk. "You can't have a program that way, Straw. You can't have people show up when they want to. That's what I'm talkin' about, son. Discipline means doin' somethin' even if you don't feel like it. You make a commitment and then you do it. You follow the program. Straw, you gotta get a grip on reality and stop that mopin' and wanderin' around."

He clenched his jaw and leaned over as though he were about to tell me a secret. "Straw," he said in a low voice, "we're this close to doin' somethin' special." He held up his thumb and index finger about an inch apart. "We could win it all. We got the talent. If I can get you disciplined and keep the Light Man healthy, we can put this program where it ought to be. Do you understand how close we are?"

This time I knew he wanted me to say something, maybe not an answer but some kind of response. The direction of the conversation wasn't going toward my notion of flexibility. "What if you just like to run," I said, trying to coax the subject back around, "but you don't want to practice with the team? I was thinking about maybe just running on my own and, if you think I'm fast enough or ready or whatever, you could let me run in the meets or not, depending on . . . ."

"Straw," he shouted, cutting me off, "sometimes, son, I don't know what to think. You're a bright boy. You have to know that doesn't make any sense." He swallowed and made an odd motion with his head as though he were carrying on a conversation in his mind. Then he contin-ued in a calm and deliberate voice. "You have to be a part of a program. If you can't practice, you're not committed enough. You can't hone your skills on your own. That's the whole thing. You commit yourself and go out there and do it." The look of frustration was still on his face, but his voice was higher and he articulated his words very carefully. His hands were folded in front of him and he moved his head emphatically as he spoke.

"I'm just trying to fit it all together, Coach," I said finally, after trying to think of something good to say and failing. The truth is I just wished the coach would go away. I hunched over and closed my eyes, and put my hands on my head with my elbows on my knees. Everything got very quiet. I wanted the coach to go away and somehow, strangely, he evaporated. He just disappeared. In my mind, all I could see was a mist, and I was alone. I could hear a sound like a voice somewhere a long, long way off, but I couldn't tell what it was saying.

I partially covered my ears and clenched my eyes together. Then, in my mind, I was looking down at the track at school, hovering over the track, and there was this boy on the track. He was sweating and straining, and he looked totally bewildered. He was pushing a stone in the middle lane, shoving the stone with all his strength and dutifully staying in his lane. He looked up at me, but he didn't say anything. I couldn't figure out where he thought he was going or what he was trying to accomplish. I wanted to shout to him: *It's an oval, a loop, and it doesn't go anywhere.* He paused like he had heard my thoughts and looked up. He looked straight at me with anguish and bewilderment all over his face, but he never said a word.

"Straw! Straw!" I heard the coach shout. "Are you all right, son?"

"Yeah," I said, trying to regroup as the boy's face disappeared into the mist and, just like that, I was back in the cluttered office staring at the coach's petulant face.

"I'm wonderin' where you go when you zone out like that, and I'm not the only one wonderin'. You're unnervin' everybody at Bridgewater. You need to get hold of yourself, Straw. Are you listening to me? Do you understand what I'm sayin'?"

"Yeah," I said. The thing is I really had no idea what he had been saying, so I asked, "What do you mean?" It was probably stupid, but I didn't know what else to say.

"Discipline," he said. "It's all about discipline."

"Okay," I said, but I still didn't know what to say. When he sat there glaring at me and looking expectant, I said, "I never seem to have enough time for what I want to do, and I can't figure out how to make everything work. Too many people want me to do too many things, and I can't figure out how to fit them all in or cut some out."

"Straw, Straw, Straw," he said, shaking his head, "you're making this too hard. It's simple. Follow the program. It only gets hard when you fly in the face of reality. All you need is to get a little discipline in your life and things will start falling into place. Do you follow me, son? It's that simple."

"Yeah, okay," I said, but I was really just giving up. I could tell that either he didn't understand what I was saying or I didn't understand what he was saying. I was trying to tell him that I didn't have time for track or rather I didn't want a lot of training when he wanted me to do it. If I spend my mornings in class and my afternoons training and my nights getting ready for the next morning's classes, I don't have time for anything else. Every time I cut out one of them, somebody gets upset. It doesn't even matter if you do something really better with your time. They only count it if it's part of the program. You could be discovering the theory of relativity, but it wouldn't count if you failed to complete your lab experiment. I'm not saying that I ever really do anything better. I'm just saying that it wouldn't make any difference anyway.

"Straw," he said, trying to look grave and solemn, "you are a product of Bridgewater Academy. This is not an ordinary institution I'm talking about. Bridgewater stands for something, Straw." *Oh, Lord,* I thought, *not that one too! Is he going to scrounge around in the barrel for every last apple?* "We are not mediocre here," he said. "You may not be mature enough to know it, but you need this program, and you need to stand up for Bridgewater. I'm not going to try to belabor the point here anymore, so let's cut to the chase. Are you in this program or not?"

He was no longer speaking in a threatening tone. His voice had almost a tone of pleading. I didn't know what I wanted to do. I couldn't see any way out, but I didn't really want to be in. I felt trapped. It isn't a commitment if you're dragged into it, is it? Or is that the point? You just take the programs as they're handed to you. Even if you want your afternoons free, you step up and get in the program. Does this make the afternoons meaningful? Or is it all just an absurdity? Anyway, I figured I might as well give up. The coach couldn't see my point. Also, I wasn't sure my idea made any sense. Besides, Lichtman would probably be bummed if I dropped track.

"Sure, Coach," I said. That's what I said but I felt like saying, "Give me my stone and let me start shoving and grunting." But I didn't. Instead, I said with all the sincerity I could manage, "I understand, Coach. You can count me in." That's not what I wanted to say.

Coach Kern's head bobbed forward a few times and his right eye closed slightly. "I think we've had a good talk, Straw. I think we're communicatin'. You know, we need to talk more often. I can teach you some things. I've been around the track a few times." He sat forward in his chair with his elbows on his desk, squinting at me for about a minute with a hint of a smile on his lips. I don't know what he was thinking. Then he settled back in his chair, propped his feet on the desk, and picked up the fly swatter.

"Okay, Straw, you need to make up some time. I want you to get started. Ten laps around the track right now. And, Straw," he said, once again with eyebrows up and the corners of his mouth down, "I want you to move your butt. Don't go out there and lollygag. And get yourself back here on Monday ready to rip." He sniffed authoritatively and nodded his head a couple of times.

"Yes, sir," I said, and headed for the door. When I got outside, I realized that I had on loafers. I had a pair of track shoes in the locker room, but I'd have to get the coach to let me in the gym. I thought about going back and telling the coach that I didn't have time to run, or just walking off. I stood on the stoop grinding my teeth for a minute or so and then I went ahead and did the laps.

A lap around the track is a quarter of a mile, so he wanted me to run only two and a half miles. I sat on the ground and thought about it for a few minutes. Then I took off my loafers and socks and rolled up my jeans to just above the knee.

I ran the first mile just about full speed because I was already going to be late and because I just felt like blowing it out. Then I got a side stitch and had to slow down some, but I was still moving pretty fast. I was supposed to meet Lichtman and the other guys at Robicheaux's house for a two-hand touch football rematch of a game we had played several weeks before. Lichtman, Q. Ball, and I had trounced Burchfield, Robicheaux, and a big guy named Chuck Breamer, and they had asked for a rematch. I wasn't really in the mood to play but I couldn't ditch Lichtman and Q. Ball. I was trying to do six-minute miles, which meant the total time would be fifteen minutes or less, which meant that I could make it to Robicheaux's house by a little after four.

A good thing about running is you do it by yourself, and you can mull things over in your mind. Ordinarily when I ran, I used the time to work out problems. The coach had so irritated and disconcerted me that I had difficulty concentrating on anything. The only thing I could think about was the coach's advice. The thing that puzzles me is, if you don't know where you're going, what difference does it make whether you have discipline? I had this nagging feeling that I ought to be doing something, going in some particular direction, but I couldn't figure out either the something or the direction. I might have been making it too hard, but, even if the coach is right that you just follow the program, whose program do you follow? I was thinking there has to be a better answer.

When I finished my laps, I went back and picked up my shoes. A note from the coach was stuck in my left loafer:

> Straw,
>
> Go by Mr. Marcus' office when you
> finish your laps.
>
> > Kern

I wadded up the note and threw it on the ground. Mr. Marcus' office is in the English department, which has offices in a building adjacent to the administration building. I hustled over to the English offices only to find Mr. Marcus' office dark. A note was taped to his door:

> Kit,
>
> I'll be back at 4:30. If you can't wait,
> please leave a note on the message
> board letting me know when we can
> get together. I have read your poem.
>
> > Ira Marcus

I pulled the note off the door and stared at it. A statement like "I have read your poem" is not very satisfying.

It doesn't say "I think your poem stinks" and it doesn't say "I like your poem." I thought the statement needed an adjective: "I have read your [crummy, superb, depressing, puzzling, etc.] poem."

Even if I hadn't had a football game, I wouldn't have wanted to hang around all afternoon. After considering the alternatives, I decided to leave Mr. Marcus a note. I went down to the message board, took a piece of paper from the pad, and, using the pencil in the little trough, I wrote this note:

> *Mr. Marcus,*
>
> *Sorry I had to leave. I'll drop by your office tomorrow (Saturday) afternoon at 3:00. I've got some stuff to do in the morning, but I'll be free in the afternoon. If that is not convenient, please let me know.*
>
> > *Kit Biddle*

I tacked my note to the board, hurried out of the building, and took off as fast as I could move toward Roby's house. I was running barefooted, trying to avoid the lines in the sidewalk and stepping around broken glass and other sharp edges, and I was carrying my loafers tucked against my chest like a football. All the distractions threw my timing off, and dodging the sidewalk lines and the treacherous debris threw my stride off, but I moved pretty well considering the circumstances.

CATALEPSIS

Roby lives in a white frame house with square white columns in the front. The house has a long, narrow porch in the back overlooking what they call the lawn. The lawn is actually a part of Roby's yard and a part of the backyards of eight or ten other houses inside Willis Circle. About a hundred yards behind Roby's house the field dips into a swale that drains water off into Catawpa Creek. The field is pretty good for touch football because it's flat before you reach the swale and because somebody keeps the grass cut close. When I rounded the house, I saw Roby hit Q. Ball with a pass out in the field.

The first guy to see me was Burch. When I first got to know him in the fall of 1953, he begged me to go to Bridgewater and then stopped being my friend a couple of years later. Some of us call him Burch but he doesn't like it. He says it makes him sound like a tree. When we don't want to hear him whine, we call him Burchfield and sometimes even Harry. Burch is about my height, with wiry dishwater-blond hair. His mouth is small for his face and, to make it worse, he has a habit of tightening his lips when he talks, particularly if he's irritated or trying to act serious about something. His father does his mouth the same way, so it may be genetic. His shoulders are narrow and for some reason he holds his shoulders sort of hunched up around his head.

When Burch saw me, he shouted out, "Hey, you schmuck, where you been? I thought you were gonna forfeit." I couldn't see his mouth, but I'm sure it was tightened up. Since Lichtman was already there, I was sure Burch knew exactly where I had been.

Roby turned around as I ran up behind him. "Come on, man, you're holding up the game," he said and greeted me with one of his elaborate sniffs.

"Let's go," I said. "I'm ready." Roby is dark like his father, but totally lacks his father's massive build. Roby seems to have sinus problems. It's not just that he sniffs. He raises the whole side of his face so that his teeth show when he sniffs, and he sometimes makes a snorting noise.

"Hey, Chuck, let's get the show on the road," Roby said. When he got no response, he repeated, "Hey, Chuck, let's go." Chuck was lurking behind the bushes next to the house, probably peeing. Chuck is more Roby's friend than anybody else's. He is huge, and he has these great big lips. He keeps his mouth hanging open a lot and his brow furrowed, so he has a perplexed expression most of the time. Chuck is a real football player. He's a nose guard on the team at the Catholic high school where he and Roby go. I think Burch thought that Chuck's size gave his team the edge, but in touch football size doesn't mean as much as you might think. The most important things are speed and quickness. If both teams have someone who can throw the ball, the team with the most speed is probably going to win.

"We won the toss," Roby said. Lichtman, Q. Ball, and I then moved to the far end of the field. Lichtman kicked the ball high and to the left, trying to get the ball to Chuck, but Burch cut him off and grabbed the ball two seconds before I downed him with a two-hand touch.

Burch scowled. "Were you offsides, Biddle?" he snapped. "Robicheaux, you gon' need to help me watch Biddle. He cheats." He gave me his most menacing scowl. I didn't respond. Running in general and speed in particular are sensitive subjects for Burch. When he didn't make varsity either his freshman or sophomore year, he dropped track.

"Come on, Burch, let's play ball," Roby said.

"And don't call me Burch." He tightened his lips and hunched his shoulders.

"I think that I shall ever search," said Lichtman in a soft but audible tenor, "for a tree as fruitless as a Burch." He then looked skyward and said, "Forgive me, Kilmer, I know that hurts."

"Come on, let's play ball," Roby repeated. Burch glowered and hunched. They huddled a minute and then came out with Burch wide, Roby passing, and Chuck centering and blocking. Roby went back in a shotgun stance, and Chuck got in position to snap the ball. Chuck called out, "Ten-count before the rush." What he meant was that the defender at the line of scrimmage had to count to ten slowly before crossing the line and rushing the passer. He snapped the ball back to Roby, and Burch took off downfield. Lichtman stayed with him step for step, and I stood at the line counting. Just as I reached ten, Roby heaved the ball in the direction Burch was running. Burch spread his arms to catch it but the ball never arrived. In about four quick steps, Lichtman dashed in front of Burch, cradled the ball under his arm, and took off back down the field.

The goal line at that end of the field was marked by a little pine tree that's not far from the back of the house, so it got a little tricky. To make matters worse, Roby's father had been putting in new shrubs and trees. I was trying to block Chuck, who was running across the field to cut Lichtman off. Chuck hit me and knocked me into Lichtman, who sidestepped to stay on his feet. He didn't see this guy-wire holding up one of Mr. Robicheaux's new trees. He caught the wire with the top of his left foot. Lichtman did a perfect flip in the air and landed on his back. The ball popped out of his hands and landed at the edge of the azaleas.

"Damn," said Burch, and he kicked the ball as hard as he could through the azaleas toward the back of the house. "Roby, that was one sorry pass." He hunched his shoulders and pressed his lips, ignoring Lichtman, who was lying on the ground not moving. The top of Lichtman's left foot was gushing blood. He lay there on his back completely still, eyes closed, not moving.

After his accident, my father was *in a coma* (people kept saying that) for a long time before he died. I remember seeing him with his eyes closed and his face completely immobile. I know it doesn't make any sense, but I don't like to see people with their eyes closed unless I know why, like they're sleeping or something; then it doesn't bother me so much. I was getting nervous, when Lichtman finally opened his eyes. I said, "You all right, man?"

He sat up slowly. "Yeah, I think so." I could tell that he was doing a mental inventory to determine what parts were still functioning. "Roby, you trying to kill people with these wires?" He turned toward me. "The guy will do anything to win a game."

"Hey, man, you're out of bounds," Roby said. "My old man's gonna be pissed about his landscaping. If you hurt that tree, I can tell you it's gonna be ugly." He sniffed and smiled at the same time.

I helped Lichtman up, and he leaned on me and hobbled around to Roby's back door. Mrs. Robicheaux was standing in the kitchen when we got to the door. "Stay right there, Eddie," she said. "Don't track blood in the house. What in the world have you done?" Mrs. Robicheaux is really pretty for an older lady. She brought some tape and gauze out on the porch and squatted down to wrap Lichtman's foot. She wore a loose blue jersey that hung down in front and Burch was standing on the top step of the porch craning to see down her shirt. Nobody noticed except me. I was standing behind Lichtman, who was sitting on the bottom step. Lichtman had a large gash across the top of his foot. "You're going to need stitches. How're you getting home?" Then without pausing, she said, "Harry, can you give Eddie a ride home?"

Burch stuck out his lips and didn't say anything at first. I could tell he didn't want to. Finally, he grumped, "Yeah, okay." Then he turned to Lichtman, "You can't get blood in my car." I helped Lichtman out to Burch's car. Burch gave Lichtman a newspaper he had gotten from Mrs. Robicheaux and said, "Put that under your foot, man. I don't want any blood dripping on my seat." Lichtman climbed into the back seat, holding the newspaper under his foot. "Watch out, now," said Burch, "don't let that blood drip on the seat." Lichtman looked up at me and shook his head. Chuck went with them because he wanted a ride home and our game was over anyway.

After Lichtman left I went into the azaleas and retrieved the football, and then Q. Ball, Roby, and I began tossing the ball around. We took turns throwing the ball while the other two went deep for passes. We had been jocking around behind Roby's house for thirty or forty minutes when the ball sailed through the azaleas again. Q. Ball had thrown the ball five feet over my head. I looked in the azaleas and all around but didn't see the ball. Then I saw the opening in the lattice screen covering the crawl space under Roby's house. A portion of the screen had been removed, leaving an opening about six feet wide. I kneeled down and squinted through the opening in the crawl space and, after my eyes adjusted to the light, I could see the ball about ten feet away.

I sat there frozen at the prospect of having to crawl under the house. I have trouble with close spaces, so I wanted to wait a little bit and see if I couldn't steady my nerves. I don't know where the claustrophobia comes from, but it's been there a long time. The first time I experienced it was when I was nine years old. Nathan hadn't started wandering off at that point, so everybody was really upset when he disappeared one afternoon. Uncle Nat was about to call the sheriff when we found him squatting under the house. Uncle Nat's house was about four feet off the ground, with brick covering most of the crawl space around the house. Uncle Nat asked me to go in and get Nathan, who was ignoring everybody. I said sure and then knelt down and crawled through the small opening. I was under the house and a few feet from Nathan when the panic struck, and I experienced my first freeze-up. Uncle Nat had to crawl under the house and get both of us out.

"You see it, Biddle?" Roby had come up behind me while I crouched in the small opening.

"Yeah, I've got it." Then, I steeled my nerves and plunged through the opening in the lattice screen. I wasn't going to admit to Roby that I couldn't crawl under a house.

"Okay, man," he said. "I'm going to get us some water."

I went only about five feet under the house before totally freezing up. My chest constricted, and I began to sweat. I closed my eyes and took a few deep breaths. I don't know how long I was under there staring at the ball a few feet away and trying to overcome a sense that the floor joists were closing in on me. At some point I heard raised voices. I looked around but no one was there. I closed my eyes and used my elbows to inch toward the ball. I had to stop every few seconds because I would get so constricted in the chest that I couldn't breathe. The effort to crawl those few feet was so great that I bumped the football with my head when I reached it. It may have been easier crawling out than crawling in, but I still had to worm most of the way with my eyes shut.

I had almost reached the opening in the lattice screen when I heard the raised voices again. I looked up, and I could see legs through the azaleas. A group of people had assembled behind Roby's house. I can't tell you how good it felt when I reached the opening in the lattice. I walked around the azaleas into the yard feeling like a mountain climber who had made it to the top. I was wiping the dirt off my elbows, grinning and holding the ball like a trophy.

I was so relieved to be out from under the house and so proud to have retrieved the ball that I didn't immediately appreciate the drama in progress in Roby's backyard. Professor Ball was standing about ten feet from Roby's father. Both of them were scowling. The first person I got to was Burch, who had just gotten back from taking Lichtman and Chuck home.

"You ain't gonna believe this one, Biddle," Burch whispered conspiratorially. "Robicheaux's daddy has been fooling around with Q. Ball's momma, and Dr. Ball is over here to fight."

It took me awhile to digest this information. I thought at first that Burch was being Burch. Then I was sort of stunned. I knew that Mr. Robicheaux and Mrs. Ball were both from somewhere in Louisiana, but I didn't know they knew one another very well. The whole thing was stupefying. I couldn't understand why Professor Ball was talking to Mr. Robicheaux rather than to Mrs. Ball and, to be candid, I found it unbelievable that Professor Ball would threaten Mr. Robicheaux. Mr. Robicheaux is a monster of a man. Professor Ball, not so much. He looks like an old math teacher. His red hair is getting gray and thin, and his pale, freckled skin has begun to droop under his chin and on the backs of his arms. It didn't look good. Mr. Robicheaux was wearing jeans and tennis shoes but no shirt. His tanned muscles rippled in his chest and arms. Blood vessels stood out on the sides of his neck and the muscles in his back forced his arms out so that he looked like a wrestler.

Professor Ball was wearing Bermuda shorts and one of those white undershirts with the narrow straps over the shoulders. His white skinny legs looked as though they were hanging from the bottom of his shorts, and his knees looked like white knobs centered between the hem of his shorts and the top of his argyle socks. His stomach hung out over his belt, and his face was even redder than usual. I think that Professor Ball wanted to look menacing, but he was wearing half-moon glasses on his forehead like he had been reading right before deciding to pick a fight with the burliest guy in the neighborhood. He can't even make a real fist with his right hand because the index finger won't bend. The finger is pink and hairless and looks like it was caught in a machine or something. In a way I was proud of Professor Ball for standing his ground, even if he did look pitiful.

"You stay away from my wife, Robicheaux," he said, tilting his head and clenching his teeth.

Mr. Robicheaux didn't move, and he didn't look frightened. He said very calmly, "You came down here to fight, Professor? Well, here I am." Professor Ball continued to scowl, holding his fists forward with his stiff finger pointing strangely at a bald spot of ground in front of him. I looked reflexively at the ground where Professor Ball's stiff finger was pointing. The lawn mower had shaved the grass away and left a barren plateau exposed. A small army of fire ants circled on the barren spot between the scowling men. Everything was so tense around me that I may be wrong about what I thought I saw, but the ants didn't seem to be running about chaotically. They seemed to be moving slowly, almost resolutely.

"I'm not coming in your yard, Robicheaux." Professor Ball's strained voice jarred my attention away from the ground. "You come out here." It didn't occur to me then, but looking back, I don't know how Professor Ball knew where Mr. Robicheaux's yard began because the grass all looked the same. I have a feeling Professor Ball really didn't want to fight but had to make a point at the risk of getting hurt. I'm glad Mr. Robicheaux didn't come out of his yard, because if he had stepped forward, I'm afraid Professor Ball might have done something foolish.

Lines of sweat had formed across Professor Ball's brow and upper lip, and his face showed strain, as though he were lifting some enormous weight. But he stood face-to-face with Mr. Robicheaux for a good while. You have to give him credit for that much. He raised the stiff index finger, pointed toward Mr. Robicheaux, and said, "Stay away from my wife." Then he turned and walked back through the field toward his house. His Bermuda shorts were pushed down beneath his stomach, and his boxer shorts were visible in the back where his undershirt was bunched. I felt sorry for him. Mr. Robicheaux looked like a bronzed warrior, and Professor Ball seemed even more nerdish than usual because he tried to seem valiant.

Q. Ball followed his father across the field without saying anything or even looking back. When Mr. Robicheaux
turned back toward his house, Mrs. Robicheaux was
standing on the back steps with a distressed expression
on her face. The rest of us were standing around looking
uncomfortable and out of place. Mr. Robicheaux looked
at Mrs. Robicheaux and, without looking away, said,
"You boys go on home now. Jimbo, I want you to go to
your room." Nobody said a word. It looked like a fire drill
the way we hustled our butts out of the yard. When we
got around to the street, Burch said, "Biddle, you need a
ride?" Burch was the only one of us who had a car. His
father gave him a red Pontiac convertible for his sixteenth
birthday. I have to admit I was pretty envious.

"I need to jog," I said. "Thanks anyway." I lived right
down the street and over a block and I needed to be
alone. I sure didn't feel like talking to Burch. I jogged
around the corner and then walked the rest of the way
home. I was sort of depressed. It really bothered me
about Mr. Robicheaux and Mrs. Ball. Poor old Professor
Ball doesn't smile much, and he sits around a lot with his
stiff finger pointing off in some strange direction. He just
looks so flaccid and pitiful, and Mr. Robicheaux looks
like something out of mythology and also seems to have
everything, including maybe Mrs. Ball.

She never mentioned it, but I suspect that my mother
heard about the Robicheaux-Ball situation almost immediately. Out of nowhere I got a lecture on character and

integrity. When something happens that provides the occasion for a lecture, it's like the whole dam bursts and all the other complaints come pouring out. In the last year or so, my schoolwork has come up about half the time. It makes no difference that there's no possible connection between my grades and Mr. Robicheaux. My mother seems to think that every evil has some insidious connection with every other one. Her usual exhortation to me is "be mature," which means do schoolwork, etc. With Anna on my mind that Friday, I heard only intermittent snatches of her lecture.

QUANTUM YEARNING

By the time I got through showering, dressing, and eating, it was almost seven. I had told Anna in my last letter that I would be at her house at seven-thirty. Of course, she didn't respond, but that's a different problem. The main irritant Friday evening was that I had to ride the bus. We don't have a car. My mother doesn't even drive, which is completely beyond comprehension. We have neither a car nor a television set because both make her nervous and, she says, both are a waste of money. We end up walking a lot, riding buses and pacing while we wait for people to come by and give us a ride. Unlike me, she has friends who have cars, including particularly the unctuous Dr. Bob. Other than Q. Ball, who has an old motor scooter, I don't have a real friend who has anything mobile. Lichtman's parents have promised to buy him a car for graduation if he jumps through all the right hoops. I have neither a vehicle nor a promise. I was nursing these wounds when

I went out the front door. I yelled over my shoulder, "I'm off to Anna's. I'll be back before twelve."

From somewhere in the house I heard my mother say, "You be careful and don't you be late. Kit?" I didn't answer because I was afraid she might still be in lecture mode, and the bus was due at our stop at seven. I was hustling down the sidewalk when I saw Burch's fancy convertible pulling into the driveway.

"What's up?" he said.

"Nothing," I said but I stupidly stopped beside his car and waited for him to tell me why he was there.

"Thought we might do something." He gave me his half-sneer smile.

"I'm on my way to Anna's," I said.

"You sure she wants to see you?" he asked, giving me the half-lip grin. Then, without waiting for a reply, he said, "Hop in, I'll give you a ride." I was about to say no when I saw the bus pass in front of my house. I almost broke into a sprint to try to catch it, but I just gave up and walked around and got in Burch's car. He didn't move for a few seconds and then, without saying anything, he looked back over his right shoulder and whipped his car out of the driveway. We had gone only a few blocks when he said, "Can you believe old Mr. Robicheaux making it with Q. Ball's mother?" I didn't say anything. If Burch thought they were guilty, they probably were innocent, because Burch is always wrong. Professor Ball probably had drawn the wrong conclusions. Misunderstandings happen. Burch let a little silence escape and then said, "You know, come to think of it, I'd like to bang Q. Ball's momma." I still didn't say anything, but I was thinking what a real nut tree Burch is and wondering why I was in his car and how I had ever thought he was a friend.

After we turned into Anna's driveway, Burch said, "You want me to hang around in case she's not even home?" I didn't answer but instead reached over and opened the car door. Then Burch grabbed my arm and said, "Biddle, we aren't always on the same page. You probably don't understand what your situation is, but I just want you to know I didn't have anything to do with it."

"I don't know what you're talking about," I said.

"I know," he said and pulled away.

Anna still lived in the same apartment she lived in when I met her delivering furniture. The apartment is nice, particularly for just three people and a dog. I haven't mentioned the dog because he's another irritant. Anna's dog stands probably less than a foot high and you can't see his eyes. He is one of those yippy, irritating dogs, but Mrs. Goolsby (or Myrna, as she insisted that I call her) and Anna both love the little hairball. I have never gotten along with little yippy dogs. They get on my nerves, and I seem to get on theirs.

My dog was a big black mongrel we named Beowulf and called Wulfie. He had a ferocious bark, but he was loyal and friendly. Wulfie was with Nathan when the murder happened. I like to think Wulfie wouldn't have let it happen if he had understood. He was also in the car with my father when he crashed into the bridge abutment. They said Wulfie was in the back seat when the accident happened, and he was thrown forward into my father and through the windshield. My father's neck was broken, but Wulfie was hardly hurt at all. Wulfie died a couple of months after Nathan was murdered. The vet wasn't sure what he died of, but he may have been bitten by a snake. It was one of those things that make no sense but just happen.

As I walked up the driveway, I looked for Myrna's car, but it was ominously missing. I was afraid Anna wasn't even at home. I went on up the stairs anyway. A large screened porch covers the entire front of the apartment. The porch has a leather couch on the end next to the stairs and a hanging two-seater swing on the other end, with a couple of chairs and a small table between them. When I got to the top of the stairs, I saw Anna on the swing with the little yip beside her. I said, "Hello," and stepped inside the screen door. The goofy yip leaped off the swing and began a whiny high-pitched bark. Anna jumped off the swing and said, "Hippo, you bad boy, come here." She opened the door into the apartment and Hippo (full name, Hippocrates) scooted in, apparently on the assumption that Anna was also going inside. For a minute or so after she closed the door behind him, Hippo yipped and whined and scratched at the door.

Anna went back to the swing and I followed and sat

down beside her. She was barefooted, and her fingernails and toenails were painted the same bright red. I looked at her and I had some difficulty breathing. I also had difficulty thinking of anything to say. It was as though my lungs and my brain had both jammed. It was like when I first started going to Bridgewater, and the most beautiful teacher in the school taught calculus. We would be having a test, and Miss Grace would lean down close to my face, press her breast into my shoulder and whisper something in a low, mellifluous voice. I don't know what she said, and I couldn't speak. I could smell the scent of her perfume and feel the softness of her breast, but nothing else entered my mind, certainly nothing about calculus or any other branch of mathematics.

"Anna, I have missed you so much," I managed to squeak out.

Anna tossed her head to one side, so that her long dark hair was swept over her shoulder in one dramatic movement. Then she narrowed her eyes so that I could just barely see the bright green of her irises. "We need to talk," she said without smiling or saying hello. I felt very uneasy. Even in ordinary circumstances, I found it difficult to talk or think in her presence, but I knew what she wanted to talk about. In early August she had written me a letter from camp suggesting that we have a more "relaxed" relationship and using the word "friends" to describe the new relaxation. I didn't like the idea and I didn't know what to say in response, so I ignored it. She had said similar stuff before and I had ignored her, so I thought the tactic might work again. "You got my letter, didn't you?"

"Your 'friends' letter?"

"That's the one," she said.

"I don't like the idea. I don't want to be friends."

"You've decided and that's the end of it, huh?"

"Anna," I said in a voice reeking of desperation, "at this point, we can't have a 'friends' relationship. I don't even know what that means."

"So, you've decided! You've decided unilaterally what our relationship is going to be."

"I don't want it to be unilateral."

"You know," she said with exasperation, "you are beyond hopeless."

"I'm sorry," I said, and took her hand and kissed it. I probably should have gotten up and left. I should have been irked rather than rattled, but I am a mere human being and she is a goddess. "I'm sorry," I repeated earnestly and kissed her hand again.

"I wish you at least had your own car. If we could just go somewhere and do something, for heaven's sake." I was crushed. I knew that I had no way of coming up with a car, short of stealing one. I'm almost surprised that I didn't heist a car. If Anna wanted me to have a car, then I wanted me to have a car even more than she did. The situation was a prime example of the quantum yearning axiom. The Biddle-Lichtman theory of quantum yearning holds that the desirability of a thing is inversely proportional to its availability. In the circumstances, the confirmation of the axiom was no comfort at all. I sat there looking pained and stupid, holding Anna's hand like it was the Holy Grail.

Finally, she pulled me toward her and said, "I don't know what to do. I like you a lot. I like spending time with you, but just not all the time. And you're so intense. You're so intense it's disturbing. You're damn near incorrigible." I didn't say anything. I don't know whether it was my state of mind or just that I didn't want to say anything.

"Okay," she said after I sat there looking lame and stupid, "here's the deal. We will be together when we're together. Okay?" I said nothing and did nothing. "We're together tonight but that doesn't mean everything is the same. Tomorrow is another day. You understand me? You can't decide what our relationship is going to be. Do you understand?"

I would like to report that I pushed back, responded with indignation or at least made some witty comment or pithy observation. I didn't. I rolled over like a trained seal. Arf. Arf. I couldn't think or talk but I could feel. The electricity leaped from her aura and ripped through my body. My senses were completely absorbed in her and everything else ceased to exist. Paradise had been regained, and I reveled in it. I leaned over and kissed her and, glory of glories, she returned the kiss.

After we had fooled around on the swing for a while, she asked if I would like a Coke. She didn't wait for an answer. She got out of the swing and walked toward the door leading into the apartment. She was wearing a short pleated skirt and her little butt made the skirt flounce around as she walked. I managed to choke out a squeaky "Sure" as she disappeared into the apartment. When she came back, she put two glasses down on the little table near the couch. "Come over here," she said, "and bring my book. The couch is more comfortable." I noticed for the first time the book on the swing. It was *The Autobiography of John Stuart Mill.* I decided not to say anything about it, because I sure wasn't in the mood to talk about a book.

"Where are your parents?"

"Mother went to run some errands. She's going to pick up the ghoul at twelve." Anna referred to her stepfather as "the ghoul" or sometimes "the feckless ghoul," a humorous but harsh play on the surname Goolsby. "You have to be gone before he gets here."

We resumed where we had left off but now in a reclining position. At first, she stretched out with her elbow on the couch cushion, and I sat on the edge of the couch in front of her with one foot touching the floor. Then I swung my legs over and onto the couch so that I lay beside her. We lay with our legs entwined and our mouths pressed together. We had been in that position for twenty or thirty minutes when she pushed me away and looked at me with a peculiar smirk.

She then reached under the back of her blouse and unsnapped her bra. We had rolled around on the sofa before, but she had never done that. She said, "Well?" and smirked again. I assumed that she wanted me to do something, so I unbuttoned her blouse and pushed it off her shoulders. Her bra was hanging loosely on her, drooping down so that I could see the wonderful contrast between the deep brown of her shoulders and the pale white of her breasts. She then slipped her arms out of the blouse and the bra straps and draped the blouse and bra over the back of the couch.

She lay back on the couch and again gave me the wry smile. I was in such awe that I hardly knew what I was doing, but I leaned over and kissed her. Then I rolled over on top of her and settled between her legs. She put her feet behind my calves and her hands on my butt and pulled me against her. Moby clearly liked the position. I looked down at her pretty face and I said, "Anna, I love you. Do you know that I love you more than anything in the world?" She didn't answer. She gently pushed my body upward and reached down and pulled her skirt up to her waist. I was above her like someone about to do push-ups. She then pushed her panties down as far as she could with me between her legs. I could see her white panties with little hearts on them rolled up across her pubic hair.

I know this sounds strange, but I was thinking that she would appreciate how much I loved her if I protected her and kept her from doing something she might regret. Also I felt like someone about to violate a sacred temple. It is astonishing now that I could think at all with Moby screaming like a madman, but my mind was clear, and I was focused only on Anna. I could no more have had sex with Anna than I could have murdered her. "I love you too much to do this," I said. I was raised on my arms looking down at her beautiful face and, if I glanced downward, I could see the ivory mounds of her breasts. I could hardly speak at all. She just stared at me almost expressionless. I was afraid she might be feeling embarrassment or rejection, so I said, "If I didn't love you so much . . . ," and then I just stopped.

She didn't say anything for a while. She just lay there staring at me with that blank expression. Then she said, "That's what I expected. I don't suppose you know the definition of the word 'feckless'?" When I tried to kiss her, she turned her head and said, "Get up." I immediately rolled over and sat up on the couch. She pulled her panties up and her skirt down and then put her bra back on. I held her blouse for her to put her arms in and she let me help button it. I felt very noble buttoning her blouse, but I don't think she appreciated my nobility. It was about then that I became aware that her book was lodged between the cushions and gouging me in the butt. I pulled it out from under me and held it without speaking for what seemed like a long time. I couldn't think of anything else, so I said, "What's this about?"

When she answered she had flint in her voice. "If you keep sitting on it, maybe you'll find out. It'll seep through your butt into your brain. I think it's called posterior osmosis." I didn't say anything because I was afraid she was going to ask me to leave. She raised her hands in apparent bewilderment, looked toward the ceiling, and shook her head. Then, as though talking to the light fixture, she said, "The Mill autobiography is a significant part of intellectual history. You wouldn't know that because you don't really have any intellectual curiosity. You're really just another fake intellectual."

That last comment floored me. I couldn't think of anything to say. I tried to take her hand, but she moved away when I reached over toward her. We sat in silence for a period that was so agonizing I'm sure it wasn't as long as it seemed. She finally looked up. I guess she read the look of distress and puzzlement on my face because she said in the same tone, "You walk around trying to make people think you're deep in thought and you really aren't thinking at all. You're just befuddled."

As ridiculous as it sounds now, I was flattered. I hadn't even considered that she thought I was bright. I had been dropped from most of the honors program and hadn't done anything other than write a few short poems, some of which I never even showed to anybody. I was thinking she must have talked to somebody who knew me earlier when some people thought I was smart. But I couldn't think of anybody who would have said much, except maybe Mr. Marcus, and I didn't really know what he would say. To be honest, I am in fact befuddled most of the time, and I had assumed she knew it. The thing that was going through my mind was, "If she wants me to be an intellectual, fine, I'll be an intellectual." If she had wanted me to be a clown, I was ready to paint my nose.

WAYWARD MARL

I sat with the left side of my behind on the couch because I wanted to face Anna as much as I could. I was sitting there trying to think of something good to say when I saw Myrna opening the screen door and right behind her a man with greasy dark hair and a red plaid shirt. She said, "Hey, Kit, you cutie." Her voice startled Anna. Perhaps because of the noise of the air conditioner under the apartment, we hadn't heard them coming up the stairs and, for some reason, we hadn't noticed the car lights. Anna jumped up, grinning in a phony way.

"Kit, this is Mike, also known as Dr. Michael Worth, a friend of Daddy's," she said, smiling and twisting like a little girl who's been told she's pretty. "Mike, this is Kit, a friend of mine."

"A close friend," said Myrna, spreading the word "close" so much it was clear Anna had not told her about our situation. "I've missed you this summer, Kit. You could have come by, you know." She hugged me and kissed me on the cheek. According to Anna, Myrna makes a good deal of money selling her landscape paintings. She had obviously been pretty in the past, but time and cigarettes have taken their toll. She smokes a lot and she always has her hair tied up in a bandanna. Her clothes seem too young for her, maybe because she and Anna wear the same stuff. Greasy Mike went into the apartment as though he were at home. Myrna turned to Anna and said, "Ooo, I envy you," and winked. Anna faked a big smile.

"Boy, that was close," Anna said in a whisper after Myrna went into the apartment. She exhaled in an exaggerated way. "They weren't supposed to be back until they picked up the ghoul at the airport." I didn't say what I was thinking. I was just happy that she didn't seem to be angry anymore. She leaned over and whispered, "That could have been awkward."

"Yeah," I said, "that could have been awkward." I looked at her beautiful face and smiled faintly but I was thinking about what would have happened if we hadn't stopped. Awkward? She seemed to have forgotten that we might have been *in flagrante delicto* when Myrna and Greasy Mike materialized out of nowhere at the top of the stairs. It didn't occur to me then, but I now wonder whether she really intended to get that far, whether she was really just taunting, playing a game to prove that I was a feckless slug. Does anything else really make sense?

"Anybody out here want a daiquiri?" Greasy Mike said,

leaning into the room dramatically. "I make the meanest daiquiris in town."

"Mike, now you know Anna can't have a daiquiri," I heard Myrna say from inside the apartment.

"I don't want a daiquiri," Anna said.

"Well, how about you, Christopher?"

"No, Mike," Anna said. "Kit isn't from Christopher; it's from Kittridge. He's Kittridge Carr Biddle. Now, say 'Kit Carr Biddle' real fast and then tell me what Daddy calls him. This is a quiz."

Greasy Mike mouthed my name silently. "Kit and caboodle," he said, grinning like a jerk.

"Bingo!" Anna said, laughing hysterically. "And I can tell you, he's the whole kit and caboodle. Poet, raconteur, furniture man, you name it, he does it." She fell back on the couch and buried her face in a pillow, still laughing, and Greasy Mike joined in the fun with a husky laugh.

"My mother's maiden name was Kittridge and my grandmother's was Carr," I said. I knew it was a stupid and lame thing to say as soon as I blurted it out.

"Well, how about it, Kit Caboodle? How about a daiquiri?" Greasy Mike said. I tried to smile and act as though I didn't mind the joke, but I can tell you I did. I should have left long before then but, as you've already figured out, I couldn't.

"Yeah, I'd like one. I sure would." Since I had never had a daiquiri, I didn't know whether I wanted one or not, but I wasn't about to decline an entrée into Anna's life, no matter how trivial or inane.

"Kit, are you sure your mother won't mind?" Myrna said. She had come into the doorway behind Greasy Mike and put her arm around his waist as though trying to talk past him. I thought the gesture was familiar, even affectionate.

"It's all right. She knows I drink some." Well, it was half true. My mother does know that I drink beer sometimes; she's not very happy about it, but she knows.

"Okay, you boys get acquainted. Anna and I will make the drinks and the goodies," Myrna said. Greasy Mike looked slightly disconcerted, but he pulled a chair around and sat down at a right angle to the sofa where I was sitting and smiled awkwardly. I didn't know what to say so I said nothing.

"I've heard a lot about you," he said. "Myrna says you're a bit of a contradiction." That comment sort of startled me and made me slightly uncomfortable and uneasy. Myrna had never said anything like that to me, but maybe she wouldn't because it would be rude. I assumed that Greasy Mike had had enough to drink not to worry about rudeness.

"I don't know what that means," I said.

"She says you're a fairly bright kid." I didn't say anything. "But she says you have quaint notions about things." I still didn't say anything, and he sat there looking at me expectantly.

"Quaint like what?" I said after a slight pause.

"Well, like she says you don't believe in evolution. Don't you think that's a paradox? Bright people aren't usually clueless."

"I don't think I've said anything about evolution," I said, trying to remember what I may have said to Anna that she would have repeated to her mother.

"Oh, okay," he said and sat back in his chair. He sat in silence for about a minute and then he leaned forward again and said, "What did you say that would make Myrna say that about you?" Now I was really getting uneasy.

"I'm trying to think," I said. "The only thing I remember is an observation to Anna that Ptolemy had developed a geocentric theory of the universe in the second century. I don't remember anything about evolution." At that particular moment, the most important thing for me was to fit in Anna's life. I didn't want to get in a fight with Greasy Mike or her mother. I started to say, "Look, I don't really know anything. I'm just trying to piece stuff together," but I didn't.

"What?" he said, wrinkling his face like I had stuck him with a pin. "What the hell's Ptolemy got to do with evolution?"

"Well, nothing directly." I didn't want to argue with him. I was just repeating the stuff Newt had said about Ptolemy. "I don't really know anything, and I sometimes repeat stuff that other people have said. My uncle says we should be cautious about new theories."

"Well, I hate to break it to you, but evolution is not a theory and it's not new," Greasy Mike said gruffly. "It's a fact that's been around a long time."

"I think that's the point my uncle was making about Ptolemy," I said as diffidently as possible. "The Ptolemaic theory of the universe was around for more than a thousand years. It was the fully accepted and unassailable truth before Copernicus and Galileo and others showed that it was flawed and untenable. *The Origin of Species* was published only a hundred years ago."

"I think evolution is clearly tenable," he said, "and I don't think the situations are comparable."

"I don't know," I said, "maybe not, but don't you think what my uncle said makes sense? You know that Galileo's proofs that the earth goes around the sun were debunked initially by most of the establishment. The geocentric notion of the universe had been around so long that other scientists derided Galileo and the church tried him for heresy."

"Okay," Greasy Mike said, "scientists sometimes get things wrong, but I don't think anybody has suggested a flaw in evolutionary science. Can you name anybody today, anybody with credentials, anybody not impaired, who has raised a question about evolution?"

"Well, yes," I said. "Charles Darwin."

"What?" he almost shouted, incredulity all over his bunched-up face. "You're saying Darwin questioned his own findings?"

"Well, yes and no. My uncle says people who read *The Origin of Species* should begin with Chapter 9, so that's what I did. I read Chapter 9 first and then I went back to Chapter 1."

"You've read *The Origin of Species* and you think Darwin questions his own theory?" I made a mental note that Greasy Mike had slipped up and called evolution a theory. I also wanted to ask him if he had read the book, but I thought that might be impudent so I didn't.

"In Chapter 9, Darwin confronted a quandary, an uncomfortable fact, that is, that the fossil record does not support evolution. He predicted that the fossil record will, with more intense exploration in the future, ultimately support the theory, but he admits that at the time of publication of his findings, the fossil record contained nothing to suggest that living things evolve from one species to another."

"The fossil record supports evolutionary theory," Greasy Mike said gruffly. "That's what *The Origin of Species* is all about."

"No, sir," I said. "It's really not about evolution." I don't know where I got the courage to say that, but I can tell you I would never have said it to Anna. If she had told me that Chapter 9 didn't exist or that *The Origin of Species* didn't exist, I wouldn't have contradicted her. Greasy Mike wasn't Anna. He was just another person with an opinion and, as Newt used to observe, opinions are like noses: Everybody has one but they're not all beautiful.

"Darwin noticed something very important," I said, "and documented his findings: Living things adapt to their environment or they have a hard time surviving change. His findings are about adaptation. In the fossil record, species are shown to change in color, configuration, and function, and species are shown to come and go but none appears to progress from one kind of thing to another. My Uncle Newt says that in the last hundred years nobody has found anything really new in the fossil record to support an evolutionary process. I'm not saying I know the answers, but I can tell you that my Uncle Newt is really smart, and he says that Chapter 9 is the screaming loose end, the puzzle piece that doesn't fit—the equivalent of the regression of the planets in the Ptolemaic system—that most scientists today have chosen, apparently deliberately, to ignore." Peculiarly, Greasy Mike sat there looking disgruntled but saying nothing.

"Uncle Newt says Darwin's work is about adaptation," I said, "not evolution of species. Darwin proved beyond any doubt that species adapt (change color and other features); but what he didn't prove is that species either evolve or devolve from one kind of creature to another. I frankly could not care less whether evolutionary theory is sound, and I'm not saying I know anything. I'm just saying . . . ."

Just then, Myrna stuck her head in the door and said, "Okay, boys, this obviously serious discussion will have to be put on hold. The ladies of the house have prepared libations and hors d'oeuvres." Greasy Mike stood up, snorted and frowned, and said, "We'll have to take this up later. You're a bright boy." He paused and then said, "But, of course, you're wrong." He patted me on the back patronizingly. "I don't know who your Uncle Newt is, but at this point in time in modern science, which you should recognize is qualitatively different from the ancient past, I think it is just foolish to question evolution."

"Science has become more sophisticated," I said, smiling as benignly as possible. I wanted to point out to him that Galileo was pretty sophisticated, and people called him foolish, but I didn't say a word. I was happy I had been rescued by Myrna. We followed her into the kitchen where she filled three glasses from a large pitcher and then took two of the glasses and a small plate of cookies, and left Anna and me alone in the kitchen with about half a pitcher. Anna's mood seemed to have changed. She smiled at me, and I picked up the glass from the counter. I sipped my drink cautiously at first. It tasted like frozen lemonade with a little tang, so I took a few large gulps. I leaned back against the kitchen counter, and Anna put her hands on my shoulders. She raised herself on her toes and kissed me.

When my glass was almost empty, Anna stepped away and looked at me; the wry grin, the same expression as when she lay back topless on the sofa, was again on her face. She said, "You need another daiquiri," and refilled my glass. I took a long drink. The old frozen lemonade was getting better all the time. We stood in the kitchen for a long time with her body pressed against mine. I leaned back and stretched out my legs so that we were almost the same height. She moved up and down on her tiptoes, which caused Moby to start throbbing again. I was kissing and sipping and having a grand old time. Anna kept refilling my glass, and I kept sipping away. I didn't notice when the room began to tilt. I think I must have drunk almost the entire half pitcher in a little over an hour.

Anna's back was toward the door and I was pretty dizzy, so I don't know how long Burch had been standing in the doorway of the kitchen when I noticed him. Apparently, Myrna had let him in and sent him to the kitchen. He said, "Hey, that looks good," and he hunched his shoulders and gave us his silly half-lip smile. Anna turned around and smiled at Burch. Even then it struck me as odd that she didn't seem surprised by his sudden appearance in her kitchen.

"Oh, hi, Harry," she said in a sweet little voice. I looked at my watch. I had to squint to see what time it was because my eyes weren't focusing very well.

"Biddle, you're drunk," Burch said and turned to Anna. "He's drunk, isn't he?"

"Burch," I said, "what the hell are you doing here?" I was leaning against the counter and then, all of a sudden, I slipped and my butt hit the kitchen floor. I was holding my half-full daiquiri glass that spattered the front of my shirt. I tried to get up but the floor was moving so I just sat still a minute. Burch laughed and pointed toward me and leaned over and whispered something to Anna. She giggled and looked down at me.

Myrna appeared in the doorway and I heard her say, "Mike, come here. Kit's had too much to drink. I knew I shouldn't let him drink." I looked up at Anna from the floor. I was embarrassed for her to see me, and I was furious with Burch. I could hear every word they said, and I knew what they were saying, but I felt as though I didn't have any control over my body.

"I'll take him home," Burch said.

"No, Burch," I said. "You dumb ass, what are you doing here?" He grinned and Anna winked at him. At that, I reached up and grabbed the counter and pulled myself up. The room was spinning and I was having a hard time, but I was determined to get rid of Burch. I said, "Burch, get out of here."

"Go ahead," Myrna said to Burch. "We'll take care of him."

"That's all right," he said, looking directly at me. "I'm going." Then he hunched his shoulders, pursed his lips, and raised his hand and punched his index finger toward me several times. "You got it coming, Straw boy. You got it coming." He didn't say anything clsc. Hc just shook his head and walked out the door.

"Okay, Kit," Myrna said, "now you come out here on the porch and get some air and I'll make some coffee."

Greasy Mike put my left arm around his neck and his right arm around my waist and started dragging me toward the porch. When we reached the porch, he dropped me on the couch. Anna sat down beside me.

"I've really made an ass of myself," I said. The room was still spinning and I was tipsy, but I was thinking. They were treating me like I was a piece of furniture, but I knew what was going on. I was still irritated about that wink because I knew even then that something was amiss, and I thought Anna was flirting with Burch. I sat on the couch for just a few minutes and then said, "Good night. I'm going home." I got up and started for the door.

"Kit, you're drunk," Anna said, grabbing my arm. "You can't go home like this."

"Trust me, I can," I said very precisely, trying to pronounce the words without slurring. I pulled my arm away, steadied myself, and walked out the door. I held on to the banister going down the steps. I was all right when I reached the driveway.

"Momma, Kit's trying to walk home," I heard Anna shout.

I had gone only a half a block when I realized that I was about to wet my pants, so I stepped between two large azalea bushes near the sidewalk and started watering the ground. When I finished, I turned around and Myrna's car was pulling up next to the sidewalk. Myrna and Greasy Mike were in the front and Anna was in the back. Greasy Mike yelled, "Come on, champ, get in!"

"Kit, please get in," Myrna said. "I can't let you go home like this. We're just gonna ride around a little and let you get some air." Myrna's car was an old Cadillac convertible. They had the top back and the radio on. Myrna and Greasy Mike were holding glasses, still sipping daiquiris. I climbed into the back seat beside Anna and she took my hand and smiled. I don't know why but I wasn't angry anymore. The tough-guy resolution had dissolved. I leaned over and kissed Anna on the cheek. Greasy Mike was driving. I didn't know where we were going, but we rode around a long time and ended up on a deserted back road. Greasy Mike pulled over and stopped. Myrna said, "Anna, take Kit for a little walk and see if that won't help some."

Anna and I got out of the car and started off down the road holding hands. The moon was almost full so we could see pretty well. The road was made of compacted chert that was almost as smooth as concrete. A wire fence topped with a strand of barbed wire ran along both sides of the road. I could see some kind of crop in the fields. The night air was very pleasant and fragrant. We walked along holding hands for about a quarter of a mile and then just stopped and stood in the road for a while. I tried to see my watch in the dark and it looked like eleven-twenty. "We'd better head back. Your mother has to pick up Dr. Goolsby at twelve."

We started back toward the car, walking with my arm around her waist. We stopped a few times and I tried to kiss her, but she mostly turned her face into my shoulder and hugged me. When we were about fifteen feet from the car, I realized that Myrna and Greasy Mike were lying on the front seat. The car was rocking back and forth, and they were moaning and breathing hard. I took Anna's hand and started back down the road. We went back to where we had been before and then stood in the middle of the road.

I put my arms around her and held her close to me. She didn't say anything. Nothing about her mother. Nothing about Greasy Mike. She offered no observation and voiced no objection. She may have tensed a little, but I'm not really sure about it. She did hold on to me, and she also got quiet and passive. "Anna, it's all right. I love you." I had sobered up pretty much by then, but I had no idea what was in her mind. She may have been offended or embarrassed. I don't know. I doubt it.

We stood near the edge of the road for what seemed like a long time. I kept repeating to her that I loved her. I wanted to take her away and hold her and protect her. She seemed a little upset in some way about her mother and Greasy Mike, but she didn't say a word. I didn't know what to make of it then, and I still don't know. Not long after I met her, she said, "The ghoul thinks my mother is a magnet for mischief. He's very jealous. I think that's really why we move so often."

What she said didn't seem to make any sense at the time, and afterward I decided that she must have been exaggerating or joking. Anyway, I hadn't thought any more about it, probably because I hadn't seen anything particularly mischievous or magnetic about her mother. We were still standing in the same spot when we saw the car lights edging toward us. As the car pulled up beside us, Myrna said, "You guys about ready? You feeling better, Kit?"

"Yeah, I'm okay." Anna and I got in the back seat and she sat stiffly not looking at me. I was leaning over holding her in both arms and the radio was moaning a schmaltzy love song, and I disappeared into her aura. I had never felt so much love. I kept saying, "I love you" over and over in her ear. She smiled faintly a few times. At the time, I attributed her reaction to humiliation and unhappiness with her mother, but I'm now inclined to think she was annoyed with me more than anything else. I've thought about it a lot. Some things never get clearer.

When we were back in the city I gave Greasy Mike directions. He pulled up in front of my house and Myrna said, "It's almost twelve, Kit. I hope your mother's not going to be furious with me."

"Nah," I said, "she's probably asleep anyway." Myrna got out and folded the seat down for me to get out. Anna was closest to the door, so she got out ahead of me. "I'll see you tomorrow, okay?"

"Well," she said, "no, that's not the way it's going to work. We clearly need to talk, Kit." Then she turned to her mother and said, "I'll be right back," and then took my arm and sort of ushered me toward my front door.

When we reached the stoop, she said, "Kit, I meant it about being just friends and not seeing each other exclusively. We're not going together, whatever that means, anymore. We're just friends. I know you don't like it but that's the way it is."

"Okay," I said, mostly because I didn't know what else to say. "Can I call you and talk about it?"

"No, I don't want to talk about it anymore."

"Okay," I said, but I can tell you I did not feel okay. "Good night." Then she turned and walked down the sidewalk and got in the car. I stood on the walk for a few minutes after the taillights of Myrna's car disappeared, and then I walked up the steps and unlocked the front door. The house was dark and quiet, so I took off my loafers and went straight to my room. I took off my clothes, turned off the lights, and lay back on the bed. I lay there for a long time staring into the darkness and thinking about my strange evening. I was very tired but I couldn't sleep. I wanted to think that things would work out, but even I couldn't see how that was going to happen.

TRINK

The next thing I heard was music, very loud music. I put a pillow over my head to shut it out and drifted back to sleep. When I woke up again, I kicked the cover off but I didn't get up. I stared at the ceiling fan and the familiar irregularities in the beadboard ceiling, trying to get my eyes to focus, thinking about the night before. I liked the part about holding Anna after the Greasy Mike incident but the denouement was devastating. It may sound strange, but I also woke up worrying about the willy-nilly verses. I don't know how to explain it in the circumstances, unless I was just trying not to confront the disappearance of Anna from my life, my ugly new reality. Maybe it was just an extension of my inability to understand Anna that I focused on the fact that I could understand almost nothing.

And I was out there alone again, Lichtman having abandoned the struggle with meaning. He had proclaimed himself an existentialist with almost an air of triumph while conceding that we had really found nothing at all.

His epitaph on our two-year effort: "We've taken this search to the end—over the pavement and passable chert, on foot through ever-thickening underbrush, through deserts and swamps—and we've ended up miles from nowhere at a totally impenetrable dead end." Okay, a little dramatic but probably a fairly accurate assessment. It was like a race we'd tried to run until we discovered that there was no finish line.

When I got to the kitchen, my mother had juice and cereal on the table. From my mother's room I could hear one of the records she plays a lot; it's something about a variation and fugue on a theme of Mozart or something like that. I poured a cup of coffee and emptied the cereal box into my bowl. I wolfed it down not only because I was hungry but also because I was in a hurry. I wanted to go by a bookstore and get a copy of the Mill autobiography, as Anna dubbed it. It seems strange now that I felt compelled to read that book simply because Anna was reading it. I certainly didn't have any particular interest in John Stuart Mill. To tell you the truth, I still don't. Mrs. Hargis opened her bookstore at nine on Saturday mornings. My idea was to jog over to the Hargis Book Shop, try to find the book in paperback, and spend a part of the day reading it. Then, if the occasion presented itself, I could show myself to Anna as a newly enlightened worthy. You don't have to tell me it sounds crazy. I know.

I was still eating when I heard the music stop, and my

mother came into the kitchen carrying a tote bag. "Good morning, or what's left of it," she said cheerfully. Almost simultaneously a car horn sounded out in the driveway. "That's Dr. Bob. We're going over to the island. What are you doing today?"

"I'm going to the bookstore," I said.

"Can we drop you at the bookstore? You're talking about Mrs. Hargis' shop?" I had actually intended to jog, but after she asked me, I thought I might just take a ride and jog later.

"Yeah, sure, it's on the way."

"Well, let's go. We're wasting a beautiful day." The estimable Dr. Bob had pulled his car around to the front of the house when I came out. Anna calls people "the estimable" and I've picked it up, particularly when I don't like the person very much, a category into which the estimable Dr. Bob fits very neatly. My mother calls him Dr. Bob because he's an orthopedist. His last name is Glans, which he says was anglicized or shortened from Glansanovsky (or something like that) by his ancestors. He looks like a Glansanovsky. I hate to say it, but she met him because of me.

Coach Kern thought I had a stress fracture and recommended Dr. Bob. As it turned out, I didn't have a stress fracture at all. The pain apparently resulted in some way because I had grown about five inches in one year. The pain went away but Dr. Bob didn't. He is now a permanent irritant: He and my mother are planning to get married over Christmas break. Dr. Bob's first wife was probably smarter than my mother. She left him and ran off to Mexico, according to Dr. Bob, "to find herself." It has occurred to me that my mother might benefit from a trip to Acapulco but I haven't said it.

"We're running a little late," Dr. Bob said after I got in the car, a comment I assumed was intended for me. He grunted, wheezed, and wiggled around behind the steering wheel.

"Speaking of late," my mother said, "weren't you sort of on the wrong side of midnight getting in?"

"It was probably about midnight," I said. Then I made another mistake. I could have said nothing more, but I stumbled into the mire. "We went riding with Anna's mother and a friend of her stepfather." As soon as I said it, I knew it was a dumb thing to say. I didn't want to talk about the night before, the midnight ride, or the purported friend.

"A friend of her stepfather?" She has a special little antenna for these things. "Who was the friend?" The thing is I knew she would ask that question.

"Some guy named Mike, a doctor who works with Dr. Goolsby."

"How interesting. Where was Dr. Goolsby?"

"He was out of town. They were going to pick him up at the airport after they dropped me off."

"I see," she said, but it wasn't clear what she saw, and I wasn't going to ask her.

"I know a Goolsby at the university," Dr. Bob said. "What does Anna's stepfather do?"

"All I know is he's a trauma doctor," I said. It had occurred to me that Dr. Bob might know Dr. Goolsby, but I had never talked to him about it because I usually avoided talking to him.

"Right," said Dr. Bob. "The university brought him in. Feck Goolsby. They brought him in to head up the trauma unit. Impressive credentials. He'd been head of trauma at the medical center in Roanoke, and before that he taught at the Columbia medical school."

"He's pretty impressed with himself," I said. "I didn't know anybody else was."

Dr. Bob grunted his disapproval. Perhaps sensing a confrontation, my mother shifted gears. "I know you like track, Kit, but I don't want you to do it if you can't get your work done." This one threw me off. Since she had encouraged me to run track, she wasn't very likely talking about track. But I was so relieved and happy to get off the subject of the events of the previous night that I hoped she had another subject on her mind. She didn't disappoint. "Kit, I want you to try harder this year. You have so much potential, and you really aren't trying." That wasn't entirely true. I had been trying in my own way. I mean I really wanted to concentrate on the stuff everybody wanted me to work on, but I kept getting shunted off the track. What I wanted to do hardly ever fit the program, which, in my judgment, was the source of most of the trouble. I was so glad to move on to another subject that I fed her what she wanted to hear.

"Mom," I said in as sincere a voice as I could manage, "I'm going to work hard this year." It's what she wanted me to say, and I may have meant it. I was sort of proud of myself. She smiled and reached over and patted my hand. I could tell that I had made her a little happier. Dr. Bob coughed and grunted. I had a feeling he wanted to say, *You may be able to fool your mother but you don't fool me, young man,* but he didn't. He just coughed and grunted a couple of times.

As I was getting out of the car in front of the bookstore, my mother said, "When will you be home?"

"Well, I told Q. Ball I'd come over to his house this afternoon." I didn't want to tell her about my meeting with Mr. Marcus.

"Okay, but don't you be late."

"Where are you guys going?" I asked nonchalantly. I don't usually get into her stuff but I had noticed that her tote bag had a quilted blanket in it.

"We're going on a picnic for lunch."

"Where?" I said. Dr. Bob grunted impatiently and wiggled around behind the wheel.

"We're going to ride over to the island with some friends," she said. "Why are you so curious all of a sudden?"

"I'm not." I don't know whether I was curious or just mischievous. I hate to admit it but I was probably trying to make Dr. Bob uncomfortable—you know, a little retribution for unwanted intrusions into my life.

"I'll be home before you are, I'm sure," my mother said.

"Okay," I said. "Have a good time." She blew me a kiss. Dr. Bob grunted again and audibly exhaled. They drove off without looking back.

I glanced at my watch. It was ten-fifty and the bookstore was dark. I stood around outside the door for a few minutes and then sat with my back against a support column at the edge of the sidewalk in front of the bookstore. I was sitting on the built-up front walk with my legs stretched out in the parking area when I saw Mrs. Hargis pulling in. I could barely see her head because her eyes were about level with the dashboard of her car. She obviously didn't see me, because she pulled all the way up to the support column. If I hadn't moved, she would have run her front bumper over my legs and pinned my chest against the column.

She was parked for what seemed like minutes before the car door opened and she emerged carrying a large canvas purse. I was waiting at the door of the bookstore, but she didn't see me because she was stooped over so far she had to pull her head way back to look straight ahead. According to my mother, Mrs. Hargis had taught linguistics at a college in New England until she retired and bought the bookstore. She has always owned the bookstore since I've known her, and she has always looked the same. She has a little string tied to each side of the frame of her eyeglasses, so they won't hit the floor when they fall off. She holds on to her eyeglasses with one hand when she reads. She looks decrepit but she's really a sharp old lady. I overheard my mother tell someone that Mrs. Hargis was one of the smartest people she had ever met.

"Kit Biddle!" she said excitedly when she saw me. "I haven't seen you in a while. You must need a special book to be here on a Saturday morning. Sorry to make you wait. I know the sign says nine but today let's pretend it says eleven."

"I'm looking for a paperback edition of the Mill autobiography." I was trying to sound as learned and accomplished as Anna.

"I presume you mean *The Autobiography of John Stuart Mill*. I think I can help you with that." She held her head back so she could look at my eyes. She unlocked the door to the bookstore and laboriously pulled it open. I held the door as she rubbed the wall beside the door to flip the light switches. Then she hunched on down the main aisle toward the back of the store. The second most remarkable thing about the Hargis Book Shop is the number of books crammed into one small room; the most remarkable thing is that Mrs. Hargis seems to know where every book is. It took her two seconds to find the book, despite the fact that it was piled up with a large number of biographies and autobiographies that had overrun the shelf space.

"Here you are, Kit. It's a paperback but it's pretty expensive. Can you afford seventy-five cents?"

"Yeah," I said, "I guess so."

"I had a customer in here yesterday who told me my paperback prices are too high and that I'd make more money if I lowered my prices. I told him that people who need money shouldn't be in business." She screeched with laughter, raising her head to see if I was joining in. I smiled but I must not have gotten the full impact of the joke. She started off toward the front of the store continuing her broken, high-pitched laugh.

"You need anything else, Kit?" she asked without turning around.

"No, that's about it." While we were walking toward the front counter it occurred to me that I had never talked to Mrs. Hargis about books on existence and meaning. I didn't know whether I wanted to get into it. I thought about maybe talking to her later, but I decided while waiting for my change that I would mention the subject to her. One of the problems was trying to figure out how to ask the question.

"By the way," I said casually, "I've been studying meaning and stuff. If you've got anything good, I could pick it up when I come back in."

"I've got a lot of books on philosophy. What do you need?" She struggled to hold her head up so our eyes would meet. "Do you mean something in the area of ontology or are you thinking more about linguistics?"

"I've been reading ontology, and I haven't really found anything," I said earnestly. "To be perfectly blunt, I've read a lot of rationalizations and mumbo-jumbo that isn't very helpful." I hadn't intended to get into it but I couldn't resist. "I've been reading and reading and I haven't found any real answers to the real questions."

"Well," she said, spreading the word into several broken syllables. "You want a clear answer, huh?" She put her crooked index finger to her lips and appeared to be thinking. "The only thing that comes to mind, that is, that really provides an answer, is the Holy Bottle sequence in *Gargantua and Pantagruel.* It's the only thing that provides a clear and definite answer." She was looking down at the counter where she was counting out my change.

"What kind of answer?" I asked skeptically. I knew the word "gargantuan" and I had heard of the book but never read it; and the reference to the "holy bottle" made me suspicious. I thought she was about to give me a sermon and echo my mother's notion that the world was created as an expression of divine love.

"Trink," she said, chuckling lightly.

"I'm sorry. What?"

"Trink!" she said, almost shrieking. "They ask the Holy Bottle to explain the meaning of life and the Bottle says, 'Trink'!" She began cackling and repeated "Trink" a couple of times while she laughed. "It's the best answer I've heard so far." It wasn't what I had expected.

"Trink?" I thought I might have misunderstood.

"Trink," she repeated, laughing so hard she could hardly talk.

"I get it." I smiled as much as I could. "Well, I've got to be going." Then I headed for the door.

She was still chortling when I left. I didn't think it was funny, and I'm not very old. How can you get old and laugh about something like that? Does that make sense? I don't understand it at all. Mrs. Hargis is a smart old lady who's been around forever, but that's the point. She's close to the end of the line. I'd like to ask her how she can joke about the meaning of her life like that. It seems to me that a person ought to become increasingly focused and maybe even morose as the years go by and the impenetrable darkness creeps in closer and closer. I get the distinct feeling that I'm missing something.

MALEDICTION

When I left the bookstore, I was trying to think of a good place to sit and read until my meeting with Mr. Marcus at three o'clock. I was hungry again, so I decided to walk down to the Frost Bite. It's not that far from the Hargis Book Shop, and I was going that way anyhow. When I got there, I took a booth toward the back of the restaurant and ordered two hotdogs, some French fries, and a Coke. Then I took out my book and started reading. I didn't know anybody there except the waitresses. Other than my waitress, nobody said anything to me. I sat in the Frost Bite reading and sipping a Coke until almost two-thirty. My food and Cokes cost me a buck and a half.

I put a quarter on the table for the waitress and dropped a quarter in the jukebox. I played some junk songs with schmaltzy lyrics, as my mother calls them. She has tried to get me interested in "real music," but it hasn't worked out exactly right. I hate to say it, but I wouldn't be crushed if I didn't hear any music at all. A lot of the time it gets on my nerves, particularly if it's very loud or repetitious. I really don't like the schmaltz much either, but my mother's music sounds like cacophony, and I can't make sense of it. I'm convinced that Schopenhauer's noise tolerance axiom is sound: He said that a person's tolerance for noise is inversely proportional to his intelligence quotient. My mother says real music isn't noise, but at a certain decibel level it's all noise. Of course, she's deaf in one ear, so maybe she gets excused from the axiom anyway.

Mr. Marcus' office was dark and locked when I got there but I was fifteen minutes early. My note was gone from the message board and there was no new note, so I was pretty sure he would show up. I took my book out of my back pocket and sat down on the floor. The main lights in the hall were off, but there were small light fixtures about waist high every hundred feet or so all the way down the hall. I sat under the fixture closest to Mr. Marcus' door. I had only read ten or twelve pages when I heard him open the main door into the building. I stood up and stuck my book in my back pocket just as the main hall lights came on.

He was smiling as he came down the hall, so some of my apprehension went away, but not all of it. I have trouble relaxing when I know I'm being scrutinized or critiqued, even if it's by somebody I know well. He shook my hand and said, "Hello, Kit. I appreciate your coming by. How are you?" Mr. Marcus is a fairly young guy and a pretty distinguished-looking guy. He plays tennis a lot so he has a good tan, and he walks like a jock. He's also very smart. My mother says he'll be gone as soon as he gets his Ph.D. and the only thing he has left to do is finish his doctoral thesis. His wife is a dark-haired woman who teaches algebra and geometry. I skipped algebra and geometry at Bridgewater, so I never had her but I'm told she's a really good math teacher. She doesn't smile very much.

"Sorry I missed you," he said. "I was out of town until yesterday and everything in the world was piled up here." I made a mental note about his being out of town until Friday. The Thursday night peeping tom episode was still on my mind.

"I'm doing okay, Mr. Marcus, thank you." He unlocked the door and I followed him into his office. I looked around for a place to sit, but every surface in the room was covered with books and papers.

"Let's see if we can clear a couple of chairs." He wedged himself between some books on a small sofa, and I cleared a chair across from him. He had picked up two sheets of paper off his desk and sat holding the papers with both hands. He looked at me pensively and then said, "I have your poem here, and I want to chat with you about it."

"I left it at your house Thursday evening but apparently you weren't there." I mentioned Thursday because I was hoping maybe he would offer some explanation of what I had seen.

"Right," he said. "We flew in a little after noon on

Friday after two glorious weeks on the coast of Maine. But I'm back now, so let's have a go at this poem." I squirmed a little in my chair because, instead of explaining what I had seen, the "We flew in . . . Friday" left me dangling somewhere between darkness and light. I wanted to ask him, if "we" came back on Friday, who was in his house Thursday night? I didn't want to start giving him the third degree about everything, but I really needed to know something. So I just blurted it out.

"I thought I saw somebody go in your house on Thursday night." I watched him closely for a reaction.

"Oh," he said without changing tone or expression, "you saw my brother Lawrence. We gave him a key and asked him to watch the place. You should have visited with him if he was there. He's sort of lonely, I think. He's a Jesuit scholastic in residence at the college, but he doesn't seem happy."

"I was sort of in a hurry," I lied. I didn't know what I was supposed to say. I wasn't sure and I decided not to say anything to him or anybody else. If Lawrence was the peeping tom, somebody else would have to deal with it. I didn't know whether that was the right thing but that's what I did.

"Okay," he said, still holding the papers with both hands, "let's get to work."

"I thought you probably wouldn't like my poem, but I wanted you to read it anyway," I said, trying to shift my mind from peeping tomfoolery to poetry.

"Quite the contrary," he said, leaning forward and speaking ingenuously and thoughtfully. "I find your poem to be an impressive piece of work. You are a fine young poet. I have taken the liberty of showing your poem to several other teachers, and I can tell you they are impressed. The consensus is we might as well go ahead and give you the senior poetry award now. Nobody else in your class can do this. Very few anywhere can."

I sat back in my chair and tried not to smile. I had been getting my butt kicked by a lot of people, and I had been worried that my poem would offend Mr. Marcus.

"Before we get to your poem," he said, "let me mention a couple of things. As you probably know, we have had our preregistration conference and, you may or may not be pleased to know, you have been discussed extensively. There's a feeling that we are letting you down, and to be candid, that you are letting yourself down. Our culpability is that we may have provided inadequate guidance to you for your next step. The feeling is that your gifts would be best applied at a very selective college, but frankly your curriculum vitae is thin on extracurriculars and getting thinner on academics."

"I don't know what you're talking about." Any smile I had stifled no longer needed stifling. Mr. Marcus had been my refuge, and now I was getting it from him too. Of course, I really knew what he was talking about.

"After this year, you're off to college. What I'm talking about is your college application. If you're going to apply where you ought to apply, you need to show something other than just grades, and you won't have grades if you stumble as much as you did last year." I shifted around in my chair and tried to think of something to say. "You're in no clubs. You've rejected the *Pierian* staff. I understand from Coach Kern that you're a track star who refuses to perform, so you may not even have athletics going for you. It's your life and you can do with it as you see fit, but you need to be prepared for the consequences. Your peers are going to go on. If you aren't careful, you'll be left behind."

"What peers? Behind what?" I knew what peers and I knew what he meant, but I had to say something, and those lame defensive questions were all I could come up with.

"Take your friend Eddie Lichtman. He's probably going to follow his brother to Amherst. And your friend Anna. I understand she's probably going to Barnard but she can go just about anywhere she wants to go. I know she means a lot to you." I might have been able to talk about Lichtman and compare myself to him, but I wasn't prepared to talk about Anna. First a hammer on the head, then a gig through the heart. I sat there gasping like a gigged flounder in the bottom of the boat, my mouth opening and closing but no words coming out.

"They're different from me," I said after struggling to come up with something and failing.

"Okay," he said. "I don't want to belabor the point

or make you unnecessarily uncomfortable. I do think that you need to think about the next stage of your life and to make plans. Even with last year's subpar performance, you're still in the race. My advice to you is to try to pull things together this year. I don't know what's best for you, but I don't want to fail you by not urging you to think ahead."

"Okay," I said but I didn't really feel okay.

"Now," he said, "I've done my duty. Let's turn to your poem. I think this is the best you've ever written. At least, the best you've shown me."

"I'm glad you like it," I said, recovering somewhat.

"What I'd like to do is to go over your poem and discuss some of its implications. As you know, I am not associated with this school as a counselor, and I'm uncomfortable even trying to talk about psychological issues. I'm not suggesting anything in particular, but after I read your poem, I wondered whether you might be having a serious spiritual crisis. I know you've been presented with some incredibly difficult spiritual problems in your life. You lost your father when you were very young. As you may know, it is established fact that people who have no father, or even a distant father, often have difficulty with the concept of God. Maybe it's because a person's first idea of God is his father." The paper he handed me was a copy of my poem. I could see that the paper he kept was just another copy of the poem. He held his copy calmly but mine rattled in my hands like a sail in a breeze.

"First, tell me what you intended by the title. What does 'A Clerical Malediction' refer to?"

To start off talking about counseling and a "spiritual crisis" and my father and then focus on my title felt like a series of punches in the gut. I didn't know what to say, so I didn't say anything. The poem is about a priest who is trying to administer last rites at a funeral, but he gets off track and says not what he's supposed to say but what's in his mind. I figured that Mr. Marcus was thinking that the priest was cursing the dead or something, but I didn't intend it that way. He's actually cursing darkness. I was starting to try to organize my thoughts when he said, "Well, let's leap over those issues and focus on your poem. Let me read the poem aloud. Is that all right with you?"

I squeaked out, "Okay," and he started reading:

> *A Clerical Malediction*
> *As you beseeched, I've come to offer balm,*
> *So let us bow and never question why,*
> *Deferring now without a mortal qualm,*
> *As I explain just what it means to die.*

I had sounded the words in my mind but, of course, I had never heard it read aloud. I don't know what Mr. Marcus was thinking, but I thought he made it sound pretty good. He continued to read:

> *Forget the bromides, promises and lies:*
> *This corpse, my friends, has heard no trumpet sound,*

For the dull roll of time, as each spark dies,
Just clicks a condolence as it goes round
And flushes the inert rubble of past
Depleted essence through a soundless dark
Tunnel that empties all into a vast
And boundless void behind a question mark.

He looked up at me, paused slightly, then read the concluding couplet:

Thus ends the grunts and grasps of harried life
And one more baffling tale of aimless strife.

I tried to discern his feelings but I couldn't tell anything. He read my poem the same way he read poetry in class. He may as well have been reading Gerard Manley Hopkins. When he finished, he squinted as though trying to decide what to say or how to say it. "I presume you intended irony in the form. Despair and nihilism are unusual subjects for a sonnet," he said, smiling slightly.

"It wasn't a sonnet at first. It was a series of quatrains and it was several pages long. I shortened it because some of the quatrains clanked and wobbled and I couldn't fix them."

"I didn't get to see the quatrains, but I like the sonnet. Your poem is truly a fine piece of work." He paused and folded his hands. "I'm not going to pretend to be unaware of the tragic death of your cousin. I can hardly imagine the impact that must have had on you. It is not at all surprising that you've reacted by doubting God's benevolence, maybe even God's existence, and I have no idea what to say to help you work through that crisis. I also don't want to be tone-deaf to a cry for help." He paused again, but I didn't say anything. I was about to say, *Hey, wait, this is just a poem,* but he cut me off. "I don't suppose you've been reading nihilist philosophy? Or maybe some of the neo-existentialists?" He smiled and added, "My view is all existentialists are neo after Kierkegaard."

"Well, last summer I read *The Stranger* and *The Myth of Sisyphus,* but to tell you the truth, I didn't like them that much and I'm not sure I know what Camus is talking about. I hate the Sisyphus metaphor. Lichtman and I have read a lot of stuff the last couple of years, but we really haven't come up with much in the way of answers." I thought about telling him about the other things I had read, but I decided against it. I also thought about trying to explain that nothing I had read depressed me as a result of convincing me of something. If I was nihilistic, which had not occurred to me, it was because I hadn't found any good answers, and I wasn't happy with my own experiences. I wasn't satisfied with the notion that beyond the opaque wall is nothingness and that you have to create your own essence by blind, remorseless commitment. I wasn't looking for an accommodation of the unknowable by a pathetic denial of its existence. Frankly, it appeared to me that everybody was trying to create meaning out of commitment.

They didn't need a philosopher to tell them how to do it. As the coach could tell them, it's called the program.

"You know, my doctoral thesis is on Kierkegaard. If I had known you were interested, I'd have let you read it. I could have used another critical eye, and you might have found it to be interesting, maybe even helpful in your own search."

"Really?" I said. I had actually considered talking to Mr. Marcus, but I had hesitated because I thought he might make too much of it. I knew he wouldn't just brush me off like my mother or take my questions lightly as Newt and Mrs. Hargis had. I just didn't know what he would say, and I didn't want to jeopardize my relationship with him. "I probably should have talked to you first. Other than Lichtman, I've had a hard time finding anybody to talk to. I'm sort of like old Omar Khayyam. I can't figure anything out, and I'm not very happy about it. I feel like I've been thrown in a game that I don't know how to play. I don't know the rules or why I'm playing, so the game itself is absurd."

"I like the game metaphor," he said. "I don't like Sisyphus as a metaphor either. I think it conveys a false concept."

"Lichtman thinks he's an existentialist," I said.

"Well, I think I'm an existentialist. I think everybody is, whether or not the terminology is used."

"Which means you stay with the program and create your essence?"

"In practical terms, it means that the game is one of self-discovery. You actuate your potentialities by striving."

"But what if you didn't want to play in the first place?"

"Well," he said after a pause, "I don't think that works. A person can't wish not to exist before he exists. After he comes into existence, he may want to terminate his life— for any number of reasons—but that is different from your point."

"But don't you think it's absurd that we have a brain and we can communicate with each other, but otherwise we're pretty much incommunicado?"

"Are you sure you're incommunicado? If you hear God speaking to you in English, I think you have to be concerned about your mental health, but I don't think God's messages for us are inaccessible." He paused, probably to let me say something if I wanted to.

"I don't know what that means," I said.

"I know," he said, looking at me intently. "I'm not sure I do either. And the hard part is that, even in the best of circumstances, you're going to find that some things continue to be incomprehensible. It seems likely that humanness per se imposes limits on what we can perceive. We are like the ant that has never seen a sunset and wouldn't be an ant if it had. Our 'reality' is severely restricted by our powers of perception."

"That's right out of the *Rubáiyát* almost," I said. "We're under this dome and we live amidst this stuff we call materiality. And we judge how well we're doing and how smart we are by how well we manipulate the stuff. The stuff may be complex but ultimately it's finite, it's a closed set. It's just stuff."

"For the most part, I agree, it's a closed set, but the dome admits glimmers and occasionally flashes of light." He paused and then he said, "Spiritual light also comes from within when you don't block it." He paused and bit his bottom lip. "I don't have many answers for you, Kit, and I don't think you're going to find any in ontology or anywhere else. I have gradually formed a belief system that, I will candidly admit to you, is not susceptible of verification. I think that we are here for a purpose that unfortunately remains shrouded, and I think God has expectations of us that he reveals to us in his time and only if we listen. For some reason, the hard part seems to be learning how to listen. I think the thing you need to do is to listen to what he's trying to tell you."

"Is he going to give me orders like he gave Uncle Nat?" I said, not trying to hide my anger.

"I take it Uncle Nat is the uncle who murdered your cousin?"

"Yes, he says he was instructed by God to hang his son, and I think that's crazy."

"Of course, it's insane. Isn't your uncle in a mental institution?"

"Yes, but Uncle Nat remains convinced that he had no choice, that he was called by God to be an alien in this world. What if he isn't insane? What does that say about God? What would that mean?"

"Kit, your uncle was delusional. The story of Abraham and Isaac is a dramatic illustration of the furthest reach of faith, and the story has a context that limits its applicability. Your uncle was, and maybe is, insane. Any other hypothesis is simply too awful, too contradictory, too evil to contemplate."

I bent over because I was feeling very sad and I was choking up. It only took me a few seconds to get control of myself. Mr. Marcus didn't say anything while I was bent over. He was still sitting with his hands folded when I sat up. My eyes were moist, and I was a little embarrassed. "I'm glad you could come by," he said after a few seconds. "I think we've done enough today. Let's get back together in the next few weeks."

That's the great thing about Mr. Marcus. He knows when the show is over. If he'd just wanted to beat me up some more, he could have done it. He reached out and shook my hand and said, "Keep writing poetry," and gave me a warm smile. I walked over to the door and held the knob for a moment, trying to decide whether to say anything else. Somehow, I found the whole thing depressing. As I opened the door to go out, he said, "You have great potentialities, Kit. God has a plan."

"Yes, sir," I said. "I just hope he knows what he's doing," and I closed the door behind me. My eyes felt watery again, but I saw Q. Ball waiting for me down the hall, so I dried up pretty quickly. I waved to Q. Ball and yelled, "Hang on a minute," and then dodged into the closest restroom. I wanted to see if my eyes were red. I washed my face and looked in the mirror. I stood looking at my face for a minute or so. I had a curious feeling that I didn't know the person staring back at me. I felt protean rather than static and I found the feeling unsettling. I looked intently at my face and then said aloud, "Who are you?" I stared into the mirror and I repeated in the same pained voice, "Who are you?" Then I was startled by a woman's voice.

"Who's out there?" A woman whose voice I didn't recognize was in one of the toilet stalls. I looked around the bathroom and observed for the first time that it had no urinals. I had blundered into the women's restroom. I went over to the door and turned back toward the toilet stalls just as the voice came again, "Who is there?"

I paused a second at the door, then said, "I have no idea," and quickly exited the bathroom and walked toward the glass doors at the end of the hall.

PHANTASM

Q. Ball was sitting on his motor scooter when I got outside. Ironically, his eyes were redder than mine. Of course, I didn't mention it. I assumed that things might not be going all that great at his house. "Hey, man, what do you say we go down to the river?" He was trying to be jaunty but it was an act and I knew it. The river is only a few miles from school. You can get there by going over to the Loop and then down a path beside the railroad track a quarter of a mile or so. I really didn't feel like going swimming. The truth is we hadn't been to the river in probably a year or more, but I could tell Q. Ball needed to do something and needed a friend.

I threw my leg over his old motor scooter and said, "Let's do it." Q. Ball's scooter is a faded red Cushman. It whined and strained, and I gave a few pushes with my foot. Q. Ball says it has just lost "compression" because it needs a new set of rings, but I expect it needs a lot more than rings, whatever they are. The old Cushman thumped and made more noise than you can believe, but here's the truth: When it got going, it was a lot faster than a pair of track shoes, which is all I've got.

The path by the railroad track is bumpy and rough, and the gravel that washes down from the track makes it tricky to ride on. My butt took a pounding. I was relieved when we finally turned off the main path and started down toward the river. The track goes over the river on a trestle that's about twenty feet above the water. The path that winds down to the river goes through the woods bordering the track and into a little clearing beside the river. About twenty yards from the trestle, the riverbank juts out abruptly and then curves back, forming a little promontory at the clearing.

Right next to the river two large logs lie in an L-shape along the bank. The ground behind the logs is usually scattered with debris from floodwater because the clearing is in a low-lying area. Large live oaks and cypress trees line the riverbank. Moss hangs from the oaks and cypress knees protrude out of the water in the shallows near the bank. The trees behind the clearing are spindly and encased in tall weeds and blackberry vines.

We took off all our clothes except our jockey shorts and stacked them in piles on the nearest log. The four-thirty train, approaching the trestle from the south, sounded its warning whistle. We sat on the log looking up at the trestle as the noise of the engine got louder and louder. You can't talk while the engine's going past. The engineer blew the train whistle to warn anybody who might be on the trestle. Then as the engine went across, he waved to us and we waved back.

In a few seconds the engine noise began to fade in the distance and all you could hear was the clack, clack, clack of the boxcars on the track. We picked up some gravel and tried to hit the passing boxcars, then sat back on the log and watched the cars clack on away. The last boxcar before the caboose had printed in large white letters on the side, "Poccotola Well Supply Company, Poccotola, Mississippi," and then in smaller letters, "We Mean Well." It was sort of depressing to watch the cars disappear beyond the trestle, leaving us sitting alone together on a petrified log.

When the caboose had crossed the trestle, Q. Ball said, "What do you think, man? Was my mom having an affair with Roby's daddy?"

I really didn't know what to say. I wasn't exactly surprised by the question, but how was I supposed to know? You can't tell what the truth is sometimes. Newt told me a couple of years ago that my father's wreck wasn't an accident and that he had intended to kill himself. Newt has turned into a jerk who hassles me a lot, so I don't know whether to believe him. Sometimes he says things just to shock or irritate me. I told him I thought he was full of it, but I really don't know what to think. All I can remember of my father is a brooding, mysterious person, but I wasn't even five years old when he died. I asked my mother about it but she brushed it off and said, "Your Uncle Newt has a vivid imagination." But, let's face it, a high-speed crash into a bridge abutment on a clear day is a peculiar accident even for a drunk ex-soldier.

I know about some people, but I really don't know about Mrs. Ball. The truth is I could believe it. I had never told Q. Ball about the incident that happened right before I started going to Bridgewater. His father had given me an exam sheet and left me at the desk in their study to do the problems. Professor Ball was gone maybe fifteen minutes when Mrs. Ball came into the room wearing shorts and an exercise bra and carrying tennis shoes in one hand and white socks in the other. "I'm having trouble hooking this thing," she said. "Can you help?" Then she turned around in front of me revealing a pretty back and dangling bra straps. I fumbled around until I got the straps hooked and then she turned around and kissed me on the lips. "You're a doll," she said. "You haven't seen my ankle weights, have you?" As she went out the door, she said, "I'm going jogging if Dr. Doodah inquires."

After Mrs. Ball left, I stared at the linear equations problems for a while and then I just got up and left. I told Professor Ball later I had been too distracted to do the problems, but I didn't say what had distracted me. I also didn't tell Q. Ball about his mother's using the phone for an hour in Morrow's Drugstore. This whole thing just shows you one of the problems with trying to do the right thing. Everybody's always saying you're supposed to tell the truth. Then, when you do, you hurt somebody. So I didn't tell him what I was thinking, which I guess means I didn't tell him the truth. I said, "Nah, you know how things get all confused and people misunderstand things."

Q. Ball looked glumly out across the river. "I don't know what's going to happen, man. My parents may get a divorce. They're really fighting a lot." He was quiet a minute. "My momma goes off by herself all the time. That's what happened last weekend. She just had to get away. Roby's daddy was supposed to be fishing." He paused and then said, "Why does she go off like that?" Because I didn't know what to do or say, I stared blankly in the direction of the trestle. I could just as well have been staring at a cypress knee. The trestle didn't have anything to do with anything, but Q. Ball seemed to think I was thinking about the trestle because he said, "Let's jump. How about it?"

He got up without waiting for a response and headed toward the trestle. We had jumped off before, but I was nervous about it. The trestle is only about twenty feet high, but from the track it feels like three hundred feet. I didn't worry about the depth of the river. I knew it was deep enough. What bothered me was the stuff floating down the river. I had seen all kinds of things floating on the water and some things partially submerged. I saw a large log one time just barely visible beneath the surface, like an ominous shadow on the river. I noticed it because a little branch was sticking up out of the water like a periscope on a submarine.

"Hey, man, hang on, just wait a minute," I said.

"Come on, man, let's jump."

"Q. Ball, don't jump. You know what would happen if we jumped on a log from up there."

Q. Ball had already reached the base of the trestle. He looked back at me and said, "Yeah, I know what would happen, and it might not be all bad." He started climbing up the side of the trestle. The creosoted support beams overlap and form stair steps up to the track. Q. Ball climbed to the top of the trestle and then walked out over the river. I didn't want to jump but I didn't want Q. Ball thinking I was chicken, so I decided to go on over and climb the trestle. I looked up as Q. Ball reached the center of the trestle. He was framed against the setting sun, looking skinny and vulnerable in his jockeys.

He had maneuvered down to the edge of the trestle and stood with his head bent over and his red hair hanging forward over his brow, holding his pale, thin arms out like a frail, featherless bird about to fly. He looked down at me and then, instead of jumping into the water feet first as I expected him to, he made a little spring step and fell into a swan dive right into the middle of the current. I was so surprised I stood there looking apprehensively at the surface of the water. After a little bit, the top of his head came up but his face stayed under water. All I could see was a mop of disheveled red hair on the surface.

I shouted, "Q. Ball!" and then I dove in the water and began flailing as hard as I could.

I had swum about halfway to the red hair when Q. Ball's face came out of the water wearing one of the goofiest grins you ever saw. I stopped swimming and he started laughing. "Q. Ball, you are a total loon." I couldn't think of anything nasty enough. I turned around and swam back to the bank. I got out of the water and sat on the log, glaring at Q. Ball, who was whooping and hollering. I shouted, "That wasn't funny, Q. Ball. That was crazy." He was treading water in the middle of the channel, laughing like a maniac. "You told me not to jump," he said, grinning inanely, "so I decided to dive." I must have been expecting something bad to happen. I was relieved and angry at the same time. "I'm going to kick your butt, Q. Ball," I shouted.

From behind me, I heard a girlish giggle. I turned sideways and straddled the log. Girls don't usually come to the trestle. I thought about reaching for my jeans but when I turned around it was too late. Two girls stood at the edge of the woods staring at me curiously, one of them dark and one sort of bronze like someone with a deep tan. I said, "Hi." The pretty bronze girl had her arms folded under her breasts.

"Is his name really 'Cue Ball'?" she asked, her head cocked to one side. Both girls were barefooted and wearing denim shorts and tee shirts cut off about three inches above the navel. They were dressed alike but didn't look much alike. The lighter girl was lithe and perky. The other one was plump and shy.

I turned my head toward the river and yelled, "Hey, there are some girls up here who want to know your name."

"Tell them the demand is always great, but I try to accommodate," Q. Ball yelled back.

"Cassandra, we got to go now," the darker girl said.

Cassandra ignored her and came over and sat on the log about three feet from me. "It's hot out here."

"It's cooler if you dangle your feet in the water," I said. She swung her legs over the log and dipped her feet just below the surface.

After a few seconds, she said, "You're right, that's pretty cool. Come on, Rolanda, put your feet in the water. It'll cool you off." Rolanda came a few steps forward, and then stopped about three feet from the log.

"There's snakes in that water, Cassandra."

Cassandra paid her no attention except to say offhand-edly, "My sister is scared of everything." Then she turned toward me and said, "Can I touch your hair?" At first, I didn't know what to think, but then it occurred to me that she probably hadn't had a whole lot of contact with blond hair.

"Sure," I said. She reached over and gave it a brush with her open hand and then ran her fingers through the hair on the right side of my head.

"Cassandra, you are crazy," Rolanda said. "Come on,

now. We need to get ourselves home." Cassandra didn't even look back at her.

"You know," she said, "your hair looks a little like straw."

"Yeah, that's what I'm told." I was thinking the coach would love that one.

"I'm sorry," she said, smiling. "I didn't hurt your feelings, did I?" Her teeth were bright and even and the two front incisors were almost a quarter of an inch longer than the adjacent teeth.

"Nah, I'm used to it," I said. "Your hair is really beautiful." It was. Deep waves of thick, shiny black hair fell to her shoulders and swirled hauntingly around her face.

"Thank you," she said simply. I clearly wasn't the first person to tell her that her hair was beautiful.

"Can I touch it?" I said.

"Sure," she said, and I reached over and felt the texture and ran my fingers through the curls.

"It's very beautiful," I said. Q. Ball had swum over close to the bank and I said, "Cassandra and Rolanda," pointing to them one at a time, "meet my friend Q. Ball." Cassandra giggled. "I have to tell you, he's not the kind of 'cue ball' you're thinking about. It's the initial 'Q' and his last name is Ball," and I spelled it for them. "His full name is Ronald Quincy Ball."

"I like it better the other way," Cassandra said, smiling broadly.

"Come on in and say that," Q. Ball said.

She looked a little impish and said, "If I had my bathing suit, I probably would."

"We don't have any bathing suits," Q. Ball said. "Why do you need one?"

"Well, maybe I don't," Cassandra said.

Rolanda came over closer to the log, frowning. She said, almost in a whisper, "Cassandra, we gotta go now. You're gonna get skinned. You know what Momma said."

Cassandra turned around on the log and said in an angry voice, "Yeah, I know what she says, but you know, Rolanda, she don't take her own advice."

Rolanda frowned and stuck out her lips. "Cassandra, you are awful talking like that. You better come on," she said, and started back up the path through the trees.

Cassandra's eyebrows went down and she stuck her tongue out at the departing Rolanda. Then she walked around to the other log and looked thoughtfully toward the water. She glanced at me across the little inlet separating us and then took the bottom of her cut-off tee shirt in her hands, pulled it over her head and dropped it on the log. Next, she unsnapped and zipped down her shorts and let them fall to the ground. She stepped out of her shorts and put them on the log with her shirt. I almost fell off the log. She was incredible. I was staring at her like a drooling idiot. "What's the matter," she said, "never seen boobs before?" She climbed up on the log and pranced back and forth a couple of times wearing nothing but plain cotton panties and an impish grin. She held her shoulders back and stuck out her little behind like a gymnast about to perform.

I continued to stare until I became self-conscious. I lowered my gaze to the river only to find that she was there, re-created by the mirror in the stream. I looked intently at the undulating image and I had an eerie feeling about the image on the water. Cassandra knew I was looking at her reflection because the image was smiling at me. I saw her arms go out and above her head and her body curve forward and then disappear into the image on the river. I continued to stare at the water, but the phantom was gone. Cassandra swam out about twenty yards and started treading water. "Hey, this is nice, isn't it, Q. Ball?" Q. Ball was about as disconcerted as he had been the day before when he was watching his father threatening to beat up Mr. Robicheaux.

"Yeah, it's great," Q. Ball squeaked out. She dog-paddled around a few minutes, smiling broadly the whole time, then started swimming back toward the bank.

When she was back on the log, she quickly put her tee shirt back on. She used her hands to brush water off her legs and wring out her long curly hair. Then she slipped her shorts on and started walking up the path. "I'd better go catch Rolanda. Nice to meet you."

"Nice to meet you too," I said. She stopped after she had gone almost to the trees and turned around.

"What's your name?"

"Kit," I said. "Kit Biddle."

She walked a little farther, gave me a mischievous grin and a cheesecake curtsy with one shoulder up and her mouth open. "Your hair's a mess, but I like it," she said and disappeared in the woods.

"Thanks," I yelled out. "I like yours too." She then reappeared from the woods but she was no longer barefooted. She was wearing boots, which I thought was peculiar except for the fact that she was walking in the woods.

"I'm kidding you. It's nathan," she said. Then she turned back toward the opening in the trees and shouted, "I didn't mean nathan."

"What? Did you say nothing?" I shouted at her as she walked back toward the tree line. She turned and looked at me without smiling. The grinning, frolicsome Cassandra had disappeared. The girl in the boots was serious, the same girl but somehow different.

"Don't pay me any mind. You know I couldn't really mean nathan." She then disappeared into the woods again.

"What?" I shouted again. *Did I misunderstand again*? I turned to Q. Ball, who was still treading water. "Q. Ball, did she say Nathan or nothin'?"

Q. Ball gave a little yelp and shouted, "I don't know, man, but can you believe that? That's unreal." Except for the strange exit, I had to agree. It was almost too perfect. I felt a twinge of guilt, as though I had gotten something I wasn't entitled to. Something special had appeared and then vanished, probably forever. I didn't tell Q. Ball about the image in the river, and I didn't tell him that she seemed to be calling me Nathan. I just chalked it up: Cassandra was just being a coquette who was having fun turning our heads. An exquisite random squib had appeared in the dark of my life, and I was grateful. I can't remember some things and I'm sure I'm going to forget some more, but I'll bet I won't ever forget Cassandra prancing on that log wearing her plain cotton panties and a devilish grin. Maybe the really beautiful things are like that: little glowing sparks in the mundane darkness of everyday existence. I also won't ever forget what she said.

"Hey, man, what do you think about that?" said Q. Ball.

"She was playing with us. I don't think she meant anything at all."

"I don't know, Biddle. A girl doesn't just take off her clothes like that. She had to mean something."

He was treading water and I was sitting on a log. Both of us were slightly disconcerted. I thought about Anna. Cassandra was beautiful but remarkably she bore only a slight resemblance to Anna, the real perfect form. Q. Ball's thoughts seemed to go off somewhere too because he got quiet. After he treaded water awhile he climbed out of the river and sat beside me on the log. In the past we had swum naked, so we wouldn't have to let our jockeys dry. It was getting late, and I began to regret that we got our underwear wet.

Cassandra disconcerted me in a number of ways, not the least of which was my physical attraction to her. I found Cassandra tantalizing in a purely sensual way. Of course, Anna was a goddess, while Cassandra was only a temptress with a beautiful body of clay. Or do I have it backwards? I really don't know but that's when the idea came into my mind to go by Anna's, not to go in but just to be there. I don't know what I expected, but I had to do it. Q. Ball and I sat in silence for a while. I don't think either of us had a grip on anything. The appearance of Cassandra had diverted my thoughts for a moment, but her departure seemed to magnify a growing sense of uneasiness.

"I'll probably go with my daddy," Q. Ball muttered stolidly.

Since I was thinking about Anna, I didn't have any idea what he was talking about. "Go where?" I asked. Q. Ball gave me an impatient shrug.

"Where do you think? If they get a divorce, I don't think I want to live with my mother."

I slipped off my jockeys and wrung as much water out as I could and then started putting on my clothes. Q. Ball wanted to talk about his parents and I didn't know what to say. When I finished putting on my tennis shoes, I went over to the river and looked across the water at the trestle. I had been coming to the river since shortly after we moved from the country house. In the beginning it was a great adventure, probably because we weren't sup- posed to do it. After the thrill wore off, we went to the river when we were bored, particularly in the summer when everything came to a standstill. I was standing in the same place I had stood before, and I couldn't think of why I was there. Even with the tantalizing magic of Cassandra, the river was no longer the same. It wasn't a relic of the past like the country house, but it produced the same feeling. I wondered why I was at the river, and I knew I would never come back again.

When I turned around, Q. Ball was standing by his scooter waiting for me. We started back up the trail to the railroad track, pushing the old Cushman. It had no hope of climbing the hill on its own power. The sun was an orange semicircular splotch on the horizon when we reached the track. The reddish glow filtered through the branches jutting up from the far side of the river that lay like a dark shadow beneath the trees. I sat on Q. Ball's scooter looking beyond the river at the sunset while he struggled to crank the gasping old machine.

You have to turn the throttle on the right handlebar at the same time that you step down on the foot crank. Q. Ball had to repeat the process five or six times before the scooter gasped into life. It was getting dark when we started bumping along the path back toward the Loop. In the twilight, Q. Ball couldn't see very well. We must have hit most of the holes in the path. A couple of times I thought the grunting old scooter was going to bounce out from under us or veer off the path down into the underbrush.

As we approached the Loop, I said, "Q. Ball, can you drop me off at Anna's?"

"I told my dad I'd be back by seven. I don't know whether I can make it."

Even before I said anything, he turned the old scooter onto Regency Street toward Anna's, and I said, "Thanks," and patted his shoulder. When we were almost to her driveway, I said, "Just let me off on the next corner and you go on."

He glanced back over his shoulder and said, "You sure, man?"

"I'm okay, Q. Ball. Just let me off here." He pulled over and I got off. The red Cushman strained and whined, and I gave it a shove as Q. Ball turned the throttle. He waved his left hand in the air as the old scooter eased off down the street.

"See you tomorrow, man," he yelled back at me.

"Thanks," I said but I don't think he heard me. I felt lonely as Q. Ball was pulling away, and I almost regretted not going on home. I was pretty sure that Anna wasn't at home and, even if she were, I had no intention of barging in on her. She said she didn't even want to talk.

TWILIGHT TIME

Twilight had thickened into darkness when I got off Q. Ball's scooter. I stood at the edge of the road and watched the light on the back of the old scooter disappear into the night. Then I walked slowly over to the sidewalk and started down toward Anna's driveway. I don't know what I intended or what I expected. Maybe I just wanted to look up at her apartment and think about her. I was only a few yards from her driveway, walking along under a large magnolia that spread over the sidewalk like an umbrella, when a white sedan came out of the alley and stopped before proceeding onto Carapace. I stopped walking.

There were two couples in the car. Under the streetlight I could see Burch's face in the back seat, and Anna was in the front seat sitting beside a guy I didn't recognize. The car pulled out and left me standing in the shadows beside her driveway, holding my heart in my hand. She had told me, but I was nonetheless stunned. I don't know why, but I went on down the driveway and climbed the stairs. I rang the bell and knocked on the door. No one answered. I could hear Hippo running around in the apartment barking. I went back down the stairs and sat on the bottom step.

When I sat down, I realized my paperback was still in my back pocket. I took it out and sat on the bottom step fondling it for probably five minutes or more before getting up and starting for home. My head hurt and my insides felt like a huge void. I walked along holding my book, feeling sorry for myself. I passed a garbage can and threw the book into it. I thought, *To hell with John Stuart Mill.* The burst of anger gave me an immediate sense of release, but the loss of the book seemed to intensify the desolation. I went back and fished my book out of the trash. Maybe I just needed something to hang on to or maybe I thought that Mill might be a kindred soul, someone who had fumbled around in the dark and ended up with his guts on fire.

I was slouching along, sort of hangdog, looking at the ground and not paying attention to anything except my own feelings. Until the wind began blowing harder, I didn't notice that clouds were blocking out the moon and the stars. The streetlights are about a hundred yards apart along that stretch of the road, so a large part of the time I was in almost total darkness. The wind groaned ominously and the leaves rustled in the trees and crackled along the ground.

A few large drops of rain hit the sidewalk around me. I moved into the street and started running. The night brightened with lightning, then went dark again. The thunder followed within a few seconds each time a streak zigzagged across the sky. I imagined I was in a meet, and I measured in my mind the distance to my house so that I could find the right pace. My body was taut with emotion. It was easy to run, and I just let it out. It's too bad I wasn't in a meet. I probably would've done my best time ever.

Burch's house is on a street perpendicular to mine. I didn't have to pass it, but it is on one of the cross streets. Anyway, I turned when I got to Burch's street. I don't know whether I thought that Anna might be at Burch's house or what I was thinking. A couple of blocks before I got to his house, a steady drizzle began. I thought vaguely about using his carport for shelter, but I had almost rejected the idea when the rain started falling in huge drops. I sprinted the remaining distance to Burch's house and ran under his carport.

Two cars were in the driveway, one parked behind the other. Burch's fancy convertible was closest to the road and in front of it was a dark coupe. Neither car was the evil white sedan. I thought about standing under the carport until the rain stopped and then running on home, but I was afraid somebody might drive up and find me standing in the dark in their carport. So, I rang the doorbell. I heard movement inside and the outside light came on. The blinds on the glass pane in the door parted slightly and I saw a fingertip and an eye.

The door opened, and Sarah appeared in the doorway smiling broadly. "Kit," she said with obvious approval, "what on earth are you doing out in the rain?" I felt strange standing there pretending to be making a visit. Except for the entanglement in the Frost Bite the day before, I had seen Sarah only randomly in the last couple of years, probably because Burch had become Burch. She wore a pink slip and her horn-rimmed glasses and had her hair pulled back in a ponytail tied with a pink ribbon. She looked like somebody who was getting ready to go to bed. Before I could think of anything to say, she said, "Come on in. This is a nice surprise."

"I was just passing by, and it started raining. Is Harry at home?" Of course, I knew he wasn't, but I had to say something.

"No, he's not." She tilted her head slightly to the right, looking sort of disappointed. "Come on in, for heaven's sake. You don't need Harry to come in." She reached down and took my arm and pulled me toward the door. "Harry took our cousin John on a double date. John's going to be a freshman at the university too." She looked uncomfortable, or maybe I just thought she should. I was wondering if she knew about Anna, but if she did, she didn't admit it. I was about to throw up.

We went through the kitchen and dining room and into their den. I sat down in one of Mrs. Burchfield's prized antique chairs and propped my feet on a shaky antique stool. "What a nice surprise," Sarah said again. "Can I get you anything?"

My stomach was so tight I could hardly breathe. I wasn't in the mood for chitchat with Sarah or anybody else. "No," I said sullenly and then remembered Newt's dictum about beer soothing frets. "How about beer?"

"Well, I don't think I can give you beer. There are only a few bottles, and they're my father's. How about a Coke?"

"Forget it," I said petulantly, "I'm all right." My mood was down and dark. I was angry and willing to hate the whole Burchfield family, including Sarah, who had done nothing at all so far as I knew.

"Don't be mad," she said. She pulled a black wooden rocker around so that it was almost facing my chair and sat on the front edge of the seat. She stood up again almost immediately. "How about wine? We have cabernet, Chablis, and some others. I don't think my folks would miss a bottle of wine."

"Wine would be good." I had never had any wine, so of course I didn't know one kind from the other. And I wasn't even sure I wanted any.

She smiled and did the head tilt again, then walked toward the cellar door. She's a little different, but she's really a good-looking girl. Burch used to alternate between bragging that she's brilliant and complaining that she's crazy. You can't pay much attention to what Burch says because he's usually wrong about everything. She came back with a glass filled with dark red wine.

"That's cabernet," she said. "There are so many bottles of cabernet in the cellar, they can't miss one little bottle." This time she sat back in the rocker and pulled her legs up with her arms wrapped around her knees. Her red-painted toes stuck out over the rocker seat. She wiggled them and smiled at me again. "I enjoyed our conversation in the Frost Bite. I'm still working on nothingness. So far, I've come up with nothing, so to speak. I know you have to exist to think about nothingness. 'Cogito, ergo sum,' as the man said." When I sat in silence, she smiled at me and said, "Can I have a sip of wine?"

"It's your wine," I said. I handed her the glass, and she took a tiny sip, grimaced, and handed the glass back to me.

"I know it's not the same," she said.

"What's not the same?"

"I can easily conceive of my own nonexistence, and yours . . . just barely," she said, smiling. "I can't really conceive of absolute nothingness." The truth is I could remember entangled legs, but I could hardly remember any conversation beyond a mention of the concept of nothingness.

"Do you ever feel movement in your brain," I said, "like when you shift from mathematics to poetry? Maybe movement isn't the right word. I feel a shift, maybe like electromagnetic activity, from one part of the brain to another."

"I've never felt that. Maybe I'm always staying put, using the same gray matter. Mostly I do math. It's tidy and tautological and comforting. I don't write poetry."

The hem of her slip had slid down her thighs, and she sat in the rocker hugging her bare legs. I could see white lace trim on her pink panties, but I was trying not to stare. Maybe because Moby began to intrude, I started having difficulty ignoring the tantalizing pink panties and the long, sleek legs in the rocker across from me. I emptied the glass and handed it to Sarah for more wine. She hesitated a moment. I was still depressed and angry about Anna, but the wine had softened the edges. She got up gracefully. "Don't drink too much, okay? Be back in a sec."

Sarah had obviously put a record on the player. From somewhere in the house, I heard The Platters crooning the first strains of "Twilight Time." Sarah reappeared and held out the refilled wine glass. "Want to dance? It may not be as interesting as nothingness, but I promise it's a lot more fun."

"I don't dance," I said, taking the wine glass and ignoring her witticism.

"Sure, you do. It requires virtually nothing," she said, probably carrying the pun too far. "You just move with the music." She pulled me up and snuggled in close. With her arms around my waist, she came up on her tiptoes and our mouths came together. It was probably about that point in the evening that Moby took control. It wasn't a matter of getting back at Burch or anything like that. Moby really doesn't do revenge. I remember thinking that what I had done with Anna was foolish and that I should have gone with my urges. The supernal form that had controlled me had vanished, leaving unchecked lust surging through my body like a tsunami. I could think of no reason even to try to repress my urges. Perhaps just to see what Sarah would say, I pushed the straps of her slip from her shoulders so that her slip slid down and clung to the tips of her breasts. She made no protest but looked uncomfortable and, after a few seconds, she reached down and put her straps back on her shoulders.

I had never been to a dance (another of those group things that made me uncomfortable), but Sarah and I did a simple two-step that even I could do. I put both my arms around her and pulled her in so that my right leg was between her legs. We didn't move more than three feet in any direction. We danced slowly, alternately kissing and sipping wine. It was thirty or forty minutes later when she looked at her watch and said, "My parents will be here in a few minutes. Suppose I give you a ride home?"

"Okay," I said. She left the den, this time toward the back of the house. I continued sipping the wine, which made me feel progressively better and less and less inhibited.

She came back wearing a white sundress with tiny little straps over the shoulders and white sandals. The zipper on the dress was in the front, and she had zipped it to the point right below her breasts. She wasn't wearing a bra. We stopped in the kitchen on the way to the carport. "Want to take the wine bottle with us? We might as well." She picked up the wine bottle and handed it to me. I drained the glass, and she then washed it and returned it to the cabinet. When we were under the carport, she said, "Harry's car is blocking me, so we'll just take his. He won't mind."

"Do you know how to get to my house?" I asked, as we got in Burch's car.

"You're kidding, right?"

"Go that way," I said, pointing to the left. She looked puzzled.

"You don't live that way," she said.

"I think I know where I live," I said. "Go that way anyway." She smiled and turned the car in the direction I had indicated.

FLAGON THROES

The rain made a dull drumming noise on the convertible top of Burch's car. When we reached Carapace, I told Sarah to hang a left toward the Frost Bite. Then, as we approached the railroad overpass, I said, "Turn under the viaduct and park." She stopped at the overpass and pulled off the road about twenty yards. When we were under the viaduct, she turned off the windshield wipers, parked parallel with the bridge, and switched off the engine and the lights. We rolled down the windows and sat quietly looking out at the darkness.

I could hear the rain's rhythmic patter around the viaduct. In the absence of the wine and the burst of testosterone, I think the moment would have been oppressively sad, but Moby doesn't do sadness very well either. I swigged on the wine and then handed the bottle to Sarah. She held it between her thumb and index finger and craned her neck forward when she sipped it.

She turned around on the seat so that her back was to the dashboard and her legs were on the driver's side of the seat, and then snuggled in with her head on my shoulder and her arms around my neck.

"This is cozy," she said and kissed me. We had been kissing for only a short time when I pushed the straps of her sundress off her shoulders and pushed the zipper down. The dress slid down to her waist. She looked at me apprehensively and then, after I pulled my tee shirt over my head, she said, "What are you going to do?"

"The question is, what are we going to do?" I threw my tee shirt on the back seat. At this point, you might have to ask Moby what my plan was. My emotions were caught in a potent vortex of lust, mourning, and pain. I unfastened the button on my Levi's and pushed them down with my still-damp jockeys and threw them in the back seat with my tee shirt.

"I don't know about this, Kit," Sarah said. "We'd better stop." I ignored her. I reached under her dress, and she lifted her hips slightly when I grabbed the pink panties with the white lace. I threw the panties on the back seat with my clothes. My energy level surged on a mixture of adrenaline and testosterone. Sarah seemed almost passive but at the same time noticeably appre-hensive. She didn't resist when I pulled her over so that she was straddling me with her knees on the seat. When I tried to pull her sundress over her head, she wouldn't raise her arms, so I bunched it around her waist. She laid her head on my shoulder and clung to me tightly, pressing her breasts into my chest. I wanted to maneuver her into position, but she had me in such a grip I could hardly move at all.

"You're going to have to loosen your grip," I said testily.

"I'm afraid," she said, holding me in a vice of tense muscles. I tried to move her around, but she was remarkably strong and she wouldn't budge. We sat in that awkward clench maybe ten or fifteen minutes. She didn't say anything. She just clung to me like someone on a precipice.

"Okay," I said, "get up." She didn't move. I waited a minute or so, then repeated, "Get up."

"No," she said quietly.

"What do you mean no?"

"No," she repeated.

"This is ridiculous," I said.

"No, it's not. I like it here. Just be quiet. You're going too fast. And you're scaring me." At that point, I thought I'd miscalculated the possibilities. I lifted the bottle and drank some wine over her shoulder, and then I began idly stroking her back. Somewhat surprisingly, I felt her muscles loosening.

"Okay, it's your show," I said. I wanted to see if she'd ask for her clothes back.

"What do you mean it's my show?"

"You've complained about everything, so make yourself happy. It's now your show."

"Why is it now my show?" She sat up straight and looked at me intently. "You took our clothes off." At that, I guessed she wasn't likely to go anywhere or ask for her clothes.

"I got us this far. Now, either we put our clothes back on or you can tell me what we're doing." By this time I was no longer thinking about Anna or anything else. The combination of wine and the proximity of Sarah's body blotted out everything except Moby's wild, soundless groaning. "Here, you need some wine," and I handed her the bottle. This time she grabbed the bottle and gulped several times before handing it back to me. I took the bottle and drank the few remaining drops and then reached out the window and threw the bottle down the slope toward the road. I resumed the gentle stroking of Sarah's back, and she began kissing my face and breathing in little gasps.

Then she pulled back, held my face between her hands and said very softly, "Are you sure about this?" The question strangely presumed that I was postured for rationality. By this point in the evening, Moby could have produced a syllogism about as readily as I could.

I wasn't exactly looking around during all this but, just as Sarah began to maneuver around on top of me, I became aware of two shadowy figures under the viaduct near the road, maybe twenty or thirty yards in front of the car. I don't know whether I heard their voices first or saw them. I was slumped on the seat, but my eyes were still over the level of the dashboard, so I could see over Sarah's shoulder out the front window. I could tell by the muffled tone of their voices and their jerky movements that they were arguing. They gave no sign of noticing Burch's car. In a low, strained voice, I said, "We have company." Sarah twisted around and looked at them and, remarkably, she turned back around and kissed me.

"They don't know we're here," she said softly. She was right about that. We were in the dark under the overpass, and they were in the edge of the glow from the streetlight. One of the shadows was a big man, well over six feet tall and stocky, and the other was medium height and thin, probably not more than a hundred fifty pounds. I heard a gravelly voice and saw the big guy reach down and pick up a bottle by the neck and raise it back over his head. The smaller guy fell backwards as though he had stumbled, but he got up and started walking down the road. When Sarah finally got us more or less aligned, she began easing down on me. Almost involuntarily, I thrust my hips upward, causing her to groan and pull back.

"That hurt," she said softly in a pained voice. She raised up and repeated the peculiar question she had already asked: "Are you really sure about this?" After I remained silent, she started moving her hips forward but had hardly caused any penetration when she groaned again. Out near the road, the big guy swung the bottle and the little guy staggered. The big guy raised the bottle again and I heard a loud sound like "splat," and I could see droplets of blood or something spray into the air. Sarah pulled back again and, just then, Moby erupted ecstatically, spewing randomly but mostly on Sarah's dress. Sarah seemed to know immediately what had happened. She stopped her hip movements, kissed me, and lay her head on my shoulder.

When I recovered enough, I looked back toward the road and saw the little guy lying on the ground next to the pavement. I waited a couple of seconds and then I whispered, "I think that big guy may have killed the little guy."

"What?" Sarah said and turned toward the road, still straddling me. The big guy looked around furtively, dropped the bottle on the ground, and then appeared to be taking something out of the little guy's pocket. Then he walked out from under the viaduct and went off down the road. I couldn't see any movement on the ground where the little guy was lying.

"We've got to do something," I said and pushed Sarah off me and onto the seat beside me.

"Well," she said in a tone that was probably part offense and part bafflement. I found my jeans on the back floorboard and started pulling them up. I felt something wet in my crotch and flipped on the interior light to see what it was. Blood was all between my legs and on the seat. "Oh, my goodness," Sarah said when she saw the blood, "I'm bleeding." She got up on her knees and reached back over the seat for her panties. "I've got blood on my dress." She held her dress up, and

I could see that it was smeared with blood and spattered with semen. I found my shirt and wiped the blood and semen off her dress as well as I could.

"Sarah, we've got to do something," I repeated. Immediately after my eruption, I had begun to feel panicky. It was as though I had been doing things in the dark where I thought no one could see, but all of a sudden I discovered that the light had been on the entire time. My mind had cleared and I had an acute sense that something was wrong. I had an almost uncontrollable urge to help the little guy under the viaduct. I felt no particular need to help Sarah; instead, I had a vague sense of estrangement from her.

"I think we should call the police," she said. "I've got to do something about this dress."

I frantically pulled on my bloody tee shirt and slipped on my tennis shoes without the socks. "Turn the lights on and pull the car up some," I said with intensity. I got out and started walking toward the shadow on the ground. Sarah cranked the car and edged it forward. The lights came on when the car was about ten feet from the little guy on the ground. He was a slightly built black man who appeared to be about thirty-five years old. I could see a bloody gash along his left temple. He wasn't moving. Beside him on the ground was the bloody wine bottle. The man had been beaten with our empty wine bottle. *I'll be damned*, I thought. I yelled back at Sarah, "Move the car forward. We've got to get this guy to the hospital."

"We should just notify the police." She got out of the car and stood by the door. I couldn't think of anything other than that I couldn't leave the guy there bleeding and unconscious.

"Sarah, we're not going to leave him here to die. Now pull the car up so I can get him on the seat." She was clearly startled by the vehemence in my voice. She got in the car and pulled alongside the inert body. He was totally limp and it felt like he weighed three hundred fifty pounds, but I got him on the front passenger seat, and I got in the back. He had a stifling odor that combined the smells of whiskey, grime, and sweat. I asked Sarah whether she knew how to get to the hospital. She didn't answer, but she was driving in the right direction. I took off my tee shirt and wrapped it around the little guy's head. Blood poured from his temple all over the car seat. I could tell he was alive, because his eyelids fluttered a little, and I thought I could see his chest moving. I don't think I was afraid, but my shoulders twitched and my neck was so tight I could hardly turn my head. I don't know what hysteria is like, but I must have been close. I had blotted everything out of my mind except the rescue of the battered man.

"Go in the emergency entrance," I said. A neon sign pointed the way. Sarah stopped at the glass doors, and I went in to get help. Since I was a bloody mess, I got immediate notice but no instant action. I had to ask a skinny old lady behind the desk for help. She acted almost uninterested, but she did call for an attendant to bring a gurney. In the emergency room a stocky nurse with tired eyes stuck something under the man's nose and his head jerked back.

"He's alive," the nurse said stolidly to the crone behind the desk. She rolled the gurney toward the double doors into the interior of the emergency room.

"What happened to him?" she asked.

"A guy robbed him, hit him with a wine bottle," I said. "Hit him hard several times."

"How long ago?"

"Just a few minutes, maybe twenty minutes." The nurse disappeared behind the double doors, and I turned back to the crone.

"Fill these out," the crone said in a bored voice, handing me some papers on a clipboard.

"I don't know anything about this man. We saw him get beaten and brought him here, but I don't know him." I put the clipboard back on the desk.

"Somebody's going to fill out these forms." She glared at me. "If you don't know this boy, why did you bring him in here? If this is somebody's yard man, they are responsible. Now, is that the case here?"

"I saw him get beaten with a wine bottle, but I've never seen him before."

"Well, this is not a colored hospital. You wait right here until I get an officer in here. The restrooms are right down the hall. You can get yourselves cleaned up, but don't you go anywhere."

If I could have figured out how to do it, I might have sprinted for the door, but the restrooms were down a dead end. Sarah and I walked silently down the hall and into our respective restrooms. When I had cleaned myself up as much as possible, I walked down the hall and stood in front of the ladies' room and waited for Sarah.

An overweight policeman with a rubbery face was standing at the counter when we got back to the waiting room. "I'm Officer Fine," he said. "Can you come back here so I can get your statement and the young lady's at the same time?"

"Sure," I said. We walked down the hall and into a little conference room. Sarah sat in a chair across the table from me looking nervous and glum.

"Okay, first gimme your names and addresses." Officer Fine had pulled out a pad and sat down at the head of the table. We gave him the information and he said, "Well, tell me how all this happened. You're a mess, son. You get in a fight with this boy?"

"No, sir," I said, and then told him the story, at least most of it. I told him that we had driven under the viaduct to park and that we saw a big guy hit the little guy with a bottle and take something out of his pocket. He made notes as I talked.

Sarah didn't say anything. When I finished my story, he turned to her and said, "You got anything to add to that?"

"No, officer," she said glumly, "that's pretty much it."

"You disagree with anything he said?"

"No, officer, I agree with everything he said."

"Thank you both. I may have to get back in touch with you, but that's all for now."

Sarah didn't say anything the whole time we were in the car. When she stopped in front of my house, I said, "I'm sorry about everything tonight. You know we couldn't leave him there." She looked tense. "I hope you're not going to be in too much trouble." I don't know what I expected but she surprised me. She leaned over and kissed me.

"I'll be all right," she said. "I know we did the right thing." I wasn't sure what all she intended to cover by her statement.

"Good night," I said and got out of the car.

"Kit," she said, sliding over to the passenger-side window. I leaned down and she kissed me and said, "Are your evenings all like this?"

"No, this one was a little extreme." She pulled me down toward the window and kissed me again. "Good," she said. "That's good. Well, good night." I returned the kiss.

"Good night," I said. "I'm sorry." She then drove off slowly down the street.

My mother was reading in the living room when I walked in. I thought she was going to faint. I had to assure her that I was all right and then tell the story I had told the cop. She actually listened fairly calmly. She asked about Anna and why this and that but she didn't yell or fuss.

"Kit," she said, "you are tired now so go on to bed, but tomorrow we've got to talk some more. Do you understand?" I reached over and gave her a hug.

"Yes, Mom."

"I love you, Kit. You've had a somewhat bumpy road. Everybody has trials and tribulations, and most people have things that happen that are hard to digest. But I worry that I've failed you, that you've not gotten the help you need." I just held her.

"I love you, Mom." That was the truth. "I'm okay," I said. That was a lie.

I went to my room and took off my jeans and shoes. I had left my jockeys and socks in Burch's car. My book was still stuck in the back pocket of my jeans. It was slightly battered but still in one piece. I threw it on the bed and turned off the overhead light, leaving my lamp on. I lay on the bed thinking that maybe I would read a few words and then go to sleep. I had a lot of adrenaline flowing and knew I couldn't get to sleep right away. I started reading and just kept on reading. I didn't think the book was all that great, and I couldn't see any particular importance to intellectual history, as Anna had suggested, but I got caught up in old John Stuart's story. Somehow I felt better knowing that a really smart guy like Mill had hard times too. Even with all he had going for him, he didn't seem to have figured out anything either. He barely mentioned the unanswerable questions. I could hardly believe what he said about the idea of the uncaused first cause. He said his father told him the idea was bogus because you always have to ask what caused the first cause, which can't be true, can it? If that were true, wouldn't it necessarily follow that nothing exists? If the first cause requires a cause, then it doesn't exist and neither does anything else, and we know that's not true, don't we? I thought about Lichtman, whose father had also weighed in with guidance, and I wondered what my father would have said. I have no way of knowing, but I'm guessing nothing worth remembering. Old John Stuart may not have known it, but he was also an ant randomly crawling around under the glass dome.

I finished the book at about four-thirty. I laid it on my night table and turned off the lamp. I was terribly depressed about the evening. My head was pounding and I was totally exhausted. I pulled the covers up to my waist. My eyes felt gritty behind the closed lids. As I was finishing the book, I felt as though my adrenaline level was falling so that I could sleep, but after I lay back and closed my eyes, my mind kept going. I wasn't obsessing about anything in particular, but I could feel the impulses flitting about in my brain, nudging random thoughts into my consciousness like an electronic machine going berserk. I may have been asleep for some part of the time that I thought I was awake.

PART TWO

In Praise of Calamity

WHISTLING WIND

After Nathan's death, we left the country house. The move just added to the pain. I don't know why I loved the country house, but maybe it was because I had never known anything else. It was never anything special except as an idea or an illusion. It has pretty white columns on the front porch and ancient live oaks in the front yard, but it's just an old frame house. It was built by my grandfather, with the help of my father and my Uncle Nat, to function as a farmhouse. It's hardly insulated at all so it's almost always too hot or too cold. It sits on what's left of the large tract Papa had farmed and logged and hunted, diagonally across the road from the house that had belonged first to Papa and then, after Papa's death, to Uncle Nat. The old house seems increasingly like something from another time and now more than ever feels like a mostly abandoned relic in the backwoods of nowhere. About three-fourths of the remaining land is still farmed, and the other fourth is covered with scrub oaks and hickories laced with blackberry vines, and here and there a stand of pines aproned with turpentine cups nailed a few feet above a thick bed of brown pine straw.

The last time I visited the country house was in November of the year before last. My mother and I went to the country to make sure the pump was drained and the house was locked up for the winter. Dr. Bob drove us to the country on a Saturday afternoon. A cold front had moved in and brought a gusty chilly wind and sullen gray clouds. I wasn't ready for the overwhelming desolation of the place. I stood in the front yard under a massive and gnarled old oak outside the split-rail fence and looked across the road toward Uncle Nat's old house and the hill where Nathan had run and chanted and died. It was awful. I don't know what I was expecting, but the whole thing was depressing.

All I want to remember are the happy times in the country: Uncle Sid, a gruff old sharecropper not really our uncle, fussing about Kate the mule or about Nathan and me messing up the barn or scattering his supplies and tools; the animal sounds, cows and chickens and hogs; and the voices of people complaining about the heat or laughing about some droll occurrence. But that cold November afternoon there were no sounds of joy around the bleak and cheerless relic. The only sound was the eerie whistling of the wind rushing at the edges of an old house that had become a shabby and forlorn symbol of the loss of the essence of something meaningful, something only partially discernible in the fog of another time.

"I hear wind whistling," I said into the darkness. The room was dark but I could see in the dim light a blue curtain and other beds with white linens. A woman in a white uniform appeared from somewhere in the room. "Where am I?" I said. The woman picked up a clipboard from somewhere toward the end of my bed and walked around and put her hand to my forehead.

"You're in recovery," the woman said. "Your chart says you're Dr. Glans' patient."

"I hear wind," I said. "I'm cold."

"It's just the air conditioner vent making that noise," she said. "You're cold because of the loss of blood. I'll get some blankets." Within seconds I felt warm blankets being piled on me. "There, that should help. While you're awake, I need to get your temp and blood pressure."

"I'm in pain," I said.

"I'm sorry, but I can't give you anything for pain yet."

I was really groggy and my mouth was dry. "I need some water."

"You can't have water either. You're getting fluids in the IV. I know your mouth is dry. As soon as I get your temperature I'll give you some ice chips. I don't want you to throw up." She stuck a thermometer in my mouth and pumped up the rubber cuff around my right arm. "Don't bite the thermometer. Can you hold it okay?" I managed to shake my head. Each of my arms was taped to a cloth-covered board and a needle was in the crook of each arm. The needles were attached to tubes that ran up to two containers on stands. One of the containers held a red substance and the other held a clear substance.

"What happened?" I said, trying to maneuver the thermometer around in my mouth with my tongue.

"I don't know. It looks like you were in an accident. You don't know?"

"I can't remember." I started to say, "I remember a dog," but I didn't. "I may have been in a truck."

"You think you might have been hit by a train? You were muttering something about a train."

I was getting warm and drowsy. By the time she took the thermometer out of my mouth, I was drifting back into sleep. She patted my arm and said, "Are you warm now?"

"Yeah, I'm okay," I said.

The next time I woke up it was daylight, and I was in a small room with white walls and ceiling. I was groggy, but I could see the top of a door across from the foot of my bed and a larger one over to the right of the bed. Over to the left, I could see the top of a window and sunlight glinting on particles of dust. At first I thought I was alone but as soon as I moved, my mother stood up beside the bed. She leaned over and said, "How do you feel?" I tried to sit up and discovered that a strap was across my chest.

"What's this?" I had this feeling that the room was beginning to close in on me. "I can't move. What is this?"

"Now, Kit, you just wait. Let me find a nurse."

She came back in a few minutes with a smiling young nurse who had the word "Bloom" on a little tag pinned to her uniform above her right breast. "What in the world are you fussing about?" said nurse Bloom. She unbuckled the belt somewhere on the left side of the bed and pulled it around to the other side. She was smiling but I probably looked like a wild animal. "This belt is to keep you from knocking the IV out." The container with the clear liquid was still attached to my left arm; the other container was gone. "I'm going to take off your belt now, but your momma's going to have to put it back when you fall asleep. How're you doing?"

"I'm thirsty and I'm in a lot of pain." I tried sitting up but nurse Bloom put her hand on my chest.

"Hold on, sport. If you want to sit up, we'll crank the bed up. You can't move your arm." She leaned over with her eyes narrowed intently and said, "You got that?" I gave her a faint smile and nodded my head. She picked up a little switch dangling beside the bed and said, "This is how you do it," and pressed the switch. The back of the bed started rising. When it was at about a forty-five-degree angle, she said, "Here, make yourself happy," and handed me the switch. The rising bed had caused me to slide down a little, and my right leg felt uncomfortable, so I let the bed back down several degrees. My mother held a water glass with a straw up to my mouth. I took the glass from her with my right hand and sipped.

Nurse Bloom was on the other side of the bed rubbing alcohol on my left upper arm. She stuck a hypodermic needle in my arm and pressed down on the plunger. "That's morphine to help with pain. It'll make you feel better but you may get drowsy pretty quickly. So if you've got anything to talk about, you might want to say it in the next fifteen minutes or so." She turned to my mother. "Call me if he needs anything. You can either come down to the nurse's station or you can push this little button." She pointed to a little black tube with a red button on it dangling by the bed. "And the bedpan is right in here." She reached under a little table and picked up a steel pan that looked like a toilet seat and handed it to me. "You probably need this about now." Nurse Bloom and my mother both left the room.

I stuck the bedpan between my legs and discovered that I had been shaved from the waist all the way down my right leg. My crotch looked like a plucked chicken. I couldn't figure out what to do with the bedpan after emptying my bladder, so I just put it on the bedside table. My mother came back into the room and leaned over and brushed the hair off my forehead. I reached up and felt my head. I had a bandage around my head but my hair was hanging down over the bandage. "Well, they didn't shave your head. I think you only have the one cut on the right side of your forehead."

The morphine lifted my mood and eased the pain almost immediately. I began to feel better except that I was sort of itchy. My mother reached down toward the floor and came back up holding some books. She looked at me wistfully and said, "Do you remember how I used to read to you? I read to you every day, well, until you took over the reading. Do you remember? I'm going to read to you until you can take over again." She held the books up so that I could see the spines and said, "You have your choice. What will it be? *Ivanhoe*? *The Count of Monte Cristo*? Or *Don Quixote*?" She held them up one at a time as she announced the titles. "I can get some others if you want something else. Some books you'll need to read on your own."

"I read *Ivanhoe* and *The Count* a long time ago," I said. I didn't want to tell her but I really wasn't in the mood for a book. In addition to my various pains, of which the pain in my leg was certainly the most severe, I was sore all over and getting groggier by the second.

"Well, how about *Don Quixote*? It's probably more suitable anyway. You know what it's about, don't you?"

"Yeah, I think so. Probably."

"It's about a senile old romantic who has trouble distinguishing between reality and illusion. It's kind and sardonic and moving and incredibly wise."

"Yeah," I said, trying to focus on what she was saying. She pulled her chair around so that I could see at least her head and shoulders. I pressed the bed switch and lowered the bed flat. My mother took my hand and looked at me anxiously.

"It's going to get better." I'm not sure what she was talking about, but I assume she meant my physical ailments. She knew about some of my problems but she had no way of knowing about my other stuff. "A wonderful thing about life," she said, "is that every problem is transient. Someone mentioned a story the other day about a king who asked his wise men to give him a statement that would be true and pertinent in all circumstances and at all times. The statement they presented to him was: 'And this, too, shall pass away.'"

She was trying to comfort me but my mind wandered. Maybe if I hadn't remembered when she told me that my father had "passed away," I would have stayed focused on the point. But sometimes my memory retains peculiar things from the past and then randomly thrusts them into my consciousness. I was only four years old, but I remember very vividly the day my father died. It was an early winter morning. I was lying in my bed in the country house under a mound of blankets. My face was cold, but if I lay still, my body heat created a warm cocoon under the covers. If I moved my legs, I could feel the cold in the sheets. I remember lying in bed for a while listening to tense movement and hushed murmurings and then slipping out of bed and going out into the hall. I can almost feel the cold of those wooden floors.

I pushed open the door to my father's room and stood in the doorway trying to see in the pale flickering light that was coming from a fire burning in the fireplace.

Several people were standing or sitting in the shadows of the room and my mother was sitting on a stool crying. I couldn't see my father at all; I could only see the covers where he was lying. My mother picked me up without speaking and carried me back to my room. "Your father has passed away," she said. I didn't understand so I said, "Away where?" She held me in her arms and rocked back and forth on the edge of the bed. "When you're a little older, you will understand."

"Isn't that a wonderful thought?" She patted my hand. "And this, too, shall pass away." I didn't answer but I did open my eyes and give her a little smile, which was probably all she really expected. "Now for *Don Quixote*," she said. "Prologue," she announced and then began to read: "Idling reader, you may believe me when I tell you . . . ." I didn't understand anything she read after that. I didn't fall asleep immediately but my concentration disintegrated. I had this incredible floating feeling. I could still feel some pain and discomfort, but they didn't seem to make any difference. My concentration was totally absorbed in my own feelings, and I gradually ceased to be aware of anything other than the blissful floating sensation. My mother's voice became a drone and then gradually faded away. She had said I would understand my father's death when I was a little older. The last thing I remember thinking was that maybe I wasn't a little older yet.

A DULL CLACKING

I could hear voices and hospital noises, but I couldn't get my eyes open. Then, after I managed to open my eyes, I couldn't focus very well. My mind wasn't clear but I remembered that I was in the hospital. "Dr. Bob is here, Kit," I heard my mother say. I felt the same way I had felt sitting on the floor in Anna's kitchen: I could understand what was going on around me, but I was having trouble participating in the event. I wanted to say, "Whoopee for Dr. Bob" or something sarcastic like that but I was in such a haze that I couldn't form the words. "You're back in his care again," she said reassuringly. I closed my eyes because I was sure they exchanged goofy grins, and I wanted to spare myself.

Just so you understand, Dr. Bob is not new to my life. He's the designated orthopedic doctor for the sports program at Bridgewater Academy. He first intruded in my life when the track coach sent me to him a couple of years before about shin splints. To my mother, he is grand: He is not needy, he is selfless; he is not wily, he is wise; he is not a wizard of misdirection, he is subtle; he does not grunt and wheeze his thoughts, he expresses himself weightily and ponderously. He has become my mother's "special friend" whose specialness I have unfortunately failed to appreciate. Okay, I admit, my perspective is not the same as hers.

"Hello, Kit," Dr. Bob almost shouted in my face. He seemed to think I couldn't hear him because he bellowed as though I were five or ten yards away. He was leaning over me grinning like a retarded person. His bald head glistened with sweat and his beady eyes shined through the puffs of his cheeks and eyelids. Dr. Bob is bald except for a semicircle of hair right above his ears. His head is almost perfectly round and the color alternates between pale and flushed. His fleshy forehead rises about six inches above an almost unbroken row of bushy eyebrows.

"Hello," I said, squinting through the glaze over my eyes. I raised my left arm to rub my eyes and noticed immediately that the needle had been taken out of my arm and that the clear-liquid container was gone. If my mother had put the straps back on me, the person who removed the needle also removed the straps. "How am I?" I was trying to make a joke, you know, on the usual question, "How are you?" I don't think either he or my mother got it. I was trying to be witty and cavalier but maybe it wasn't all that good of a joke. I groped around by the side of the bed until I found the bed switch and then I raised the head of my bed a little.

"Well, you have a concussion, multiple dissections and lacerations, multiple abrasions and contusions, and a compound fracture of the right femur." He apparently read my list of injuries verbatim from my chart. "For a fellow who rolled a two-ton truck, you're looking pretty good."

"I'm in a lot of pain."

"We're going to take care of that as soon as I'm done here," he said. He was examining the bandage on my leg as he talked. "Everything's coming along as expected. You should be able to leave the hospital in about two weeks, depending on your progress and whether anything else comes to light. You got banged up pretty good. I had to pin your femur. It's going to be awhile before you can walk again. I don't know exactly how long, but you could be looking at four or five months. We'll have to wait and see. Your femur was shattered pretty badly."

I started to ask if I'd be able to run but decided that it didn't matter. Dr. Bob probably wouldn't tell me the truth anyway. He moved his stethoscope around on my chest and asked me to cough and then did the same with my back. "No congestion," he announced and put the instrument away. "I'll stop by and check on you regularly. You're coming along fine." He made some notes on my chart and then he told the afternoon nurse to give me a shot for pain. "You lost a lot of blood. You're very fortunate that Dr. Goolsby happened to be there. Your girlfriend's father, who just happens to be the best trauma

201

doctor in the state, just happens to be at the site of your accident? You have a guardian angel, son. You know, you could have bled to death before they got you to the hospital." I didn't tell him but I didn't know that Dr. Goolsby was there. I was about to pass out and I thought I was hallucinating. A person who looked like Dr. Goolsby was kneeling beside me on the pavement and cutting away the right leg of my jeans. That didn't make any sense. Why would Anna's stepfather be there? He wasn't involved. He didn't have anything to do with it.

"Small world," I said.

"It's small but I'm not sure it's that small."

"I'll be right back," my mother said and followed Dr. Bob into the hall. A couple of minutes went by and my mother hadn't come back, so I lowered my bed and closed my eyes. Then I heard the door open and I assumed that my mother had returned.

"What did he say?" I said without opening my eyes.

"He say love yo' neighbor as yo'self," an unfamiliar voice said in response. I opened my eyes and saw a plump, dark-skinned woman in a light blue uniform standing at the foot of my bed. "And he say a lot more that you gon' need to pay attention to. You hear me?"

"Yes, ma'am," I said, but I can tell you that's not what I was thinking.

"If you're awake, I need to get you cleaned up. You suppose to get your bath in the mornin' but you been snoozin' all day."

"You a nurse?"

"Honey, I just plain old Leola. But here's the good part you gon' miss if you ain't careful: I'm the one that the Lord sent to take care of you. We gon' start by gettin' you cleaned up. Where is your wash basin?" She opened and closed the bedside table and then went into the bathroom. "Here it is," I heard her say. "Why they put it in here I don't know." I heard water running and a pan banging into the sides of the sink. Leola came back into the room with her arms stretched out and her shoulders held back, balancing the pan in front of her. "I'm suppose to make sure you brush your teeth and bathe. We gon' get you well, honey. The good Lord gon' do the hard work and Leola gon' do the cleanin' up. The Lord does heavy. Leola does light. That's the way it always works. You understand what I'm sayin'? I'm just grateful to the Lord for grace and mercy. You hear me?"

"Yes, ma'am," I said solemnly. I was in a good deal of pain, and I didn't know whether to take her seriously but I knew I was going to like Leola.

"Soon as I get done here, I'll get Tyrone—he's the orderly—to help you finish bathin' your privates."

"Tell Tyrone to take a break. I don't need anybody to bathe my privates."

"We need to get that gown off." She came over to the side of the bed and pulled my arms from my backless gown and took it away. "Put this across your lap and I'll pull this cover down." She handed me a towel, and I slipped it under the sheet and spread it across my lap. Leola then pulled the covers down to the end of the bed.

"Okay, we wash the face first, then your arms and legs, then your back, then your chest." She soaped the cloth in the water and began washing my face. "You pretty brown for a white boy. The sun was about to get you lookin' good when you messed it up."

"I'm sorry, what?"

"Look at the color of that skin," she said. The edge of the towel was just below the point on my stomach where the top of my shorts came, so that Leola could see the tan line across my abdomen. "You were about to get brown enough to pass." She laughed as though she had told a great joke. "We'd need to give that straw-colored hair a little help too." I smiled faintly just because she seemed to expect it.

As Leola bathed me, the morphine began to take me away. She must have seen my eyes drooping. "Hey, don't you go to sleep on me. I got to put lotion on your back so you don't get bed sores. You hear me, honey?"

"Leola, I'm having a hard time . . . ," I said, my voice trailing off. She helped me lean forward as far as I could and began washing my back.

"Can you turn any more? I can't reach your lower back." I tried to rise up and turn over some more, but I couldn't move much without a lot of pain. She washed as much of my back as she could reach and then said, "I'm gon' dry off your back and go ahead and put some lotion on you.

Then you can go on to sleep." After she had finished, I lay back. I was getting lighter and drowsier. I could feel Leola bathing me but I didn't try to open my eyes. It was as though I were a child again. I have dim memories, maybe they're just feelings, of a past time before I could talk. My mother has told me that when I was a baby she bathed me in a washbasin on the kitchen counter. The kitchen was warm even in the winter because of the heat from the wood stove. The counter was in front of a window that looked out on a cornfield that was static brown in the winter and undulant green and gold in the summer. It's probably a little crazy but with my eyes closed I could see out that window while Leola was bathing me.

I heard Leola go into the bathroom and turn on the water and then come back into the room. I felt a warm, wet cloth on my arm and then on my chest. Leola moved the cloth around very gently. The sun was glistening in the corn silk and the green stalks were swaying almost imperceptibly. I could see myself lying in the grass at the edge of the cornfield underneath the clothesline, and I could hear a dull clacking like the sound of a train a long way off, but it may have been my own heartbeat. I thought I heard my mother say, "Nathan is asleep." I'm sure she didn't because she wouldn't have called me Nathan. My mother told me later that she came back in the room while Leola was bathing me and that she said, "My son is asleep." That may be corny but it's something she would have said.

HALF-SHADOWS

The next time I woke up I was shivering. I wasn't cold; I had been dreaming. In the dream I was hurt and limping down the railroad tracks toward the river, stumbling along on the cross ties. I was having trouble walking and it took a long time. When I reached the trestle, I wanted to walk down to the river but I thought I might not be able to climb back up. I limped out over the river and stood on the trestle looking down at the images and shadows on the water. The reflection of the trees on the west bank spread almost halfway across the river, leaving an irregular line dividing the lighter part of the stream from the ominous black water beneath the shadows. I eased out to the edge of the trestle and looked down at the water.

I peered at the familiar promontory at the bend in the river, and I searched the water for Cassandra's image. She wasn't there. At first the only phantom on the river was my own reflection, which looked eerily like Nathan on the water's rippled surface. Then, as I watched the current moving silently beneath me, I saw the reflection of a large heron sweep across the river and disappear into the dark shadows of the west bank. Tears formed in my eyes, and I remember thinking that if I jumped into the river the pain might go away. I raised my arms out to the side of my body and lowered my head. "Oh, God," I said, looking down at the half-shadowed stream, "why would you leave me here?" I paused a moment as though waiting for an answer, and then I woke up shivering.

"Pray, honey," Leola said. She materialized out of nowhere. I didn't know what she was talking about, and I tried to relate it to my dream. It didn't make any sense so I didn't say anything.

"My little niece was run over by her drunk daddy las' night. Pray for that baby. She barely hangin' on by a thread."

"I'm sorry, Leola. How did that happen?"

"She two years old. Followed him out to the car and he backed over her. He drunk. Didn't even know what he did till he saw her in the driveway."

"That's unbelievable. Somebody should have taken the car keys from him."

"Nobody able to stop him. He does one bad thing after another. Ever'body always making excuses for him. Phoenix say he can't help hisself."

"Phoenix?" I said.

"My husband, Phoenix Cook, I'm talking about. It's

Phoenix's brother Abner. Phoenix is a good man but he make excuses for every bad thing Abner does."

"Does your husband work at the club sometimes?"

"He does," she said. "Do you know Phoenix?"

"Yeah, I met him one time when I was working in the maintenance shop."

"Phoenix got three different jobs. He's a postman, a maintenance man, and assistant pastor at our church. Phoenix builds. Abner tears down. The only bad thing Phoenix does is bail out that sorry Abner. I told him he a contributor to the evil, but he won't listen."

"I agree with you," I said.

"Phoenix ain't the only one helpin' Abner. Jus' las' Saturday night, Abner took a man's wallet and almost got hisself killed. Man left his wallet on the bar. Abner grabbed up the wallet and went off down the road. The man caught Abner hidin' under that crossing over on Carapace and beat him with a wine bottle. Almost killed him. But some white boy come along and save Abner. Anybody else would've died under that bridge, but not Abner. A guardian devil come running up to save him."

"Maybe it wasn't a devil." I had sat in silence as long as I could. I knew as soon as she mentioned the viaduct at Carapace that I had been Abner's guardian. I thought I was doing good, maybe atoning for evil, not participating in it. "Maybe it was just somebody who happened to be there and thought he was doing good." I wanted to tell her the truth but I couldn't.

"Why would the Lord permit that? Why not send that boy somewhere to help a good person?"

"Maybe there aren't any, Leola. Maybe that's the problem." I wanted to say, "Maybe God is evil," but I didn't. I also didn't tell Leola that I was the one who had kept Abner from bleeding to death under that viaduct. I wanted to believe that the man I helped wasn't Abner, but how do you rationalize past the improbability of two wine-bottle beatings under the same viaduct on the same Saturday night?

"Leola," I said, "why didn't God protect that baby?"

"That's a mystery. That's a awful mystery."

The morphine had begun to wear off. I was again in pain, but more than anything I just wanted out. I was burdened by the chaos and pain in my life, and now Leola was telling me about a two-year-old baby whose tenuous life I had stumbled into. "I'm sorry, Leola," I said. "I'm so sorry." But I didn't confess. I couldn't.

"I know it looks terrible," Leola said before she left to order my pain shot, "but somethin' good gon' come out of this. The Lord always uses bad to make good."

In less than an hour after my pain shot, I was gone. But even before that I had left the pain of my wounds and the pain of cruelty and death and my willy-nilly existence, all in a haze of irrelevance. But it only lasted a few hours. The next time I woke up I had visitors. Q. Ball was looking at me with a bemused expression on his face and right behind him was Sarah, my reluctant accomplice in the rescue of

Abner. Q. Ball probably noticed that I stared past him at Sarah, who smiled sweetly, even sympathetically. I wasn't at all surprised to see Q. Ball but I was slightly surprised to see Sarah after the debacle Saturday night.

"How are you doing?" she said, walking over to the bedside and looking concerned and solicitous. "I brought you some things." She was clutching a bundle of books and a brown bag.

"Hi," I said. "You two come together?"

"No," Sarah said. "We just happened to get here about the same time. We've been waiting more or less patiently for you to wake up." Q. Ball stood behind Sarah and widened his eyes and raised his shoulders in an exaggerated way, presumably signifying that he didn't understand what was going on. Sarah came around to the opposite side of the bed and held up some flowers in a vase. "I cut these especially for you. I love sunflowers. They're the most gorgeous flowers in the world. They're heliotropic so I'm going to put the vase on the windowsill. Tomorrow I'm bringing special roses, aquamarine like your eyes. You just put white roses in water with food coloring and you get any color you want. I think I can get aquamarine if I mix blue and green dye. It may turn out the color of river water, but I think I can do it."

She was talking rapidly and flippantly, I guessed, because she was nervous. Q. Ball raised his shoulders again and put out his hands like someone asking for an explanation, but I said nothing. Sarah had dropped the books in a chair before pulling out the flowers. She picked up one of the books and said, "I brought you something for when you feel like reading." She held up an imposing tome titled *Master Poems of the English Language.* "I also brought my books just in case you need for me to stay. I plan to stay with you as long as you need me." She came over to the bed and took my right hand in both of hers. "Just tell me what you need." Of course, I didn't say anything, but I was thinking inverse proportionality: The less you need, the more you get.

"Well, Biddle?" said Q. Ball dramatically, raising his arms above his head again. "Maybe you'd like to say something sometime. Huh?"

"Sarah," I said, "I need to wash my face. Would you please wet this cloth for me?" I had a slight headache and my face felt oily. I really wanted to wash the sleep from my face but I also wanted her to leave the room a minute because my bladder was full. "I'll tell you when you can come back."

"Sure," she said. She then surprised me by opening my bedside table, getting the bedpan and handing it to me. She squinted at me with a thin little smile and went into the bathroom. I heard the water running as I maneuvered the bedpan into position.

"Where is Anna?" Q. Ball whispered.

"I don't know," I said.

"What's she going to think of Sarah boobs-and-brains in there?" he said, continuing a husky whisper. I'm sure I don't have to explain that the reference to boobs was an admiring dig at Sarah's imposing physique. The reference to brains was a tribute to scuttlebutt about Sarah's IQ. As for the boobs, some things are pretty obvious. I don't know about the IQ stuff but everybody says she's smart.

"I don't know," I repeated in the same monotone.

"Well, where did Sarah come from?"

"I don't know," I said.

"Well, you're just a load of valuable insight. Have you now got two girlfriends?"

"No, I'm not sure I even have one."

"Are you all right, man?" He leaned over toward me. "Some people are saying this might not have been an accident. They said you stole a truck and just rolled it on an open road."

"I don't know what people you're talking about, but they're nuts." The subject irritated me but also made me uncomfortable. I had flipped a truck in the open road. I was familiar with the road and I had been driving big trucks, including the Lichtman's furniture delivery truck, so neither the road nor the truck could explain what happened. I didn't know how to explain it. "I think I hit a dog," I said after a pause.

"You hit a dog?" he said in the same hushed voice. "And that caused you to flip a two-ton truck? Man, that must have been one big dog."

"I know I hit a dog," I repeated.

"Can I come out now?" Sarah shouted from the

bathroom. "This is a little prudish, don't you think? I'm familiar with basic bodily functions." She came back into the room without waiting for a response. I was taking the bedpan from under the covers as she approached the bed. She handed me the wet cloth, then took the bedpan and went back into the bathroom. I heard her rinse the bedpan and flush the toilet. She came back and put the bedpan under the night table. "See how easy that is?"

I put my head back and covered my face with the cloth. Sarah was washing my face when the door edged open and my mother's head appeared. "Knock, knock," she said. "How's the patient?" Until she stuck her head in the door I had almost forgotten about my pains, but as soon as I saw her I became aware of discomforts every-where, particularly in my leg.

"The patient's in pain," I said. I probably just wanted sympathy or attention or something.

"Hello, Ronnie," she said to Q. Ball and then turned toward Sarah. I don't know what she was thinking, but I hoped she wouldn't mention anything to Sarah about Saturday night.

"Mom, you know Sarah Burchfield, don't you?"

"Hello, Mrs. Biddle," said Sarah, smiling broadly.

"Yes, of course. Sarah was my star student. Sarah is everybody's star student. Sarah, if you're here to give Kit his math assignment, let me know so we don't duplicate." I thought that was very adroit, so I smiled at her and she winked at me.

"No, ma'am," Sarah said, "I'm just here to take care of him."

"Oh," my mother said, looking over at me. She was as puzzled as Q. Ball, but she didn't say it. "We need all the help we can get." She circled the room and put the books and notebooks she'd brought on the edge of the night table closest to me. "Can you reach these? You can get to work as soon as you're up to it. I also have your assignments, except one project that Mr. Marcus is going to discuss with you."

"I'm not up to it now. I'm in a lot of pain." I was in some modest pain, but I have to say that physical discomfort was only part of the problem. I also hate glossy-covered textbooks.

My mother turned to Sarah and said, "I'm trying to read *Don Quixote* to him, but he can't stay awake long enough." She looked at me and said, "How long did you last? Five minutes?"

"No way. I'm probably good for seven minutes or more."

"I'm going to have to go, man," said Q. Ball. "I just wanted to check on you." He went to the door and turned back toward me. "I'll be back later, man. You're okay, huh?"

"I've been a lot better but I'm okay. How are you doing?"

"I wasn't in a truck wreck, man."

"There are all kinds of wrecks," I said.

"Yeah, well, right now, the vehicle is careening but still in the road."

"Hang in there, my friend," I said. "This too shall pass." My mother smiled.

"I'm hanging tough," he said and then, right before closing the door behind him, "So you hit a dog, huh?"

"Hit a dog," I said.

"All right. Hit a dog." He hesitated a moment, looking puzzled, then turned to my mother and Sarah. "He hit a dog. That's his story and, as they say, he's sticking to it. Good night, ladies. Good night, my friend."

"Bye, Ronnie," my mother said, and then turning to me, "You may not want to hear *Don Quixote*. You two may have things to talk about." She was fishing for a hint from me, but I was slow. Sarah picked up the thread.

"If you have some things to do, Mrs. Biddle, I can read to him." She picked up *Don Quixote* from the night table. "Where did you leave off?"

"I think we were through the Prologue, weren't we, Kit?"

"We're going to have to start over because I can't remember anything."

"All right," Sarah said. "We start over."

"Okay, I'm going to go," my mother said and came over and kissed me on the forehead. "Do you need anything before I go?" I told her I didn't need anything. She had a faint look of concern on her face when she left but it may have been her usual maternal stress. She probably had something better to do anyway.

Sarah pulled her chair up close to the bed and smiled at me. "Where do you want me to put these?" She reached into the brown bag and pulled out my jockey shorts and socks that I had left in Burch's car after our random adventure on Saturday night. "You'll need these again sometime. I washed them for you."

"Right," I said, smiling sheepishly. "How about we put them with my other stuff?"

"Where would that be?"

"Come to think of it, I don't have any other stuff. They cut my clothes off me. How about the closet?"

"That works," she said. After she closed the closet door, she stood at the end of the bed smiling at me.

"Where did you come from?" The question popped out awkwardly, strangely, maybe because that was Q. Ball's question. It seemed odd that she had appeared, or maybe reappeared, in my life at that juncture, when everything seemed to be falling apart.

"If you don't want me here . . . ." Her smile had vanished. She looked offended or distressed or maybe both.

"I just don't know where you came from all of a sudden."

"All of a sudden? I've known you for six years. I know everything about you. Everything. You want to know something about yourself, just ask me. You love poetry but you don't like free verse. You love Yeats but you don't like Auden. Your heroes are Shakespeare, da Vinci, and Isaac Newton." She went on and on gushing stuff about who I am, at least who I am in her mind. Her description often began with "You're always" or "You're never." I was surprised and flattered, but even in a semi-groggy state I knew the universals were ill-founded and often ridiculous. I wondered what caused her to see all this stuff when everybody else, including me, saw no superlatives whatever and a tangled mess of negatives and relatives. I liked the attention but I had this feeling that she was almost assigning attributes to me. I wanted to bask in the glow of her assessments but, at the same time, I felt a need to object, to point out that she was describing someone else.

"I remember the first time I saw you but I bet you don't, do you?"

"Well," I said, straining to remember that far back. We moved to our house when I was twelve years old, and I met her brother about two months after we got there. So, she was asking me about a time with a lot of change and strain and pain. I could tell she wanted me to remember but I couldn't. I hate to say it, but my vague recollection was of a little reddish-haired girl with large glasses that Burch called his "crazy little sister," but I didn't want to give Sarah that memory.

"You and Harry had been playing touch football with Ronnie and some other boys, and you came to our house to get water. You were wearing khaki shorts and sneakers but no shirt. Your hair had grass in it and streaks from the sun. You were a sweaty mess, and you had a grass burn on your knee and elbow. Then you talked to my mother about poetry and you knew by heart some of her favorite poems. You recited 'Dover Beach' and 'Ozymandias' and 'Kubla Khan,' and you did these incredible math computations in your head. I know the math was just Trachtenberg, but you really impressed my mother. She told me after you left that you might be gifted in a special way and you were going to be interesting to watch. It was the last day of August in the summer before I started sixth grade. I wrote it in my diary."

"I'm still sort of groggy," I said hesitantly, "and I'm still having trouble remembering some things." I was fudging the truth. Of course, I remembered playing football with the guys, and I remembered her mother's questions almost every time I went to their house, but I didn't remember seeing Sarah there very often.

"I may not have been a part of your life but you've been a part of mine for a long time. I've had so many dreams. You can't read my diary but I can tell you we have a long history."

"You amaze me," I said.

"Good, I've been waiting for you to notice." She paused, probably to see if I was going to say anything, and then said, "My mother called your mother Sunday morning. Our stories may not have matched exactly about Saturday night, but they were close enough. My story had left out the part about parking. I also told my mother that the blood on my dress came from that injured man's bleeding head, which was partly true."

"In that regard, our stories matched perfectly," I said. "We weren't looking for a cover story for the blood but I guess we got one." I don't know what she was thinking, but I was thinking about the larger bullet we had dodged. "I'm glad you didn't . . . we didn't . . . ," I just stammered and stopped.

"We didn't unintentionally release motile gametes in a receptive environment?" she said, forcing a bit of a smile. "I know the biology. I'm supposed to be smarter than that and so are you."

"I'm not. Even in the best of circumstances, I'm not. And in those circumstances, I was as stupid as a squid."

"I didn't drink that much wine, so what's my excuse? Maybe I can blame it on hormones. The contradiction is I didn't want to stop and I did want to stop. And, this is going to sound a little weird, I didn't want to disappoint you: As crazy as it sounds, I was willing to risk fertilizing an untimely egg and creating a challenge for myself. I can't explain that."

"A challenge for both of us," I said. "We could have had a lot more than a theoretical biology problem." I thought about my two sexual episodes. In the case of almost anyone other than Anna, I could at least conceive a moment's irrationality, but Anna is always deliberate. My frolic with her on the porch sofa could have produced the same biology problem, but the syllogism doesn't work: Anna doesn't lose control. Random isn't in her repertoire. She certainly wasn't yielding to me reluctantly to avoid disappointing me, and she certainly had no intention of rearranging her life. What was she doing? At this point I'm sure I'll never know. I suspect that her real intent was just to see what I would do, and if I folded (as she expected and as in fact I did), to add fecklessness to her inventory of disdain.

"It wasn't what I expected," Sarah said hesitantly. "It wasn't very romantic. I'm not sure what I had in my mind but, I hate to tell you this, it was not worth remembering." She paused a few seconds and then said cheerfully, "So I've sort of done a recalibration. I want to forget the last part of Saturday night. Can we not talk about it and let it just fade away?"

"I don't know what to say."

"Say nothing. Just be quiet and I'll read to you."

She picked up my book and began reading. This time I stayed awake. I had to have a pain shot about nine o'clock. I began getting lightheaded a half hour or so after that. But I followed the story until almost ten o'clock. I began to get fuzzy right after the part where Don Quixote has routed a hapless barber. In the story, Don Quixote and Sancho see a rider approaching with something on his head gleaming like gold. The gallant and noble Quixote concludes the rider is a pagan knight wearing the wondrous helmet of Mambrino. The pagan is actually an itinerant barber riding along on his ass and wearing his basin on his head to protect his hat from rain, but the Knight of the Mournful Countenance lowers his lance and bears down on the hapless barber, who flees in terror leaving both his ass and his basin. When Sancho fetches the basin, Quixote places it on his head and rationalizes that the helmet is misshapen because some misguided person has melted down a part of the helmet for the gold.

After that, my mind continued to clench on the image of the old man wearing the barber's pan on his head and thinking it was a golden helmet. At first, I thought it was ludicrous and then I thought it was sad. I was thinking that normal people seem to see things pretty clearly. Then it occurred to me that about half the time I don't know whether I understand what I'm seeing or not. I was wondering if everybody is as confused as I am, if maybe I have a pan on my head and just don't know it. When I could no longer understand what Sarah was reading, I told her.

The last thing I remember was her holding my hand and then, right before I fell asleep, she brushed my hair and kissed me on the lips. I was flattered by her attention but I wasn't surprised by it. She didn't ask about Anna. She seemed to assume that Anna had vanished. She didn't know what I knew. The fact is she was right about Anna's being gone, but I have no idea how she knew. What she didn't know is that the perfect form, the ineffable essence of Anna, is still very present in my mind. I don't think I'll ever get rid of it. I don't think I could get rid of it even if I wanted to.

MAMBRINO

Zac Purcell's father shot himself a little over a year after Nathan's death. We didn't know the Purcells very well because they didn't go to church, but after Mr. Purcell's death the family wanted his body buried in the church cemetery. Mr. Purcell's grave is located several rows from Nathan's grave, back toward the highway along the cemetery access road. My mother and I visited the cemetery on a Sunday not long after the Purcell funeral. When we pulled into the access road, we could see Zac balancing himself on the Purcell monument, holding a bottle of beer in his right hand and his penis in his left hand. He was very clearly peeing on his father's grave, moving his hips back and forth to splatter urine over as much area as possible. When he saw us, he yelled something that sounded like a war whoop and waved the beer bottle in the air, peeing and grinning like a madman. We drove on by, and I waved at Zac. I didn't know what else to do. My mother then said, "Well, the statement is clear enough but the purpose is ambiguous."

It is somewhat peculiar that I was musing about Zac's dramatic *statement* when Burch opened the door to my hospital room and snarled, "That was a real cute statement Saturday night." I was awake but a little groggy. The words sounded like something in a dream uttered somewhere in the shadows. Almost every time I fell asleep I had dreams. They weren't nightmares exactly, but bizarre rearrangements of things as I'd perceived them.

The dreams went away as soon as I woke. Some phantoms are part of what we regard as reality, and they are harder to get rid of. Burch is one of the latter. When I focused on him, his upper lip curled up in a forced half-smile. He didn't sit down or say hello. He stood at the end of my bed sneering. "Real cute," he said, "and I just want you to know I got the message."

"What?" I said. Of course, I knew that Burch was no bad dream. He is clearly a bad fragment of reality. And I knew what he was talking about. My question back to him was just a dodge, almost a pretense of innocence.

"You know what I'm talking about. Getting Sarah to pick up that drunk and getting blood all over my car. If you weren't already busted up, I'd bust you up." I didn't say anything, but I was thinking that if I weren't busted up he couldn't bust me up. I wasn't at all sure he wasn't going to take the opportunity to hit me. "Well, here's the fun part. I got a message for you." He gave me a little half grin. "Anna sends her greetings." I flinched. The mention of her name always causes some tension but Burch added an extra measure of stress.

It didn't take a genius to figure out that Burch got some perverse pleasure out of the situation with Anna. "You know she was with my cousin John while you were trying to destroy my car." He shook his head up and down in almost imperceptible movements and squinted at me knowingly. "She said to give you this." He handed me an envelope with my name written across the front in a clearly feminine cursive. "I'm sure it begins 'Dear John,' but it ain't intended for my cousin." I felt as though Burch had punched me very hard right below the sternum.

"Burch," I said as calmly as I could, "get out of here."

He hunched his shoulders and tightened his mouth and gave me his most baleful sneer. "I oughta bust you anyway." He walked over to the door and turned back toward me. "You really are a piece of work. Your wacko uncle killed your retarded cousin, and I won't be surprised if you do something just about that crazy someday. You haven't been hearing voices by any chance, have you?" He pointed at me the same way he had in Anna's kitchen when I told him to get out. "See you around, weirdo junior." In the six or so years I had known Burch, he had irritated me hundreds of times. But the irritants of the past were blocked from my memory by a wall of almost demented wrath. I am certain that I would have committed a violent crime if I had been able to get out of bed.

After Burch left, I lay there holding Anna's letter in both hands. I didn't want to open the envelope. My heart was pounding. Nerves jumped erratically in my face. The thought of Anna always made me tense, and I had added fuel for tension. Since she had gotten Burch to deliver the letter, I knew she wasn't writing to beg forgiveness. I may have been holding on to some deluded hope that her letter would provide a means to be joyfully reunited, but I actually knew the letter was going to be more pain. I thought about throwing it in the trash. I lay there waiting for something, anything other than reality, staring straight ahead, listening to the hospital sounds around me, holding the letter like it was a lifeline. The truth is I knew what she was going to say, not precisely everything and not exactly the words she would use, but the basic message:

> *Dear Kit,*
>
> *The ghoul told us about your wreck and injuries when he got home Sunday afternoon. He had wandered off, purportedly to look at farmland in Escambia County, and came upon your accident on the way back. I spoke with your mother as soon as I could reach her. She told me you would probably be out of it for a couple of days, so I decided to take a little time before writing you.*
>
> *As you know, I've been trying to talk to you for months without noticeable success. I'm not sure why it's so hard but maybe it's*

because you don't like to listen. Maybe you don't intend to be so wound up but you are a wad. This is a little strange because you're not really a particularly focused person. I don't want to be unkind but you seem to enjoy fretting and looking unhappy.

The more serious problem is that I am not the person you've created in your mind. I've tried to explain this problem to you. I've even tried to show you that the person you have in your mind does not exist. Most of the time I feel like someone in a straitjacket who's been given a small area to function in, and I can't get out of either the jacket or the area.

My mother says I'm crazy. You know what she thinks about you but I'm afraid she doesn't understand the problem. I'm very fond of you too but we're trains on different tracks. I want to be your friend, even a close friend, but the intensity of your fixation disturbs me. We both need to explore relationships and feelings. We have other periods of our lives for commitments and exclusivity.

I'd like to come by and see you in the hospital. If I do, I want you to understand: It's on my terms. Just write me a note or call me. I'm sorry I have to write this letter

*at this difficult time. I hope it doesn't hurt
your feelings too much, and I hope you get
well very soon.*

Fondly,
Anna

I folded the letter and put it back in the envelope.
The 'Fondly' hurt as much as having Burch deliver the
letter. I wasn't surprised by the other stuff except maybe
the part about the straitjacket. Burch was right; it was
a Dear John letter. It had a little fluff to carry the news
but it was goodbye. I let the bed back down and looked
in the direction of the ceiling, holding the letter against
my chest with my hands folded. I waited awhile and then
read the letter again.

I was thinking about whether I wanted to see her on
her terms, by which she clearly meant that we were going
to be pals. When I tried to think of her in the other role,
it was almost as though another person had been substi-
tuted for Anna. I had an intense sense of loss but I knew
it wouldn't go away just by seeing Anna as a chum on
random occasions. I didn't decide not to see Anna; she
simply disappeared. I could see the form fairly clearly, but
I could only see Anna in my mind in vague silhouette.
The pain was excruciating.

I am plagued by these thoughts and, from time to time,
I have felt like calling Anna and telling her that I want to
see her. I haven't done it because I can't. I know what I
really want back is the person who fits the specifications

and acts out the attributes of the form. The thought has occurred to me that maybe I couldn't have sex with Anna because it would have impaired or violated the form. If a person exists as mostly an idea, maybe everything is constrained by it. In any case, I didn't contact Anna.

I was in a deep funk when Sarah walked in an hour later. "What in the world is wrong?" she asked as soon as she walked into the room and saw my face.

"Burch," I said between clenched teeth. "It's your oafish brother. He makes me sick." I didn't want to talk about Anna's letter, which I had stashed in the drawer of the night table, so I decided to talk about Burch. The residual anger from his offenses was right beneath the surface of my despair over Anna, so it was easy to shift the focus of my feelings to him. I didn't want to talk about Anna with Sarah. Apparently Sarah didn't want to talk about her either. I was confident Sarah knew the whole story, at least the external story, but she didn't say a word about it.

"What did Harry do this time?"

The thought of Burch almost choked me with rage but I really didn't know then and I still don't know why. He didn't make Anna do anything. He just happened to be there when things began to collapse around me and, accordingly, he was a worthy receptacle for my wrath. He had become a symbol of the malevolent forces that were rearranging the elements of my life because I am a noble and long-suffering soul.

"I don't know what he did," I said after I had recovered

enough to speak. "I think he's one of the evil enchanters hectoring me. It's hard to organize your life with enchanters everywhere you turn."

"Yeah, I know about the evil enchanters," she said, squinting and glancing about furtively. "They're here. We can't see them but we can feel them." I reached over and got the washbasin from my night table and put it on my head. "Now, that's not only becoming, it's truly fitting," Sarah said. "This is no doubt the helmet of righteousness."

"The helm of Mambrino is worn with honor," I corrected. She raised the mirror in my serving table so that I could see myself. I looked really goofy, but I left the pan on my head for a while. In fact, it didn't come off until Sarah removed it.

"You look distinguished, and I'm sure the helm provides crucial protections and all that." She leaned over and kissed me. "But the logistics are awkwardly challenging. Maybe we could run a little risk. Remove the helm, not permanently, mind you, but just for a brief interlude."

"Admit it, you're an enchantress trying to find weakness and vulnerability."

"You're so clever, and yet so weak and wan."

"Maimed and mournful," I said.

"Too bad," she said, removing the pan from my head and leaning in to kiss me again. "The noble are frequently called upon to suffer."

Sarah was hovering over me when my mother came in

at nine. Slightly flustered, Sarah got off the bed immediately. "Dr. Bob is downstairs waiting for me, but I wanted to check on you before going home. I see you're in good hands." She brushed the hair off my forehead. I glanced over at Sarah, who was fidgeting. "It doesn't look like you need any help from me here." Then she opened her large purse and began rummaging through the contents. "Your Uncle Nat wrote you a letter that's in here somewhere. It is addressed to you, but I will tell you I hesitate to give it to you. He is not well. I want to protect you from his mad ravings but I don't feel comfortable withholding your mail. You are a mature young man, and I want to treat you with the respect you deserve. I just want you to keep in mind that he is not well."

"Mom, would you just give me the letter? You're acting like it's from an alien." She handed me the envelope and kissed me on the forehead.

"I have trouble with his ravings, and I expect you do too. I'm just trying to prepare you."

"I just don't know why he would write me." I tore open the envelope and read the letter through quickly. My mother stood beside the bed looking at me expectantly. "What in the world? This removes all remaining doubt. He's off-the-chart nuts."

"What? I'm almost afraid to ask what he said."

"You're not going to believe this. He thinks I may be his son, that I may be Nathan. We were changelings! Is that crazy or what?"

"I wish Nat hadn't done that. But I should have known." She looked at me without speaking. I could tell she was struggling. "Kit," she said finally, "there was some confusion at the hospital but it is ridiculous to suggest that a switch occurred. The same nurse assisted both deliveries and she was certain."

"I can leave," Sarah said, picking up her glasses. "I've got to go anyway."

"No, Sarah," my mother said, "this has nothing to do with you."

"What was the confusion?" I said.

"You and Nathan were born within hours of each other. The obstetrics nurse had to return to the delivery room to assist the doctor with Hannah. A practical nurse in the unit moved the babies before they were tagged. She was also certain which baby was which, and we all agreed before we left the hospital. Your Uncle Nat's mind has been festering in that mental ward, and he's convinced himself of another absurdity."

"Why have I never heard anything about this?"

"It's just another one of Nat's delusional phantoms without substance or reality. It's just nonsense."

"The fact that I may be Nathan is nonsense?"

"Kit, you are not Nathan. For heaven's sake, you're you."

"I know I'm me but who in the world is that? What about blood tests? Why didn't that clear it up?"

"You and Nathan were both O positive, so that was no

help. But that's not important. Both nurses were certain you were my baby."

"But how? If they scrambled us, how could you know?"

"For one thing, Hannah had a harder delivery. The babies looked different. The forceps had made an imprint on Nathan's head, and his skin had serious discoloration. Trust me, Kit, there was no mistake."

Uncle Nat's letter was two pages long. The first part was mostly an expression of concern for my well-being and regret that I had been hurt, followed by some preachy stuff. Then, in the last paragraph he wrote:

> *You know how dear you are to me but*
> *I suspect that you have never understood*
> *the depth of my affection or the basis of the*
> *emotion. Since we were one large family*
> *unit I thought it made no difference, but*
> *now it seems of singular importance that*
> *I mention something that I'm sure no one*
> *has ever told you. You and Nathaniel may*
> *have been switched at birth. I have always*
> *felt in my bones that you were my son. The*
> *truth may never be known but the facts*
> *point in that direction.*

"There were two newborns in the ward that night," my mother said. "You and Nathan. Only two. One of those babies clearly bore the marks of a hard delivery. Nat knows that full well. His delusions are spreading. This is all nonsense, and I want you to put it out of your mind. Can you do that, Kit?"

"Okay, I guess, maybe," I said, but I can tell you I wasn't sure what to make of it.

"Thank you," she said and kissed me on the cheek. "I'll see you in the morning. Good night, Sarah." Then she left the room and I could hear the rapid clicks of her heels in the corridor as she hurried away.

"I'm sorry," Sarah said.

"About what?"

"Well, everything seemed awkward with your mother. I felt like I shouldn't have been here."

"It was an awkward moment, but it was not awkward because you were here." I was thinking that it just seemed like more of the same stuff: I have no idea who I am. "You know who my Uncle Nat is, I presume."

"I assume he's the uncle who killed his son. The crazy Isaac-sacrifice man."

"How long have you known about it?"

"I've always known about it. Why does it matter? Everybody has crazy relatives."

"Yeah, but not everybody has one that crazy."

"I thought it made you maybe more exotic than other people, but mostly it's just not relevant."

Sarah left a little after nine, and I decided to try to read. I wasn't sleepy and for a while I wasn't in too much pain. I had trouble concentrating on my book because of my letters. Anna's was crushing but not really unexpected.

Uncle Nat's was out of nowhere, and I had a hard time dealing with it. It is a strange feeling to have something like that rise up like a monster out of the past. What clung to my mind was that Nathan and I looked so much alike. I don't want to be Uncle Nat's son, and I don't need to add to the vagaries of my being. As I lay there, I wondered who else knew about the confusion.

Newt jerks me around with all sorts of random stuff, but even he never mentioned that I might be Nathan (which would mean that Uncle Nat murdered Kit), so he probably never heard the story either. I decided not to say anything to him about it, and I think that's just as well for several reasons. First, he would probably have just done the usual, i.e., jerk me around. Second, he probably didn't know anything anyway. Third, he only visited me once while I was in the hospital. I learned later that he'd been trying to cope with the dawning of an epiphany: His latest, a sweet lady named Ruby, had reached Stage Four in their relationship and thrown his clothes and books out on the lawn of her house.

When Mrs. Pitts came to check on me at eleven, I asked for a pain shot. I probably didn't really need it at that time, but I wanted out. I wanted to float away and stop worrying about things for a while. She didn't even look at my chart. Maybe she saw that I was distressed. After she gave me the shot, she told me about her beautiful granddaughter who was attending a high school in Memphis. She said she wanted to bring her granddaughter up to see me (whoever I may be) before I left the hospital. I apparently blew my best chance by having the accident late in the summer; her granddaughter had spent a week with Granny Pitts in early June.

After Mrs. Pitts left, my mind wandered back to the accident. I wanted to remember how the wreck happened, but I was having trouble. When I started thinking about that Sunday, I got absorbed by a lot of strange emotions. The truth is I couldn't piece things together in my mind. I had been able to remember Saturday night and the compulsive reading of John Stuart Mill's autobiography in the early morning hours of Sunday. I remembered the anxiety and pain, the terrible oppressive pain, and I couldn't think of a way out. But the rest of Sunday was hazy. It was as though my mind had tried to blot Sunday out. I remembered lying on the hot pavement and all the people gawking at me. I remembered the strange apparition that looked like Dr. Goolsby crouching beside me and talking to me about blood.

DOLOROSO

I had a feeling of being smothered and I snapped awake. At first, I didn't recognize Leola. My eyes seemed to have a film over them, and I was still disoriented by a peculiar dream. I had been having strange dreams almost every time I fell asleep. Maybe it was the morphine. I don't remember all the dreams, but that one was very vivid. In the dream I was under Roby's house. I was crawling in the dark toward a football that had come to rest in a large hole. When I reached the hole, the lights came on. I could see a glass wall several yards on the other side of the hole running left and right and up as far as I could see. The hole was empty except for the ball and a bunch of ants at the very bottom that were marching resolutely in a circle around the ball. I sat fascinated by the circling pismires.

"What a wonderful circus," I said.

"This is it," said a familiar voice. "You end where you began." I looked up and saw Cassandra standing on the other side of the wall with her hands on her hips, wearing nothing but white cotton panties and a subtle smile. She was incredible.

"But where did I begin?"

"Come back in the water," she said, ignoring my question. Then I noticed that she was standing by the river, which lay behind her like a darkly shadowed mirror. I could see her reflection lying like a wraith on the water among the shadows of trees and the intimation of orange twilight. I got up and walked toward the wall but I stopped because I saw that the wall had glass doors labeled "IN" and "OUT." A large lamp swung back and forth above my head, and I was sometimes in glaring light and sometimes in total darkness. I didn't know what to do, so I brought my right knee up and hugged it tightly against my chest. I stood on my left leg for a long time, gazing at the doors, watching the lamp swing back and forth like a pendulum. I couldn't hear a sound.

"Where am I?" I said. My voice echoed as though I were in a tunnel.

"No," Cassandra said, "that's not the question." She gave me a coquettish grin and said, "I didn't mean anything." Then she dove into the river. I watched the rippled surface but she didn't come up, so I lay on the ground and pulled my knees up against my chest. The wind began to blow hard, and sand and dust pelted my face. I looked back toward the wall, and I could see Cassandra lying on the riverbank with her legs spread and her head tilted back. The muscles in her neck were tensed and her jaw was clenched.

The sand was piling up around my body, and I was having difficulty breathing. I awoke gasping for breath.

"My niece died," Leola said.

"What?" I said, trying to get my mind oriented.

"Abner's little baby didn't make it, and Phoenix is so upset he stopped eatin'."

"I'm sorry, Leola." I picked up the damp cloth on my serving tray and began wiping my face. "I'm so sorry."

"It's terrible. It's so terrible I can hardly bear it. But I feel in my bones somethin' good gon' come out of it. One thing, Abner is finally gonna reap what he sowed. They gon' charge him with homicide 'cause he drunk when he killed that baby."

"That's so tragic."

"Yeah, it's tragic all around. You know a sad thing about Abner, he was the smart one. He was the little brother who was golden. He could count when he was three, and he could read when he was four. Phoenix used to tell me when we were goin' together that Abner was special. Abner gonna soar like an eagle. The dark moods started when he was about sixteen, and he wouldn't listen to nobody. He ignored ever'body and applied to the university. Phoenix and ever'body told him that was a mistake, the university don't admit colored."

"They turned him down?" I said.

"They say they los' his application," Leola said. "Same result as turn down. He applied twice and they kept losin' his application. Then Abner joined the army. But he was only in the army about a year when he went AWOL and got a dishonorable discharge."

"That's terrible."

"He ain't never recovered. He all about booze and self-pity. He caught tragedy and now he spreads it like a virus." Her lip quivered a little, and she looked away. "I'm sorry to put this on you, but I thought you might like to know about that baby. Please pray. Pray for all of us. Pray for Abner." Leola walked over to the door just as Coach Kern appeared in the doorway.

"May I come in?" he said, sort of stooping over and acting humbler than I had ever seen him. The coach is not known for his humility.

"You sure can," said Leola. "In fact, you here at jus' the right time. Maybe you can bring some joy and encouragement. This is one fine young man, I guess you know. But right about now he could use a helpin' hand. I'm here but I'm jus' plain ol' Leola." Then she turned to me. "I'll be back to check on you in a little bit. You call me if you need anything."

"Thanks, Leola." I probably wouldn't have been in the mood for the coach in any circumstances, but I can tell you I was not happy to see him at that moment. He stood beside my bed, fidgeting with his baseball cap, looking strange and out of place. Finally, I said, "Hey, Coach." He was wearing a coat and tie instead of his Marine Corps pullover. He looked, well, different, like he was wearing clothes from his college days. His coat seemed to be too small across the shoulders and around the chest, and his shirt collar appeared to be choking him. His coat was tan and looked like polished cotton and his shirt was plaid, mostly blue and red. His tie was solid yellow and squared at the bottom rather than pointed. I could see the bottom of his tie because the coat didn't reach all the way around him and the bottom button was straining to hold the coat together in the front.

"Hey, Kit," he said in a strange, meek falsetto. I had never heard the coach speak with such unction. He had never called me "Kit" before. The closest he ever got was the first time he ever called me anything. The first day of gym in my first year at Bridgewater we started with calisthenics and then the coach had us sit on the gym floor in little rows. He was calling out our names from a list and we were supposed to stand up and say "yo." I thought that was pretty corny, so when he said, "Kittridge Biddle," I said, "It's Kit," and raised my hand.

"Where is Kittridge?" He squinted in my direction. "I can't see you, Kittridge." His voice overflowed with derision. "Are we shy, Kittridge?" He said Kittridge with emphasis to be sure I got the point: It didn't matter what I wanted to be called. He would assign the name he chose.

"Here, Coach," I said meekly, waving my hand again. I was sitting about five rows back so he could see little more than my head.

"Is that timid little voice coming from that straw head I see back there? Kittridge Biddle sounds like a big-city law firm, but what I'm seeing looks more like a little pile of straw." A titter of laughter went across the gym floor. "Stand up, Straw, so I can get a look at you." I stood up and another ripple of snickers went across the floor. I had sweated and my hair probably looked a little like hay. "You know how to say 'yo,' Straw?"

"Yes, sir," I said. Another chorus of chuckles broke out around me. The coach was really enjoying himself.

"Well, Straw, let's hear it!"

"Yo," I said in a sort of flat conversational tone.

"You need to practice your yo, Straw. Sit down." The class hooted with laughter.

If I hadn't been looking at his face, I'd have said that a different man was standing in my hospital room. "You doin' all right, son? I'm awfully sorry about your leg." He paused and moved his head around strangely. "And your other injuries. I don't know what all." He looked embarrassed that he didn't know my full list of maladies.

"I'm all right, I guess. I can't run very fast." I reached over and got the bed switch and cranked myself up a little more.

While we exchanged greetings, Sarah came in smiling like somebody who'd just won a prize. She came to the bedside opposite the coach and said, "Hey, Coach," and picked up my cloth and went into the bathroom. I heard the water running and then she came back and started to wash my face.

"Hi, Sarah. Let me do that." I took the cloth from her,

and she picked up a comb and began combing my hair while I washed my face. I glanced at the coach and saw that he was looking at Sarah or perhaps he was looking at her green sleeveless sweater. She seems self-conscious about the size of her boobs because she holds her shoulders over, but even that didn't work with the clinging green sweater. She took my face in her hands. "Now, hold still a minute while I get this part straight." She combed carefully down the middle of my head.

"There," she said, "that does it," and kissed me lightly on the lips. She was wearing bright red lipstick that had apparently come off on my mouth because she wiped my lips with her fingers.

"You know Sarah, don't you, Coach?"

"I do. Good to see you, young lady. Straw, I came in here feelin' sorry for you, but you're doin' all right for yourself." The coach's tone had changed. I went from "Kit" back to "Straw" in less than two minutes. "You're propped up here like a prince and you got this good-looking girl pamperin' you. So why was I feelin' sorry for you? I talked to Mr. Marcus. He said you were depressed and frettin' about everything. Straw, you don't look all that depressed to me."

"Not if I can help it," Sarah said.

"Young lady, if you can't do it, I don't think it can be done."

Sarah smiled and held her shoulders back. She was pleased with herself. She stood beside the bed with her mouth open in a sultry smile and her boobs jutted forward. Her sweater contrasted with the auburn hair that fell over her shoulders and her Levi's appeared to have been shrunk on her. The coach was right: Sarah had become a bombshell.

The door leading into the hall was ajar, and Lichtman's face appeared in the crack. "I'm looking for the Biddle symposium on meaning and reality," he said.

"Sorry," I said, "we've got admission standards, and you didn't make the cut."

"Hey, Coach," he said, and then made his way toward Sarah. "Let me hug this ravishing redhead." He seized Sarah and held her body against his. "Oh, I can't stand it," he moaned. "You're astute, Biddle. Giving up an irritating palindrome for two spectacular meanings. Talk about trading up." When he hugged Sarah I felt no threat, no jealousy, nothing. If he had hugged Anna and made some remark about her breasts, I'd have dissolved in jealousy and exploded in fury. Lichtman seemed instinctively to have known that, because he never said or did anything like that with Anna. Of course, Anna showed total disdain for old Lickmore, as she called him, so he probably didn't have much of an opening.

"Hello, Eddie." Sarah pushed Lichtman back but smiled at his witticisms.

"Coach," Lichtman said, "does this guy know how to screw up a track team?" Before the coach could answer, Lichtman turned to me and said, "Boy, is Burch unhappy with you." He turned to Sarah and said, "Have you told him?" Sarah shrugged and said nothing.

"What's Burchfield's problem?" said the coach. "He's not on the team. He already graduated." The coach didn't like Burch a whole lot, but only because Burch had dropped track. It had nothing to do with Burch's real deficiencies.

"No, wait, hold the phone," said Lichtman. "Burch is mad about the blood in his car. I'm the one who's pissed about the track team, including in particular this wound." He held up his left foot so that we could see that he was wearing a tennis shoe with the top cut out. "I got this wound because Biddle doesn't know how to play touch football."

"What blood?" the coach asked.

"According to Burch," said Lichtman, once again seizing center stage, "as reported to me by parties of the second part, Sarah here offered Biddle here," he motioned elaborately as he spoke, "a ride home in Burch's fancy convertible, and the diabolic Biddle forced her to stop and pick up a bloody wino who bled all over Burch's beautiful interiors. I said the story sounded apocryphal but the parties of the second part are adamant and they are usually reliable reporters. So here's my question to the duo involved: Is any part of the story true?" He looked at me, then Sarah, then back at me.

"Well, yeah," I said. "We helped this guy who was hurt." I said "we" to loop Sarah into the project. "I thought we had to help him." I tried to make myself sound noble, but in my behalf, let me say I did experience some discomfort, a modest quantum of queasy conscience.

"That's pretty dangerous, Straw," said the coach. "You could have gotten in a bad situation."

"You can't do an inverse proportionality analysis in that situation," said Lichtman gravely. "You have to do a risk-reward analysis, weighing the one against the other. The risk was that the wino would pull a knife or something. The reward was getting blood all over Burch's car." He held up his hands as though balancing incorporeal weights and struck a reflective pose. He put his chin out and then said, "I think you guys did the right thing. I'm proud of you both. Burch deserved it."

"Harry was mad but we did the right thing helping that man," Sarah said in what I thought was a sincere tone. "Kit is one of the good guys." I squirmed.

"I hate to tell you this, Lichtman, but I didn't intend to get blood in Burch's car." I don't know why I wanted to grope for a little more nobility, but I do that sort of thing all the time. I have a compulsion to try to make people think I'm noble and long-suffering, but it's all a fraud; the august and longanimous Biddle doesn't exist. As should be clear by now, I don't know which Biddle really exists. It's like that joke about the guy who looks up in the sky and plaintively shouts, "Who am I?" and a booming voice answers, "Who wants to know?" The joke is really on me because I don't know who wants to know.

"Don't feel bad about it, Biddle," Lichtman said. "You have to take your bounties where you find them. *Felix culpa.* The moral is still the same: A prick's car will be washed in the blood of a wino. No offense, Sarah."

"I'm not in this," Sarah said. "Harry can take up for himself. I'm not his apologist." She may have wanted to come to Harry's defense but she probably didn't. She looked at Lichtman with her arms folded, a stance of disinterested objectivity. The coach frowned and then came over and punched my left arm lightly and said, "I'm gonna have to be goin', Straw. I'm glad you're doin' okay. We're gonna miss you on the track team. We're not gonna have as good a year without you."

"Thanks," I said and reached over to shake his hand.

"Hang on, Coach," said Lichtman. "Don't you want to stay and hear about meaning and deep and pithy axioms like 'existence precedes essence' and 'darkness is inversely proportional to light' and other heady and profound insights? Biddle and I have the answers. We are full of heady sayings and philosophical stuff."

"Light Man," said the coach, "you are full of very little other than yourself. I just hope you'll get your foot out of that gauze and get your butt back on the track next week." Lichtman had finally gotten on the coach's nerves. "Nice to scc you again, young lady," hc said to Sarah. "I'll check on you again later, Straw. If you need anything, let me know."

"Thanks, Coach." The coach who left the room was not the one who entered.

"Boy, that's a large, smelly vat of horse piss," said Lichtman.

"Yes," I said, "and you get to soak in it. Lichtman, I'm finally seeing a benefit from these injuries: I don't have to go to track practice. I don't have to see the coach's pretty face every afternoon. I not only escape the smelly vat, I get the pleasure of knowing you're soaking in it daily without me. Is that nice or what?"

"Umbrage!" said Lichtman dramatically. "That's brutally harsh, Biddle, totally unfeeling. I face the Kernish nightmare alone and you gleefully revel in the knowledge. Sarah, have you ever seen a more blatant example of schadenfreude?" He was being cynical and comical but he looked more morose than I'd ever seen Lichtman. After a moment of silence, he said, "Comedy is always a mask of darker currents. The truth is I'm about as flat as a river rock. Even you may be more cheerful than I am, Biddle, as hard to conceive as that may be. I don't like upheavals in my life, and I can feel them coming in shocks and convulsions. I'm beginning to want off the bus." He held his hand up as though waving to an invisible bus driver. "The times seem to be harder, guys. Much, much harder. Either times are harder or I'm faltering. Teetering. Tottering." Behind him, Sarah raised her arms and pretended to play a violin and, almost telepathically, Lichtman added, "*Doloroso*, maybe even *lacrimoso*."

COGITO, ERGO POSSUM

We sat in the odor of antiseptics and the distant sounds of machines beeping and the echoes of steps in the hallways. The mood of the room had turned somber almost immediately after the coach left. Finally, Lichtman said, "Today we went to counseling sessions about college, and I got this hollow feeling in my stomach. It's not worry about disappointment. I think I've got that covered. It's change. Radical change. I was just getting used to this game, and now we're about to head off to a totally new playing field." I don't know what he expected from me but I didn't have anything to contribute.

"Of course," he said turning to Sarah, "Biddle doesn't know anything about college angst. He's just going to slide into old Hammock Community College, where they'll welcome him not because he has a brain but solely because he managed to find the place. You know he's just riding the tide, don't you? The curriculum at Hammock Community will only be six inches deep, so he won't even get wet. He'll ride the genetic tube right on through and won't even touch the water. But his momma is going to tell him he's the most wonderful boy that ever made a footprint. And you're probably going to say, '*Ecce puer*, he's just so smart,' when you know damn well he's hardly making a stroke."

"Wow," I said, "you are wound up." I wanted to pretend that Lichtman was being overly dramatic, but even before my meeting with Mr. Marcus, I had been thinking vaguely about what I was going to do. At that point I had a lot of other things on my mind. Lichtman's parents do have higher expectations of him. He has known since the eighth grade that he is supposed to go to a school that rejects most applicants. Lichtman's older brother set the bar for him three years ago: He's a junior at Amherst. It would be ugly for Lichtman to do less; at least, that's what Lichtman thinks. The truth is that other than my mother and Mr. Marcus, nobody has talked to me about college.

Of course, there seems always to have been the general but persistent notion in my family that one should attend the University of Virginia, an imperative that Newt blithely ignored. Maybe it would be different if I hadn't caved academically. I was thinking that Mr. Marcus probably regarded me as a marginal case. But I had begun to feel something new rising inside me, something I'd never felt before. I don't know where it came from but my focus had begun to sharpen. I felt a compulsive drive to plunder and pillage intellectually, to push the limits, to read and analyze everything. For the first time, my mind felt the way my body used to feel at the meets: taut, trembling with anticipation, waiting for the gun. I had a strange new focus, a new intensity.

"You probably ought not to count me out just yet," I said. "I may surprise you." The truth is I was getting sort of sensitive about the jabs that seemed to be coming from all directions: Mr. Marcus' suggestion that I was directionless, Lichtman accusing me of taking the easy way through, and, worst of all, Anna calling me a fake intellectual, whatever that is. I had actually begun to see all those programs in a new light, not as a way to provide meaning or substance to my life but as a schedule of intellectual meets to test my acumen and endurance and something perhaps equally important: a means of refuting the palindromic assessment that had begun to weigh upon me even more heavily than my willy-nilly life. "I've decided to raise the bar," I said.

"That ain't saying much," Lichtman responded immediately. "The bar is on the nether side of the sod. You'd have to raise the bar to make it visible. Give me something tangible. I don't want to hear some cop-out like the honors program at Backwater State. Give us something real. You've hit some homers but you can't just say you're gonna bat a thousand. Nobody wants to hear about the homeruns you hit last year. We want to know about now.

We want to hear something real, something inspirational, something relevant to serious angst. Help me out here, Sarah. What should we expect from the boy wonder? How high should the bar go?"

"Ivy League or equivalent," I said before Sarah could answer. The unfortunate truth is that I had hardly given it any thought. I didn't know where I could even get in, but Lichtman had forced me to verbalize what I had merely begun to think about. Or maybe I was just puffing in front of Sarah, who stood beside the bed silently watching what she probably thought was some kind of egghead strut by a couple of outsized egos.

"Okay," said Lichtman, "but you may recall that you did an implosion last year, chasing the palindrome. You only have one semester to recover."

"Not less than fifth in the class. Ninety-ninth percentile on the SAT. And I may do some resumé padding, you know, join some of your clubs." I threw in this last as a dig at Lichtman.

"Whoa," said Lichtman, "something has stirred the somnolent beast! Am I witnessing a resurrection? The question yet remains: How do you crawl out of the hole you dug for yourself last year?"

"Knock, knock," my mother said, sticking her head through the door. "My, this is a solemn group. Is this a wake?"

"Sort of," I said. "We were observing a moment of relative silence in honor of the death of innocence."

"I'm not sure I want to hear about this. I hope you're not involved in the demise, Sarah."

"No, ma'am, I'm just a spectator." Sarah smiled but she always seems to look uncomfortable around my mother.

"Hello, Eddie," my mother said. "Aren't you and Sarah supposed to be at the math team meeting? You're not playing hooky, are you?"

"All in good time, Mrs. B," said Lichtman. "In a caring society, we first attend the halt and the lame, with respect to whom, it is to be noted, you also are here making an obligatory visit." Say what you will, Lichtman may be as witty as Newt. I could hardly control the laugh despite the pain in my leg. My mother also smiled at his witticism.

"Well," she said, turning toward me, "how are the halt and the lame doing?"

"I'm okay, I guess. Lichtman's trying to add college angst to my load."

"Pay no attention to such foolishness," she said, hugging me. "You are a special young man. You'll find your way and succeed wonderfully without adding fruitless stress to your life."

"What did I just say?" Lichtman said, spreading his arms and looking from Sarah to me. "Didn't I just say that? He's such a wonderful boy. Didn't I foretell the maternal assessment? All right, Sarah, we're ready for your line. Let's hear it."

"*Ecce puer*," Sarah said in a high-pitched mock, "he's just such a smart boy."

"There, we've got that out of the way. I can now toddle off to arithmetic with complete reassurance and full confirmation of my prescience. Sorry you can't go, Biddle. I know you're seriously tweaked about that." He walked over to the bedside and stuck out his hand. "Welcome back, mon ami. I thought you might have disappeared eternally in the palindromic abyss. But I think you're beginning to rise to the top, carried upward, no doubt, by large and buoyant meanings."

"Can we give you and Sarah a ride, Eddie?" my mother said. "We're headed your way."

"I've got my car," Sarah said. "But thanks anyway."

"I'll take a ride with the double meanings," Lichtman said.

"The meanings are going to stay behind and say goodbye," I said.

Lichtman put his arm around Sarah's waist and said, "Biddle, it's getting late. We have an important arithmetic meeting to attend."

"I keep having the feeling I'm missing things in these conversations," my mother said.

"Me too," said Sarah. I'm fairly confident, however, that Sarah hadn't missed anything and I doubt my mother had either. Sarah extricated herself from Lichtman and came to my bedside.

"In the circumstances, Mrs. B, I accept the offer of a lift, but I leave with grave misgivings for the cripple."

Sarah took Lichtman by the arm and led him to the door.

"Don't leave the lad unprotected," Lichtman said.

"Can I do anything for you?" my mother asked.

"Yes, you can take Lichtman to arithmetic."

"He's in a weakened condition, Sarah, and he's a sensitive and impressionable youth." Then before exiting behind my mother, Lichtman turned back toward me. "You're serious, aren't you?"

"The train is back on track," I said, "even if it looks slightly derailed at the moment."

"You sound like a fellow I met back in the tenth grade. You may remember him. He dazzled us all without even trying. I liked that guy. I thought he had been kidnapped, confined in a palindromic Château d'If. I knew he could dig his way out. I just didn't know whether he would. *Cogito, ergo possum.* The question now is whether you can hang by your tail."

After my mother and Lichtman left, Sarah pulled the guest chair up next to the bed, then stepped up and sat on the edge of the bed. "Wherever you go to college, I'm going too. You're not going to leave me behind." I pulled her over toward me.

"I'm serious. Where do you want to go?"

"I was really thinking about the University of Virginia."

"Virginia isn't co-ed, so that won't work." Her voice had a tinge of concern. She paused a few seconds and then said, "You knew that, didn't you?" I smiled and she kissed me. "Okay, let's see. Cambridge is a nice place. Philadelphia is a nice place. There are lots of really nice places we can both go."

"I'll probably have to go where somebody will offer me some money. I don't even know what I have, and I don't know where I can get in."

"I'm sure you'll get plenty of offers and money." She sat on the bed smiling broadly and looked at me with a curious expression on her face. She is a startlingly statuesque girl. The irony is that I was thinking about unbuttoning Anna's blouse and then feeling as though I were doing something sacrilegious. Believe me, I can't explain it. I have no way of judging objectively, but some people might say that Sarah is as pretty as Anna. She is certainly more curvaceous. But the truth remains that Sarah could strip naked, and it wouldn't provide as much excitement as Anna's smile. I don't like it. I hate it. But I can't help it.

"I'm going to have to go too," she said. She sat on the bed looking at me. Then she took my right hand and placed it on her left breast, holding my wrist in both her hands. "Do you know what that is?" she said.

"Okay," I said, "this is a trick question, right?"

"No, it's not," she said solemnly, "and I'll give you the answer: That's my heart. Only superficially is it my breast." I said nothing because I had not seen this side of her and I didn't know what to make of it. Then she repeated, "That's my heart. Do you understand? That's my heart. That's why it's meaningful. That's my heart and you are in it."

"Okay," I said. She took my hand from her breast and held it in both her hands.

"I love you and I want to please you but I want you to be real," she said. "I want you to see me as a person, not an object. I can't explain it but I've loved you from the first moment I saw you." She took my face in her hands and kissed all around before ending with my lips. Then she climbed down off the bed. "I've got to go to math club." She kissed me again and said, "I'll see you tomorrow," and went out the door walking backwards, looking at me intently and smiling broadly.

She was hardly out the door when I finally got it. The revelation: When Sarah said she wanted me to be real, she meant her reality, not mine. I had lodged in Sarah's brain the same way Anna had lodged in mine. She had developed an idea of me, and I had already violated the restraints. I finally grasped that she loved her idea of me and I had to infer that she may or may not love any other version of Kit Biddle. I had been flattered by her attention and the obviously ingenuous compliments, but I already knew I couldn't live up to her notion of me, and I could already feel the pinch of the bonds. I was troubled and uncomfortable, maybe because a fictitious persona is a spirit-breaking load that gets heavier by the mile. It's very hard to be a phantom in a world of real people.

After Sarah left, I picked up my book and found my

place. I propped the book on my chest and began where I had left off. I wasn't tired or sleepy. I started reading and kept on reading until finally I had to get a shot for pain. I bogged down when I got to the part where Don Quixote has sent Sancho into the village of El Toboso to find the beauteous Dulcinea. Sancho reasons that, since Dulcinea doesn't really exist except in Don Quixote's mind, he might as well spare himself the trouble of searching. So, he waits by the side of the road until some peasant girls come along and then convinces Quixote that one of them is the wondrous Dulcinea, whom the evil enchanter has transformed in Quixote's sight from the essence of beauty and grace to a coarse farm girl. When the valiant Knight of the Mournful Countenance presents himself to the girls, they scorn him and hasten away, leaving him to rationalize that his ideal is veiled from him because the wicked enchanters hate him.

Maybe because the morphine had made me slightly giddy, I started laughing and couldn't stop. The night nurse came in with some pills, and I was laughing so hard that I could hardly swallow them.

"Something sure is funny," she said.

I nodded my head, laughing almost hysterically. She left looking bewildered. I read the same passage over again and continued to laugh. I put the bookmark back in place and dropped the book on the night table. I laughed until I started to cry. I turned off the lamp and stared into the half-light with tears running down my face. The idea of gallantly bowing before the illusion of Dulcinea had seemed so ludicrous, and then it seemed so unbearably sad that I could hardly stand the thought of it. The pain in my leg eased but not the feeling of emptiness. I rolled my bed back up to a sitting position and then put my arms around my pillow and sat there in the shadowed room crying.

I was bent over hugging my pillow and didn't hear the night nurse come back in. "Are you all right, young man?" I was sobbing uncontrollably, and I didn't answer. She came over to the bed and patted my shoulder. "It's gonna be all right," she said, stroking my head. I tried to get control of myself but I couldn't. She put her arms around my shoulders and repeated, "It's gonna be all right. You'll see." When finally my sobbing subsided, she said, "Can I get you anything?" I didn't answer because I just couldn't talk right then. "Did something bad happen?" I shook my head because I couldn't form words without beginning to sob again.

"Dulcinea doesn't really exist," I said. My voice was shaky and high pitched because my throat was tight, and a sob was rising in my chest.

"What?" she said, obviously perplexed.

"It's something I was reading. This girl was very important to this guy, see, but she wasn't real. You see what I'm saying?"

"Well, no, I don't see what you're saying. How could somebody be important who wasn't real?"

"I don't know," I said and began to sob again.

"Sometimes sadness isn't related to anything real," she said. I was hunched over with my face in my pillow when she came out of the bathroom with a wet cloth. "Here, let me wash your face. Lean back." I released my grip on the pillow and lay back against the bed with my eyes closed. She took the cloth and wiped across my forehead, down each cheek, under my eyes, across my chin, and then repeated the motion several times.

"I think I'm all right," I said.

"Maybe you can get some sleep now. You want me to turn off your night-light?"

"Yes, please." She smiled and turned off the night-light and closed the door behind her. I sat there in the oppressive gloom staring into the darkness. Except for a sliver of light under the door and a diffused glow behind the curtains, the room was dark. If I turned away from the window, I could close my eyes and see more than when they were open. With my eyes shut I could see images and shapes of unfamiliar objects that danced about in the ether before my face, uncontrolled and uncontrollable. My impulse was to impose some kind of order on them but they were too full of energy to be ordered by me. I fell asleep watching a circus of images that were not intimidated by the whip of my will or the prod of my mind. I could not coax them through the hoops.

THE GLASS WALL

I didn't wake up until I heard the breakfast cart and the banging of trays. My tray appeared a few seconds after I opened my eyes, and I decided to try to eat some of the food. The orange juice had a metallic taste and the smell of the scrambled eggs made me nauseous. I picked up my notebook and started looking over the assignment sheets that my mother had gathered from my teachers. I went over my assignments with a peculiar new intensity. It was not merely Anna's disdain of my intellect that goaded me. True, I was determined to prove to her, and perhaps to me, that I wasn't as mentally impoverished as she thought. But there was something more, something truly elemental, nudging my mind awake. While I was reviewing my workload, Mr. Marcus came in. When he walked in, I thought, *Oh, no*, not so much because of him but because I wasn't in the mood to talk to anybody. I was overloaded, and Mr. Marcus wasn't likely to help carry any of it.

"I've brought you a few books," he said almost apologetically. He was clutching several books under his arm. It occurred to me that my mental image of him was just that: a jaunty, upbeat guy carrying an armload of books and wearing a sport coat and hat. "Tell me if you've read them. They're just for fun." He had brought Wodehouse's *Much Obliged, Jeeves*, Erasmus' *The Praise of Folly*, and a paperback of e. e. cummings' poems. "I almost brought you some heavier work, but I decided to hold off till you're feeling better."

"Thanks," I said and took all the books and stacked them beside my breakfast tray.

"I've spoken with your mother about your work and your physical and emotional condition. I see no reason why you can't complete your schoolwork from home so that you can graduate with your class. She tells me that you may not be able to get around well for five or six months. That surprised me. I am not concerned about your ability to keep up with the class. I am concerned about her view of your emotional state." I think that he expected some comment from me, but I didn't feel like getting into it. "Your mother thinks you're very depressed. Is she right?"

"I don't know. Probably not 'very depressed.' But I'm probably a little down at the moment. I can't figure anything out, and I seem to be having to make a lot of rearrangements in my life. Nothing seems fixed anymore. I've been thinking about our conversations, and I don't know what to make of it all. I've been struggling with a lot of stuff, trying to find some basic answers. I haven't found anything except attempts to rationalize. All these smart people. All these years. I thought I'd find some book by somebody who did more than rationalize the questions and quandaries. It's pathetic. Unbelievably pathetic."

"I know. Like everybody else, I have no answers for you. My only advice is stay engaged. Life is like swimming. You have to get in the water."

"I don't think I can swim."

"If you assume that you can't, you can't. Once you get in the water, you may discover something about yourself that you never suspected."

"If that's faith, I can tell you I'm going to drown."

"I suspect that 'faith' has a largely intellectual meaning to you; that you think of faith in terms of ignoring rational doubts or engaging in a suspension of disbelief. Faith in the true sense has almost nothing to do with the intellect and a great deal to do with a higher communion."

Mr. Marcus didn't know it, but the reference to "communion" threw me into another realm. I drifted into the past and I could feel the rhythm of Nathan's Sunday chant. The family called it his Sunday chant because he did it on Sunday morning when the rest of the family was leaving for church. He would run back and forth, pulling his tether along the cable, frantically chanting over and over:

God has made the union,
Got to take communion.

Like Nathan's other chants, it didn't make a whole lot of sense. He probably understood something about theology. Uncle Nat had tried to teach him the basics of the faith. The chant began when, about a year before the murder, Uncle Nat had to stop taking Nathan to church. It wasn't Uncle Nat's idea to stop taking him. A delegation from the church came out and met with Uncle Nat because of Nathan's rhymes. Nathan refused to believe that he wasn't supposed to talk in church, so he rhymed there the same as everywhere else. In fact, it may have been worse in church. The problem had grown over the years until it was impossible for Uncle Nat or any other preacher to say anything with emphasis without evoking a rhyme. When Nathan began rhyming in church, some members of the congregation protested. But Uncle Nat felt so strongly that Nathan should attend his services that he temporarily abandoned his usual subject of sin and preached a series of sermons on the spirituality and faith of the afflicted.

In the ensuing months, Uncle Nat began to look increasingly desperate. He structured his sermons so that emphatic phrases were limited, and unless Nathan was out sick or something, he would struggle to minimize the rhyming. His sermons, already as dull as a hum, became marvels of monotone. At first the rhyming was reduced to an occasional mimic of the last words before a pause and to stand-alone phrases like "please stand," which would evoke some nonsense rhyme from Nathan like "peas canned." It got worse and worse until even the Lord's Prayer had a strange nonsensical echo:

> *Congregation: "Our Father, who art in heaven."*
> *Nathan: "Dour pother, true heart of leaven."*
> [Rhymed in the same reverent tone.]
> *Congregation: "Hallowed be thy name."*
> *Nathan: "Harrowed by the game."*
> *Congregation: "Thy kingdom come."*
> *Nathan: "Why wring some dumb?"*
> *Congregation: "Thy will be done."*
> *Nathan: "Why kill the son?"*

Uncle Nat knew even before the elders showed up at his house that Nathan had to be left at home.

Nathan's nonsense rhymes didn't have anything to do with the point Mr. Marcus was trying to make, but the rhymes are strung across my mind like spider webs that tend to catch randomly flying thoughts. As I understood what Mr. Marcus was saying, I was supposed to think or communicate with something other than my brain. I started to tell him that I had a hard enough time using my brain and that I would probably have even less luck with some other organ. But I didn't. You can say things like that to cynical people like Lichtman, but they fall flat if you try them on a guy like Mr. Marcus. So I just said, "I'm having a hard time with that."

"Well, do me a favor. Don't reject it out of hand. Think about it."

Injection of another irony: I need to think about finding answers some way other than thinking. I don't know whether he's right or not, but I sensed a problem. Sometimes I feel as though I'm in one of those dreams in which you're trying to get something that stays forever out of reach. I have conversations and I may as well be alone talking to a reflection in the water or a passing train. One thing for sure, I was worn out with the effort. I decided I would try to shift to something else.

"I just need to think about it," I said, trying to lay the foundation for a transition. "Right now, I've got a kind of reality crisis, but I can work through it. Give me a little while and let's talk about it again."

"I'm not sure I have a very good grasp of all the things that are troubling you, but I am confident that time, thought, and prayer will help you distill them and deal with them. I want to urge you not to try to force an answer. Relax a little and let your intellect roam in high spirits. Stop trying to pry the hinges off. To be candid, one of the reasons I brought Wodehouse and Erasmus is to try to brighten your outlook." He picked up *The Praise of Folly* and held it out as though offering it to me a second time. "There's a lot more wisdom here than the tone might suggest. This may not be the best translation, but it's probably the most interesting. Sometimes the translator seems to be going sort of off-roading." He thumbed the pages of the book a few seconds and then said, "Here's an example of what I'm talking about: 'It is folly alone that stays the fugue of youth . . . .' So, is *fugue* a good thing? That is close to being literally meaningless."

"A lot of things seem to be that way," I said.

"Yes, but this translation has a lot of charm. You can love something like that. Something with shrouded intent and implication. It's the way life really is. We live in a penumbra rather than in total darkness or total light. The interesting thing is that, in spite of the fact that 'fugue of youth' is almost a nonsense phrase, you not only get the idea but you get an interesting intimation of other meaning." I didn't respond because, frankly, I didn't know what the phrase meant. He was quiet a minute and then picked up his hat and stood up. "Anyway, it's a fun book and I think you'll enjoy it." He paused a moment at the door, which made me think he was trying to come up with something else to say, maybe some way to make a pleasant exit. "I didn't tell you last Saturday, but you've been provisionally readmitted to the honors program."

"You're kidding me." I was honestly surprised by this turn in the conversation. "My mother didn't say anything about it."

"I know. I was delegated to talk to you at her suggestion. She thought I was the person to do it. It was the consensus of the faculty that last year was a fluke and that the honors program was designed for people like you. We've considered the possibility that the failure is ours rather than yours, and we want to confront that possibility in a real way."

"I'm not sure I deserve that kind of confidence."

"Only you can determine that. I've been trying to decide how you can do your honors paper. I'd like to see you do something that analyzes your struggle with meaning, sort of a review of the Kit Biddle climacteric. Think about it and give me your thoughts."

"Isn't a climacteric supposed to be a multiple of seven? I'm not a multiple of seven."

"I meant it in the general sense of a crossroads, a period of challenge, which I think you've had in a very serious way. I don't take astrology seriously but, as I recall, the multiple-of-seven years are unfavorable periods. Aren't the trines climacteric and multiples of nine? Eighteen may be a period of favorable change. Maybe you have something to look forward to."

"Look at me," I said. "I'm a heap of calamities. I don't think 'favorable' works for me."

"We'll see," he said. "Plants thrive after pruning. And crops grow best in manure. Don't dismiss calamity until you can look over your shoulder and see what it has produced."

"I really don't know whether I can do the kind of paper you're talking about but I'd like to try." I had actually thought about maybe trying to write something on the issues I'd been worrying about. One of the things that I found surprising about John Stuart Mill's autobiography was that he didn't struggle enough with the problem of meaning or, if he did, he decided to leave it out of his book.

"Give it a shot. Have large aspirations. I don't want a few pages of inconsequential happenings. You might take a segment of your life and maybe trace your intellectual development or your struggle with meaning, which I hope you recognize is really a spiritual struggle. I want you to challenge yourself. The research can be waived only if you think and write comprehensively."

I knew that Mr. Marcus had no real idea what my life was like. He and my mother had obviously talked about some of my ghosts; but even she didn't know everything bothering me. He might be shocked or offended or alternately one and then the other. From my perspective, it would clearly be more fun and less contrived than a research paper. The more I thought about it, the more I liked the idea. I tried to make sure he and I were talking about the same kind of paper. After going over it with him, I was almost convinced by his attitude that he really didn't care what it was about so long as it was substantial. I told him I was thinking about taking some themes and counterpoints and blending them autobiographically into the recent events of my life. He said that was what he had in mind, but he may have just wanted to make it easier for me.

I have been working on the manuscript off and on for the past five months. It's longer than I expected it to be, and I still haven't finished. During a large part of every day

I am alone because everybody is busy. Of course, Sarah visits me several hours each day—she calls it our *cinq-a-neuf*—and for a little longer on the weekends. Lichtman and Q. Ball visited almost every day for a while, but their visits have steadily declined as they've restructured their lives without me. Of course, Anna has never visited me at all. I have not asked her to. I've been told that my leg is not mending properly and that I will probably have to have another operation that involves grafting bone from my hip onto the shattered femur. I've asked whether I may lose my leg, and I've gotten a lot of bobbing and weaving. I don't sleep much because I don't get tired lying in my bed or sitting in a chair with my leg propped up. I spend a lot of time every day working. I also read a lot. When I started writing, I was determined to prove that I am not a fake intellectual, as Anna said, but I'm now way past that objective. The climacteric project has now become an obsession unto itself.

I've learned to type but I write everything out in longhand first. I agreed to let my mother be the courier of my scribblings if she promised not to read the manuscript. She probably hasn't kept her promise. At this point, it doesn't much matter. The only person I've given permission to read it is Mr. Marcus, who has become a helpful critic and editor. He gets the cursive pages from my mother first, and then we go over the stuff and make changes. He has also helped me recall our conversations, some of which I had trouble remembering in any detail.

After Mr. Marcus finishes with my draft, I type the edited material and then go back to writing the narrative. I have not shown any of the manuscript to Sarah despite her repeated requests. I don't know whether our relationship will survive when she finally does read it, but that's not why I haven't given it to her. The real reason is that I'm afraid of getting bogged down and distracted from the work if her feelings are hurt and we spend too much time and energy talking about it. I really enjoy Sarah's company, but unfortunately I am sometimes concerned about her expectations.

After Mr. Marcus left, I lay there worrying about everything for a long time. I hadn't thought about a climacteric, and I had a hard time thinking of my situation as a crossroads. I was thinking that it was more like a wasteland, i.e., nothing but desiccated prairie in all directions. A crossroads seemed to imply a point of decision; a wasteland just meant that you were nowhere at all. Before I fell asleep I was thinking that maybe it doesn't make any difference whether it's a crossroads or a wasteland: In either case, I'm lost.

GROSS AND FINE

66 "This is Dr. Gross of Psychiatry Associates," my mother said. I had woken early and spent some time reading *Don Quixote,* but my eyes had gotten heavy. I had placed the book on my chest and closed my eyes for a bit. I opened my eyes and was immediately greeted with those ominous words. When you have a lot of evidence of impending disaster, it's not really a premonition. Sometimes you can't expect anything else; in some circumstances, calamity is just the next thing that happens in a sequence of events. It's like my rope-swing accident when I was a kid. To add to the thrill, I twisted the rope tightly, so the swing seat would spin in addition to making the usual sweep from the tree limb to the top of the arc, a point about twenty feet above the ground. The result was that the instant I left the limb the seat began to spin violently and I lost my grip at the top of the arc. For the instant that I was suspended in

midair, I knew I was in trouble, but you couldn't really call it a premonition.

"Are you awake, Kit?" my mother asked sweetly. I had opened my eyes and I was looking directly at her, so she had to know perfectly well that I was awake. What she really meant was, "Are you ready for a bomb, Kit?"

"Kit, this is Dr. Herschel Gross. Dr. Gross, this is my son, Kit."

"How are you, young man?" Dr. Gross said, patting me on the shoulder a couple of times.

"Dr. Gross is a psychiatrist and one of Dr. Bob's friends from medical school. Dr. Bob asked him to talk to you. I've got to run or I'll be late for my class." She stopped at the door just as an attendant was bringing in the breakfast tray. "Dr. Bob says you have to eat or he's going to put you back on glucose. So, eat." Then she left me with Dr. Gross and the smell of scrambled eggs. I tried to think of some way to avoid both. Of course, I could ignore the scrambled eggs but not the shrink. He sat down in the armchair back to my left near the head of the bed. I raised my bed to a sitting position, which caused him to be completely behind me. To twist around to see him put pressure on my leg and caused a good deal of pain, so I couldn't see him at all. He was reading something and making guttural noises in his throat. We sat in semi-silence for what seemed like a long time.

"Your mother has asked me to meet with you, but I can only help someone who wants my help. Is it agreeable with you if I review some things with you?" I felt more than a little ridiculous sitting in bed, staring forward at a blank wall, talking to the invisible man. You would have thought he'd come around so that I could see him but he didn't.

"I'm not crazy, and I don't need a psychiatrist."

"Well, you're not intellectually impaired. Indeed, your mother tells me you're exceptionally gifted. I am not here to address intellectual prowess. I met with your mother and Dr. Glans and we agreed that you might benefit from an unburdening of the difficult events in your life. Some of life's issues are easier to address with an objective listener and trained counselor."

"I've had some stuff, but everybody has stuff. I still don't know what there is to talk about."

"Why don't we just explore? And, if you want to stop, just tell me."

"I don't know what there is to explore but okay, I guess."

"You've taken some pretty hard knocks. Are you having any double vision, vertigo, or headaches?"

"Nothing unusual. I have a slight headache after the pain medicine wears off, and my forehead hurts a little where I got cut in the wreck, but that's about it."

"When you were twelve years old, your uncle suffered a mental breakdown of some sort. Would you like to talk about how that affected you?"

"No, I wouldn't."

"A cousin close to you died as a result of your uncle's illness. You must have feelings about it."

"Look!" I was nearly shouting. "The crazy loon killed him, murdered one of the sweetest, most innocent people in the world. For God knows what. Is that what you want to know? Do I hate him? I do. I probably hate him more than anyone has ever hated anyone. And you won't ever understand it, so why don't you take your goofy clipboard and leave me alone." My voice had begun to crack by the end of my outburst. I struggled to keep from crying. I could hear scribbling and paper rattling but Dr. Gross said nothing for a long time.

"Why don't we shift gears here. My information is that you may have been somewhat disoriented after the accident."

"I don't know. I don't think so."

"It says here you gave some passerby the wrong name and that you seemed not to know who you were."

"Who said that? The sun was glaring and I couldn't see, that's all. I was on the hot pavement and blood was everywhere, and it was hard to see. It was a difficult situation. I don't know what people expect."

"I see," he said and everything got very quiet. I couldn't see him and I couldn't hear him, and I had a nervous feeling in my stomach, so I glanced around at him. He was bent over, writing on his clipboard. All I could see was the top of his head. "Do you remember what happened to you? How the accident happened?"

It sounded like an accusation. I felt defensive but I don't know why.

"Sure," I said after I gathered my thoughts. "I was driving the maintenance truck from the golf course." I was faking it, at least a little bit. I had been trying to remember what happened, but it was confusing, almost like trying to remember a dream. I kept thinking I had hit my dog, Wulfie, but I knew that was not possible. Wulfie ate a poisonous plant or something and died shortly after Nathan's death.

"How did you wreck the truck?"

"I'm a little fuzzy on some things, but I know enough."

"You know it was a one-vehicle accident, don't you?" Again, I detected an accusatory tone.

"I didn't try to kill myself," I snapped.

"I haven't suggested that you did." He was making me very nervous.

"Well, I didn't," I said, my voice breaking.

"Your father died in a car accident, didn't he?" Just like that. I could see where he was going: Father kills himself in a car, and son follows the pattern.

"Why are you talking about my father?" I turned around in the bed to look at him, and a pain shot through my leg. "This invisible-man game is stupid. I don't want to talk anymore." I waited for him to say something but he said nothing. He continued rattling papers and lurking behind me like some specter. When he just sat there, I shouted, "I'm not going to talk to you anymore."

A nurse stuck her head in the door and said, "Is everything all right in here?"

"Everything's fine," Dr. Gross said. "Thank you." Then he shuffled out from behind me. "I will talk to Dr. Glans and, if you want to meet with me again, we can all get together on objectives." He disappeared out the door before I could say anything. I was so disconcerted I probably couldn't have said anything anyway. After he left, I thought about his questions. At first, I thought he was ridiculous. Then I thought that maybe he wasn't, that maybe I'm the one who's absurd. I try to make my life rational but I have to admit that it doesn't seem particularly sane to me either. I've been trying to piece together the recent events in my life and I'm having a hard time understanding a lot of it.

I pushed my call button and nurse Bloom came in wearing her usual smile. "Mr. Biddle, you can't have anything for pain until you eat your breakfast. Those orders are straight from your mother."

"Oh, Lord, I can't eat this stuff right now."

"How about ice cream? Let's try some ice cream."

"Okay, let me try some ice cream. I'm really not very hungry."

She left and came back a few minutes later carrying three little cartons of vanilla ice cream and a hypodermic needle. "You get your shot if you promise to eat all three."

"All right, give 'em to me." She pushed the food table across my chest and put the cartons on it along with a spoon. Then she swabbed my right arm with alcohol and gave me the injection. I took off the top of one of the cartons and spooned out some ice cream. I had eaten so little that my stomach felt as though it was being invaded, but I kept eating until I had finished all three cartons. I picked up my book and found my place, but I couldn't concentrate so I put it back on the night table. An acute sense of loss was only partially relieved by the morphine. Dr. Gross was right about one thing: I have some things that rankle. I could see Nathan's face almost any time I closed my eyes, and of course Anna was another ghost that lurked in the shadows of my mind. Nathan and Anna had both seemed like such a large part of my life, at least as I had perceived it. They were major props that had somehow disappeared. I don't know what you do when you lose props like that, and the place they occupied seems unbearably empty. I lingered in a semi-conscious haze for a long time, reviewing in my mind the losses I had suffered. The morphine finally took away the sense of loss and everything else.

I woke up after noon. My mother was reading a magazine in the chair beside the bed. As soon as I moved she got up and walked over to the bed. "Kit," she said, "a police officer is on his way here. Do you feel like answering questions about your accident?"

"Yeah, sure," I said, but I was thinking that the pain seemed incessant. Nathan dies, Anna disappears, I cripple myself, and then I get painful letters and painful visitors.

My mother stood beside my bed looking stricken, and I stared at the opposite wall, trying to coax my mind to deal with the strange disorganization of my life. Uncle Nat had taught me to question both pain and pleasure, and it seemed to make sense back then. Now, I don't know. At the time, I had not experienced the death of Nathan or the touch of Anna, so maybe I didn't know much about pain or pleasure.

"When is pain bad and when is pleasure good?" The question was presented to Newt and me in August 1952, a month before Newt left for college and about a month after my eleventh birthday. Uncle Nat's question disconcerted me because I thought it was asked backwards.

"Always," I said.

"Sometimes," said Newt.

"An absolutist and a relativist," said Uncle Nat. "Or perhaps an innocent and a trickster. Kit, please defend your position."

"Who wants pain?" I said.

"How about pain as a warning that you've been hurt or contracted disease? Isn't there good in being warned? When you disparage pain, aren't you just attacking a very useful messenger?"

"I think of death and pain as the same."

"Good," Uncle Nat said. "That's very good, Kit. Now, why is death bad?"

I didn't have an answer to that question, and I don't remember any being offered by Uncle Nat or Newt. I

remember Uncle Nat's disparagement of pleasure, epit-
omized in his mind by intoxication and "feel good"
delusions. I also remember that Newt seized the opportunity to take a serious question on a farcical romp.

"I am convinced," Newt opined gravely, "that pain and
pleasure are debits and credits, i.e., in the great balance
sheet of life, pain and pleasure always balance out." As
usual, Uncle Nat frowned and fretted but allowed Newt
to proceed, maybe because he had come grudgingly to
respect Newt's wit. I still don't know whether Newt was
serious, but the theory, which Newt called the Third Law
of Hedonics (he never revealed the first and second laws),
is that for every pleasure there is an equal and opposite
pain. Conversely, according to the theory, for every pain
there is an equal and opposite pleasure. Thus, pain and
pleasure always balance out, so that a person can take
heart in travail because he's building up an account of
pleasure due, which means that, at the appropriate time,
he will become the beneficiary of a compensating joy.

"I think the officer's trying to clarify some of the facts."
My mother's voice intruded into my musings. "Dr. Bob
has spoken to the president of the club. They're not going
to press charges." She paused and then said, "I've spoken
with the officer. Interestingly, he's the same one who took
your statement Saturday night when you took that man
to the emergency room. He still has some concerns."

My tension level was high when the officer got there a
few minutes later. Sure enough, it was the same overweight

cop who talked to Sarah and me in the emergency room. When he came through the door he was holding his handheld radio to his ear. I had a hard time understanding what the person on the other end was saying, but I heard him say he was at the hospital following up Sunday afternoon's truck theft. My sphincter tightened. If Newt's Third Law of Hedonics is valid, an offsetting pleasure, approaching rapture, had to be in my near future.

"I'm Officer Fine," he said. "It is unfortunate, but I believe we've met before, and I ain't that happy to see you again." He twisted his face into a frown and stood glowering at me, maybe waiting for me to say something. I didn't know what to say. "What I'm doing is follow-up on the events of last Sunday afternoon involving a stolen truck in a one-vehicle accident. I've got the patrolman's report, so I know the who, the where, and the when. What I don't know is the why and the how. One witness said you thought you hit a dog. I went all up and down that road and I couldn't find a dog."

"I hit a dog and lost control of the truck," I said. "That's all I know. I can't remember anything else."

"Okay," he said. "You hit a dog." He paused. "You were alone in the truck, right?"

"Yes, sir."

"And nobody, no other car hit the truck or anything?"

"No, sir."

"What did the dog look like?" he said and then, "Aw, it doesn't matter. Here's the serious part as far as

I'm concerned: Why were you driving the country club's maintenance truck?"

"I borrowed it. I don't know where I was going. I was just driving."

"As I mentioned, Officer, we've spoken with the club," my mother interjected.

"Yes, ma'am, I understand. But you know that the maintenance superintendent," he looked at his note pad, "a Mr. Harbo Wallace, said your son didn't have permission. In fact, Mr. Wallace says your son was discharged from the maintenance crew for improper behavior."

"We've spoken with the club management," my mother said, "and they're not making an issue of it."

"Well," he said, "we aren't bound by their wishes. The D.A. can prosecute even if the victim doesn't want it to happen. The important thing is the public interest, not private influence. Even if the D.A. chooses not to go forward, I think you need to make an issue of it. You need to see the pattern. Saturday night he's in the emergency room covered in blood at midnight, and Sunday he steals a truck."

"He helped an injured man Saturday night. Surely you're not saying he did anything wrong."

"I'm trying to alert you to a pattern, ma'am. I've seen it before, and I'd be concerned if I was you."

"I assure you, Officer Fine, I am concerned, and we are going to address these issues."

"Well, bailing him out may not be addressing the

issues. Somebody pulled some strings here, and I don't think it does this boy any good. He stole a truck."

"I appreciate your admonition, and I assure you we will take it to heart. In general, I totally agree with you about bailouts, but we may have some extenuating circumstances that we need to explore before deciding what is best."

"That's all I've got." He looked at my mother and shook his head. As he walked to the door, he turned to me. "You need to watch yourself, fella. I hope you recover soon and that you've learned something from all this. I'm not going to recommend that the D.A. pursue this, but I don't want to see you again. Do you understand me?"

"Yes, sir. You won't see me again." I meant every word I said. He would never see me again.

"Okay," he said, "I hope you recover real soon. Ma'am, ya'll have a good day." His radio blared unintelligibly and he held it to his ear as he walked out the door.

"There's a lot to be concerned about here," my mother said when the cop was out the door. "I don't know what concerns me more. You know, if Dr. Bob hadn't intervened on your behalf, you would have been charged with grand larceny. Do you understand how serious this is?"

"Yeah, I know, but I didn't intend to take the truck." I knew that didn't make any sense when I said it. My mother just looked bewildered. She didn't say anything for a long time. She just sat there looking stumped and worried. "I'm sorry," I said. "I know that was embarrassing to you.

It was to me too. It won't happen again." She smiled and patted my hand but her face still showed strain and worry.

"Did you intend to wreck that truck, Kit?" she asked, her voice quavering for the first time I can remember.

"I didn't intend to wreck the truck, and I don't know why I took it."

"Okay," she said. "Let's drop it for now."

After she left I struggled again to remember what had happened. I had been nervous and sad, and I hadn't had much sleep. I couldn't remember why I took the maintenance truck. I couldn't remember much about the wreck except right before the crash and then afterward when I was sitting in the blood on the hot pavement. I remembered going by Anna's that morning and then running on the golf course, and I remembered driving away in the truck. But I don't know why. I also remembered hitting the black dog and losing control. The whole thing had a dream-like quality, sort of gauzy and vague.

PART THREE

Shrinkage

GENEALOGY

After Nathan's death I started killing ants. I didn't spray them with insecticide or pour motor oil on them; I bludgeoned them with the butt of an old tobacco pipe I found in my grandfather's desk drawer. I had first tried a sort of fratricide by hauling shovelfuls of roiling fire ants from one mound and dropping them like conscripted dragoons on another mound. The strategy produced the expected havoc but it never produced destruction. Immediately after dispatching the disoriented conscripts, the invaded mound always returned to the remorseless functionality it had before the incursion. I switched to the cudgel not only because my invaders failed but also because I wanted to be more than an instrument of transitory chaos.

I wanted to be the hand of annihilation, the unseen but implacable shadow of death. Generally, I killed ants one by one except when they swarmed toward me in such a tight phalanx that multiples were crushed by a single blow. I wouldn't say the tobacco pipe was particularly efficient but I will say it was lethally effective. Day after day I would taunt the targeted mound until the ants crawled frantically and heedlessly into oblivion. Sometimes the carnage lasted for weeks; but the end was always the same. Ultimately, I reduced the mound to a pile of perforated dirt surrounded by a moat of crumpled brown bodies.

I thought about my ant wars when I saw Dr. Gross' meerschaum propped upside down on his desk. His pipe was larger than my makeshift weapon and the stem was more curved, but the shape of the bowl was essentially the same. I was staring absently at his pipe when he cleared his throat and said, "Good morning, Mr. Biddle." He didn't look up but remained hunched over his desk, pinching his bottom lip with his left thumb and index finger and making postnasal-drip noises in his throat while he flipped through pages in a manila folder. Hair trimmed neatly enough to please a mother, even his trousers had a perfect crease. I had some difficulty seeing him as the doctor who had done the skulking invisible-man routine at the hospital. I would say he looked basically normal, sitting there all formal and well combed in his mahogany captain's chair. I sat across from him in an upholstered leather chair. I also had an ottoman and I wanted to prop up my right leg, which had a vague, intermittent ache, but I was too anxious to do anything but lean forward with my fingers interlaced in front of me like someone praying. My crutches were propped against the wall behind me to my left.

Before he had a chance to say anything else, I said, "I don't think I know who I am." His expression, something like impatience mixed with boredom, did not change. "Do you understand?" I said. He took off his glasses and massaged his forehead with his bushy eyebrows raised just slightly. My voice sounded thin and whiny, and I knew it.

He was looking at me when his folder slipped off his lap and fell to the carpet almost soundlessly. He reached down and picked it up and began straightening his papers. The only sounds in the room were the swishing of the papers being reassembled and the hum of the air conditioner in the window beyond his rolltop desk. After he had the papers straight, he sat back in his chair and sighed audibly, giving me the impression he was already exasperated. He sat staring at me like I was an intruder.

"Do you understand?" I repeated. My mewling felt like pleading. He rubbed the side of his chin with his right thumb, his jaw forward in a dismissive jut. Then he bent over and scribbled something in his notes, ignoring me and my question. All I could see were the top of his head and his bony fingers moving his ballpoint pen around on the folder.

"I can help you with that," he said finally.

"With what?" I said.

"You said you don't know who you are." Without looking up, he flipped to the first page in the file folder he had retrieved from the floor. Then, in a tone that sounded like someone reading to a small child, he said, "You are Kittridge Carr Biddle." He looked up, raised his eyebrows slightly as though expecting me to respond. "You are an eighteen-year-old Caucasian male, mentally alert, apparently sound physically except for a compound fracture of the right femur currently secured with an intramedullary nail." He made the guttural noises and pinched his upper lip. "Is there something else to know?"

"That's not what I meant. That's not what I'm talking about." When he kept staring at me, I said, "I think I may have died."

He placed a new sheet of lined paper in his folder and scribbled more notes I couldn't read from where I sat. When I didn't say anything, he raised his head. "Well, I can help you with that too. You didn't die. You're very much alive."

"Okay," I said, "but I was lying in the road." My head began aching at the base of my skull. I could hear my pulse in my ears. I tried to concentrate on what he had said but I couldn't remember whether it was a statement or a question.

"Okay," he said, "not a great place to be, but lying in the road is not really extraordinary."

"Lying in the road isn't what I'm talking about. I know you're going to think I'm nuts." He didn't say anything. He sat there looking at me expectantly. "I was lying in the road in a puddle of blood but I was also standing on a hill beside the road." I didn't tell him everything. I stopped to see what he would say about that part of it.

"You suffered a serious loss of blood," he said nonchalantly. "The blood loss deprived your brain of its usual supply of oxygen and you hallucinated. It's not unusual and therefore not really strange. We can talk about this phenomenon if you want, but I think it's really peripheral to our purpose."

"Maybe I don't need to be here. I can tell you we're wasting time if all we're going to talk about is suicide. I didn't try to kill myself. I wrecked a truck." I reached behind my chair for my crutches. "The crazy thing is, I think I know more about what's important than you do." I struggled to my feet and put the crutches under my arms.

"Okay," he said, "I think that's fair." Instead of hobbling toward the door, I stood there on my left foot looking at him. I hadn't expected him to say something like that. "It's also fairly meaningless. It means we've begun. It doesn't mean we're done." I stood there on one leg staring at him for a few seconds, and then I repropped my crutches and sat back down in my chair. "There are questions that have not been addressed totally apart from your experience as a modern-day Lazarus."

"I don't think that's funny," I said.

"I'm sorry if that sounded flippant to you, but scientifically the Lazarus cases we deal with are not miracles but symptoms."

"I know what happened. You don't have to believe me. Frankly, I don't care."

"I didn't say I don't believe you. In fact, I believe everything you've said. I'm just suggesting that you not get carried away with your interpretation of your perceptions." He leaned forward with his elbow on the desk and pinched his bottom lip again. "From time to time, people have experiences that are, shall we say, outside the bubble." He squinted at me like he was looking into a bright light. "As you probably know, you are not the first case involving a so-called out-of-body experience. You have to understand that we have no basis for dealing with something like that. We are forced to ignore those phenomena without regard to our interest in them or our attitude toward them. We ignore them because they fit no pattern of reality that we can analyze or explain, and therefore they cannot add or subtract anything. They are outside our understanding and we are thus constrained to ignore them. Science has nothing to offer with regard to them."

"You think I'm nuts, don't you?" I said.

"No, I definitely do not think you're insane. I've only begun to try to get to know you, and as you are well aware, virtually everything I know has come to me secondhand. If it appears that you have a problem that falls into my area of medical practice, I will do what I can to help. My guess is you've hit a rough patch and you just need to talk to a trained counselor. The facts will emerge as we go forward at a pace appropriate for you. We need discussion and analysis sufficient to provide clarity. I will then give you as much guidance as may be available from the facts that have emerged. At the moment, I couldn't possibly reach a conclusion of any kind on the basis of the information in this file."

"I'm probably not crazy," I said.

"You had a serious concussion. You lost a lot of blood. Those are facts I do have in this file. Let me suggest that we drop back a bit and get oriented. We can get back to the roadside incident if we need to, but for now, I would like to start with your assertion that I don't know what is important. I think that premise is sound, and I think it provides a good foundation for going forward. Before we explore anything else, let's try to sort out the peripheral from the central. I need foundational material, and I suspect that you need to talk. I want you to tell me who you are."

"Well, that's a turnaround. I say I don't know who I am, and you say tell me who you are."

"You don't have any memory loss, do you?"

"No," I said, "I don't think so."

"Okay, tell me what you know about you. Tell me something not in this file."

He looked at me like I was a mental patient. I didn't know what to say, and I felt strangely like an animal in a trap. I could feel my eyes moving back and forth like a cornered ferret. My mind began to sort the various options for avoidance or escape. I couldn't think of anything other than that I should have left when I had my crutches under my arms. I turned toward the door to my right and thought vaguely of reasons for excusing myself. I thought about maybe saying I had to use the bathroom. His office door was ajar about a foot and a half, and I could see "Dr. Herschel Gross" engraved on a brass plate about a third of the way down. If I could have thought of a way to do it, I would have slipped out, disappeared like a phantom in a fog. As it was, I was too hobbled bodily and emotionally to do anything, so I sat there fidgeting, looking pained and perplexed, but uttering not a word.

"Let's try something else," he said. "Let's leave you out for the moment and talk about the people around you. Tell me about your family." My first thought was, *he wants to talk about Nathan*. I started to ask but then stopped. I just sat there looking stupid and he sat there staring at me. "Just tell me something mundane, nothing unpleasant, just something, anything, about your family." After the eerie silence persisted, he said, "Okay, let's drop back in time. Tell me something about your grandparents or even your great-grandparents."

I still didn't say anything immediately, but I began to reach back in my memory for something to talk about—names, dates, places, events, anything just to have something to say. The simple act of focusing my mind seemed to reduce the tension in my neck. When I thought about things in the distant past and the stuff

I knew or thought I knew, I relaxed a little. Distant and detached recollections were almost comforting. At first there was a slow lapping at the boundaries of my memory and, after some thrusts and falls, a growing surge of fairly ordered thoughts. I felt a sense of release when I started talking, like I was putting down an enormous load I'd carried for miles, and I began spilling out family history in a deluge of facts, assumptions, and maybe distortions.

"My mother has a large number of genealogy books," I said, "and, according to her, the earliest ancestor in the family tree on this continent was Captain Hugh Biddle, who went to Barbados in the early 1600s and then later went to Virginia."

"That's a bit further back than I had in mind," Dr. Gross said. "How about something a little closer to home? If we start in 1600, we won't get to your generation for a couple of years. What about one of your grandparents? I don't care which one."

"My grandfather on my father's side was Nathaniel Tyler Biddle. I know about him, but I never knew him. He died seven months before I was born. He was called Papa. My mother has photographs of him. He was a tall, thin man with a long, narrow head, who looked a bit like Bertrand Russell with baggy eyes." I then told him what I knew about Papa, who also shared Russell's love of mathematics. I don't know what else they had in common, but Papa was a Presbyterian minister, a devout and disciplined man, certainly not a libertine or an atheist. His ancestors on this continent were all from Virginia, the family having moved at some point from Isle of Wight County to Albemarle County. He was a graduate in mathematics, with a minor in theology, from Mr. Jefferson's University, as my Uncle Nat calls the University of Virginia.

He sat there looking expectant so I kept talking. I told him how my father and Uncle Nat both went back to Charlottesville to become "educated gentlemen" at the university. But that was more than two decades after Papa left Virginia. Papa moved from Albemarle County to Alabama in 1910 after the tract of land called Biddle's Mountain was sold for division among the family members. According to my mother, the joint owners of the property decided that the continued use of the land for farming wasn't practical. Papa used his proceeds from the sale of Biddle's Mountain to buy 9,000 acres of farm and timber land straddling the Tombigbee River in Alabama. At the age of twenty-five, Papa left a comfortable, structured life and moved to the hinterland of a state he had visited only once before.

I also told Dr. Gross about my grandmother, whose maiden name was Virginia Carr ("of the Virginia Carrs," as Newt has sardonically quipped). The story in the family is that when Papa told Ginnie about his Alabama plan, she terminated their engagement. A year's separation, enhanced by ardent correspondence, finally changed her mind, and they were married in 1913 in Charlottesville. Papa and Ginnie produced my Uncle Nat in 1915 and my father in 1918. They also worked the farm, built silos and mills, and founded the Bigbee Baptist Church, for which Papa provided the spiritual leadership and the land for the sanctuary and cemetery.

Ginnie died in 1930 of typhoid fever and left Papa with a large farm, a little rural church, and two teenagers. The boys had been taught at home by Papa and Ginnie because they lacked confidence in the county school system. After Ginnie's death, Papa sent the boys to the local school, where they excelled in academics and athletics. Three years after Ginnie's death, Papa married Millie Ogden, a schoolteacher and parishioner almost half his age, and later that same year Millie died giving birth to my Uncle Newt. Papa died of heart failure in 1940 when Newt was eight years old.

I stopped talking when I got to Papa's death. I didn't know what else to say or, more pertinently, what Dr. Gross wanted to hear. I couldn't understand what issues any of it was relevant to. Everything in the distant past was fairly straightforward and normal, not smooth and painless but, on the other hand, not strange stuff.

"Your father," Dr. Gross said, flipping back through his notes, "Thomas Carr Biddle, died in a car crash." He spoke, apparently trying to reenter as gently as possible the discussion that had terminated our session in the hospital. The question seemed simple enough. I couldn't even remember why it bothered me when he asked about it before.

"He crashed his car into a bridge abutment," I said. "He hit the abutment dead-on. He was drunk. He apparently only started drinking after the war."

"The war ended in 1945, so . . . ."

"Yeah, I was born in 1941 and he joined the army in 1942." Then I told him the stuff my mother had told me. "He went to officer training camp at Fort Benning and then to Europe as part of the First Army. He was wounded in the Battle of Hürtgen Forest in 1944 and then spent almost a year in military hospitals. He came back to Bigbee in 1945. I don't remember him very well. Newt says he and Uncle Nat fought a lot, and he stopped shaving and bathing and looked and acted like Bigfoot on a moonshine binge. He says my father wandered the woods along the banks of the Tombigbee, acting like he was looking for something he'd lost. I don't remember much about him. That's about all I know."

"And your mother?"

"She's still alive," I said inanely. "Of course, you know that."

"Yes. She's been helpful in providing background information. Tell me about her. How did your parents meet?"

"I don't know. They met in Charlottesville when my father was at the university. My mother was already out of college working as a tutor in French and English literature. She's younger than my father was but she skipped some grades. She went to Wellesley College in

Massachusetts. I think they married in Charlottesville right after my father graduated. Her last name was Kittridge. I'm named after her."

"Okay, now, let's defer talking about your Uncle Nathaniel. Tell me about your Uncle Newton. He was almost a member of your household, I understand."

"Yeah, we were one big unhappy family." My half-witticism had no apparent effect on him. "My mother acted as his substitute mother, 'in loco parentis,' as Newt says, 'with the emphasis on loco.' Technically he lived across the road from us, but he stayed with us a lot of the time. Until his death, Papa was Newt's main tutor, and then Uncle Nat and my mother became his tutors. They tutored us all, me, Newt, even Nathan. Of course, Nathan wasn't exactly a student. And Newt wasn't exactly a tutor, but he's probably the smartest, so he taught a lot without trying. By the time I was four, he was twelve, and I thought he knew everything. He probably thought so too. My mother taught us English, French, history, and gardening—what she called 'applied botany,' but it was really just gardening. Uncle Nat was supposed to teach Latin, mathematics, science, and theology."

"Why do you say 'supposed'? Was he not a good teacher?"

"It wasn't that. It's just that he was sort of inflexible and stern. Or maybe I should say mechanical and humorless. I can't tell you the stuff he had me memorize. Newt saved me from some of it. He told me why I memorized the stuff. He explained what it meant. He could make it more like play than work. I memorized the stuff Uncle Nat gave me, but Newt made it real. He talked about why, not just what. I don't know how but he knows all kinds of stuff. I memorized mathematics formulas but Newt understands math. Quantitative relationships are real in his mind. I worked at grasping and then applying concepts, but he just reads math books. It isn't just math though. He knows language too. Why an iamb plods and an anapest dances."

"Okay," Dr. Gross said dismissively. I had the feeling he thought I was exaggerating about Newt. I wasn't.

"You need to meet Newt. He's read everything and somehow it stays in his head. He used to wake us up in the morning with lines from the *Rubáiyát*: 'Wake! For the sun, who scattered into flight/The stars before him from the field of night/. . . strikes/The Sultan's turret with a shaft of light.' He went to Harvard College for a couple of years, but he didn't go back after Nathan's death. He just locked himself up in the house. Now he just reads books and drinks beer. Maybe he ought to be here instead of me. Uncle Nat's craziness affected everybody."

"Your Uncle Nat had a mental breakdown." I couldn't tell whether he was making a statement or asking a question.

"He went crazy," I said.

"And Nathan's mother?"

"She's dead," I said. "She died when I was nine."

"What did she die of?"

"Uncle Nat says she died of a broken heart. Actually, she had breast cancer. She was a lady named Hannah that Uncle Nat met because she was the daughter of Papa's nurse. She and her mother lived with the family in Bigbee until Papa's death. I never met her, but in her pictures she looks like a movie star. Long blonde hair and beautiful face. She was from Mississippi, a little podunk town a lot like Bigbee. When Uncle Nat joined the army, she went back to Mississippi. She left Nathan and everybody else. My mother says that after the war Uncle Nat went to Mississippi to get her but it didn't work. She wouldn't come back."

"You and your cousin Nathan were born on the same day, I understand."

"Yeah. He may have been premature. He had a lot of problems. Uncle Nat and Hannah were married six or seven months when Nathan was born. Newt says they were married right after Papa's death, in December 1940. Hannah was only eighteen years old when they married. Nathan was born in July 1941, so the math doesn't work very well."

"I see," Dr. Gross said noncommittally. "Did your Uncle Nat also have post-traumatic stress from the war?"

"He had something. He always seemed detached and rigid. I don't know how he was before the war, but he stopped farming after the war, I know that. He spent a lot of time on sermons, particularly sermons about sin. He talked about the nature of sin and the causes of sin and the consequences of sin, over and over."

"He took over the church after your grandfather died?"

"Yeah, he tutored and preached. And his sermons got longer and longer. Some people grumbled but he just got more and more intense. He preached to us a lot too."

"Do you know whether anyone in your family suspected that your Uncle Nat was unstable?"

"I didn't. Newt said once that Uncle Nat was a half bubble off plumb. He put it in one of his limericks. Newt writes limericks, particularly to make fun of people or dumb ideas. The Uncle Nat limerick goes like this:

> *There was once an old preacher named Glum*
> *Who was thought to be grumpy and dumb,*
> *But the church members knew*
> *Why his pews were askew:*
> *He was just a half bubble off plumb.*

Newt was angry with Uncle Nat at the time. I thought Uncle Nat was a little strange talking over and over about obedience to God, but I didn't think he was crazy. I thought he was stern but a very kind person who was just religious. He'd say things like you have to be obedient to God, even if what you did was absurd in the eyes of society."

"What happened after the murder?"

"What you'd expect. Everything went crazy. We had the sheriff and deputies and newspaper people and gapers riding by in cars. The newspapers called it the 'Isaac

Sacrifice' and then everybody started calling it that. We left Bigbee after a few weeks. My mother found a house, the house we now live in, and we moved away. We agreed we weren't going to talk about it to anybody. We tried to be anonymous and, for the most part, people didn't mention it even if they knew about it. Then I started getting what my mother calls 'random animadversions' after I started going to Bridgewater."

"When did you enter Bridgewater?"

"Three years ago. My mother went back to teaching to support us, and I got free tuition. When we first moved to the city, my mother was my main tutor. Dr. Ball taught me math and science but she taught everything else."

"Okay," he said but I'm not sure he was listening. He was looking intently at pages he'd flipped forward in my file.

"Dr. Ball's son is one of my friends, but he's in the marines now because his family got all messed up." I didn't say anything for a while. When he finally looked up, I said, "His nickname is Q. Ball."

"I'm sorry," Dr. Gross said, "whose name is cue ball?" As I had suspected, he had not been listening. He had, as Newt says, left the main road.

"I said Dr. Ball's son is a friend of mine. His name is Ronald Q. Ball so we call him Q. Ball, sort of a pun on his name."

"I see," he said.

"We were doing okay but my mother says we ran out

of money. She started selling the land at Bigbee and that's how we lived for a while. She still owns the country house and about four hundred acres, but that's all that's left."

"So, you would have been in what grade when you started at Bridgewater?"

"The tenth. I already knew most of the stuff in my classes, so I probably should have entered a higher grade, but I guess it worked out okay. I had trouble adjusting when I started because I was nervous and I wasn't used to the way they did things."

"Did you have depression problems?"

"I probably thought too much about death. But mostly I just didn't want to be around people, and I felt uncomfortable with all the herding and schedules and the bells going off and all those people talking all the time."

"Okay," he said and hunched over and scribbled some notes on his clipboard. I had begun to sweat, and the room felt stuffy and humid. He didn't say anything for a while. "We've not talked about your mother's family," he said finally.

"She hardly has any except me and in-laws. She has a couple of uncles, one in Richmond and one somewhere in Montana. She's an only child and her parents are dead. They were killed in a flash flood the same year my father died. I wasn't even five years old and I went to two funerals within a few months of each other. They lived in Virginia. We visited from time to time, but the truth is I hardly remember anything about them. They were both schoolteachers, I know that."

"Okay," he said, again hunched over his clipboard, and making those postnasal guttural noises. He scribbled for a while and then looked up and said quietly, "That's all we're going to do today. We'll take it up again next week and keep going."

"Are we going to keep talking about my family?"

"Yes, as well as other relationships important to you."

"Like what?"

"Any relationship that's important to you. Your mother mentioned that you had a difficult experience with a girlfriend. We might want to talk about that."

"You mean my former girlfriend."

"Yes, the girl you went with for a year or so."

"Eleven months. I only went with her off and on for eleven months."

"I was given the impression she meant a lot to you."

"For a while, yes, but I'm over her," I lied. I tried not to show any emotion. "I have a new girlfriend now. I've got a lot of stuff going on but I'm okay. I worry more about the willy-nilly verses."

"The what?"

"The willy-nilly verses from the *Rubáiyát*. They've bothered me for a long time because I can't figure anything out. I don't know who I am, and I feel like . . . ." I paused because I didn't know how to explain it. Then I said, "There was this heron at the beach one summer." I looked at Dr. Gross before I said anything else. I didn't want him to think I was crazy or obsessing about something strange. "This heron was standing on one leg at the edge of the floodlight looking wary and puzzled. That's what I feel like most of the time." I wanted to seem normal and I didn't want Dr. Gross to think I was obsessing about really insignificant stuff. When you don't know what's significant, it's sort of hard.

He glanced at his watch and said, "I see. Well, okay, we can address those things too. I'll see you next week, then?"

"Yeah, I guess. I hope we do more next time."

"We did quite a lot today. It's background but it's the fabric of your life. Very important. We've done very well." He smiled for the first time since his Lazarus joke. "This is not a race," he said, continuing to smile. I don't know why, but I was actually pleased that he thought we had done well. I felt strangely exultant, as though I had inadvertently accomplished something. We had seemed to be meandering aimlessly in the family graveyard. I wasn't sure exactly where we had arrived, but it felt more like penumbra and less like darkness. I had no sense of clarity, but I could see flickering, like flecks of sunlight, in my mind. I felt almost like swaggering. As it was, I gathered my crutches from behind my chair and hobbled out the door.

NATHAN

The first time I visited Dr. Gross' office I felt like a person going to jail. The next session was more like going to the dentist. The reception area was familiar, and the routine was essentially the same. I sat in the waiting room for a while, flipping the pages of old magazines without reading anything in them, thinking with a mild degree of apprehension about what Dr. Gross might want to talk about, until the receptionist told me to go down the hall to his office. Then I sat in the same chair as before, fidgeting while Dr. Gross thumbed through his notes making his allergy noises and looking grave and doctoral. I noticed for the first time that the room was painted a pale blue and that the fluorescent lamp closest to the window was humming. The air conditioner wasn't running but everything else was just as I had observed the week before. After I sat waiting for what seemed like five minutes or more, Dr. Gross looked up at me, smiled slightly, and said, "Good afternoon. How are you today?"

"I'm okay," I said. "I'm getting pretty good on the crutches. I could probably win a race."

"When you are ready," he said, ignoring my joke, "we need to talk about your cousin Nathaniel. I don't want to talk about difficult relationships before you're ready, but . . . ."

"I'm okay. I'm ready. What do you want to know?"

"Start with your earliest recollections."

"He was always there so that's all the way back. He was like me and yet different. We looked a lot alike, but he wasn't normal. We were born on the same day in the same hospital, but something went wrong, terribly wrong, and he couldn't be normal."

"He lived across the road from you?"

"Yes, we lived in a sort of isolated area, on the outskirts of Bigbee. Are you familiar with Bigbee?"

"I'm aware of its existence," he said, "but I've never been there."

"I wouldn't think so. It's a farming and logging community. Bigbee is the outskirts, so it doesn't make any sense to say something is on its outskirts. Nathan was my only playmate much of the time. We were also sort of fellow students except that he couldn't really be a student. He wasn't normal. My mother and Uncle Nat taught us, but Nathan wouldn't really participate. They mostly worked on what they called his verbal skills. At first, I was the only real participant because Nathan wouldn't respond. He hardly said a word until he was five or six years old."

"How did you feel about that disparity?"

"I didn't think much about it."

"The fact that you were able to read and he wasn't, that didn't affect you?"

"He may have been able to read before I was. He just wouldn't communicate it. We had this big fat tome titled *Webster's New Twentieth Century Dictionary of the English Language*. Nathan started going through it before he was three years old. He may have been just looking at lines of type at first, but he kept getting more and more of it in his head. When he was five, you could give him a definition and he would turn to the word in the dictionary. He might not say anything, but if you looked, you'd see he had turned to the right page and was pointing to the word. By the time he started talking, he'd gone through the whole thing, and by the time he started memorizing poetry, he may have known every word in the dictionary and the page number where the word appeared."

"How did they test his knowledge? How did you know what he knew?"

"Trust me, he knew it. The question is how he knew it. He didn't seem to be paying attention most of the time. He wouldn't answer you if you asked him for a definition, but if you gave him a definition, he'd go right to the word in the dictionary. And if there were synonyms, he'd do them consecutively in order of their appearance in the dictionary. He knew words that nobody uses, what Newt calls Thomas Hardy words. Really unusual words. Foreign words. He knew everything in the dictionary and the appendix. Of course, sometimes he was gone, somewhere in his mind, and you couldn't find or follow him. And if he was gone, he'd just ignore you. But if he wasn't gone, he liked the word games. Everybody liked the word games. People who visited us wanted to play, and they were always amazed. I was amazed. It was fun, and it was amazing."

"When did he begin to read other books, the books you were reading?"

"Never. He just read his dictionary. That was where he started and ended. He loved his dictionary, and he didn't seem to need anything else."

"Did you have a dictionary for your use, or did you share Nathan's dictionary?"

"Nobody shared Nathan's dictionary. I had a small paperback dictionary, which was all I needed. Nathan would get upset if you tried to take his dictionary. It sat in the center of his desk and he'd sit there like a worshipper at a shrine and rock back and forth staring at it intently and occasionally turning a page. He was probably five or six years old before he could carry the fat tome, but he wouldn't leave it. If Uncle Nat wanted him to eat at the table with the rest of us, he'd have to haul the Webster's out and prop it up near Nathan's plate. Nathan would eat and turn pages and ignore the conversation at the table. His dictionary had a lot of food smudges on it."

"He began to talk at what age?"

"He would say words before he would actually talk.

He didn't like conversation very much. He finally started memorizing poetry when he was about nine, at least that's about when he began reciting. By the time Nathan began responding, I had memorized and proudly recited parts of long narrative poems, a large number of shorter poems, and a bunch of nursery rhymes and jingles. I was racking up little gold stars—I got ten stars for memorizing 'The Raven' alone—and Nathan was racking up nothing. He'd sort of listen to me sometimes. Mostly he'd just sit there with his dictionary ignoring us. I remember my mother telling Uncle Nat that she thought Nathan was on the verge of responding. I didn't see anything responsive, but she turned out to be right.

"At first, he wouldn't look up from his dictionary. He'd just repeat a rhyme you read to him. He didn't care a lick about the gold stars, but after he got the hang of it he repeated and rhymed everything. It's funny, but he didn't like music—he'd sometimes cover his ears—but he loved the sound of words. He'd rhyme a series of words and repeat them over and over with the emphasis at different syllables and at different pitches."

"His name was Nathaniel Tyler Biddle," Dr. Gross said, flipping a page in his notes.

"Nathaniel Tyler Biddle, the third," I corrected. "He was named after my grandfather and Uncle Nat, who were the first and second. I don't know who started calling him Nathan, but that's what everybody called him except Uncle Nat, who always called him Nathaniel."

"Nathan was diagnosed as autistic, which is consistent with everything you've said."

"That's what they said later. At first, they said he was just slow. Let me tell you, he wasn't slow. He had problems, but he wasn't slow. He also had epilepsy. He had seizures."

"Were they petit mal or grand mal seizures? Do you know the terminology?"

"They were bad. He'd fall on the floor, gritting his teeth and rolling his eyes back in his head, with every muscle tensed. He didn't have them often. When he did, it was intense."

"In an environment of relatively high intellectual achievement, he must have presented interpersonal challenges."

"We didn't talk about it because that was just the way things were. Other people probably talked about him. I think most people understood and tried to be polite, but I heard some dimwits call him things, like 'disturbed,' 'deranged,' and sometimes worse. He was definitely different but he wasn't crazy. You couldn't talk to him very well because he wouldn't converse. If you read something to him or said something in his presence, he had it forever. He could repeat long passages of prose and pages of poetry. Then when he was about ten years old he started the responsive rhyming."

"Responsive rhyming?"

"Yeah, you'd need to witness it. If you said something that caught in his mind, he'd come out with a word that rhymed with what you said. If somebody said something like, 'Tell the truth,' Nathan might say 'snaggletooth' or 'shell of youth' or some nonsense rhyme like that. Sometimes he'd just ignore you, but if you said something excitedly or with emphasis, he almost always gave you a rhyme, sometimes the most strange and exotic stuff. He knew words nobody else could remember."

"Did Nathan have a nanny or someone to look after him?"

"Just my mother and Uncle Nat, and, of course, Newt. When we were small, he was easy to take care of. Mostly he just wanted to sit with his dictionary. When we went outside, he would stay right with me and usually do what I told him to do. We played like other kids, I guess. Later, he became more difficult because he wouldn't always listen to me and he started wandering off if somebody didn't watch him. That's when Uncle Nat came up with the harness."

"What kind of harness?"

"It was almost like a straitjacket but with the arms free. Uncle Nat strung a cable from a live oak at the top of the hill behind his house to a massive old oak in the front yard, and he would tether Nathan to the cable. The tether was attached to the back of the harness and the other end was fastened to a steel ring on the cable. Nathan could run back and forth beside the house and the ring would slide along the cable. He'd run and run. He did a kind of shuffle-run with jerks against the cable when he got to the end of the tether. They said it was necessary, but

I didn't like it. It was strange watching him. It was like he was a dog, but Wulfie, my dog, wasn't tethered at all. They'd run along together. Nathan would run and chant strange stuff and Wulfie would run along with him, barking and howling."

"What did he chant?"

"Strange stuff. Some of the stuff he did over and over, and some of it didn't seem to get repeated. We knew some of the chants because he kept repeating them, like the Poccotola train chant."

"The what?"

"I knew that would throw you. We don't know what it means either, except that Poccotola is a little town in Mississippi that nobody ever mentioned around Nathan because his mother lived there. She had been gone since Nathan was a baby, so the chant probably had nothing to do with her. But it was strange for him to chant about it."

"What was the chant? Did you hear it enough to repeat it?"

"Sure, we all knew it. 'Poccotola train broke down,' repeated over and over until he seemed to be satisfied with it and then he'd stop and say, 'Ipse dixit gotta fix it' and smile and raise his head, as though looking for something in the sky or on the ceiling."

"And nobody knew what it meant?"

"We didn't know whether it was supposed to mean something. Some of his stuff seemed to be gibberish. I thought they were just words he liked. He didn't know anything about trains breaking down. One time the locomotive on the GM&O passenger train broke down but I don't think Nathan even knew it. The train doesn't even stop in Poccotola. The closest it gets is Tontopoc or Oxford. So there really isn't a Poccotola train. Not really."

"I don't suppose anybody ever asked him what he meant."

"I did. I didn't expect an answer but I asked him. He ignored me until I repeated the question a few times. Then he just gave me one of his responsive rhymes, something that sounded like 'block a toll of pain' and started rocking back and forth and repeating it over and over. I just dropped it because it really didn't matter anyway."

"Nathan's date of death, according to my notes, was . . . ."

"June 30, 1953," I said. "That was a terrible day."

"Do you feel like discussing it?"

"It's like a shroud on my life, and I can't get out from under it." I felt pressure in my face and my eyes got blurry. I didn't want to start crying, so I sat for a moment looking toward the back of the office like I was interested in the air conditioner. Dr. Gross said nothing. When I looked back at him, he was making a note in his file. "Nathan would have been twelve the next month," I said, my voice shaky and weak.

"If this is too difficult, we can talk about it some other time. Why don't we switch gears and . . . ."

"No, I want to tell you about it. Hang on a second.

I'm trying to think how to tell you." My eyes watered again and I looked toward the air conditioner again. "Just give me a minute."

"All right," he said. "When you're ready." I really don't know what I told Dr. Gross but I tried to tell him the truth about what happened. It was a Tuesday morning on June 30, 1953. I don't know why I remember the day of the week but I do. Uncle Nat had given me some math problems to do. It was a timed test. We had been working on Trachtenberg for almost a year and I had gotten pretty good at doing computations in my head with the algorithms. Uncle Nat gave me a hundred twenty problems in ascending difficulty, and I was supposed to write down all the answers in one hour, an average of thirty seconds for each problem. I did them all in forty-five minutes. I was very proud, and I decided to walk over and show Uncle Nat my solutions. I felt as though I had entered a contest and won really big. I had a sense of jubilation, and I knew Uncle Nat was going to be impressed.

It was a late spring morning without a cloud in the sky. The temperature had not reached 80 and a gentle breeze stirred in the trees. I remember smiling as I stood on our porch looking across the road where I would present my triumph and receive my well-earned praise. When I got to the road, I saw Nathan at the top of the hill beside Uncle Nat's house. He was hanging limply from his cable, and I thought he'd been left outside too long and had fallen asleep standing up. I thought he was just hanging there in his harness. When I was halfway up the hill I knew something wasn't right. Nathan was wearing shorts and a tee shirt and he was barefooted. His feet were just barely touching the ground. The tether was wrapped around his neck, and his head was slumped over at a peculiar angle. His left foot was just brushing the top of an anthill, and his foot and leg were covered with ants. There seemed to be hundreds of them hunched over chewing on him.

Uncle Nat was sitting at the base of the oak that the cable was fastened to, and Wulfie was curled up beside him whimpering. I threw my math solution sheets on the ground and ran over and grabbed Nathan around the midriff and unhooked the tether. I dragged him away from the anthill and began to rub the ants off him. I screamed, "Help me," but Uncle Nat sat there. I said, "The ants are all over him."

"We are all like ants," Uncle Nat said, "crawling around in the darkness."

"What in God's name?" I shouted.

"I got it all wrong," Uncle Nat said calmly. "The Lord . . . . I knew the lie. I knew there was no basis for a ram in the thicket. I'm sorry, I know you don't under-stand. I have failed the truth."

"What are you talking about?" I shouted at him. "What have you done?"

"God told me what to do. He told me what to do, but . . . oh, my God, our lives are so confused. I intended to obey, but the terrible web of deception. I don't know how . . . ." Then I heard him say "Nathaniel" like he was talking to Nathan. That was scary. He didn't get up. He just sat there looking crazy. He was holding a bundle of moss, some that the wind had blown out of the oak, and he held it up as though offering it to me. "I was in the vine, but somehow I became separated by lies and treachery. I am left to draw life from thin air." He looked up from the ground. "Did you know that Spanish moss is also an epiphyte? It has no roots, no channel of life. It draws its meager existence from the atmosphere, from the dust and moisture in its surroundings." I backed away from him and started to run. I didn't know whether to be afraid but I wasn't taking any chances. I looked back over my shoulder a couple of times to be sure he wasn't after me. Even if he had been, I knew Uncle Nat couldn't catch me. The one thing I used to be able to do well was run. Nobody could have outrun me that day.

When the sheriff got there, Uncle Nat told him what he'd done and why he had done it. The sheriff refused to believe him. "Somebody's gotta convince me Brother Nathaniel did such a thing." It took about an hour of questions and answers, but I guess Uncle Nat finally convinced him. The sheriff took Uncle Nat in his patrol car and the rescue squad loaded Nathan's body into an ambulance. Everything was upside down. I couldn't make any sense of it. Everybody cried but Newt. He locked himself in Uncle Nat's house and wouldn't come out and wouldn't let anybody in except the sheriff. He wouldn't even go to the funeral. I probably shouldn't have gone either. I didn't do well.

The only people at the funeral were the church's officers, my mother and I, Uncle Nat, and the sheriff and a deputy. A minister from Haltom preached the funeral service. He was well meaning but almost as strange as Uncle Nat. He said Nathan was "one of the least of these" and, as such, much beloved of God. He kept talking about Mount Moriah and how we all have to make the journey. "We all stand before God with fear and trembling," he said. "We all must work out our salvation, and we all must have a Moriah moment." I thought he was nuts too. Uncle Nat had started calling that little hill behind his house Mount Moriah a few months before the murder. It was part of the delusion, and the crazy preacher at the funeral just kept it going like it made sense.

I know a funeral is supposed to help with closure. Maybe it did. I don't know. My mother cried the whole time. Uncle Nat sat there like a statue. Everybody handled it pretty well except me. The coffin was in the chancel where the communion table usually sat, and the strangest thing happened: I started thinking I was in the coffin. The mortician had put makeup on Nathan's face and pushed his long blond hair back with a neat part down the middle. They had arranged him so that his smudged and frayed volume of *Webster's Dictionary* was cradled in his right arm like he was holding a baby. By the time the preacher concluded his sermon, the face in the coffin was mine. When the ushers came forward to close the coffin lid, I came off the pew howling.

One of the ushers grabbed me, and everything got quiet. Then another usher started to close the coffin lid, and I went berserk again. I shoved the usher over the first pew and he landed on one of the elders in the second row. When one of the other ushers tried to close the coffin lid, I grabbed it and held it open. I was staring at Nathan's face when the sheriff's deputy reached for me. I don't know what I did but he ended up on the floor in the aisle. Then I heard my mother's voice like a siren in a fog, and I stopped. "Kit," she said, and I looked up at her. Then I looked at the coffin, and I understood the chaos I had caused. "It's time to go. The funeral's over." I looked at my mother and then at Nathan's face and I began to cry. I knew I wasn't in the coffin. My mother took my arm and led me out the side door of the church. It was raining. We stood in the rain crying with our arms around each other.

When I finished my story, Dr. Gross said, "I know that was difficult, but you handled it well." I was looking at the floor, my head in my hands. He reached over and patted my shoulder and said, "Perhaps we should stop for the day. The time's almost up anyway."

"I wanted to tell you this stuff."

"I know. You've been holding it for long enough. When we grieve, we need to confront the loss and accept the new reality, not just the fact of death but also the circumstances in which death occurred. Have you visited Nathan's grave?"

"My mother and I have been there a lot. My father's grave is right next to Nathan's, so we have two reasons for visiting. My mother put Nathan's chant on his headstone."

"The train chant?"

"Yeah, the headstone has his name, Nathaniel Tyler Biddle III, then the dates of his birth and death, and then 'Poccotola Train Broke Down, Ipse Dixit Gotta Fix It.'"

"That's interesting. Do you suppose your mother ascribes some meaning to the chant?"

"I doubt it. If she does, she's never said anything. She probably just wanted to put something on his headstone that came from Nathan. Maybe it sums up his strange life. His death wasn't really any more tragic than his life. He was all alone, sort of in a bubble of words. You know, at first, I could communicate with him. He knew exactly what I was saying. Later on, he withdrew. He would ignore me and everybody else. We looked like twins almost. We were about the same size, had the same eyes and hair. He was just more abstracted and absent. The stuff we memorized didn't seem to have any effect on him. The willy-nilly lyrics didn't bother him a bit. He didn't seem to wonder where he'd come from or where he was going. Maybe he knew but couldn't tell me."

"Your Uncle Nat, I understand, is incarcerated for the murder of Nathan."

"He's in the loony bin. He's in the wing for the criminally insane at Bryce Hospital."

"Have you visited him, attempted to make your peace with him?"

"My mother and I visited him a few months after he was incarcerated but I haven't gone back because the visit was a disaster. It started off well enough, with Uncle Nat greeting us as though he were at a revival meeting. He began to bubble over about the new ministry that God had opened up for him. He compared himself to the apostle Paul. When he started talking about Nathan, I couldn't take it anymore."

"What did he say?"

"He said, 'That dear boy. Oh, God, that dear boy,' like he was talking about somebody else's son, like Nathan had been struck by lightning or something. Then he said, 'I was called to be an alien and a stranger in the world and, though I'm faulted, I have earnestly striven to glorify God. I've tried to be an obedient servant even if the demands were preposterous, even if I failed the test of faith, even if I failed terribly.'

"I couldn't sit there any longer. I shouted at him: 'What test did you fail? You killed Nathan, for God's sake. I think you are a damned alien.' My mother grabbed my arm and said, 'Kit, I think it best . . . ,' but I cut her off. I said, 'I want to know how in God's name this happened.' Uncle Nat looked surprised that anyone would even ask such a question.

"He said, 'Nathaniel,' like he was talking to Nathan. 'You are spiritually immature.' He shook his head like he was talking to a small recalcitrant child, 'and you have an inadequate grasp of . . . .' I shouted at him, 'How could you kill Nathan?' My mother then jumped up and started shoving me toward the door. Uncle Nat was still talking as I left.

"He said, 'These events are more problematic than you may suppose. The truth is elusive. I have tried to obey God, who works in me to will and to act according to his good purpose. I have tried to stand in an absolute relation to God . . . .' As he babbled, my mother pushed me out the door and I heard him say, 'Nathaniel' again."

"And how did you feel about that encounter?"

"Like I'd talked to a psychopath who had no idea what he'd done. Uncle Nat had always been stern but he was, underneath an inflexible surface, a kind and considerate person. Even in discipline, I knew that he wanted to guide me, to tell me the truth. He never even spanked me or any of us. In our studies, he had a set and unalterable approach, but he was always concerned and involved. He was responsive and available. When he made a commitment to you, you could count on him. I can't remember my father very well, so Uncle Nat was the closest thing to a father I knew. To tell you the truth, my image of God was always Uncle Nat, a distinguished, kindly person who always stood for truth and good."

"Did anything good come of the visit?"

"If it did, I don't know what it was. It got worse and worse. My mother stayed with Uncle Nat for a while and I went to the reception area. The receptionist asked me if she could help me, and I told her I was waiting for my mother. She was acting sort of goofy so I went outside to wait. I was out there maybe ten minutes when a security guard came up acting like I was an inmate trying to escape. I went back inside, and he stayed with me until the receptionist told him I wasn't a patient. 'He's waitin' for his momma,' she said. I started pacing back and forth in the waiting area, which seemed to get on the nerves of the receptionist.

"She asked if she could get me something, and we were about to get into it when my mother came down the hall looking disconcerted. 'I should not have brought you here, Kit,' she said. 'This was a mistake.' By then, I had lumped the asylum personnel and the inmates into the same pile. 'He's a psychopath,' I said, and then loud enough for the receptionist to hear, I added, 'Everybody here is nuts.' We never went back. At least, I never went back. My mother may have, but if she did, she didn't mention it to me."

DULCINEA

I hadn't noticed the painting above the couch opposite my chair in Dr. Gross' office. I was in the familiar start-up mode for the session: I fidgeted while he thumbed through my folder making his strange guttural sounds. The picture on the opposite wall depicts five dogs of different breeds frolicking in a beautiful field of grass and flowers like children playing follow-the-leader. The day my mother and I left Bigbee, I saw dogs in a similar random line. We were on our way to the city in a car driven by one of the elders of the church, and right behind us was the moving van carrying our stuff. As we were driving down the highway, we passed the dogs meandering along the right side of the road. It appeared to me that a female was in heat and that a pack of about five male dogs was following her, with a big chocolate lab closest behind her.

When our car passed the dogs, I turned around on the seat to watch them. They had been running along more or less parallel to the road, but just after we passed, the female abruptly turned and started across the highway. The trailing males turned as if drawn by a lodestone and followed like nothing else existed in the world. The bitch made it across the road unscathed, but the big lab leading the pack ran right in front of the moving van. The van's right front wheel went over the lab's head and the back tires bounced over his body. When I turned back around in the seat to face forward, I saw that my mother had also watched the lab get crushed by the truck. "The van hit that dog," I said. My mother just turned around in the front seat. "That was terrible," she said. "It happens more often than it should." I looked back again and I could see the dark blob in the bend of the road.

"I know you've said your former girlfriend, Anna, is past history," Dr. Gross said, mispronouncing her name, "but tell me about her anyway." The room suddenly felt sticky, and I wanted to ask him whether the air conditioner was broken. The fluorescent lights buzzed like a chain saw, and a car horn blared somewhere near the building. Even more strange, my eyes began to burn.

"Have you been talking to my mother?"

"Of course, I have. She is your mother, and she is vitally interested in your well-being. However, anything you say is confidential. I would never repeat anything you tell me or violate the confidentiality of these sessions. My conversations with your mother are decidedly one-sided. She opines that the onset of your present emotional state coincided with your breakup with Anna. I think it appropriate that we explore the nature of your response to that personal interaction."

"She's wrong," I said and then sat in silence for a moment. This is going to sound strange, but I wanted Dr. Gross to think I was reluctant to talk about Anna. The truth is I wanted to talk about Anna more than anything else. Of course, I only wanted to talk about the things I could talk about. Some things I would never tell him or anyone else. If I told him everything, he might really think I was nuts. It's probably goofy to worry about whether a shrink thinks you're crazy, but I did. I wanted him to see me as a stable, normal person, even if I didn't really feel totally sane. There were problems with talking about Anna. A lot of what I think about her now isn't what I thought at first. I had been enchanted, even enraptured, but I didn't think she wasn't real. I didn't think she was a phantasm. I didn't think she was a product of my own obsessive mind. She had shown up in my life when I was already having trouble distinguishing the real from the imaginary.

Lichtman and I had talked about Platonic forms and people who didn't seem to be real, people like Michelangelo and Newton and Shakespeare. We talked about whether they might be evolutionary forecasts of what humanity would ultimately become. We talked about whether they might not be human at all, but actually sort of nephilim who were here to show us things ordinary people couldn't, to provide light in the darkness, to give us a sense of the feasible. It may sound strange that Anna would get mixed in with these broodings, but somehow she did: She became a kind of Platonic form, a melding of the sensible and the supernal. Did I tell Dr. Gross any of that stuff? No, I didn't. I also didn't mention the other stuff Lichtman and I had talked about that Dr. Gross might not regard as normal.

"Let's begin obliquely," Dr. Gross said after a pause. "Why don't you tell me what Anna looks like?"

"Sure," I said and took my wallet out of my back pocket, pulled out my only photograph of Anna, and handed it over to him. He looked a little surprised but he took it. The photo doesn't do her justice, but a photograph could never capture the essence of Anna. Her mother took the picture in front of their apartment not long after Anna and I started going together. Originally, I was also in the picture, but I cropped me out so the photo would fit in my wallet. The photograph shows Anna in shorts and a blouse with little epaulettes at the shoulders, barefooted, hip displaced to one side, almost laughing at the camera. From the photo, you can tell that she is a little over average height, perfectly proportioned, exquisite in form, and dramatic in pose.

You cannot tell from the photo that she has green eyes like her mother, but you can discern the dark complexion of her Italian father. From the photo, you might assume that Anna is indistinguishable from thousands of other pretty girls in the world, but you would be wrong. The essence of the form is obscured by the shroud of the lens. A photograph could never reveal the infinite glorious details that are Anna. It certainly couldn't reveal the scintillating intellect: I hardly ever saw her study, yet she exuded mathematics, music, physics, literally everything. How did she do that? The only thing I can say is that she is one of those people like Newt, for whom almost everything seems to be innate, like bees that know how to make perfectly symmetrical hexagons without ever being taught anything by anybody. How do they do that? I don't know. They don't have to learn it; they are epiphytes of data and principles the rest of us have to struggle to grasp.

I didn't try to tell Dr. Gross any of this stuff. I didn't even tell him how the teachers maneuvered around Anna cautiously, apparently trying to avoid being embarrassed in their own subjects. I learned to circle her too. Early on I learned not to argue with her about anything. If she said something I questioned, I just pretended to agree. I never brought up difficult subjects (like the death of Nathan or the willy-nilly verses) because I didn't want her to know how insecure and confused I am. If she commented that something I said was foolish, I would blush and my throat would get tight and I would want to kick myself for having said such an inane thing.

Sometimes I was perplexed and bemused when I later replayed the conversation in my mind. Without the aura of Anna, I often saw an obvious and disturbing incongruity, and occasionally something she said seemed completely ridiculous. From time to time, I would intend to revisit one of her apparently faulty premises, but I never did. Once in her presence, I could no longer see anything wrong with what she had said. The meaning seemed to change when viewed against the reference of the perfect form.

"She's very pretty," Dr. Gross said. "I understand she's also bright."

"She's one of those people like Newt. She's almost unreal."

"That's quite a compliment." I couldn't tell by his tone whether he believed me, and I started to elaborate, but I just let it go. "Did you meet her at school?"

"No, I met her delivering furniture to her parents' apartment. The first thing she ever called me was 'furniture man' and that remained my name forever, particularly when she was annoyed with me."

"You worked at a furniture store?"

"Yeah, my friend Eddie Lichtman got me a job in the summers at his father's company, Lichtman's Galleries. You know Lichtman's. Everybody does. I met Anna before my second year at Bridgewater. It was one of those days. Newt calls them climacteric days. You know, from astrology, crossroads in your life." I paused because I thought he might have some comment. I didn't know what he wanted me to talk about. He didn't say anything and he didn't do anything but sit there looking at me expectantly, so I told him about Anna. Not everything, of course, just how I got to know her. I really wanted to tell him and he seemed to want to hear it, so I told him as much as I could pull together in my mind.

I was the furniture man because I met her one day when Lichtman and I were delivering furniture. It was late in July, about five o'clock in the afternoon, and we were making the last delivery of the day to an address on Carapace Boulevard for a person named Dr. T. Feck Goolsby. The invoice indicated we were delivering a sofa, an end table, a coffee table, and a lamp, but when we got there the sofa wasn't on the truck. I told Lichtman that we should leave the stuff we had and then come back later with the sofa, but he said that wasn't store policy and that we had to deliver the sofa.

The plan we came up with was for him to go back to the warehouse for the sofa and for me to go ahead and deliver the pieces we had on the truck. So that's what we tried to do. We off-loaded the end table, the coffee table, and the lamp in the front yard of the house on Carapace, and Lichtman then drove the truck back to the warehouse. I went over and rang the doorbell to explain the situation to the people. An old lady came to the door after I'd rung the bell several times. She looked at me suspiciously and said, "Yes?" I held up the invoice and said, "I've got the furniture you ordered from Lichtman's. If you'll tell me where you want it, I'll bring it in for you." She looked at the invoice and said, "I'm sorry, young man, this isn't for me. It's for the Goolsbys in the apartment in the back. If you'll go down the alley, you'll see it."

I thanked her and walked back and picked up the lamp and carried it down the alley to the apartment. I didn't see anybody, so I left the lamp beside the stairs and returned for the coffee table. The last piece I hauled down the alley was the end table. I took it last because it weighed a ton and it was awkward to hold. It was solid oak and octagonal, with little doors in front. I decided to go ahead and take it up the stairs because I already had it in my arms, and it wasn't going to get any lighter on the ground.

I had to regrip the thing several times on the stairs because it was so heavy and unwieldy, and the stairs were so steep and narrow. Then, when I got to the top of the stairs, the landing wasn't large enough for me to put the table down, so I tried to open the door, which was unfortunately locked. Since I couldn't go forward and I couldn't very easily go back down the stairs, I partially rested the end table on the banister and kicked on the door. I had to kick several times before I heard someone walking toward the door.

Then she walked out onto the screened porch. My legs got weak. I'll be honest. I didn't think something like that could even exist. I used to wonder what it would be like to be Anna, to live in that body, all that incredible splendor all the time. How would you do that? She was wearing shorts and a tee shirt, and she was holding a book to her breast with her left hand. She had pushed her glasses up into the edge of her hair just above her forehead. I was expecting a Mrs. Goolsby, a name that suggested a woman who couldn't get a catcall on a construction site.

Instead, I was staring at a work of art, a definition of beauty, a living aesthetic standard beyond my imagination. She walked over to the screen door and looked at me without smiling or speaking. I was standing on the narrow landing clutching the leaden end table, afraid that any minute I was going to lose my grip. A bead of sweat had run down my forehead and into my right eye. My eye stung from the salt, my face must have been red from the strain, and my throat was constricted. I tried to speak but suffered a strange laryngeal paralysis.

"You must be the furniture man," she said coolly. If she had not been a goddess, I would have said something like, "No, I was just out for a walk and happened to climb these stairs carrying this ninety-pound end table." Instead, I stood there like the cigar-store Indian. She was so stunning I couldn't speak, much less whip out a witty zinger. I stood there gripping and regripping the end table, looking stupid and saying nothing at all. "Well," she said in a cultured, mellifluous alto, "he's sort of cute even if he's dumb as a stump." I tried to smile. "Must be a Norwegian mute who's copped a job in home furnishings. I would try sign language, but his hands are dutifully occupied."

"I've got your pieces from Lichtman's," I finally squeaked out. She then reached up and unlocked the door.

"Well, okay," she said, "he speaks. He's vocal if not voluble. We're making progress and at *chez* Goolsby, like other beacons of cultural leadership, progress is our most important product." She was being sarcastic, but she was smiling angelically. "Let me show you where to place those treasures." I followed her into the apartment, face glowing red and arms I could no longer feel. Once inside, she stood with her index finger pressed against her lips, looking first at one side of the apartment and then at the other.

Every furniture surface in the room was covered with books and most floor surfaces were covered with opened and unopened boxes. Meanwhile, I was still holding the end table and certain that my arms were going to fall off. "I think it goes over here," she said finally. "If it doesn't, the ghoul can move it." At the time, I didn't know what she meant by "the ghoul," but I can tell you I was happy to put the table anywhere. After depositing the end table, I stood for a few seconds rubbing the circulation back into my arms. I tried to think of something interesting to say but I couldn't, so I went down and successively brought up the coffee table and the lamp.

"We somehow left the sofa," I strained out with great effort. "It wasn't on the truck. He'll be back in just a couple of minutes with the sofa."

She was looking at me with an amused expression, her head tilted to one side and her long dark hair hanging straight down beside her face. "Would you like some tea?" she said sweetly. "I was about to have some. You look hot." In ordinary circumstances, you'd think I'd jump at the chance to have tea or anything else with her, but I could hardly breathe.

"No, thanks." My voice was peculiarly husky because my throat was constricted. "I'm all right." I wanted to say something interesting, but I couldn't think of anything so I walked out onto the porch. I was stalling, hoping something good would come into my mind. Since I was waiting for the truck to come back, I figured it wouldn't seem too awkward if I stood on the screened porch while I waited. The idea was that if I stood there long enough something would eventually occur to me. As I had hoped, she followed me out onto the porch. She was pulling her hair back in a ponytail as she came through the door, an action that thrust her boobs out and revealed her long delicate neck. My brain was paralyzed. When I say that I couldn't think of anything to say, I don't mean that I couldn't think of anything brilliant to say; I mean that I couldn't think of anything at all.

"I am Anna," she said, pronouncing her name "ah'nah," and she extended her hand toward me. She has beautiful hands, straight, tapered fingers and perfect nails. I took her small hand and gave it a gentle squeeze. She smiled at me. The apotheosis probably occurred at that moment if it had not already occurred. I was too flustered to do much, but I was about to introduce myself when a man appeared at the top of the stairs and opened the screen door. He was dressed spiffily in a navy blazer and a little narrow bow tie. I recognized him even before he rolled his shoulder and wobbled his head. I thought, *Oh, Lord, it's the goofy golfer,* and I began a desperate search of my mind for a way to dissemble or become a different person.

At first, he didn't recognize me because he was ignoring me. He said in a tone of exasperation, "Anna, you know you're not allowed to have company in the apartment when your mother and I are not present. I'm stunned at the alacrity with which you attract . . . ." He didn't finish what he was saying. He had turned toward me and was staring at me like I was a cockroach that had crawled out of his cereal box.

"Father figure," she said in a tone that was very close to his, "this is the furniture man." Then with an elegant sweep of her arm, sort of like a ballet dancer, she turned to me and said, "Furniture man, this is my stepfather, the estimable Dr. Defect Goolsby." I had by then remembered the name "Goolsby" from the golf course encounter. I picked up the "Defect" and the implication that they didn't get along very well. I can tell you I was pleased to perceive the antagonism. I was also relieved to hear the word "stepfather," not only from my own vantage point but also from the standpoint of genetics: If Dr. Goolsby had been Anna's biological father, new laws would have to be formulated in the science of genetics.

"Young lady," he said, "you are again pushing the envelope."

Since I recognized Dr. Goolsby, I assumed that he recognized me. I was waiting for the explosion, not knowing what to do. I couldn't think of anything else, so I stepped forward with my hand out and said, "My name is Kit Biddle. I work for Lichtman's Furniture Gallery." He looked at me tentatively and skeptically, and I could tell that he was debating whether to continue the diatribe he had started while standing soaking wet beside Catawpa Creek a few weeks earlier. But he didn't. After a slight pause, he shook my hand and immediately took a handkerchief from his coat pocket and wiped his hand as though he had handled a turd. He continued to look at me balefully, probably trying to decide whether and/ or how to deal with this irritant that had somehow reappeared in his life. Ultimately, he did nothing but roll his shoulder, grimace, and growl at me.

"If your function is to deliver furniture, why are you not doing it?" he snapped. He was probably trying to look menacing, but that would be a stretch in any circumstances. Dr. Goolsby is a little balding guy, probably five feet six and a hundred forty pounds, with a combover and a nervous shoulder tic. That day, he was wearing a little narrow bow tic and saddle oxfords. He obviously wanted to intimidate me. He clenched his jaw like someone really mad, and I fully expected at least a semblance of a snarl. Instead, like Perry Mason in a courtroom gotcha, he said, "May I ask why you are here and your delivery truck is idling on the street out front?"

"He's here?" I said. "I didn't know he was back." I'm sure I sounded as confused as I felt. Truthfully, I was relieved that he was talking about the truck and not the golf course. "We didn't bring the sofa, and he had to go back for it. I'll be right up with your sofa." I turned toward the stairs but stopped because Dr. Goolsby said something over his shoulder while walking into the adjacent room. "I'm sorry. I didn't hear you."

"Where did you put the other pieces?" he shouted irritably. I stopped because the question was obviously addressed to me. Anna smiled at me, and I smiled back. I didn't know whether to go get the sofa or to wait, so I did what I wanted to do, namely, stand there staring at Anna. "This piece is improperly placed," he said from the living room where I had deposited the pieces in accordance with Anna's instruction. "Young man, please come here."

"You're being summoned," Anna whispered, one thick eyebrow raised and a faint smile on her face. "Trust me, it was inevitable." I followed her back to the living room like an automaton, entranced by her graceful movements and virtually oblivious to furniture in general and Dr. Goolsby's interior design preferences in particular.

"I want the end table over here, if you would be so kind. When you manage to deliver the sofa, it goes here." He pointed to an area next to the area designated for the end table.

"Yes, sir," I said obsequiously and picked up the leaden end table, carried it across the room, and put it down where he was pointing.

"Thank you," he said. "Now, if you would retrieve the sofa from your truck, we can wrap up this little project, and you can be on your way."

"Yes, sir," I said again and went out the door, down the steps, and out to the street. The truck was nowhere in sight. I waited a few minutes, looking both ways down Carapace to see if Lichtman was turning around or something, and then I went back down the driveway to the apartment. Dr. Goolsby was standing on the landing at the top of the stairs, and I could see the vague silhouette of Anna behind the porch screen. I thought she might be looking at me so I smiled broadly at the screen.

"Well, young man, why are you standing in my driveway grinning? Are you planning to bring up the sofa or are you posing for a picture?"

"No, sir. I mean yes, sir." I was confused but it really had nothing to do with his sarcasm. My mind was on Anna, so I hardly knew what he was saying. "The truck's gone. I guess he couldn't find us. I don't know what happened." I learned from Lichtman later that night that he had left after no one answered his knock at the house on the street. He had been irked that I had apparently delivered the three small pieces and then abandoned the project.

"Well, that's a stunning performance," Dr. Goolsby snapped. "I presume that delivering furniture can be a challenge at a certain level of function." He retrieved his handkerchief from his inside coat pocket again and wiped his forehead and rolled his shoulder several times. "Have I made a terrible error?" he asked, apparently addressing the doorpost. "Is this life in the backwater? Is there a silver lining I cannot perceive?" He was looking at the doorpost but I don't think he expected it to answer. I didn't know whether he wanted me to say something, but I didn't know what to say. I could address the problem of the furniture delivery but I didn't have any other answers. Anyway, he didn't wait for me to say anything. "Can we make another run at it tomorrow?" He whipped his handkerchief from his pocket and wiped his forehead several times, looking more than mildly distressed, and rolled his shoulder in an agitated manner.

"Yes, sir, I'll have the sofa here first thing in the morning. Is eight o'clock too early?"

"Eight will do fine. And please, let's not make this a career project. You can do this," he said reassuringly. He then opened the screen door and stepped onto the porch. I heard him say, "Anna, you need to get ready. We must be at the gallery downtown in thirty minutes. We don't want to perturb your mother." I waved at the screen, hoping Anna was watching, and then I began walking toward the street. I looked back at the screened porch a couple of times, and I could just barely see her through the screen. She was still standing on the porch when I reached the street because I looked back one last time before I turned toward home. I waved but I couldn't tell whether she waved back.

I didn't see Anna the next day. She was either asleep or already gone when we delivered the sofa. I tried to drag out the delivery as long as possible in the hope that, if she were asleep, she'd wake up and come out of her room yawning and stretching in all her splendor. But it didn't work. She never appeared. After that, I tried to get up the courage to call her. I actually found her phone number but for some reason I couldn't do it. The beginning of school solved the problem, because she was sitting in the front row in my history class when I walked in. "Hey," she said when she saw me, "it's the furniture man."

I still couldn't talk to her very well. A part of my problem was that I really believed the physical-attraction axioms that Lichtman and I had formulated. The basic physical-attraction axiom (we called it the "special theory of physical attraction") is that the attractiveness of a girl is inversely proportional to your attractiveness to her. And the second law (the "general theory") is equally true and immutable: The number of girls you find attractive is inversely proportional to the number who find you attractive. My attraction to Anna was so intense, you can imagine what I expected, but at first everything seemed to fall into place.

We were both in the honors program, so we were in most of the same classes. I was with her a large part of the day. I talked with her before class and sat next to her during class. I also walked with her between classes and, on days when I didn't have track practice or when I skipped track practice, I walked her home. Since she was a new student, I was her first friend, and for a while, her only friend. In spite of all this togetherness, we remained mere friends for several weeks. In fact, I had been hanging around her like a puppy for almost a month before I even held her hand.

The breakthrough came on a field trip to Fort Ryan. Our history teacher arranged for an excursion to the fort as a part of our study of the Civil War. Everybody chipped in a couple of dollars and the school chartered a Greyhound bus. The teacher handed out a mimeographed diagram of the fort and spent the time in transit describing how the fort functioned and how it was supposed to guard the entrance to the harbor. I had read a little bit (including a book on the *Merrimack* and the *Monitor*, the ironclad warships) and Anna, as usual, seemed to have read everything. I tried to seem interested, but it wasn't easy. My leg was against Anna's on the bus seat and occasionally she would lean over against me to whisper something in my ear. My body was electrified and my brain was completely numb.

We arrived at the fort a little before ten o'clock and the teacher gave us some basic instruction. We were supposed to tour the fort in groups and then convene on the rampart at noon for a picnic lunch. Truthfully, I don't remember much about the fort except the powder room, and the only thing I remember about it is that it was in the interior of the fort and dark. We started out in a group of six or seven, but Anna and I dropped out of our group. I didn't want to be in a group, and Anna didn't want to be in a group with Lichtman. He had been banished for committing the unpardonable sin: According to Anna, Lichtman had condescended to her at a math club meeting. He started calling her "the palindrome" (and other things) and she began referring to him as "Lickmore." I hate to admit it, but I was glad they didn't get along. I really didn't want her to like Lichtman, but I wouldn't have told either of them how I felt.

We walked slowly through the old fort, with Anna acting as tour guide and commentator. I was far more interested in the guide than the tour. She was radiant. The powder room is on a lower level of the fort and off a covered walkway. Anna and I walked along in the wonderful gloom of the walkway, passing occasionally through shards of light that slanted in from the courtyard through the arched openings in the bulwark. Anna edged over close to me and I took her hand and held it as we walked along. We reached a doorway to an interior room that was totally dark except for a small arrowhead of light that streamed across the limestone floor of the walkway and into the room a foot or so. We stopped at the threshold to allow our eyes to adjust.

"This is where they kept the gunpowder," Anna said, her voice reverberating in the dark room. "They had to keep the powder dry, so the room has no exposures other than this door." She smiled and then said, "Let's go in."

"I don't think we can see anything in there," I said, pretending to study the diagram. I didn't want to tell her that I don't like close places, and I sure didn't want to have one of my freeze-ups. The room wasn't small, but the darkness created a sense of closeness, so I was a little uneasy. I don't do well with close places. I begin to sweat and shake if the walls start closing in on me. Anna smiled mischievously.

"Let's go in anyway," she whispered. What was I going to do? I stood there for a second and then turned toward the dark open door. She gave me a little shove, and after a brief moment of resistance, I began edging into the room despite a modest but growing unease. She was behind me almost shoving so I choked it down. I held on to her hand and inched forward into total darkness. Apart from the sense of closeness, I was concerned about falling in a hole or stepping on a snake or stumbling over something, so I slid my feet along the floor a few inches at a time. The sensations from holding Anna's hand and creeping into the black unknown were almost overwhelming. We were silent until we had edged into the room about eight feet.

"We probably ought not to go any farther," I said. Truthfully, I don't think I could have forced my legs to take another step. I stopped and turned back toward Anna but she kept edging forward until she was touching me. It was so quiet that I could hear her breathing. She nuzzled in against me and I put my arms around her and kissed her on the forehead and then, as she tilted her head back, I kissed her on the nose and the lips.

The powder room was the high point of the field trip. I didn't forget about the closeness and the darkness, but I ignored them. I would have stayed in there the rest of the day. Unfortunately, after about fifteen minutes Anna insisted we had to finish the tour and join the class for the picnic. I enjoyed the afternoon, but it wasn't the same as the powder room. After the picnic, the whole class went down to the beach, where we took off our shoes and waded in the surf. Anna and I walked off down the beach but she wouldn't do anything other than hold hands. She said kissing in public is gauche. But she was very nice to me. Even when she called me "F.M." or "furniture man," it seemed endearing and without the cynicism that some-times infused the things she said later in the year.

My story ended when Dr. Gross interjected, "We're almost out of time but I have a couple of notes. You did remarkably well with that, by the way." He flipped back a page on his clipboard. "I infer that you had met Dr. Goolsby before you met Anna," he said, this time pronouncing her name correctly.

"Encountered would be a better word than met. I ran into him at the golf course earlier in the summer before I got the job at Lichtman's. It didn't go well."

"So I gather. I'd like to hear about that. Next time maybe? Did your relationship with Dr. Goolsby ever improve?"

"No, not that I could tell. After Anna and I started going together, I ignored and avoided him. I'm sure he remembered me from the golf course, but he never mentioned it and I certainly didn't bring it up. He avoided me, and I avoided him. It's a strange family unit. Dr. Goolsby isn't Anna's first stepfather. He's number two. Anna's real father was a medical student at Columbia University when Anna's mother met him. His name is Giovanni Paolo Bentravato. Her name is actually Anna Bentravato. That's Italian, huh? He was from Milan, Italy, and he was on a student visa when they married. Anna showed me pictures of him, sort of old and grainy photographs of a good-looking, dark-complexioned guy variously attired in jeans or tennis shorts or hospital greens. Anna called him 'gloriously handsome but frustratingly unfeasible.' He left Anna's mother and went back to Milan when Anna was still a baby. I never understood why, but I guess it had something to do with the 'frustratingly unfeasible' part of him. I don't know when the first stepfather entered and exited the picture, but Dr. Goolsby had been around for almost ten years."

"One last thing," Dr. Gross said. "I take it you are claustrophobic?"

"Yes, I have trouble with close places."

"You actually handled the situation well in the circumstances."

"Yeah, I guess, but I really didn't have much choice in the circumstances. What was I going to do?"

"Your will overcame your emotions. That's good. Sometimes the circumstances overwhelm us."

"It was Anna, remember. I don't know what I'd have done if it had been someone else."

"Okay, but you did well," Dr. Gross said abruptly and glanced at his watch. We had in fact overrun my allotted time. "Did you really find that hard? You really didn't seem to."

"Well, not really so much."

"You're certainly not as reticent as you profess. We're making exceptional progress. I hope you understand what we're doing. It is very important that you follow when I'm leading and that I follow when you lead, as you must in some areas. Do you understand? Think about our last sessions, and next week let's talk about where we've been and where we need to go." When I started to speak, he held up his hand. "Hold that thought until next week."

"I was just going to say, 'See you next week.'"

"Oh," he said. "Okay, see you next week."

BURCHFIELDS

"Why do sunflowers tilt toward the river in the morning and in the opposite direction in the afternoon?" Uncle Nat was repeating my question. My mother and I had planted the flowers on the road side of the fence in the front yard of the country house in the summer of 1948 when I was seven years old and Newt was fifteen. I had raised the question to my mother, who passed it along to Uncle Nat for my botany lesson. The question was now directed to Newt, whose answer was characteristic.

"It's the spiritual inclination of sunflowers," he said, his tone assured though not the full baritone it is today. "Everybody knows that sunflowers are devotees and worshippers of the great river god, Aqua-Molech. They are, however, morally fickle, so that by afternoon they've fallen away, much like the chosen people in the wilderness, and bow down to Arbor-Chemosh, the licentious tree god who twists their stamens and taunts their pistils."

I laughed, because, as usual, Newt was the wittiest person in the world.

Uncle Nat frowned and said, "I'm certain, Newton, that you enjoy these efforts at drollery, but I persist in being unmoved. Would you like to try again, keeping in mind that we don't have all day to spend on a simple botanical principle?" My mother and I looked at Newt expectantly. You never knew what he was going to say but he usually made it funny and informative. He must have been tired or something, because he just answered the question.

"The river," he said, looking directly at me and pointing toward the river, "is to the east of us where the sun is wont to rise. These pretty yellow blossoms are sunflowers, which are solisequious plants, that is, the sun causes a biophysical reaction in the stem and the plant is thrust toward the rays of the sun. As the sun rises, the flowers angle toward its rays and then follow its path devotedly throughout the day."

"Thank you, Newton." Uncle Nat forced out a thin smile. "You've added the word 'solisequious' to our young nephew's vocabulary and a concept to his understanding." He was right about that. I know what solisequious means; I even know what it feels like. Dr. Gross' voice interrupted my reverie.

"You seem distracted today." He had been writing on my folder, and I had been waiting patiently for him to begin our session. My mind had drifted off to other things, so I was sort of startled by his comment.

"No," I said, "I don't think so. No more than usual." He was probably right, but the fact is I'm probably distracted most of the time.

"Okay, now that you've joined us, where would you like to go today? Did you think about my question at the end of our last session? Are we headed in the right direction or do we need to change course?"

"Well, I did think about it, but I don't know where we're going, so I don't know whether we're on course or not. I was sort of hoping you knew."

"Fair enough," he said. "Let's continue hacking our way through the jungle, and see where we come out. What about that?"

"We may just get lost."

"True, but if that happens, we'll hack our way back and more than likely have learned something from the struggle. Tell me about your new girlfriend." He flipped through the notes on the right side of my folder. "Her name is Sarah?"

"Yeah," I said, "Sarah Burchfield."

"I am confused by something. Your mother has told me that Sarah is the closest thing to a real prodigy in your school, that her intelligence quotient as measured by standardized testing is extraordinary. Your mother has access to information that we don't have, so I'm inclined to give her assertion some credence."

"You're wondering why I talk about Anna's brilliance and haven't mentioned Sarah's?"

"Well, I didn't mean that precisely, but if you would like to address that point, I'd like to hear it."

"I don't know whether I want to address it or not. Anna is gone. Maybe she was never really here. I'm not even sure she's real. She doesn't seem real. Maybe I'm Pygmalion. It's like I made her up, but I don't know how. What did my mother say?"

"She said things similar to what you've said. She didn't suggest that Anna wasn't real or that you had sculpted her out of imagination."

"Why is this stuff relevant?" I asked. For some reason, the subject was unpleasant, and it was making me edgy.

"I am interested in your perceptions, particularly your perception of yourself and your perception of those around you. Let me pose a hypothetical: If it were true that you actually score higher than Anna on standardized tests and that Sarah scores higher than either of you, would you find those propositions unlikely or incongruous?"

"If that were so, I'd say the tests are not measuring the right stuff, probably missing the point."

"That's a lot of confidence in your perception. With all the shadows and ambiguities in your everyday experience, you're that confident?"

"You would have to have met Anna. You'd see what I mean. Anna isn't like other people. I don't know how to explain it but she's different. I don't care what the standardized tests say."

"It is true, of course, that standardized tests have limited value as indicators of empirical finesse. In the empirical world, the amount of sand you move does not necessarily correspond to the size of the shovel you use. Nonetheless, I wonder about your assessment. Is it as objective as you seem to assume?"

"What difference does it make?" I said. "Anna is gone. She's past tense. It doesn't even matter whether she was real. I assure you she won't ever reappear." I did not tell him how much pain I felt just saying those words.

"Okay, let's work in the present tense. Tell me about Sarah. Do you have a photograph of her?"

"No, I don't have one yet."

"Did you just recently meet her?"

"No, I've known her about six years."

"That's interesting," he said.

"Her crazy brother, Burch, was the first guy I met when we moved here and supposedly my best friend for a while."

"Supposedly?"

"He's not a real friend, probably never was. At first, we did stuff together. He's a year older than I am, but we were about the same size. He's not like Sarah. He hasn't read much, and he struggles with everything. I don't know why we even tried to be friends. We started off playing scrub football with a couple of other guys in the neighborhood. I used to be able to run. Before my injuries I was fast, so I was pretty good at some sports. When we first met, he had never heard of a person being homeschooled, and he was bemused by the fact that I'd never been in a schoolhouse. I was kind of a novelty, maybe even a little strange. Some of it may have been that more people than I had assumed knew we were related to 'Abraham of Bigbee,' as one newspaper referred to Uncle Nat. I don't know. I hardly saw Sarah. She was always sort of lurking in the background, reading books through those large glasses she used to wear. She'd come out and stand there when Mrs. Burchfield did the interrogations, but she didn't say anything and she didn't smile."

"Interrogations? What kind? Was Mrs. Burchfield antagonistic?"

"Oh, no. She really likes me. The truth is, of all the Burchfields, I thought she liked me the most and that Mr. Burchfield liked me the least. Every time I went to their house, Mrs. Burchfield would ask me to come into her study and then she'd ask me about stuff."

"What kind of stuff?"

"A lot of math questions, mostly just Trachtenberg, and books I'd read and poetry I'd memorized. Sarah has said that sometimes her mother was asking questions that Sarah was too shy to ask me. Mrs. Burchfield is a freelance writer for magazines. She's like Sarah, interested in all kinds of stuff. The thing I really didn't like was when she'd call Mr. Burchfield and say, 'Come here, Burchie, and listen to this.' Then she'd ask me to repeat the answer to a question she'd asked me or get me to recite a poem again. Mr. Burchfield is a former army colonel, but he now works at an insurance agency. I don't think he reads anything except occasionally the *Wall Street Journal* or maybe a military book, but he would dutifully report when she summoned him and pretend to be fascinated with the subject. Burch stood there smiling almost proudly at first, like the owner of a circus pony. But after awhile he started acting like I was trying to compete with him for his family's attention. Until the wheels started coming off our friendship, Burch called me 'the brain.' Later, I became 'weirdo,' 'kook,' 'nutball' and, maybe worst of all, 'Isaac's crazy cousin.'"

"Isaac's cousin? He was taunting you about Nathan's murder?"

"Yeah, the paper called it the 'Isaac Sacrifice.' The other members of Burch's family never said anything."

"Did he bring up the murder when you first became acquainted or only later?"

"Later, when things got really bad between us."

"Sometimes people just grow apart and sometimes there's a big blowup, but friendships don't always last, you know."

"After about a year, we started bumping into each other. When we first moved to the city, Burch was bigger than I was, but I was much faster. Then I started growing, and without even noticing the change I got taller and stronger and so much faster that he would fall behind three or four yards in a sprint and disappear altogether in a cross-country race. When I made varsity track my first year at Bridgewater, he dropped track. Shortly after he gave up track, he got the fancy convertible for his birthday. If he saw me walking somewhere, he'd toot the horn but he wouldn't stop. Track was part of the problem, but the antagonism got really bad after the Dayla Peterson thing."

"I presume Dayla is a girl the two of you jousted over?"

"She was his girlfriend. I didn't joust. I had been hanging around and sort of going with a girl named Carol that I liked pretty well, and Burch was going with Dayla and was completely obsessed with her. I really couldn't see it, but I can tell you Burch thought Dayla was perfect. She's not. She's pretty, but she's not bright. Lichtman described her perfectly. He said Dayla is built like an Italian sports car but her engine sputters. If you mention something more complicated than shoe size or the weather, she'll stare at you like you've said something in Swahili. If she says anything at all, it's usually so strange you don't know what to say in response."

"You didn't, by any chance, share this assessment of his girlfriend with Burch, did you?"

"No, not directly anyway. Lichtman and I talked about it but not with Burch."

"So, your perception is that you did not cause the rift. What, then, was the friendship-fracturing incident about?"

I don't think I caused the rift, but Dr. Gross' tone suggested that he thought I was probably at fault. I thought, *okay, I'll just tell him what happened and he can decide for himself.* The incident that caused the fracture happened one Saturday afternoon in early June. When Burch got to Bridgewater, he had joined a fraternity, Phi Omega Epsilon, and he had begun hanging around mostly with his "Phi O brothers," so I was sort of surprised when he came by my house. We rode around in the fancy convertible for a while and then ended up at his house, where we sat around talking about nothing. We hadn't been there fifteen minutes when Burch went over and stood in front of the full-length mirror on the back of his closet door. He combed his hair a bit, grinned approvingly and said absolutely out of nowhere, "Biddle, I'll bet I can call right now and get a date with Carol."

"I doubt it," I said. I was pretty sure he was wrong, mostly because Carol had told me she didn't like Burch very much. Sometimes what a girl says is different from what she does, but I still didn't think Carol would do it. I probably would have told Burch she wouldn't, even if I thought she might.

"Tell you what," he said. "I'll call Carol and you call Day and let's see what happens."

I said, "No, I don't think so." I was sitting on his bed, lounging back on his reading pillow.

"You're afraid of what would happen, aren't you?"

"I'm not afraid. It's just a dumb idea."

"All right, let's just see. What's Carol's number?" I didn't answer so he picked up the telephone directory and found Carol's number. He dialed the phone and gave me his half-lip grin, signifying that he was very pleased with himself.

"Hello," he said into the receiver, "may I speak with Carol?" He cupped his hand over the mouthpiece and danced around sort of stupidly, grinning like a jackass the whole time. "Carol. Hi, this is Harry. What do you mean Harry who? The Harry. Harry Burchfield. How are you?" There was a slight pause and then Burch said, "Look, Carol, I think you're really cute and I'd like to do something with you sometime." There was another pause, somewhat longer than the previous one. "The devil with Biddle." He cupped his hand over the mouthpiece and repeated his inane jig. "We won't tell him. He's dense as granite. He'll never know." After another moment of silence on Burch's end, he said, "I was just kidding you, Carol. Here's your boy." Then he handed me the phone. I hadn't intended to call Carol, so I told her that Burch was being a clown and that I'd call her later.

I then hung up the phone and handed it back to Burch. As soon as he got a dial tone, he started dialing another number. "Here," he said. "Now it's your turn." I handed the receiver back to him and he tried to shove it back to me and in the process the phone hit the floor between us. "Dammit, Biddle, you're gonna break the phone." He picked up the phone and redialed Dayla's number, and then he handed me the receiver again. "You can't bail out now. Not after your girl's stiff-armed me."

By that time, I was really annoyed, so I took the phone and held it against my ear. Burch ran out of the room and I heard the click of the extension phone when he picked up. Dayla answered two seconds after he picked up the extension.

"Dayla, this is Kit Biddle. How are you?" I didn't really know what to say, and I had the feeling that anything I said was going to sound stupid.

"I'm fine, Kit," she said hesitantly. "How are you?" There was an awkward pause while I tried to come up with something to talk about, and she said, "I'm a little surprised to hear from you."

"Well, I just wanted to talk to you. I usually don't get a chance to say much to you." Then I remembered that when Burch first started talking monomaniacally about Dayla, I had thought about "La Belle Dame sans Merci." You know, the Keats poem. So, I seized the idea and said, "I was just thinking, you remind me of one of my favorite Keats poems."

"Oh," she said, almost squealing, "how sweet." It probably wouldn't have made any difference if she had asked me which poem. "Didn't you write some poems for the literary magazine?"

"Yeah," I said, "a couple."

"I wish you'd write a poem for me."

"Well," I said, feeling even more uneasy. I didn't want to promise to write a poem for her. I also didn't want to keep piling up lies. It's probably absurd but I was trying to hang on to a little integrity. "Tell you what. I'll read some poetry to you. My favorite poems."

"That would be nice."

"You want to meet me over in the park?"

"When?"

"How about an hour from now?"

"Okay," she said softly, "that sounds like fun."

"Day!" Burch bellowed into the phone. "I heard that! I heard that, Day!" Burch slammed down the phone and ran to the doorway where I was sitting in a chair, already feeling like a crumb. His face was contorted with anger. "Damn you," he shouted and stomped out of the house. I had hung up the receiver after Burch broke in on the conversation, but I didn't move for a few minutes. I still don't know why he came by my house or why he wanted me to call his purported girlfriend. Why would he want me to do that?

"People are attracted to one another," Dr. Gross interjected, "because of perceptions at the time: special gifts, perceived benefits, the satisfaction of needs in the association. In that sense, we are all meeting the needs or failing to meet the needs of others. When needs cease to be met as expected, the attractions begin to disappear, and repulsions replace them. If that's being used by someone, then we're all tools in one way or another to those in our milieu."

"Burch told me later that Dayla had known all along that he was there and that she had just been playing around. But that was really the end. After that, the repulsions really appeared. He seemed to take every opportunity to gig me. Before I started going to Bridgewater, Burch had told me that he wanted me to join his fraternity when I got there. The bid to join Phi O never came, and Burch told me later that I had been blackballed because the brothers thought I wouldn't fit in. After the Phi O brush-off, I became a part of an exclusive fraternity consisting of Lichtman, Q. Ball, and me that we called 'Tau Alpha Mu,' or TAM for short. The Greek alphabet was just fluff: TAM was actually an acronym for 'Trio of Anal Misfits.' Lichtman came up with that one. It's probably about right."

"It's interesting that your relationship with Burch didn't affect the rest of the Burchfield family," Dr. Gross said, grinning broadly. "Sarah has begun to sound like Juliet, required to foreswear her family name for her true love." It took me a few seconds to realize that Dr. Gross was having some difficulty hiding his amusement.

"I don't think so. Sarah says she has always liked me and her mother has always seemed to like me. About a year after we moved into the neighborhood, Sarah wrote me a note. It was almost a book report on some Jane Austen novel. I think I was supposed to infer something, but I just thought it was strange. It was so strange I didn't answer at all, partially because I didn't know what to say. But she seems always to have liked me. That's what she says anyway. I don't think she is much swayed by Burch's opinions. They don't have a lot in common. They don't seem to have come from the same gene pool. They don't look much alike, and they don't have the same mental apparatus. For the most part, he's irrelevant. He's now a sophomore at the university, so he's no longer around very much. When he comes home at breaks I don't see him and Sarah doesn't mention him. Some things that disappear are actually good."

"Is it significant that we've spent most of the hour talking about Sarah's brother rather than Sarah? When I asked you about Anna, we didn't end up talking about some relative."

"I don't know. I don't know the significance of any of this stuff. I'm here because everybody says I ought to be, apparently because everybody thinks I'm crazy. I didn't intentionally leave out Anna's family. I'd love to tell you about her stepfather. You know, I mentioned that I had met him before I met Anna. It wasn't funny when it happened but Lichtman and Q. Ball think it's hilarious."

"Yes," he said, "I'd like to hear it. I feel certain that it's germane to something, huh?"

"Now you want me to decide what's germane. This is your stuff. I didn't want to do it anyway. You wanted me to talk, and I'm talking. I'm talking more than I've ever talked in my life. I don't know the significance of any of this stuff. As far as I can tell, we're just like a couple of guys in a bar making jokes and telling lies."

"Are we telling lies?"

"I'm trying not to lie but I'm probably not getting

everything right. I suppose that means everything I say is either a guess or a guise."

"That's fairly perceptive. You can't get everything right. Nobody is really an objective expositor of his own experiences, but my job is not to determine accuracy. My job is to determine how you are dealing with reality as you perceive it. In that sense, I don't ever deal in the actual. I am always in the suppositional. It is important that my patient is not so divorced from reality that he or she cannot function, but I don't concern myself with the actual perception unless it is delusional on its face. You have your own nuance of perception that derives from where you are intellectually and psychologically. I want you to deal with your reality in a constructive way. If your perception is sharpened or clarified in the process, that's a lagniappe that I hope for but don't always expect and in fact is not necessary for successful therapy."

"Okay," I said. I hunched my shoulders to convey the idea that I didn't care. "I guess." I did in fact care very much. I don't know why I wanted to pretend that I didn't.

"All right, tell me how you met Anna's stepfather."

"Not if you think it's irrelevant."

"Trust me, it is relevant in our pursuit. Some things are more important than others, but you don't know before you explore them. Let's explore a little." He made a little smirking expression with his mouth, from which I inferred that he thought something else was more important. "Tell me about Dr. Goolsby, the nefarious stepfather."

"No, not if you don't want to hear it."

"I want to hear it. I particularly want to hear it because it's on your mind. We aren't going back to where we started, are we?"

"No, we're not," I said. "I just don't want to wander off the point and talk about goofy stuff that's not relevant."

"As I understand it from Dr. Glans, if it hadn't been for Dr. Goolsby, you might not have survived. You might have bled to death. So, in some significant way, Dr. Goolsby is very important in your life, totally apart from Anna. I know the details of your injuries in only rudimentary outline, but Dr. Goolsby looms large in one of the more important crossroads in your life. It appears that he has managed to be both villain and hero in the same story. That in itself is worth a few minutes of our time."

"The day I met Dr. Goolsby, he wasn't a very likely hero," I said hesitantly. "It may have been just the day, you know, one of those days. I don't know whether you have them, but I have days when everything seems like a large pit of total absurdity. Nothing goes right. I didn't meet Dr. Goolsby until the afternoon, so in a sense he was just a part of a pattern that began early and persisted.

"The first absurd event of the day occurred when I let my mother talk me into taking her to the country to put flowers on the family graves, particularly my father's and Nathan's. The cemetery is adjacent to the sanctuary of the Bigbee Baptist Church where Uncle Nat had been pastor and where Papa had been pastor before him. The cemetery plot designated for the Biddle clan is right next to a little white picket fence that separates the church from the graveyard. Dr. Glans lent us his car and I drove us to the cemetery. We got there about nine-thirty, and my mother and I put fresh flowers around the graves and removed the withered blossoms and accumulated debris. Then my mother stood at the foot of the graves with tears running down her face. That's one of the reasons I hated going to the cemetery with her. Every time she would stand there looking stricken, repeating over and over something like, 'Oh, God, my God, why?' Sometimes I choke up because sadness seems to be contagious, but mostly I just get very nervous.

"Then the first weird thing of the day happened. We were standing at the foot of Nathan's grave, snuffling and fidgeting in tandem, when I heard the cracking sound. Generally, the cemetery is quiet except for the occasional drone of a lawn mower, so the popping noise was noteworthy and ominous. I glanced over my shoulder and confirmed what I thought I was hearing: A large water oak was leaning precariously in our direction, and the popping sound was the remaining surface roots breaking as the tree edged toward the ground. My mother heard nothing. She looked startled when I started pushing her out of the path of the falling tree. For probably thirty or forty seconds after I shoved her aside, the tree hung at about a thirty-five-degree angle above the ground. Then the massive water oak came crashing down right across where we had been standing. The trunk missed my father's grave entirely but fell across Nathan's headstone and cracked it down the middle. The right side of the headstone broke off and fell backwards onto the grass at the head of the grave, leaving the left side standing with a bizarrely fragmented inscription. From the top of the headstone to the bottom, the remaining fragment said:

NATHANIEL

Born: July 22,
POCCOTOLA
IPSE DIXIT GO

"The ride back to the city was quiet, but things got even stranger when we pulled off the highway to get lunch. The usual ritual for the cemetery visits was to leave at about eight o'clock in the morning, get to the cemetery about nine-thirty, spend an hour arranging flowers and mourning, and then get back for a lunch of cheerful recovery at Mikey's Barbecue around noon. The falling tree threw us off a bit but we were basically on schedule. The problem was that when we reached our luncheon destination, Mikey's Barbecue had ceased to exist. As soon as we turned off the highway you could see the smoke from the smoldering pile of ashes that had been Mikey's.

"My mother's favorite barbecue joint had caught fire and burned to the ground during the night. It is irrelevant to her sense of loss that Mikey was subsequently found to have set the fire himself. She was so shaken by the destruction of Nathan's headstone and Mikey's Barbecue that we skipped the lunch part of the routine and drove home in almost total silence. I had a peanut butter sandwich and a glass of milk alone at our kitchen table. My mother proceeded to arrange for a tree service to remove the water oak and then began combing the yellow pages for a new headstone for Nathan's grave."

"I'm sorry," Dr. Gross broke in, "but we're over our time again."

"Oh," I said, sort of surprised to be jolted out of my story. "I'm sorry."

"Let's take it up there when we get together next week. I assume that Dr. Goolsby will ultimately show up in this narrative?"

"Sorry," I said again. "I was just trying to describe the day. I don't know why Dr. Goolsby showed up in it, but yes, he does show up. It was just a strange day."

"Well, tell me about it next time," he said and stuck out his hand. "I have a patient waiting who probably is becoming impatient. See you next week." The receptionist tapped on the door just as I was reaching for the handle. "Sorry, Frances," Dr. Gross said to her, "we were trying to find a stopping point." A surly-looking middle-aged man was standing behind the receptionist, alternately looking at his watch and glaring at me like I'd withheld oxygen from him for much of the twenty minutes I'd encroached on his appointment. I took pride in the fact that I had also had to wait when Dr. Gross had run over with the patient who preceded me and, unlike the agitated character pushing past me into Dr. Gross' office, I had never acted irritated or offended. I was thinking that, comparatively, I might be one of Dr. Gross' saner patients, perhaps even his most patient patient. I don't know whether anyone else who sees a shrink has these thoughts, but I wanted to be mature and I wanted almost desperately to be normal.

THE GHOUL

While I was in the hospital, one of the guys on the track team visited me and mentioned offhand that his sister Essie had tried to kill herself by taking sleeping pills. He said she put a suicide note in her mother's cigarette case, saying that her life wasn't worth all the pain. Her mother discovered the note sometime during the day at work and rushed home to find Essie sitting on the toilet crying. Apparently, Essie had mistaken laxative capsules for sleeping pills and had taken about twenty of them. Her goofy brother acted like he thought the pharmaceutical blunder somehow made the suicide attempt funny. I know who Essie is because she was in some of my classes at Bridgewater, but I don't really know her, so I can't tell you why I was so disconcerted when she came out of Dr. Gross' office while I was waiting to go in.

We stood face-to-face, not more than ten feet apart, staring at one another like we'd encountered an alien. I felt like someone who'd been caught doing something really embarrassing or despicable, like peeing in the water fountain or stealing from a blind man. Essie was obviously flustered, because instead of saying hello or smiling or anything normal, she turned her face away from me and virtually ran out of the office. Maybe nobody had told her that there's a back hallway that patients can use if they want privacy. I had thought about using it myself, but until I ran into Essie that morning, I had never encountered anybody familiar going in or coming out.

Almost ten minutes after I sat down in my usual chair in Dr. Gross' office, he was still writing in a folder that wasn't mine. "Hang on a sec," he said when I walked in. I could tell from the thickness and the markings on the outside of the folder that it wasn't mine, and I assumed that it was Essie's. But I couldn't see a name, so I really don't know whose folder it was and I didn't ask. When he finished, he turned to me and said, "Good morning," and then picked up the folder I had come to recognize as mine even without seeing my name on it. He flipped to the end, read the last page of his notes, and said, "Okay, let's pick up where we left off."

"One of the 'benefits' I got from Dr. Bob," I said, "was a part-time job in the maintenance department at the country club."

"Dr. Bob?" He flipped back through his notes, looking completely confused. He seemed to have forgotten where we had left off the previous week. It was the first

time since we had been meeting that he seemed disconcerted or preoccupied.

"Your friend, Dr. Glans," I said. "My mother calls
him Dr. Bob. I guess she thinks that keeps him in a
more formal-sounding role. Since they're about to get
married, I guess he's about to become Dr. Step-Bob."

"Yes," he said ignoring my cynicism. "I want to talk
about your relationship with Dr. Glans, but you were
saying something about a maintenance job?"

"When we finished last week, I was about to tell you
how I met Dr. Goolsby, remember?"

"Right," he said distractedly, clutching my folder
and running his ballpoint pen through the hair on the
right side of his head in several quick movements. "So,
Dr. Glans arranged for you to have employment after
school hours?"

"It turned out to be a fill-in job, not a regular job, and
I had to work for this redneck named Harbo Wallace.
Seventy-five cents an hour to suffer the mindless oppres-
sions of the world's only talking anus." Dr. Gross cleared
his throat but actually smiled slightly. "When you show up
at a job and your new boss calls you 'pissant,' the deduction
just isn't all that hard. Harbo resented having to hire me
and decided before I even showed up that he would find
a way to get rid of me. The summer before my junior year
at Bridgewater he finally got to fire me. He had assigned
me the job of refurbishing and trimming around the front-
nine bunkers. The day I showed up to work on the bunkers

was the afternoon of the day I started describing to you last week, the day that was already in a massive hole before I even got to the golf course."

"Yes, I'm with you," Dr. Gross said. "Go ahead."

So I did. I told him how I had originally met Dr. Goolsby. I don't know whether it was helpful for my therapy, but I wanted to tell him because my relationship with Dr. Goolsby may have been as peculiar as my relationship with Anna. Besides, Lichtman and Q. Ball love the story.

It was early July, a few weeks before I met Anna, during the summer after my first year at Bridgewater. I was on the track team, and I was supposed to do some summer running, so I ran the three miles from my house to the club's maintenance shed. It was afternoon when I got there, and the maintenance yard was empty except for one guy who was sitting in the shade eating his lunch and reading what appeared to be a small Bible. Without getting up, he extended his hand to me and said, "My name is Thomas but everybody calls me Phoenix 'cause I used to live there." I introduced myself. He said, "Nice to meet you, Kit Biddle. This is the day that the Lord made. Ain't the Lord good?"

"Not that I can tell," I said dryly. He frowned just slightly, and then smiled benignly.

"You workin' the traps?"

"Yeah," I said. "I promised Harbo I'd get the front nine done before the weekend."

"Well, he got us both on it. I done finished one, two, and three. We almost out of sand. Four and five can't be finished without sand. One of us got to go to the pit with the big truck."

"It doesn't matter to me," I said. "You want to get sand while I do the trimming?"

"Sounds good to me. That rough is so high it's probably hidin' snakes. I don't like nothin' don't have no shoulders."

It was about two o'clock when Phoenix dropped me at the fourth hole and drove off to get sand. I decided to begin with the small mower and trim around each sand trap and then come back and do the fine cutting at the edges. The fourth hole is a dogleg par five with a little lake about halfway between the tee and green. Catawpa Creek runs along the right side of the fairway and then across to the left side of the fairway in front of the green. Other than trying to watch out for flying balls, I didn't pay much attention to the golfers.

The maintenance crew is supposed to stay out of the way as much as possible. So, I don't know what caused me to notice Dr. Goolsby. It may have been that he was even goofier looking than most golfers, which is a pretty scary mouthful in itself. Dr. Goolsby was a trip. He was wearing khaki shorts, a plaid shirt, and black socks pulled all the way over his calves. Topping off the ensemble was a floppy green hat that he removed every few minutes to wipe sweat off his bald head with a hand towel, always wiping from left to right to mat down the hair that was actually growing on the left side of his head just above his left ear.

Even before he hit a ball (or, more accurately, tried to hit a ball), he cleaned his club like he was planning to eat with it. He also had a nervous habit of rotating his left shoulder and wobbling his head around. I was working at a bunker just in front of the lake and Dr. Goolsby was trying to hit across the part of the lake where the water narrows to the creek. He was in a twosome with a younger guy, maybe thirty-five years old, who had laid up in front of the lake with his first shot and then hit his ball over the lake, covering probably two hundred yards with his second shot.

Dr. Goolsby had already drubbed the ball several times when he plopped another one in the middle of the lake. Frankly, I couldn't see how he hit the ball at all. On his backswing he brought the club straight up as though he were throwing a sack over his shoulder. Then he lurched forward on the downswing, keeping his weight on his right foot. The usual and expected result was a slice off to the right. In an apparent effort to offset the slice, he addressed the ball at an angle as though planning to hit it into the woods on the left side of the fairway.

The younger guy playing with Dr. Goolsby was trying to offer consolation and golfing tips without much success. It was clear that Dr. Goolsby was the senior and that the young guy was obliged to be solicitous and diplomatic. "Doctah Goolsby," he said. The young guy had that thick, r-less drawl that some people have around here. My mother says it's a carryover from British brogue, but the Brits haven't been here in a while, so I don't know. Anyway, the young guy said, "You might want to take a nine ahn and just pop it ovah the lake."

Actually, I like accents. Uncle Nat pronounces out and about like oot and aboot. There's always some social reason for it. My mother never said oot and aboot, so I don't. Anyway, I'm watching Dr. Goolsby's effort to hit his ball over the lake and I'm thinking that he's going to take the young guy's advice and try to pop the ball over with a nine iron. But he doesn't. He ignores the advice and walks over to the golf cart and pulls out a fairway wood. He then goes into his strange windup and efficiently and inexorably places his ball in the lake not too far from where he had hit the previous ball.

Dr. Goolsby was muttering something about needing a caddy when he yelped and began jumping and running and swinging his arms. I thought he might have finally come undone after one too many bad shots into the lake. Then I saw the yellow jackets, about ten or twelve of them, making menacing sweeps at Dr. Goolsby's skinny legs. After the first couple of yellow jacket strikes, Dr. Goolsby did some free-style choreography and dashed back toward the tee. When he was sure the bees hadn't followed, he stopped and looked down at the welts on his knees and lower thighs and he made a little whimpering sound. "It might have been good to warn me about hornets," he said. The young guy didn't bother to answer. He just went to his bag and got a bottle of Benadryl. Dr. Goolsby took the bottle and sat on the ground a few yards from my mower and began dabbing his wounds.

At that point, I took the small mower and went around the lake and down the fairway to the next bunker. I wasn't supposed to run the mower in the presence of golfers, and, in spite of the fact that Dr. Goolsby didn't really qualify as a golfer, I decided that I should continue my work at a different sand trap. It seemed likely that Dr. Goolsby would resume his flailing as soon as he recovered from his stings, and I had no way of guessing how long it would take him to clear the lake. So, I hiked on down the fairway.

I was working at a fairway bunker just across the lake and on the right side of the fairway when I heard a ball do the familiar *kerplush* in the lake. I continued to work until I saw the golf cart and the younger guy signaling for me to cut the mower engine. When the sound dissipated, he said, "My friend hit a ball ovah this way. By any chance, did you see it land?"

I think I should get at least half credit for trying. I made a sincere effort. I wanted almost desperately to take the question seriously. Regrettably, I failed. "It didn't land," I said after a brief pause while I struggled for a soft answer. "It watered." I know that was not a good answer, but sometimes I just can't do any better.

"You mean I didn't clear the water?" Dr. Goolsby said.

"Well," I said, totally losing any semblance of a grip on my good intentions, "you cleared 95 percent of it. The 95th percentile ain't that bad." You don't have to tell me. I know I shouldn't have said it, but it was one of those days. To some extent, I think I was set up by circumstance. Dr. Goolsby's question required a lot of pretense about his game that I might have handled on some days, but on that particular day I couldn't muster the requisite quantity of delusion.

"Are all the hirelings at this club smart alecks?" Dr. Goolsby said, turning to the younger guy, who was already red in the face.

"No, I nevah, evah encountahed such." Then he turned to me with a stern expression. "Fellah, you'll be heahin' moah about this encountah." Then he wheeled the golf cart around and drove a few yards off where the fairway was flat. "I think you should just drop a ball and take a stroke. It's open from heah on."

When Dr. Goolsby pulled out a fairway wood and began looking for a place to drop, I started trying to figure out where to go to avoid his ball. I couldn't very easily get behind him because he was only a few yards from the lake. I knew he was likely to slice right, but his stance to the left created a quandary: What if a miracle happened and the ball inadvertently and inexplicably went straight or at least straighter? Ultimately, I decided to edge over toward Catawpa Creek on the right side of the fairway and hope for a shallow slice.

Unfortunately, the slice was not shallow at all. Fortunately, the ball that ricocheted off the maple I was standing near missed my head by a good ten inches. I heard the wet thud of the ball as it hit the bank of the creek, and I looked just in time to see it roll back into the shallow water on the far side. I was edging down the creek bank when the golf cart screeched to a stop beside me. "Did you see the ball?" the younger guy asked. I made a mental note that he avoided the word "land" in his question. I also noted that his tone was less than congenial.

"Yes, sir," I said humbly, trying to be conciliatory, "and it may be reachable." I could see a ball retriever on the back of the cart. "Your retriever may be long enough." Since I knew where the ball was and they didn't, I decided to try to earn some needed brownie points. I went over to the cart and got the ball retriever, pulled the recessed segments out of the handle to the maximum length, and started trying to pick up the ball, which was just barely visible in the murky water at the far edge of the creek. The ball had muddied the water, and I was having trouble getting the retriever under it. Dr. Goolsby had dropped another ball and was looking off down the fairway when I said, "I think we're going to have to go around to the other side to get this ball."

"I think probably not," Dr. Goolsby said brusquely. "Give me the implement." I handed him the retriever and he stalked over to the bank of the creek. He leaned forward over the creek trying to maneuver the head of the retriever and then suddenly lost his footing and stepped off the bank into Catawpa Creek. He stood there in knee-deep water looking distressed and helpless but also strangely indignant. The younger guy looked like an obstetrician who'd dropped the baby.

He was just standing there looking flustered, so I decided to help Dr. Goolsby out of the creek. I put out my hand and he gripped it and said, "Look at this," as though I had caused him to fall in the creek. He was holding my hand and seemed to be leaning backwards. He was either trying to pull me in or he was sinking in the sandy bottom of the creek. I don't know which it was, but I couldn't hold him. I tried to shift my weight to counterbalance his, but I was standing on the very edge of the bank, and I had no way of holding him or acting as a counterweight. I was about to lose my balance when I loosened my grip on his hand, and he fell backwards into the deeper water and sank like a stone.

He came up sputtering and gasping, but he managed to get over to the bank where the younger guy and I helped him out of the creek. He pointed at me and said, "You . . . ," and coughed up some water and then finished the epithet, "nitwit!" That's all he said to me. He turned to the younger fellow and said, "I've obviously got to go in. This is the way back to the clubhouse, isn't it?"

"Yeah," the young guy said, "we can cut th'ough numbah one and we'll be almost theah." Dr. Goolsby glared at me as though about to unleash another attack and then, waving his arms in a gesture of disbelief and dismissal, turned and stalked back toward the golf shop, rolling his shoulder and wobbling his head in an obvious fury. His shoes made a squish-squish sound with each step. His floppy green hat had floated off down Catawpa Creek. I confess that I intentionally let it float away. His bald head was now sparkling with beads of creek water, and his hair, which had been carefully combed over his balding head, now hung limply over his left ear almost down to his left shoulder.

"Have a nice day," I said earnestly. You probably won't believe it, but I was innocent. I really wasn't trying to be sarcastic. I can see how it might have seemed that way to them, but I just wanted to say something conciliatory and that's the best I could come up with at the time. Both Dr. Goolsby and the younger guy turned and stared at me like I had cussed them.

"Nevah," the young guy said, "have I encountahed the likes of you at this club."

After they stalked off, I went back to the mower and continued my work. I had completed all the trim work around the bunkers on the fourth and fifth fairways when Phoenix drove down the service road and got out of the truck. "I don't know what you did, Biddle, but you got trouble. Mr. Harbo wants to see you now. Come on, hop in the truck." I didn't say anything to Phoenix, but I was thinking that I had done it again. I was also worrying that

I was about to be fired and that the news would get back to Dr. Bob and by relay to my mother.

Actually, neither my mother nor Dr. Bob ever said anything about it, but I did in fact get fired. When I walked into the maintenance shed, Harbo shouted in my face, "Whatta hell do you thank you doin'? Dr. Ware's on the Grounds Committee, and he's a hell of a nahce guy. So whatchoo do? You try to drowned the guy he's recruitin' fo' the universty." He grimaced in a failed effort to fake remorse in making a tough decision. "I'm 'fraid Imo hafta letcheego, Biddle. We just ain't got no place here fo' you."

I started to try to defend myself, but I just turned and walked out of the maintenance shed. Harbo had dogged me from the first day I worked for him. Most of it wasn't justified. I sort of appreciated Dr. Bob's help getting me the job, but I knew pretty quickly that it probably wasn't going to work. Harbo was just another manifestation of the chaos that had been stalking me.

And where did my firing lead? I was hardly home an hour when my friend Lichtman called and asked whether I'd like a summer job with him at his father's furniture warehouse. I told my mother that I'd decided to work at the furniture store rather than the golf course, advertently omitting the part about being fired. I thought that a divine hand had delivered me from Harbo. I didn't understand that it wasn't a hand at all; the phalanges were actually the tentacles of the twin demons of havoc and despair maneuvering Anna into my life.

"Bravo," Dr. Gross said and started clapping like someone at a concert. "That's a great story. You've told it before, haven't you?"

"How'd you know?"

"You have it down pat, pauses and all."

"I've told both Lichtman and Q. Ball. They thought it was funny."

"Is it all true?"

"I think so. Most of it anyway."

"Did you learn anything from the encounter with Dr. Goolsby?"

"What was I supposed to learn? That Dr. Goolsby is an ass who can't play golf?"

"Did you learn anything about yourself?"

"I don't know. Did you learn anything about me from the story?"

"I ask the questions," he said, smiling broadly.

"All right, but I don't know what, if anything, I learned. Sometimes it takes me a long time to figure out what I ought to have learned."

"I see why you expected Dr. Goolsby to be, shall we say, disdainful, even antagonistic, but you may have given the episode more weight than it deserves. We all have little run-ins that seem significant at first but over time diminish virtually to nothingness, sometimes even to humor. I see why you have Dr. Goolsby in the anti-Kit contingent, but what about Dr. Glans? You seem to have conflict with him also."

"Not really," I said.

"You don't resent him?"

"I didn't say that."

"Do you regard him as an intruder?"

"Sort of, yeah."

"That's fairly common, you know?"

"So I've heard."

"Is there anything specific to Dr. Glans that would not be applicable to some other person dating your mother?"

"I don't know. He probably overdid the stress fracture ruse."

"Ruse? If you don't mind my asking, how did he overdo the stress fracture treatment?"

"Well, for one thing I really didn't have a stress fracture at all. He unnerved me. No, he scared the hell out of me."

"How did he scare you? I don't mean to press the point unduly but there has to be something you're not saying."

"You won't understand. You'll probably just think it was normal or something. But it wasn't. He had me coming to his office and he kept calling my mother. He examined me, x-rayed me, asked me questions, and then talked to my mother. Then I kept going back. He had me coming to his office almost once a week for a stress fracture. He was calling my mother all the time talking to her, which unnerved me because I thought at first that he was really talking about me. I was imagining all kinds of terrible things because Dr. Bob was calling and they were conferring, quietly and confidentially, way too much for a stress fracture. Turned out, he was talking just to be talking but nobody told me I wasn't the main subject. It was just verbal canoodling but I wasn't clued in on the ruse."

"That is unfortunate. I'm sure that neither your mother nor Dr. Glans intended to scare you. It appears you were a victim of a moment's distraction. All's well that ends well, huh?"

"I guess. You'd think they'd at least tell me."

"That would have been the thoughtful thing to do, but they probably didn't imagine that you were really worried. The good news, of course, is that they weren't really talking about you."

"I was just happy when Dr. Bob told me I didn't have to come back and that I could get back to running track. After all those weeks, Dr. Bob revealed that I did not have a stress fracture after all and that I was a growing teenager who should take aspirin for any recurring pain in my legs. He's been hanging around ever since, and I can truthfully say that the other insights he has shared with me have been equally valuable."

"I find it hard to believe that he's made no positive contribution to your life. Are you being fair to him?"

"Well, let's see. He gave me some golf lessons at the country club and played a few rounds of golf with me. And he helped me get my driver's license."

"Those are positive things, aren't they?"

"Yeah, I guess so, but those positive things produced more snorts and grunts than a pig farm."

"Yeah," he said, smiling broadly, "maybe you gotta take the snorts and grunts with the gifts and gains. I hear what you're saying." He picked up my folder and began scribbling notes. "You know you're doing well. I hope you feel that. You've shown a sense of humor and a lot of perspective that I didn't anticipate. Despite some tendency toward isolation as a solution to social interaction, you're dealing with relationships fairly well. Unless you have some other relationships to talk about, we now need to go to the incident that brought us together, the Sunday you wrecked the truck. I want you to think about it and then tell me next week if you're ready to talk about it."

"I didn't try to kill myself," I said. "I can talk about it now if you want."

"No, we're done for the day, and I want you to be sure you're ready. Next week, come prepared to tell me what happened or to tell me we need to talk about some other stuff. Either way, we go forward." He stood up and stuck out his hand. "We're even on schedule this time. How about that?"

"We're getting good at this," I said. We both smiled and shook hands. It had taken me five weeks to learn to like Dr. Gross and to get comfortable with the process. I had thought that Dr. Gross was just another of those demons that seemed always to be lurking in the shadows of my life. I didn't want to talk to him, even if I knew I needed to address some of the crazy stuff in my life. I had never talked to anybody about Nathan. My mother and I didn't discuss it, and Newt acted like it was a theological issue run amok. Of course, I didn't tell Dr. Gross everything about Anna, but I wouldn't know how to explain some of it. Our sessions together weren't perfect, but they helped me to feel normal, and I really wanted to be normal. I had come grudgingly to respect Dr. Gross and to tolerate the process. I already knew what I was going to say at the next session. I had been thinking about the wreck from the beginning, and I was ready.

THE BREAKDOWN

At our next session I told Dr. Gross everything I could remember about how I'd almost killed myself rolling the country club's maintenance truck.

I woke up that Sunday morning after only a few hours of sleep. My eyes were burning and I had a dull headache. I also had an acute sense of having lost something significant. I had never felt so bereft. It was as though a large part of the meaning in my life had disappeared, and I had been left staring into a void. I had an idea of Anna in my mind that I couldn't make work, and I had a feeling of rejection and loss. My idea of Anna was so real to me that I vacillated between trying to cling to it and despairing at the recognition that it wasn't real, that it was a phantom. But the sense of loss was less surprising than the painful guilt that hovered over me like a shroud. Somewhere a voice was telling me that I had done something wrong, and I searched for the voice and tried to make it speak more specifically. It remained vague.

My stomach had a painfully hollow feeling, and I shivered every time I thought about the night before. I lay facedown in my pillow and pushed the ends up around my head, so that I could neither see nor hear anything. I don't know how long I lay in bed fretting and feeling ineffably forlorn and lost, but ultimately I seemed to hit some kind of bottom. Almost as if carried up by some invisible force, I began to feel a modest return of strength. My first thought about the exterior world was to wonder what time it was. I got out of bed to find my watch. It was nine-thirty. I went to the kitchen to get coffee. Beside the coffee pot was a note from my mother:

> *Kit:*
>
> *I've gone to church with Dr. Bob. Please do not go anywhere. I have spoken with Mary Burchfield. We will talk after church. Sorry we are out of your cereal. There are donuts on the refrigerator.*
>
> *Love, Mom*

I poured myself a glass of orange juice and washed down two aspirins. Then I got a donut and a cup of coffee and sat down at the kitchen table. I finished my donut and got another one. After I finished, I got in the shower and ran some water over my head for a few minutes, and then put on a clean pair of jeans and my running shoes.

I took a quick swipe at my teeth with the toothbrush, picked up my watch and my money, and went back to the kitchen. I turned over my mother's note and wrote on the other side:

Mom,

I've gone running. Things are not working all that well right now. I'm having a hard time, and I don't know what to do about all this stuff. I love you.

Kit

I went out the kitchen door and rounded the house toward the street. I was a little stiff at first but after a few blocks I was okay. I sucked in my stomach and I could feel my back and abdominal muscles harden. I was running as fast as I could run. After the first mile I was drenched in sweat, but I was feeling better. I was concentrating on running, and I wasn't worrying about anything or at least not too much. I kept pushing myself to run faster and faster.

I had no plan, but I ended up running toward Carapace. I want to think I wasn't just headed for Anna's, but I might have been because that's where I went. When I got to her driveway, I stopped and looked up at the porch where I had first met her and where I had spent a lot of time. I wanted to go and knock on the door, but I couldn't. I half hoped that she would come out, but she didn't. After I had stood there for a long time looking at the screened porch, I turned and started running up Carapace. I know I had no plan after that; I was just totally out of control.

I can't tell you why but I started chanting nonsense over and over in my mind. When I got to the top of the hill on Carapace, I cut down Country Club Road and then cut over and started running down the fairway that borders the road. I crossed another fairway and, all of a sudden, I was standing at the crossroads of a cart path and the main interior road, looking right at the main-tenance shed. I had been running as hard as I could run and I was seriously winded, so I bent over and gasped for breath in front of the double doors of the shed. As soon as I looked up, I had the thought in my mind: I was going to take the maintenance truck. I don't know where the thought came from.

Nobody was in the maintenance shed when I walked in, and the keys were in the ignition of the flatbed truck. The big mower was on the truck. Its wheels were running across the truck rather than in the same direction as the truck's wheels, so I figured the mower wouldn't roll off the truck and maybe wouldn't move at all. As I pulled out of the maintenance yard, I looked back at the mower. It hadn't moved so I headed for the highway. I put my left elbow out the window and gunned the old truck to about sixty-five miles an hour. Even with the air blowing in the window, it was hot in the truck. It must have been more than 90 degrees that day, and my back and behind were sticking to the truck seat. I nudged the truck a little faster.

It seems peculiar but there was hardly any traffic. It was just before noon and the roads were empty. I saw six or eight cars maybe, all of them with people dressed up as if they had been to early church, but mostly I was just driving along by myself daydreaming, struggling with an empty feeling of meaninglessness that was exacerbated by a sense of loss and guilt. My head began to hurt again. I was going through mechanical motions, but I didn't have a purpose or a plan. The thought of wrecking the truck intentionally actually crossed my mind. I didn't hear any voices, but I had the feeling that something was tugging at me. I wanted out of the pain, out of the guilt, out of the desolation. My mind became so separated from the act of driving that I hardly knew where I was. I crested a hill, and I could see that both sides of the road led to open fields of green grass, and I remember thinking that it would be a relief to lie down in the grass and close my eyes.

At some point I became aware of a big black dog running along the middle of the road meandering in and out of the vapor haze rising from the heat of the pavement. *Wulfie*, I thought, and I strained to get a better look. He seemed to be moving erratically, jerking sideways as though pulling against the limits of an invisible tether, but his motions may have been exaggerated by the refraction of light in the steam hovering over the pavement. I remember wiping sweat out of my eyes and feeling as though I were losing my mind, because the dog looked like Wulfie, and I could hear Nathan's voice in my mind chanting nonsense. I cut close to the right shoulder of the road so that I would have plenty of room to get by the dog. But just as I was about to pass him, for no apparent reason he darted across the road in front of the truck. I heard a loud thump and a yelp and felt the impact reverberate through the truck. I looked in the rearview mirror and saw the black mongrel's limp body flung lifelessly toward the side of the road.

After that, I had no idea what I was doing. The truck was gaining speed because of the steep slope of the hill. In trying to miss the dog I had maneuvered the truck over so far that the right wheels had gone off the road and bounced along on the shoulder until I cut the wheel back left. When I did I heard the mower slam into the left rail of the flatbed. The truck swerved into the left lane of the highway and then all the way over and off the left shoulder. I tried to turn the truck back to the right and heard the mower hit the right side of the flatbed. The truck veered back across the road and off the right side, and I still had not slowed down. When I twisted the steering wheel back to the left and the truck started veering wildly toward the left side of the road, I slammed on the air brakes. I heard a loud bang and then nothingness. At first everything was black, and then I began to see a shimmering filtered light.

I was lying on my back in the middle of the road looking into a blurry sky. I raised my head and through the film over my eyes I could see blood all around me. I pulled myself up on my elbows and then on my hands and looked around. The heat of the pavement burned my hands. The flatbed and the mower were a tangled pile of metal up the hill a few yards behind me, and the cab of the truck was on its side a few yards down the hill in front of me. Blood was pouring down my face and into my eyes and mouth. I tried to wipe the blood away from my eyes but it was pouring too fast. Then I noticed that my right leg was twisted peculiarly and that blood was soaking through the right leg of my jeans.

I didn't see anybody at first. The pavement burned my hands and the sun almost blinded me. I was weak but I didn't want to lie back. The first person I saw was a portly old lady with blue hair and a blue and white dress. She stood at my feet and bent her large body over in front of me so that our eyes were on almost the same level. "Are you hurt, young man?" she asked sincerely. Even then I thought that was a peculiar question. I didn't know what might be wrong with me, but I could see a leg askew and a lot of blood, and she had a better perspective than I did. I didn't know what she could see, but I knew she had to suspect that all was not well.

"I killed Wulfie," I said. I'm not sure what I meant. I was a little confused. As soon as I said that I had killed Wulfie, I knew that it wasn't true, but I didn't correct myself because the sun was blinding me, and I couldn't see very well. I leaned forward and lowered my head and shut my eyes. I had a vague idea that things would be clearer if I stopped trying to see around me. When I opened my eyes I saw that blood had dripped from my head and covered my crotch. "Poccotola train broke down," I babbled incoherently. The lady with the blue hair got upset and started telling me over and over that I was going to be all right. Other people began gathering around me. I could see cars stopping down in front of me and people walking toward me. Somebody brought a sheet and threw it across my legs, but I threw it off. "I'm hot. Put the sheet behind me. And can you get some water?"

My mind started to get a little clearer. I remember being irritated about the gawkers. Most of them didn't say anything. They just stood there gawking. I heard somebody say, "Can we get us some water from that house?" The crowd grew larger and louder, and I heard an authoritative voice say, "Y'all stand back some so he can get some air." I was hot and in some pain but I was not short of air. A girl in tight shorts stood directly in my line of vision chewing gum very rapidly and holding a portable radio and swaying back and forth to music that I could hear only faintly. I could hear very plainly the discussion of how I looked. A woman's voice said, "My goodness, it's a wonder he's alive at all," and a flat drawl responded, "This ain't nothin' compared to the one I seen over near Niceville. This old boy hit a log truck and he was scattered all the way down the road. Blood was everwhar. Man, I'm tellin' you, that was the worst'un I ever seen."

The lady with blue hair leaned down by me and said, "I've got some water here," and held a large glass to my lips.

"Pour it back there." I motioned with my head. She looked perplexed so I repeated, "Pour it on the sheet back there." She hesitated a minute and then poured the water on the sheet behind me.

I heard the flat drawl say, "What the hay'ul is she doin'?" The water soaked through the sheet and trickled under me. I lay back on the wet sheet, and I looked up at the blue-haired lady. "Thanks, that's better." She dabbed a cloth around my eyes to wipe the blood away.

"You're going to be all right, son. Somebody'll be here in a minute. What's your name?"

"I don't know. I think my name is . . . Caboodle," I said hesitantly and then I wanted to correct myself. "No, it's . . . ." I felt very confused and I strained to remember my name. The blood was in my eyes, and I just couldn't see. "Caboodle," I said after a long pause. Then I said, "Caboodle is dead," but I don't know why I said it. My head was spinning and large, and everything seemed so far away. I was confused but I managed to push myself back into a sitting position, stabilizing myself with my hands. I wanted to understand and control what was happening. The blood was still pouring from my head, and the pavement was covered with the blood gushing from my leg. The blue-haired lady dabbed with her cloth, trying to wipe away the blood that kept running into my eyes. I was completely surrounded by gapers. I was feeling faint and having some difficulty seeing because blood was in my eyes and the glare of the sun made it difficult to keep my eyes open. I felt like somebody very far away.

I heard a siren in the distance. At first it seemed to be in my head, like a faint ringing in my ears. Then it grew louder and louder. It was approaching from behind me, so I couldn't see what was happening but I could hear car engines starting and movement. The pavement had gotten hot again, and my head was swimming. I was hot, and I felt weaker. I heard a voice say, "I'm a doctor." Then a bald-headed man bent over and began cutting away the right leg of my jeans. "I'm afraid he's dissected his femoral artery," he said to a woman who was kneeling beside me. "I've got to stanch the flow." My head was swimming, and everything seemed faint and surreal. "Let's lay him back," the man said. "I've got some work to do here."

On my back, I watched the blue sky become dimmer and dimmer until I was in total darkness. Then I opened my eyes and I was standing in a bright light on the hillside looking down at the steaming highway. I could see the pieces of the truck and the puddles and streams of blood flowing from the body on the pavement and there, on his knees in the blood, a man who appeared to be Dr. Goolsby. "What is he doing here?" I said. Then someone said, "Is he going to make it?" He held his arms out beside his body like he was welcoming someone. He smiled faintly at me and then said, "It's gushing too fast." I didn't know what he meant, and I wanted to say, *Who in the world are you*? But instead I said, "What's gushing?" Then he pointed toward the body lying in the road and said, "I think that's got it."

"What?" I asked. He smiled faintly and said, "We need to move quickly." I couldn't see him very well because it was almost like the sun was shining in my eyes. I wanted to say, *What do you mean*? But I couldn't form words. I reached my hand out toward him, but he began to fade with the light until I was alone on the hill in total darkness. I couldn't see anything or hear anything. Then I saw little streams of flickering light in the darkness, and I heard voices and the hum of a car motor. I tried to move but I was strapped down, and I could hear the high-pitched sound of a siren, and I could see a flashing red light. I was trying to make it make sense when everything went black again.

The next person I saw was the old crone who was behind the counter when Sarah and I took Phoenix's brother to the emergency room. "This must be the Biddle boy," the crone said. "If Dr. Goolsby is ready to release him, Dr. Glans wants him in X-ray as soon as possible." I thought she was going to hold me hostage in the emergency room until somebody agreed to fill out forms, but she didn't even mention forms. The ambulance attendants rolled me into a little room and maneuvered me onto a gurney. The nurse who followed us into the room wasn't the tired, stocky lady. This one was perky and freckled. She was wearing large dark-rimmed glasses, and she had short blonde hair sticking out from under her nurse's cap in two little waves. She looked at a sheet of paper on a clipboard and started putting stuff on a little table next to the bed. She lifted my arm with the plastic bracelet and said, "Okay, let's confirm who you are."

"I don't know," I said. "I think I'm . . . ," and I paused trying to concentrate.

"Don't know, huh?" She looked at my arm bracelet. "You're Biddle all right. You didn't try to fly, did you?" She took my blood pressure and my pulse and said, "This is going to smart a little, but it'll make you feel a whole lot better." She cleaned my right shoulder with a cotton ball saturated with alcohol and then stuck the needle in my arm and pushed down the plunger. She took off my running shoes and socks, removing them gently from my right foot, and then started cutting off the remnant of my jeans from the bottom up with a large pair of scissors. "Sorry," she said, "but these have got to come off." When she finished the jeans, she did the same thing with my jockey shorts. "We can save your shirt if you can get it off." I shook my head no and she said, "Okay, we'll just cut it off too." After she cut away my tee shirt, she said, "Here, let's put this on you." She helped me put on one of those backless hospital gowns. Then she carefully peeled away the fragments of my jeans and shorts.

She was right about feeling better. At first it felt like a runner's high that I used to get at about the third or fourth mile, and then the high began to expand exponentially:

I was totally beyond pain or care. I also started itching, and I ran my hands over my face and arms. I could feel dried blood down the right side of my face and along my arms. Somebody had put bandages around my head and upper arms, and I could feel tape pulled tightly around the upper part of my right thigh. The nurse wheeled me out of the little room and down a long hall, pushing from the back of the gurney. She smiled at me and said, "Are you feeling better?" By then I was really floating.

"Yeah, I'm all right."

"Good," she said and winked at me. She pushed me into the X-ray room and parked me beside a large black table. She hooked the clipboard on the end of the gurney and said, "These people have you now." Then she came around and patted me on the cheek and said, "You behave."

My eyelids were getting heavy. I smiled and closed my eyes, and I began to have dream-like images in my mind. I think I was still awake, but in my mind I could see myself running around the track at school. The track forms an oval around the soccer field and the bleachers line the long part of the oval. The stands were empty except for a man hanging on to the rail at the top of the stands. I was running along wearing a white straitjacket tethered to a cable suspended around the track. I strained to see the man who was watching me. I was hoping it wasn't my father because I didn't want him to see me like that. I was running as hard as I could run and chanting maniacally.

"Poccotola train broke down," I chanted as I ran. And no one was watching me run except the solitary figure at the top of the stands who watched in silence as I ran and chanted like a lunatic.

PART FOUR

The Heron's Song

FLIGHT

At my last session with Dr. Gross, I mentioned the great blue heron standing on one leg beside the beach house at the edge of the outdoor lamp. When I mentioned the heron, Dr. Gross seemed to think I was just making idle conversation, maybe because I had never explained that the strange bird bothered me. He asked me if the incident had any particular meaning for me, and I told him that I thought it was just empathy. He smiled and said he could see that, because "you are sort of a one-legged bird," a comment I found sort of weird.

Maybe because of the expression on my face, he realized I wasn't kidding, and he slipped back into serious shrink mode: He stroked the side of his chin and lowered his brows and, after a slight and somewhat awkward pause, he asked why I had not mentioned the bird before. In shrink world, when all else fails, you come up with a question to ask. Anyway, I told him that I thought I had mentioned it, but actually I couldn't remember any discussion about it. We had talked about so much I probably couldn't tell you half the stuff we covered in the days and hours I spent in his office. "Were you empathetic when you watched the bird standing in the darkness or did you just begin to empathize later?"

"I don't know. I know that he made me sad standing out there alone looking wary, like something might be stalking him, and I thought he also looked sort of puzzled or maybe even lost."

"I'm sure he was wary," Dr. Gross said, "because all sorts of predators roam the beach at night, and he may have been puzzled on some instinctive level. The heron brain doesn't have the capacity to contemplate the mysteries of the universe." He smiled and looked at me expectantly. "One of my hobbies is ornithology," he said. "I have a large photograph album, including pictures of the great blue heron, young and old."

"They're all over the beach and the river," I said. "The one standing beside the beach house was big but I don't know how old he was."

"It's hard to tell. He could have been a fledgling," he said. "Fledglings are almost full size when they leave the nest. Sometimes they get pushed out of the nest if they won't leave voluntarily. The parent herons have no choice. They can't feed themselves and four or five nearly grown fledglings. They'll all die. Can you imagine? For a fledgling heron, the sum total of reality extends only to the rim of the nest and the sky above. They have no way of grasping the danger of remaining in the nest or the prospects that lie beyond. Everything outside the nest is a feral, yawping marsh that reeks of terror and strife. The fledglings have no data suggesting that the outside world offers anything but shrieking, fathomless chaos and danger. They don't even know they can fly."

The session did not end at that point but I can't remember anything else that was said. In my mind, that was the end. I had begun seeing Dr. Gross a few months after my initial encounter with him in the hospital. As soon as I could get around on my crutches, I began seeing him almost every week. I saw him for almost a year, and I talked to him about almost everything. I talked a lot and he just asked questions, for the most part. By the time he declared us done, I felt better about most things, and I had come to like Dr. Gross. He's witty and smart, and he listens. We covered just about everything: my father's death (maybe suicide), Nathan's murder, Anna's disappearance and Sarah's appearance, Dr. Bob's intrusion, and my aimless life.

Some things in my life have actually improved and some irritants have persisted. My mother and Dr. Bob married in December of last year, and they have shoved me at least partway out of the nest. It is somewhat awkward because my right leg has not healed properly, and I am thus still on one leg. I had the bone graft surgery in August, and I have hope that I will soon be walking.

Since I have my mother and Sarah (not to mention the king of grunts) helping in all kinds of ways—some very annoying—I am doing fine. At my suggestion, my mother and Dr. Bob live in his house, and I live in our old house alone except that Sarah stays over most weekends. It sometimes feels a little strange but I actually like the arrangement. I assume that it's like having a large dorm room all to myself.

I've actually gotten pretty good with the crutches, so I'm not particularly restricted. My life is somewhat insular but I like it. I graduated in May with my class and I did well my last year of school. I didn't make it to fifth in the class, as I had predicted to Lichtman, but I got close. I completed the climacteric project on schedule, and Mr. Marcus gave me a high honors grade. Since I didn't attend classes, Sarah and my mother acted as couriers for me, and Mr. Marcus pitched in occasionally. My only extracurricular activity was that I edited the literary magazine, a job I found surprisingly enjoyable and satisfying.

Sarah stays with me a lot. She has a summer job in her father's insurance agency. When she's not working, she's mostly here with me. She cooks our meals, and I act as her hobbled helper. We fool around some but we also do a lot of reading and talking about things. We don't talk very much about philosophy because Sarah regards it as either tautology or opacity. She has a point. We both love symbolic logic, which has become our intellectual common ground. We're almost like a couple of old people. The painful thing is that Sarah will never be Anna. That is either the blessing or the curse. One day I will probably know which it is. Sarah has the virtue of being a real person but every other day I wonder whether that is a relevant fact. I also wonder whether I will ever be a real person to Sarah and not a phantasm created by her dreams and illusions.

At my mother's prompting, I wrote a note to Dr. Goolsby thanking him for saving my life. I don't know why I resisted writing the note, but maybe I wasn't sure he had done me a favor. When I finally wrote the note, my motive may have been more connivance than real gratitude. I had sort of hoped that it might prompt a letter or a visit from Anna. It didn't work. I have heard from Anna only once and that was four months after my note to Dr. Goolsby. She wrote a strange note complimenting me on a paper I wrote on the subject of causation that was read aloud by the teacher in one of the classes we shared but that I never physically attended. Her note evidenced very little emotion but she asked whether I wanted her to visit me. Then the note ended almost bizarrely with "Love, Anna." The note rattled me terribly, and I picked up the phone to call her several times.

I wanted desperately to call her but ultimately I couldn't do it. I'm not sure why, but every time the notion to call her came into my mind I experienced excruciating pain and unnerving agitation. The fact that I couldn't call her didn't mean I wasn't interested. Every scrap of information about her excited me, and I tried to keep up with what she was doing. I even looked for her face anytime I left the house, no matter how unlikely that she would be there. Not surprisingly, she graduated first in our class and was declared Most Cerebral in the yearbook. She was also valedictorian and president of the Math Club, to Lichtman's great chagrin. I'm told that she's at Stanford University, having decided against Barnard College, her mother's alma mater. I don't know where her mother and Dr. Goolsby live now, but I know they've moved from the apartment on Carapace. It is sad and strange but the thought of that apartment without Anna, emptied and abandoned, makes my heart hurt.

I haven't really seen all that much of Lichtman, but he used to pop in randomly and visit me for a few minutes. Anna edged him by a minuscule fraction, and he graduated second in our class. In September he went off to Amherst, which, I gather, helped him with the ongoing sibling rivalry with his brother. With his acceptance at Amherst, his angst disappeared and he seems not the least concerned about that new playing field he fretted about. Q. Ball's parents divorced in November of last year and he joined the marines the following month, despite the fact that he probably would have graduated fourth or fifth in the class. He had already been accepted at a bunch of great colleges. Roby's parents apparently patched things up. He's at Holy Cross.

Several other noteworthy things, some good and some not so good, have happened recently. First, Mr. Marcus' brother Lawrence left the novitiate and married Annie Brasher, the same one who worked at the college where Lawrence was a scholastic and who incidentally lived in the house across from Morrow's Drugstore. Lawrence apparently married her on the first day possible after her divorce. With great deductive powers of analysis, I have concluded that I caught Lawrence in a tryst, not peeping in a stranger's window. Mr. Marcus seemed very unhappy about the Lawrence development, but I was slightly lifted, just getting a little light for a change. I included the peeping tom episode in the climacteric, and Mr. Marcus edited it for me but he never mentioned it and neither did I, not even after my mother told me the Lawrence and Annie story.

The second news item I got from Leola a few days ago. She called and asked me how I was doing, and then told me that Phoenix had quit his other jobs and entered into full-time prison ministry. His new focus had begun with Abner, who was sentenced to fifteen years in prison for the death of his baby daughter. Abner had been depressed after the tragedy but had begun to regroup with the help of the prison ministry at Atmore. He has immersed himself in the Bible, which, according to Leola, he studies diligently every day. He's also begun to read every other book he can get his hands on, particularly theology, history, and books on racial injustice. He reads the speeches and follows the marches of the Reverend Martin Luther King and vows to join the Southern Christian Leadership Conference when he gets out of prison. Phoenix has helped Abner get enrolled in a correspondence-school program that he will complete long before he gets out. His plan is to be ready to join Dr. King in the movement when he becomes eligible for parole in 1968.

The third notable occurrence is truly notable: Newt has entered the University of Virginia as a junior, transferring his two years of credits from Harvard. He left for Charlottesville last summer. He told me he loved Harvard but that it was time to go home. I don't know what that means, but I know how it feels. He now says he wants to become a lawyer. Who knows? Lawyering may put a premium on talents that Newt has in great abundance, particularly including schmooze. I can't see Newt as Bartleby the Scrivener, but he may have found the perfect outlet for his gifts. A peculiar thing is that I was elated by Newt's decision to transfer to Virginia. It felt like a reconnection with a past that seems to be slipping away.

Sarah wants us to go to the same college. Since my leg has not healed, I am still not in a position to apply. I have had two surgeries, and we are now waiting to see whether the bone graft works. I probably won't get accepted at some schools because of my junior year performance. Sarah has been accepted everywhere she applied. She has a perfect 4.0 GPA, and she took the most advanced of the honors courses. She also made a perfect score on the

SAT and got her picture in the newspaper with other perfect scorers in the state. A couple of things are nudging me toward Virginia. First, I have a feeling that my father might have wanted me to go to Virginia as a matter of tradition. Second, the fact that Newt will be in Charlottesville is a huge magnet. He'll probably treat me the same way there that he does here, but even with the abrasions, he's still like a big brother, and, let's be honest about it, he's smarter than I am. I don't know what I'm going to do, and I've decided not to worry about it until I'm forced to.

From a physical standpoint, the truck wreck has been a serious ordeal (I will never run competitively again even if I don't lose my leg), but from every other perspective it has been a blessing. You might say I've become a grudging and belated fan of calamity. It really is a lot easier to see up when you're lying on your back. Maybe I should take a tip from Erasmus and write something—perhaps titled *The Praise of Calamity*. It was calamity that gave me a moment of pause, an occasion for reassessment and redirection. I suffered both a breakdown and a breakthrough. I still sense a void in my life, a sense of inexpressible loss that may never go away. Ironically, it is this longing that provides at least some of the fuel for my locomotion.

On a final note, I should mention one bit of Dr. Gross' advice that didn't work out very well. At one of our last sessions, he told me that I should visit Uncle Nat and try to find some closure. It seems likely the murder of Nathan is going to be like the disappearance of Anna: The pain won't ever go away but I have learned to live with it. After thinking about Dr. Gross' advice for about a month, I went to Tuscaloosa and visited Uncle Nat. Since I was still hobbling around on crutches, Sarah provided the transportation and physical assistance on the trip.

Uncle Nat seemed genuinely happy to see us. He was gracious, articulate, even funny at times. He told us about the Bible study he teaches and the number of people he has been privileged to witness to, including some of the guards and returning visitors. Remarkably, he has become a part of the official counseling program at the hospital, and the staff regularly refers to him as Reverend Nathaniel. Uncle Nat is tall and thin and very distinguished looking, and he has more than the usual complement of charm, which he poured on Sarah. She was almost gushing. Part of it may have been that she was expecting to meet a monster.

"This may have strange and terrible implications," she whispered during our visit, "but your uncle seems totally sane and he is very charming."

The visit might have been constructive as well as productive and therapeutic, but it ended badly. As we were about to leave, Uncle Nat maneuvered us to the corner of the reception area where I had waited for my mother during our visit in 1954. After we were seated in an isolated corner of the room, he said, "If I may, I need to address a couple of topics in private, topics that, like much of life in general, have an element of the wonderful and an element of the terrible. May I speak freely?"

"Of course you can," I said. "Sarah is virtually a member of the family." She smiled agreeably.

"First," he said, "I am pleased to report that the board here has determined in its great wisdom that I experienced a 'psychotic episode' in 1953, from which I am fully recovered, and therefore I am due to be released from this prison. That's the wonderful part. The terrible part of it is that I lied to them." He slowly moved his head back and forth like someone grudgingly answering a difficult question. "I actually told them that I realize that God did not speak to me. I can hardly tell you how painful it is for me to tell you that I lied so blatantly, so terribly. I know that was not the right thing to do. I am telling you that God spoke to me not once but repeatedly over a period of months. I stood in the presence of God, and I was shaken. I recognized the singularity of the occurrence. I know God does not speak to people in that way. As you may imagine, I doubted it was the voice of God, and I tried to avoid it and reject it, but ultimately I had no choice. Do you understand my dilemma now? Do you understand my present predicament? Do I go back to the board and tell them the truth, or do I accept my freedom based on a lie?"

By this time, Sarah's eyebrows had edged up near her hairline and I had ended up somewhere near catatonia.

Neither of us said a word. "I told them that I know that I acted out of delusion and that the voice I heard was all in my head. The truth is that the voice was in my head but it was no delusion. They want to talk about things outside my mind as though those things have more substance, more veracity, more reality than the things in my mind, but every day brings fresh evidence that those exterior things they have such faith in are illusions without substance or truth or reality. The awful thing is that I knew that I was not supposed to offer that dear boy as a sacrifice, and I did it anyway. God told me to offer my son and I didn't do it. Don't you see?"

"You mean, because Nathan wasn't really your son?" I said tentatively.

"That is exactly what I'm saying," he said. "Martha castigated me for my letter to you last August, that is, the part about the difficulties when you were born. I had previously resolved to remain silent, but silence is sometimes pernicious, and the silence in this instance seems to be devouring our family. My dear Hannah was the first to be consumed. The events at the time of your birth were consequential and fraught with emotion. The day you were born was one of the most wrenching days of my life." Considering that he had murdered Nathan, my reaction to this statement was not positive. It was part consternation, part puzzlement.

"I have gone over and over in my mind the sequence of events that caused both the uncertainty and the discord, and I want to describe those events to you." I didn't say anything, and he continued. "Martha went into labor on the morning of the 21st, a Monday, and finally gave birth early Tuesday afternoon after an excruciating labor. The tension from Martha's travail may have been a precipitating cause of Hannah's going into labor herself Tuesday morning. By three o'clock that afternoon, Hannah delivered a fine baby boy without complication or difficulty. Hannah's baby was handed over to a practical nurse for transport to the neonatal unit, and the obstetrician's nurse remained behind to help the doctor with Hannah. Of course, I stayed in the waiting area near the delivery room. When the doctor was done, I accompanied Hannah to her room, which was next door to Martha's. In due course, a baby was brought to us by the obstetrics nurse. Immediately, Hannah said, 'This is not my baby. There's been a mistake. I saw my baby in the delivery room. This is not my baby!' I was unable to comfort her." Uncle Nat paused, looking like a person in great distress. I don't know what I looked like, but I can tell you the discrepancies between his story and my mother's were not comforting.

"A part of the confusion in the hospital resulted from understaffing and a part from the changing of shifts. After finishing with Hannah, the obstetrics nurse and the neonatal staff had left the premises, having reached the end of their shift, the seven-to-three shift. A practical nurse on the next shift, the three-to-eleven shift, tagged the babies and delivered one baby to Martha and the other to Hannah. Her determination of which was which, according to her, was based solely on her 'understanding' and her visual determination of the likely birth order."

"You're saying Hannah had an easy pregnancy?" I asked, my mind having locked on a crucial discrepancy in the two versions of the facts. "I thought Hannah had almost died giving birth to Nathan."

"I'm afraid that isn't so. You have not been told the facts. I am telling you, Hannah had no difficulty at all. It was Martha who struggled."

"The nurses weren't asked about the babies?"

"Oh, yes. The three-to-eleven personnel were all questioned but they were adamant. They defended their actions vigorously. Their level of conviction was exceeded only by Hannah's. She became somewhat hysterical, and the hospital went into defense mode. An intern on duty administered a sedative to Hannah. Indeed, she was kept sedated for most of the remainder of her hospital stay. By the time the original attending nurses, the seven-to-three personnel, were questioned, Hannah had left the hospital, and Martha had bonded with you and was intractable. When I left for military service, Hannah was in deep depression. Stripped of her baby and abandoned by me, she never recovered as a mother or a wife."

By this time I was shaken by Uncle Nat's clear, disturbingly straightforward version of the story. His version of events was essentially different from my mother's. That was troubling but maybe not really all that surprising. Uncle Nat's straightforward, matter-of-fact recitation, without a hint of hesitation or question, was unsettling precisely because it sounded like the truth. I didn't know what to say at first, and then I just blurted out what had been haunting me since I got his letter: "If the babies had been tagged differently, I would have been Nathan. Wouldn't you have sacrificed me?"

Uncle Nat looked shocked by this and said, "Oh, no, that's not true at all. God instructed me to offer my son as a sacrifice, and I failed the test of faith because I really knew that you were my son. I knew that dear afflicted boy was not my son. Don't you see? That's why there was no ram in the thicket. God wouldn't allow Abraham to kill his son Isaac. God would have released me once I met the test of faith, just as he had done for Abraham. I failed both God and Hannah. The grace of God in the person of my son was to be delivered through Hannah. I knew she was right, and I failed her. I wanted to maintain harmony and in the process planted a truly evil seed. I thought that we would all participate in the lives of all our children with such immediacy that parentage was actually of secondary importance. I ignored the fact that truth has its own vitality, its own primal essence like blood, and I failed to understand that love is nourished and sustained by truth. It is precisely because of my failings that I have ended up in this eternal, nightmarish twilight."

I have no idea what Sarah thought of all this but I

suffered a kind of paraphasia. I may have been most stunned by the fact that two people whom I had thought of as truthful above all else were telling significantly different versions of the same story. The one thing Uncle Nat had stressed as virtually a theme of his life was that truth is spiritual currency and thus absolutely necessary in differentiating the real from the gloaming that envelops everything. On the other hand, my mother had also emphasized the primacy of truth. The quandary was that I couldn't conceive that either Uncle Nat or my mother would misrepresent such an important series of events.

"I know the voice I heard was in my head," Uncle Nat said with a quaver in his voice, "but the voice wasn't my voice. The terrible thing was acting counter to the truth. Don't you see? I know I got it wrong, but it wasn't because of some external reality. I was in an absolute relationship with God, and I knew that the particular superseded the universal. Now I listen for his voice and wait for his instruction, but it's like I've fallen into darkness and I can't hear anything and I can't see anything. I have lost the wonderful place I occupied, the absolute relationship I had with God, and I am now thrown back into the world of the universal, all-condemning moral law. The only direction I have is a recurrent thought in my mind, not the clear voice I had before. The notion in my mind is vague, disturbingly soundless and painfully indistinct; but the impression is unmistakable: I need to retrace time and confront the test of faith again. I cannot do it from this prison. Do you see the terrible dilemma?"

I was too stunned to talk. I didn't know what to say or how to say it. "Do you want my opinion?" Sarah asked. Her voice seemed to startle Uncle Nat. "I know I'm an outsider here but I think the answer is obvious." Uncle Nat just smiled benignly. I couldn't speak. I probably looked like someone who had grabbed the wrong wire. "I think, Reverend Biddle, that you already have the answer. You have to go back to the board and tell them the truth. You can't live a lie. You heard and followed explicit instruction from God. You have to go back to the board precisely because truth has its own vitality. That primal essence, you said yourself, is like blood. If you ignore it, you are severed from the vine and you will continue to live, not in the light, but in that nightmarish twilight." I didn't know what Uncle Nat was thinking, but I can tell you what I was thinking: *Wow, Sarah really is smart.*

"My God, young lady," Uncle Nat said, "you are obviously right. I must go back to the board and tell the truth, set matters straight, or run the risk of eternal separation. The board will just have to understand the truth. Don't you think they will?"

When we reached the parking lot, the sun had begun to set. I hobbled around to the passenger side of Sarah's car and she opened the door for me, but I didn't get in. I propped my crutches against the car door and stood there on one leg in the fading light of the day. "What in the world?" I said, and then I began talking but I don't know what I said, because I was just spewing emotion: pain, confusion, and disillusionment. Sarah said nothing while I rambled.

I was trying to process the chaos, and I just couldn't do it. It was like when I got to the top of the hill and realized that Nathan was hanging by his neck. I couldn't make it work in my mind. I wanted Uncle Nat to explain it, but he just sat there babbling about obedience to God and getting it wrong, and I had no idea what he was talking about. The only thing I knew for certain was that Sarah had it right: Uncle Nat needed to tell the board the truth, so they would know what they are dealing with. If I had been quicker, I would have told him, but I had stood there, dumb and confused. After I settled down a bit, I thanked Sarah for confronting Uncle Nat with the truth and said, "You were really quick in there."

"Your Uncle Nat proves that being smart is not inconsistent with being crazy. I guess you know he's seriously deranged. I don't know how he got where he is, maybe in the war. He is bright and knowledgeable in many areas, but in the one that counts, he's insane. Until he mentioned retracing time and confronting the test of faith again, I didn't know where he was going. When he got back to Moriah, it was clear to me that he was planning to try again using you as the sacrifice because you are the son God was referring to. In his mind, God would save you with some metaphorical ram in the thicket. No! Sometimes you just have to say no to other people's versions of reality." She reached over and took my hand. "You're my lamb, not his."

"I think I understand the sin Uncle Nat preached so much about," I said after Sarah stopped talking. "It seemed peculiar but now it sort of makes sense."

"It does?" Sarah said. "I'm not sure I know what you mean. I understand mental instability."

"I didn't know this until a couple of years ago, but Uncle Nat has a graduate certificate from the Alabama Polytechnic Institute in Auburn."

"Well," Sarah said, looking puzzled, "that's nice."

"I found the certificate in his desk drawer under his diploma from the University of Virginia."

"Okay," she said, the perplexed expression still on her face.

"The certificate acknowledges the completion of a three-month course in crop and soil science."

"I'm sure this is going somewhere," Sarah said. "It can't be as random as it sounds."

"The certificate is dated December 31, 1940. Uncle Nat and Hannah were married in early December after my grandfather's death. It's the math, the tautological and comforting math. Nathan and I were born on July 22, 1941. I don't think Uncle Nat was in Bigbee nine months before Nathan and I were born."

"I see," Sarah said softly. "Math isn't random."

"My mother said Nathan bore the marks of a hard delivery, not that he appeared to be premature. Uncle Nat's description of the births was very precise and detailed, but not once did he suggest that one of the babies was premature." I don't know what I looked like but I felt like somebody lost in dense woods in total darkness. "So who am I?" I said. "Who in the world am I?"

I just stood there on one leg in the thickening twilight, distraught and confused. I didn't say it, but I was wondering: *In what reality did I end up here*? As you have no doubt noticed, I have my own version of reality. We all seem to have our own reality, and even more disturbing and unnerving, our realities too often seem not to correspond very well. When I first focused on myself as a person, I wondered why I am. Then I began to see reflections that were hard to reconcile, and I wondered who I am. I don't have answers to either of those questions. The answers may be more jumbled, shrouded, and elusive than ever before. I seem to be stranded in darkness that is relieved only randomly, almost like a beacon in the distance, by intermittent flashes of light.

My present fleeting glimmer suggests that I don't know why I am or who I am, but I may know where I am: I think I'm clinging desperately to the rim of a nest that is no longer mine. I know I have to leave because I'm increasingly cramped and confined. My mind is trying to draw inferences about a better place, a real world with new and wonderful things where my mind and spirit can soar like a bird. But I'm not sure I know what I'm seeing. Most of what may lie beyond my limited perspective is shrouded by a dense and impenetrable fog. When I try to imagine the world outside my reality, the images in my mind are not reassuring. They are disquieting. I want to believe in the intimations but I am baffled by the shrieking, fathomless chaos and the feral yawping. And I don't know whether I can fly.